THE TIME OF THE HERO

the text of this book is printed
on 100% recycled paper

THE TIME

OF

THE HERO

MARIO VARGAS LLOSA

translated by Lysander Kemp

HARPER COLOPHON BOOKS
Harper & Row, Publishers
New York, Hagerstown, San Francisco, London

First HARPER COLOPHON edition published 1979

ISBN: 0-06-090652-9

79 80 81 82 83 10 9 8 7 6 5 4 3 2 1

PART ONE

We play the part of heroes because we're cowards, the part of saints because we're wicked: we play the killer's role because we're dying to murder our fellow man: we play at being because we're liars from the moment we're born.

—JEAN-PAUL SARTRE

1

"Four," the Jaguar said.

Their faces relaxed in the uncertain glow which the light bulb cast through the few clean pieces of glass. There was no danger for anyone now except Porfirio Cava. The dice had stopped rolling. A three and a one. Their whiteness stood out against the dirty tiles.

"Four," the Jaguar repeated. "Who is it?"

"Me," Cava muttered. "I said four."

"Get going, then. You know which one, the second on the left."

Cava felt cold. The windowless latrine was at the far end of the barracks, behind a thin wooden door. In other years the wind had only got into the barracks of the cadets, poking through the broken panes and the cracks in the walls, but this year it was stronger and hardly any place in the academy was free from it. At night it even got into the latrines, driving out the stink that accumulated during the day, and also the warmth. But Cava had been born and brought up in the mountains, cold weather was nothing new to him: it was fear that was giving him goose pimples.

"Is it over?" the Boa asked. "Can I go to bed?" He had a huge body, a deep voice, a shock of greasy hair over a narrow face. His eyes were sunken from lack of sleep, and a shred of tobacco dangled from his jutting lower lip. The Jaguar turned and looked at him.

"I have to go on guard at one," the Boa said. "I want to grab a little sleep."

7

"Go ahead, both of you," the Jaguar said. "I'll wake you up at five to."

Curly and the Boa went out. One of them tripped on the threshold and swore.

"Wake me up as soon as you get back," the Jaguar said to Cava. "And don't take too long. It's almost midnight."

"I know it." Usually Cava's face was expressionless, but now it looked exhausted. "I'm going to get dressed."

They left the latrine. The barracks was dark, but Cava could find his way along the two rows of double bunks without a light: he knew that long, tall room by heart. It was silent except for a few snores and murmurs. His bunk was the second on the right, about a yard from the outside door. As he groped in his locker for his trousers and his khaki shirt and his boots, he could smell the tobacco-sour breath of Vallano, who slept in the upper bunk. Even in the darkness he could make out the double row of the Negro's big white teeth, and they reminded him of a rat. Slowly, quietly, he took off his blue flannel pajamas and got dressed. He put on his wool jacket and went down to the Jaguar's bunk at the other end of the barracks, next to the latrine, walking carefully because his boots squeaked.

"Jaguar."

"Okay. Here, take them."

Cava's hand reached out and touched two hard, cold objects, one of them rough. He kept the flashlight in his hand and slipped the file into his pocket.

"Who's on guard?" Cava asked.

"Me and the Poet."

"You?"

"The Slave's taking my place."

"What about the ones from the other sections?"

"Are you scared?"

Cava did not answer. He tiptoed to the outside door and opened it as carefully as he could, but it still creaked on its hinges.

"A crook!" somebody shouted in the darkness. "Kill him, sentry!"

Cava could not recognize the voice. He looked out into the patio. It was completely empty in the dim light from the lamps around the parade ground, which lay between the barracks and a weed-grown field. The drifting fog obscured the outlines of the three cement hulks where the Fifth Year cadets were quartered, making them look unreal. He went outside and stood for a few moments with his back against the barracks wall. He could not count on anyone now: even the Jaguar was safe. He envied the sleeping cadets, the noncoms, the soldiers in their barracks at the other side of the stadium. He knew he would be paralyzed by fear unless he kept going. He calculated the distance: he had to cross the patio and the parade ground; then, protected by the shadows in the field, he had to skirt the mess hall, the offices and the officers' quarters; and finally he had to cross another patio—this one small and paved with cement—that faced the classroom building. The danger would end there, because the patrol never went that far. Then, the trip back to his barracks. In a confused way he wanted to lose his will and imagination and just carry out the plan like a blind machine. Sometimes he could go for several days following a routine that made all the decisions for him, gently nudging him into actions he hardly noted. This was different. What was happening tonight had been forced on him. He felt unusually clearheaded and he knew perfectly well what he was doing.

He began to walk, keeping close up to the wall. Instead of crossing the patio he went around it, following the curved wall of the Fifth's barracks. When he came to the end of it he looked around anxiously: the parade ground seemed vast and mysterious, outlined by the symmetrically-placed lamps around which the fog was gathering. He could picture the shadowy field beyond the lamps. The sentries liked to stretch out there, either to sleep or to talk in whispers, when it was not too cold. But he was sure that tonight they were all gambling in one of the latrines. He began to walk quickly in the shadows of the buildings on his left, avoiding the splotches of light. The squeaking of his boots was drowned by the crash of the surf against the cliffs bordering one side of the Academy grounds. When he reached the officers' quarters he shivered and walked even faster. Then he cut across the parade ground and plunged into the shadows of the field. A sudden movement near him, as startling as a blow, brought back all the fears he had begun to overcome. He hesitated for a moment; then he could make out the eyes of the vicuña, as bright as glowworms, regarding him with a wide, gentle stare. "Get out of here!" he said to it angrily. The animal remained motionless. That damned thing never sleeps, Cava thought. It doesn't even eat. What keeps it alive? He moved on. Two and a half years ago, when he came to Lima to finish school, he was amazed to find that creature from the mountains wandering calmly among the gray, weather-beaten walls of the Leoncio Prado Military Academy. Who had brought the vicuña to the Academy? From what part of the Andes? The cadets used him as a target, but the vicuña hardly paid any attention when the stones hit him. He simply walked away from the boys with a look of utter indifference. It looks like an Indian, Cava thought. He went up the stairs to the classrooms. He was not worried now about the sound of his boots: the building was empty except for the desks and the benches, the wind and the shadows. He crossed the upper lobby with long quick strides. Then he stopped. The faint beam of the flashlight showed him the window. The second on the left, the Jaguar had said. And yes, he was right, it was loose. Cava started gouging out the putty with the pointed end of the file, collecting it in his other hand. It felt damp and decayed. Then he carefully removed the pane of glass and laid it on the tile floor. He groped until he found the lock, and swung the window wide open. Inside, he turned his flashlight in every direction. On one of the tables, next to the mimeograph machine, there were three stacks of paper. He read: *Bimonthly Examination in Chemistry, Fifth Year. Examination Time, 40 Minutes.* The sheets had been mimeographed that afternoon and the ink was still somewhat moist. He copied the questions hurriedly into a notebook without understanding what they meant. He turned off the flashlight, went back to the window, climbed up and jumped. The pane of glass exploded into hundreds of strident splinters. "Shit!" he grunted. He remained crouching, listening, trembling with terror. But he could not hear the wild tumult he expected, the pistol-shot voices of the officers: only his own panting. He waited for a few more seconds. Then, forgetting to use the flashlight, he picked up the broken glass as well as he could and put it into his pockets. He walked back to his barracks without taking the slightest precaution. He wanted to get there as soon as he could, he wanted to climb into his bunk and shut his eyes. As he crossed the field he took the broken glass out of his pockets and threw it away, cutting his hands as he did so. He stopped for a moment in the doorway to his barracks, catching his breath. A dark shape loomed up in front of him.

"Okay?" the Jaguar asked.

"Yes."

"Let's go in the latrine."

The Jaguar went first, pushing at the double door with both hands. In the yellow light Cava could see that the Jaguar was barefoot, could see and smell his big pale feet with their long dirty toenails.

"I broke the glass," he said in a low voice.

The Jaguar's hands came at him like two white claws and fastened on the lapels of his jacket. Cava swayed backward but kept his eyes on those of the Jaguar, who was glaring at him from below his curled-up lashes.

"You peasant," the Jaguar muttered. "You're just a peasant. If they catch us, by God I'll. . ."

He was still holding on to the lapels, so Cava put his hands on the Jaguar's, timidly trying to loosen them.

"Keep your hands off!" the Jaguar said. "You're just a peasant!" Cava could feel the spit spraying his face. He lowered his hands.

"There wasn't anyone in the patio," he said. "They didn't see me."

The Jaguar released him and stood nibbling the back of his hand.

"You know I'm not a squealer, Jaguar. If they find out, I'll take the whole blame. So just forget it."

The Jaguar looked him up and down. Then he laughed. "You gutless peasant," he said. "You're so scared, you've pissed your pants. Look at them."

He had forgotten about the house on Salaverry Avenue, out in Magdalena Nueva, where he had lived until the night he arrived in Lima for the first time, and the eighteen-hour trip by car, the procession of ruined villages, dead fields, tiny valleys, occasionally the ocean, cotton fields, villages, dead fields. He sat there with his face pressed to the window, feeling a tremendous excitement: I'm going to see Lima. Sometimes his mother pulled him toward her, murmuring: "Richi, my Ricardito." Why is she crying? he wondered. The other passengers were asleep or reading, and the driver was cheerfully humming the same song over and over again. Ricardo fought off sleep all during the morning, the afternoon, the early evening, without turning his eyes from the horizon, waiting to see the lights of the city appear unexpectedly in the distance like a torchlight parade. But little by little his body grew tired, his senses dulled; he told himself, in a haze of fatigue, I won't fall asleep. And suddenly someone was gently shaking him. "Wake up, Richi, we're here." He was on his mother's lap with his head resting on her shoulder. He felt cold. Familiar lips brushed against his mouth and he had the impression that in his sleep he had been changed into a kitten. The car was moving slowly now. He saw vague houses, lights, trees, on an avenue longer than the main street in Chiclayo. It was a few moments before he realized that the other passengers had got out. The driver was still humming, but without any enthusiasm. What will it be like? he asked himself. And he felt the same fierce anxiety he had felt three days ago when his mother, calling him aside so that his Aunt Adelina would not overhear, had told him, "Your father isn't dead, that was a lie. He's just got back from a very long trip and he's waiting for us in Lima." Now his mother repeated, "We're here." "Salaverry Avenue, right?" the driver asked. "Yes, number thirty-eight," his mother said. He closed his eyes and pretended he was asleep. His mother kissed him. Why does she kiss me on the mouth? Ricardo wondered. His right hand clutched at the seat. The car finally stopped after making a number of turns. He kept his eyes closed, curling up against his mother. Suddenly his mother's body stiffened. "Beatriz," a voice said. Someone opened the door. He felt himself being lifted out and set down without any support. He opened his eyes: his mother and a man were embracing and kissing each other on the mouth. The driver had stopped humming. The street was silent and empty. He looked at them fixedly, his lips counting the moments. At last his mother stepped back from the man, came over to him, and said, "It's your father, Richi. Kiss him." Once again, two unknown masculine arms lifted him up. A face drew close to his, a voice murmured his name, dry lips pressed against his cheek. He remained rigid.

He had also forgotten the rest of that night, the chill of the sheets on that hostile bed, the loneliness he tried to overcome by forcing his eyes to make out some object, some glimmer, in the darkness of the room, and the anxiety that troubled his thoughts. His Aunt Adelina had told him once, "The foxes in the Sechura Desert always howl like demons at nightfall. Do you know why? To break the silence that terrifies them." He wanted to cry out, so that there would be some life in that room where everything seemed to be dead. He got up, barefoot, half-dressed, trembling at the thought of the shame and confusion he would feel if they suddenly came in and found him up. He went over to the door and put his ear against it, but he could not hear a sound. He went back to bed and started crying, with both hands over his mouth. When the daylight came into the bedroom and the street was alive with noises, his eyes were still open and his ears were still listening. A long time later, he heard them. They were speaking in low voices and it was only an incomprehensible murmur. Then he heard laughter and movements. Still later he sensed the door opening, footsteps, a presence, known hands that drew the sheets up to his chin, a warm breath on his cheeks. He opened his eyes: his mother was smiling at him. "Good morning," she said tenderly. "Won't you give your mother a kiss?" "No," he said.

I could go and tell him I've got to have twenty soles, but I know what'd happen, he'd get all weepy and he'd give me forty or fifty, but that'd be just like telling him I forgive you for what you've done to my mother and you can keep on whoring around all you want as long as you give me good bribes. Alberto's lips were moving silently under the wool muffler his mother had given him a few months before. His jacket and his military cap, which he had pulled down to his ears, protected him against the cold. He was so used to the weight of the rifle that he hardly felt it. I could go and tell him there's no half way, not even if he sends us a check every month, until he repents of his sins and comes back home, but then he'd just start crying and say that everyone has to bear his cross like Our Lord, and even if he agreed, they'd take a long time to get things settled and I wouldn't get my twenty soles tomorrow. The regulations said that the cadet guards had to patrol the patios in front of their own barracks and also the parade ground, but he spent his tour of duty strolling along the tall rusty fence that protected the front of the military academy. As he looked out through the bars, which reminded him of the flanks of zebras, he could see the paved road that snaked along the fence and the edge of the cliffs. He could hear the sound of the sea, and when the fog thinned for a minute he could glimpse, far off, what looked like a shining lance—it was the jetty of the bathing resort, La Punta—thrust out into the sea like a breakwater, and in the other direction the fanlike glow of Miraflores, the district where he lived. The captain of the guard checked the sentries every two hours, and at one o'clock he would find him at his post. Meanwhile, Alberto planned what he was going to do on Saturday. Maybe even ten of the guys are dreaming about that movie, and after seeing all those women in panties, all those legs and bellies and all, maybe they'll want me to write them some little stories, but they won't pay in advance and how can I write them if the chemistry exam is tomorrow, I'll have to pay the Jaguar for the questions unless Vallano whispers the answers to me if I promise to write some letters for him but who can trust a Negro. Maybe they'll want some letters but who can pay right off at this time of the week because it's only Wednesday and everybody's spent his last centavo in "La Perlita" or the poker games. I could get twenty soles to spend if the guys who're confined to the grounds ask me to buy cigarettes for them and I could pay them back with letters or stories, or it'd be even better if I could find twenty soles in a wallet somebody lost in the mess hall or the classrooms or the latrine, or right now I could sneak into the barracks where the Dogs are and go through the lockers until I found twenty soles but it would be better to take fifty centavos from each one so it wouldn't be so obvious and I'd only have to open forty lockers without waking anybody up but I'd have to find fifty centavos in each one, or I could go to one of the noncoms or a lieutenant and say, lend me twenty soles, I'm a

man now and I want to go see Golden Toes, and who's that
shit that's yelling like that. . .

It took Alberto a moment or two to identify the voice and
to remember he was away from his post. Then louder:
"Where the hell is that cadet?" This time his whole being
reacted. He raised his head and could see the walls of the
guardhouse, the soldiers sitting on a bench, the statue of the
hero defying the fog with his drawn sword, all of them
spinning around him as if in a whirlwind, and he could
picture his name written out on the punishment list, and his
heart was beating wildly, he was in a panic, his tongue and
his lips were moving imperceptibly, Lt. Remigio Huarina
was standing less than five yards away from the bronze hero,
looking over at him with his hands on his hips.

"What are you doing here?"

The lieutenant came up to Alberto, who gazed over the
officer's shoulder at the splotches of moss on the stone base
that held up the hero's statue, or rather he saw them in his
mind because the lights of the guardhouse were dim and far
away, or else he invented them, it was possible that on that
same day the soldiers on duty had scraped and scrubbed the
pedestal.

"Well?" the lieutenant asked. "What's going on?"

Alberto stood motionless, his right hand held rigid to his
cap, all of his senses alert as he faced that short dark figure.
The officer also stood motionless, his hands still on his hips.

"I'd like to ask you for some advice, Sir," Alberto said. I
could tell him I'm dying of a bellyache, I've got to have an
aspirin or something, my mother is seriously ill, somebody
killed the vicuña, I could even ask him to. . . "What I mean
is, personal advice."

"What the hell are you mumbling about?"

"I've got a problem," Alberto said, still standing at attention. I could tell him my father is a general, a rear admiral,
a marshal, and for every point I'm docked he'll lose a year
of promotion, and I could. . . "It's. . .it's personal." He

stopped, hesitated a moment, then lied: "The colonel told us once we could ask advice from our officers. I mean, about personal problems."

"Name and year," the lieutenant said. He had dropped his hands from his hips and now he looked even smaller, even more fragile. He took a step forward and Alberto could look down at him more closely. At his pouting lips. At his scowling, froglike eyes, though without the life of a frog's. At his round face, contracted in an expression that was meant to be implacable and was only pathetic, the same expression he put on when he ordered the punishment lottery, which was his own invention ("Brigadiers, give six points to all the number threes and multiples of three!").

"Alberto Fernández, Sir, Fifth Year, first section."

"All right, now get to the point."

"I think I'm sick, Lieutenant. I mean mentally, not physically. I have nightmares every night." Alberto had lowered his eyes, feigning humility, and he spoke very slowly, his mind a blank, letting his lips and tongue talk on by themselves, letting them weave a spider web, a labyrinth. "They're awful, Lieutenant. Sometimes I dream I'm a killer, or sometimes these animals with human faces are chasing me. I wake up sweating and shaking. It's horrible, Lieutenant, honest."

The officer studied the cadet's face. Alberto discovered that the frog's eyes had come to life: surprise and suspicion peered out of them like two faint stars. I could laugh, I could cry or scream, I could run away. Huarina finished his scrutiny. He took a sudden step backward, and said, "I'm not a priest, goddamn it! Go take your personal problems to your father or mother!"

"I didn't mean to bother you, Lieutenant," Alberto mumbled.

"Wait a minute, what's that arm band?" The officer pushed his snout closer, his eyes widening. "Are you on guard duty?"

"Yes, Sir."

"Don't you know you should never leave your post except when you're dead?"

"Yes, Sir."

"Personal problems! You're a fuck-up."

Alberto held his breath. The scowl had vanished from the officer's face, his mouth was open, his eyes were squinting, there were wrinkles on his forehead: he was laughing. "You're just a fuck-up, goddamn it. Get back to your post. And you should be grateful I'm not reporting you."

"Yes, Sir."

Alberto saluted, made a half turn, and glimpsed the soldiers at the guardhouse sitting huddled over on the bench. He heard from behind him, "We aren't priests, goddamn it." In front of him, toward the left, there were three cement hulks: the Fifth Year, then the Fourth, and finally the Third, which was the barracks of the Dogs. Beyond that the stadium sprawled out: the soccer field covered with weeds, the track full of hollows and holes, the wooden stands warped by the dampness. On the other side of the stadium, beyond the ruined building that was the soldiers' quarters, there was a grayish wall where the world of the Leoncio Prado Military Academy ended and the open fields of La Perla began. And if Huarina'd looked down and seen my boots, and if the Jaguar hasn't got the chemistry exam, or if he's got it and won't trust me, and if I go see Golden Toes and tell her I'm from Leoncio Prado and it's the first time I've come, I'll bring you good luck, and if I go back to the neighborhood and borrow twenty soles from one of my friends and leave him my watch in hock, and if I don't get hold of that chemistry exam, and if I don't have laces for my boots for the personal inspection tomorrow I'm screwed and that's for sure. Alberto walked slowly, dragging his feet a little. He had not had any laces in his boots for a whole week, and his boots threatened to come off at every step. He had covered about half the distance between the Fifth Year

and the statue of the hero. Two years ago the assignment of
the barracks was different: the cadets of the Fifth were in
the barracks next to the stadium, and the Dogs were nearest
to the guardhouse. The Fourth had always been in the
middle, between their enemies. But when there was a change
of directors, the new colonel decided on the present assignment, and explained it in a speech: "The privilege of sleeping near our great hero is one that ought to be earned. From
now on the cadets of the Third Year will occupy the barracks farthest away. Then each year they'll move closer to
the statue of Leoncio Prado. And I hope that when they
leave the academy they'll resemble him a little, because he
fought for the freedom of a country that wasn't even Peru.
In the army, Cadets, you've got to have respect for symbols,
damn it."

And if I steal some laces from Arróspide, I'd be a real shit
to steal from a guy from Miraflores when there's so many
peasants in the section that spend the whole year shut in as
if they're afraid of the street, they'll probably have some
laces. And if I steal them from somebody in the Circle, from
Curly or that slob of a Boa, but what about the exam, I
don't want to flunk chemistry again. And if I steal them from
the Slave, what a joke, that's what I said to Vallano and it's
true, you'd think you were pretty brave if you hit a dead
man, except you're hopeless. You can tell Vallano's a coward
like all the Negroes, you can tell it from his eyes, what eyes,
what fear, what jumping around, I'll kill the bastard that
stole my pajamas, I'll kill him, the lieutenant's coming, the
noncoms are coming, give me my pajamas back, I've got to
get a pass this weekend and I'm not saying anything to start
a fight, I'm not saying anything about your mother, I'm not
insulting you, just asking what's going on or something, but
to let somebody grab your pajamas right during inspection
without doing anything, that's too much. What the Slave
needs is for somebody to knock the fear out of him. I'll steal
the laces from Vallano instead.

He had come to the narrow passage that led to the Fifth Year's patio. In the moist darkness, that was filled with the sound of the sea, Alberto imagined the bodies curled up in their cots behind the cement walls, in the crowded shadows of the barracks. He must be in the barracks, he must be in the latrine, he must be in the field, he must be dead, where have you gone to, little Jaguar? The deserted patio, vaguely lit by the lamps on the parade ground, was like a village plaza. There were no guards in sight. He must be playing a few hands, if I just had a coin, just one fucking coin, I could win those twenty soles, maybe more. He must be gambling and I hope he'll trust me, I'll write you some letters and stories, but actually he's never asked me for anything in three years, oh hell, I'm sure they're going to flunk me in chemistry. He went through the lobby without running into anyone. He went into the barracks of the first and second sections; the latrines were empty, and one of them smelled foul. He looked into the latrines in the other barracks, deliberately making a lot of noise as he went down the aisles, but there was no change in the calm or feverish breathing of the cadets. He stopped in the fifth section, a little before he got to the door of the latrine. Someone was talking in his sleep, but he could only make out a woman's name in that babble of words: "Lidia." Lidia? I think Lidia's the name of the girl friend of that guy from Arequipa, the one that showed me the letters and photos she sent him and told me all his troubles, write her a good letter for me because I really love her, I'm not a priest, goddamn it, you're a fuck-up. Lidia? There was a ring of bundle-shaped forms in the seventh section next to the urinals: they all looked like hunchbacks as they squatted in their green jackets. There were eight rifles on the floor and another one leaning against the wall. The latrine door was open and Alberto could make them out from a distance, from the barracks door. As he went toward them a shadow intercepted him.

"What's up? Who is it?"

"I'm the colonel. Have you got permission to gamble? You should never leave your post except when you're dead."

Alberto went into the latrine. The tired faces of a dozen guards looked up at him. Smoke hovered in the room like an awning over their heads. Nobody he knew: identical faces, all dark and rough.

"Have you seen the Jaguar?"

"He hasn't been here."

"What're you playing?"

"Poker. Want in? First you've got to be the lookout for a quarter of an hour."

"I don't play poker with peasants," Alberto said. He put his hand to his penis and aimed at the players. "I just mow them down."

"Get out of here, Poet," one of them said, "you're bothering us."

"I guess I'll have to tell the captain," Alberto said, turning away. "Captain, the peasants are playing poker during guard duty."

He could hear them insulting him. He was out in the patio again. He hesitated for a few moments, then walked toward the open field. And if I'd been sleeping in the grass, and they'd stolen the exam during my tour of duty, that'd be tough to explain, or if I'd jumped the wall, and if. . . He crossed the field to the back wall of the Academy. That was where they used to jump over, because the ground was level on the other side and there was no danger of breaking your leg. At one time, you could see shadows clearing the wall every night and coming back just before dawn. But the new colonel expelled four cadets from the Fourth who were caught leaving and since then a pair of soldiers patrolled the other side every night. So there were fewer attempts to get out, and never at this spot any more. Alberto turned around. In the distance he saw the patio of the Fifth, dim and empty. Then he glimpsed a small blue flame out in the field. He walked toward it.

"Jaguar?"

There was no answer. Alberto took out his flashlight—besides their rifles, all the guards had flashlights and purple arm bands—and snapped it on. A lax face, with a smooth, beardless skin and timid eyes, was squinting up into the beam of light.

"You? What're you doing here?"

The Slave raised a hand to shield his eyes from the flashlight. Alberto turned it off.

"I'm on guard duty."

Was Alberto laughing? The sound shook in the darkness like an attack of belching, stopped for a moment, then broke out again. A sound of sheer contempt, harsh and mirthless.

"You're taking the Jaguar's place," Alberto said. "You make me sick."

"And you imitate the Jaguar's laugh," the Slave said quietly. "That ought to make you even sicker."

"I only imitate your mother," Alberto said. He unslung his rifle, laid it on the grass, turned up the lapels of his jacket, rubbed his hands together and sat down beside the Slave. "Have you got a cigarette?"

A sweaty hand brushed his and drew away, leaving him a limp cigarette without any tobacco in the tips. Alberto lit a match. "Watch out," the Slave whispered. "The patrol might see you."

"Shit," Alberto said, "I burned myself." The parade ground stretched out in front of him, glowing dimly like a great avenue in the heart of a fog-bound city.

"How do you make your cigarettes last you?" Alberto asked. "I always run out by Wednesday or even sooner."

"I don't smoke very much."

"Why are you so damned timid?" Alberto asked. "Aren't you ashamed to be taking the Jaguar's turn?"

"I do what I want," the Slave said. "What difference does it make to you?"

"They treat you like a slave," Alberto said. "Hell, they all treat you like a slave. What are you scared of?"

"I'm not scared of you."

Alberto laughed. Suddenly he cut his laughter short. "You're right," he said. "I'm laughing like the Jaguar. Why does everybody imitate him?"

"I don't imitate him," the Slave said.

"You're like his dog," Alberto said. "He's got you screwed."

Alberto tossed the butt away. It glimmered for a few moments in the grass, then went out. The patio of the Fifth was still deserted.

"Yes," Alberto said, "he's got you screwed." He opened his mouth, then closed it. He put his fingers to the tip of his tongue, picked off a shred of tobacco, cut it in two with his nails, put the two bits on his lips and spit them out. "You've never had any fights, have you?"

"Just one," the Slave said.

"Here?"

"No. Before."

"That's why you're screwed," Alberto said. "Everybody knows you're scared. You've got to slug somebody once in a while if you want them to respect you. If you don't, they walk all over you."

"I'm not going to be a soldier."

"Neither am I. But you're a soldier here whether you like it or not. And the big thing in the army is to be real tough, to have guts, see what I mean? Screw them first before they screw you. There isn't any other way. I don't like to be screwed."

"But I don't like to fight," the Slave said. "Or the thing is, I don't know how."

"It's something you can't learn," Alberto said. "It's a question of guts."

"That's what Lt. Gamboa said one day."

"And it's the truth, isn't it? I don't want to be a soldier either, but you learn how to be a man here. You learn how to take care of yourself. You find out what life's all about."

"But you don't fight very much," the Slave said, "and still you don't get screwed."

"I make believe I'm crazy. I mean I play stupid. You could do that too, so they wouldn't walk all over you. If you don't defend yourself tooth and claw they jump on you. That's the law of the jungle."

"Are you going to be a poet?" the Slave asked.

"Are you kidding? I'm going to be an engineer. My father's going to send me to the United States to study. I just write letters and stories so I can buy my cigarettes. But that doesn't mean a thing. You, what are you going to be?"

"I wanted to be a sailor," the Slave said. "But I changed my mind. I don't like the services. Maybe I'll be an engineer too."

The fog had grown thicker, and the lamps along the parade ground looked smaller and their light was dimmer than ever. Alberto fished in his pockets. He had run out of cigarettes two days before but he repeated the action automatically whenever he wanted to smoke.

"Got any cigarettes left?"

There was no answer from the Slave, but a moment later Alberto felt an arm against his stomach. He found a hand, which was holding out an almost full pack of cigarettes. He took one and put it between his lips, running the tip of his tongue over the end of it. He lit a match and brought the flame up close to the Slave's face. The light flickered gently in the little grotto of his cupped hands.

"What the fuck are you crying for?" Alberto asked. He opened his hands and dropped the match. "Goddamn it, I burned myself again!"

He took out another match and lit the cigarette, dragging the smoke in and exhaling it through his nose and mouth.

"What's the matter?" he asked.

"Nothing."

Alberto took another drag. The tip glowed and the smoke

THE TIME OF THE HERO 25

mingled with the fog, which was very low, almost hugging the ground. The patio of the Fifth had disappeared. The barracks were a huge, motionless blotch.

"What've they done to you?" Alberto asked. "You shouldn't ever cry, man."

"My jacket," the Slave said. "They've screwed me out of my pass."

Alberto turned his head. The Slave was wearing a dark brown sleeveless sweater.

"I've got to go out on pass tomorrow," the Slave said. "They've got me screwed."

"Do you know who it was?"

"No. They took it out of my locker."

"You'll get docked a hundred soles. Maybe more."

"It isn't that. There's an inspection tomorrow. Gamboa's going to put me on the shit list. I've already been two weeks without a pass."

"What time have you got?"

"Quarter to one," the Slave said. "We can go back to the barracks."

"Wait a while," Alberto said, getting up. "There's plenty of time. Let's swipe a jacket."

The Slave leaped to his feet but then stood there without taking a step, as if paralyzed.

"Let's go," Alberto said.

"But the sentries. . ."

"The hell with them," Alberto said. "Can't you see I'm going to risk my pass to get you a jacket? Yellowbellies make me sick. The sentries are in the latrine in the seventh section. There's a game going."

The Slave followed him. They walked through the thickening fog toward the invisible barracks. The nails on their boots scraped through the wet grass, and the beat of the sea, mingling with the whistle of the wind, invaded the rooms of the doorless, windowless building that stood between the classrooms and the officers' quarters.

"Let's go to the ninth or the tenth," the Slave said. "Those midgets sleep like logs."

"Do you want a jacket or a bib? We'll go to the third."

Alberto pushed gently at the door, which opened without a sound. He put his head in like an animal sniffing at a cave. There was a sound of peaceful breathing in the shadowy barracks. They closed the door behind them. "At the back," Alberto whispered, his lips touching the Slave's ear. "There's a locker that isn't close to the beds."

"What?" the Slave asked him, without moving.

"Oh, shit," Alberto said. "Come on." They went down the barracks slowly, shuffling their feet, with their hands out to avoid obstacles. If I were a blind man, I'd take out my glass eyes and I'd say to Golden Toes, I'm giving you my eyes, but trust me, my old man's got enough whores already, it's enough that you should never leave your post except when you're dead. They stopped by a locker and Alberto's fingers slid along the wood. He put his hand in his pocket, took out a skeleton key, tried to find the lock with his other hand, closed his eyes, gritted his teeth. And if I say, I swear, Lieutenant, I just came in here to get a book to study chemistry so I won't flunk it tomorrow, and I swear I'll never forgive you for the way my mother'll cry. Slave, if you ruin me just for a jacket. The skeleton key scraped across the metal, entered, caught, moved back and forth, right and left, entered a little further, stopped, there was a click and the lock was open. Alberto twisted the key out. The door of the locker began to swing open. Somewhere in the barracks an angry voice broke out into incoherent mutterings. The Slave put his hand on Alberto's arm. "Quiet," Alberto whispered, "or I'll kill you." "What?" the Slave asked. Alberto's hand carefully explored the inside of the locker, a fraction of an inch away from the woolly surface of the jacket, as if he were stroking the face or the hair of a beloved one and were relishing the pleasure of the imminent contact, still only sensing her. "Get the laces out of a pair of boots," Alberto said. "I need them." The Slave took his hand away, bent down, and started crawling. Alberto slipped the jacket off its hanger, put the lock back on the staples, and squeezed it shut with his hand over it to lessen the sound. Then he moved toward the door. When he got there, the Slave put his hand on him again, this time on his shoulder. They went outside.

"Has it got a name on it?"

The Slave turned on his flashlight and examined the jacket minutely. "No."

"Go to the latrine and see if it's got any spots on it. And make sure to use different-colored buttons."

"It's almost one o'clock," the Slave said.

Alberto nodded. When they got to the door of the first section, he turned to the other. "And the laces?"

"I only found one," the Slave said. He hesitated for a moment. "I'm sorry."

Alberto stared at him, but did not insult him or laugh at him. He merely shrugged his shoulders.

"Thanks," the Slave said. He put his hand on Alberto's arm again and looked at him, his timid, cringing face bright with a smile.

"I just did it for the fun of it," Alberto said. And he added quickly, "Have you got the questions for the exam? I don't know beans about chemistry."

"No," the Slave said. "But the Circle must have them. Cava went out a while back and he was heading for the classrooms. They must be working out the answers."

"I haven't got any money. That Jaguar is a crook."

"Do you want me to lend you some?" the Slave asked.

"You've really got money?"

"A little."

"Can you lend me twenty soles?"

"Twenty soles? Yes."

"Great, great! I didn't have a centavo. If you want, I can pay you back with some stories."

"No," the Slave said. He lowered his eyes. "I'd rather have letters."

"Letters? You? Have you got a girl?"

"Not yet," the Slave said. "But maybe I will have."

"That's fine, man. I'll write you twenty of them. But you'll have to show me hers, so I can tell what she's like."

The barracks was coming alive. In the various sections there were sounds of footsteps, of lockers closing, even a few jokes.

"They're changing the guard," Alberto said. "Let's go."

They went into the barracks. Alberto went over to Vallano's bunk, squatted down and took the lace out of one of his boots. Then he began shaking the Negro with both hands.

"Motherfucker, motherfucker!" Vallano shouted.

"Come on, it's one o'clock," Alberto said. "You're on duty."

"If you woke me up too soon, I'll murder you."

At the other end of the barracks, the Boa was shouting at the Slave, who had just awakened him.

"Here's the rifle and the flashlight," Alberto said. "Go back to sleep if you want to, but the patrol's in the second section."

"No shit?" Vallano said, getting up.

Alberto went over to his own bunk and undressed.

"Everybody's so sweet around here," Vallano said. "Very, very sweet."

"What's the matter?" Alberto asked.

"Somebody swiped one of my laces."

"Shut up!" a voice shouted. "Sentry, tell those fairies to shut up!"

Alberto could tell that Vallano was walking on tiptoe. Then he heard a telltale sound. "They're stealing laces!" he shouted.

"One of these days I'm going to break your jaw, Poet," Vallano said, yawning.

A few minutes later the Officer of the Guard blew a sharp blast on his whistle. Alberto did not hear it. He was asleep.

Diego Ferré Street was less than three hundred yards long, and a stranger to it would have thought it was an alley with a dead end. In fact, if you looked down it from the corner of Larco Avenue, where it began, you could see a two-story house closing off the other end two blocks away, with a small garden protected by a green railing. At a distance, that house seemed to end Diego Ferré, but actually it stood on a narrow cross street, Porta. Two other parallel streets, Colón and Ocharán, cut across Diego Ferré between Porta and Larco Avenue. After crossing Diego Ferré they ended abruptly two hundred yards to the east at the Malecón de la Reserva, the serpentine that enclosed the Miraflores district with a belt of red brick. It marked the farthest limits of the city, for it was built along the edge of the cliffs, above the clean, gray, noisy waters of the Bay of Lima.

There were half a dozen blocks between Larco Avenue, the Malecón and Porta Street: about a hundred houses, two or three grocery stores, a drugstore, a soft-drink stand, a shoe repair shop half hidden between a garage and a projecting wall, and a walled lot that was used as a private laundry. The cross streets had trees along both sides of the pavement, but not Diego Ferré. The neighborhood lacked a name. When the boys organized a soccer team to compete in the annual tournament held by the Terrazas Club, they named their team "The Happy Neighborhood." But when the tournament was over, the name was not used any longer. Also, the crime reporters used "The Happy Neighborhood" to describe the long row of houses called Huatica de la Victoria, the street of the whores, which made it somewhat embarrassing. So the boys simply called it the neighborhood, and when somebody asked them which one, they distinguished it from the other neighborhoods in Miraflores, like the 28th of July or Reducto or Francia Street or Alcanfores, by saying: "The Diego Ferré."

Alberto's house was the third house on the second block of Diego Ferré, on the left-hand side. The first time he saw it was at night, when almost all the furniture from the previous house, in San Isidro, had already been moved. It seemed to him a lot larger than the other one, and it had two obvious advantages: his bedroom was further away from that of his parents, and since there was an inner garden they would probably let him have a dog. But the new house would also have its disadvantages. Every morning, the father of one of his friends had driven both of them from San Isidro to La Salle Academy. From now on he would have to take the express, get off at Wilson Avenue, then walk at least ten blocks to Arica Avenue, since La Salle, although it was a very respectable school, was located in the heart of the Breña district, with its zombos—half-Indian, half-Chinese—and its swarm of workers. He would have to get up earlier, and leave right after breakfast. And there had been a bookstore across from his house in San Isidro, where the owner had let him read the *Penecas* and *Billiken* behind the counter, and had even lent them to him for a day, warning him not to crease them or get them dirty. Also, the moving would deprive him of an exciting pastime: that of going up onto the roof to watch what went on in the Nájar family's yard. When the weather was good they ate breakfast in the garden under bright-colored umbrellas, and played tennis, and gave dances at night, and when they gave dances he could spy on the couples who sneaked off to the tennis court to neck.

On the day they moved he got up early and went to school in a good mood. When he got out he went straight to the new house. He got off the express at Salazar Park—he still had not learned the name of that grassy esplanade hung out over the sea—and walked along Diego Ferré, which was deserted at that hour. At home he found his mother threatening to fire the maid if she started spending her time with the neighboring cooks and chauffeurs the way she had in San Isidro. After lunch his father said, "I've got to leave. It's very important business." His mother cried, "You're lying again! How can you look me in the face?" And then, with the help of the servant and the maid, she began a very careful inspection to make sure that nothing had been lost or damaged by the movers. Alberto went up to his room and stretched out on the bed, aimlessly doodling on the jackets of his books. A little later he heard the voices of boys through the open window. The voices stopped, there was only the sound of a kick and the hum and slap of a ball as it bounced against the door. Then the voices again. He got up from the bed and looked out. One of the boys wore a flaming shirt, red and yellow stripes, and the other wore a white silk shirt with the buttons open. The former was taller, with blond hair, and his voice and looks and gestures were insolent. The other was short and stocky, with curly black hair, and he was extremely quick. The blond boy was playing goalkeeper in the door of a garage. The dark boy kicked the brand-new soccer ball at him, shouting, "Stop this one, Pluto!" Pluto, with a dramatic grimace, wiped his forehead and his nose with the back of his hand and pretended to fling himself at the ball, and if he stopped a goal he laughed uproariously. "You're an old lady, Tico, I could block your kicks with my little finger." Tico stopped the ball skillfully with his foot, set it, measured the distance, and kicked, and almost every kick was a goal. "Butterfingers!" he jeered. "Fairy! Look out for this next one. It's going to the right, and boom!" At first Alberto watched them without much interest, and apparently they had not noticed him. But little by little he began to study their styles, and when Tico kicked a goal or Pluto intercepted the ball, he nodded without smiling, like a veteran fan. Then he began to pay attention to the jokes the two boys were making. He reacted the way they did, and at times the players gave signs that they knew he was watching: they turned their heads toward him as if they had

long way so as not to go past the barracks. Do you see them, are you coming, the bastard said, look at all those different-colored chickens, what more do you want, do you want anything more? Which one'll we take, the black one or the yellow one? The yellow one's bigger. What're you waiting for, idiot? I'll grab her and hold her wings. Come on, Boa, grab her beak. As if that was so easy. Don't run away, little chick, come here, come here. She's afraid of him, she's giving him a dirty look, she's turning her tail on him, just look at that, the bastard said. But it was true that she pecked my fingers. Let's go to the stadium and tie up her beak for good. And what if Curly buggers the fatboy? The best thing, the Jaguar said, is to tie up their legs and beak. But what about the wings? What'll they say if she cuts somebody's balls off when she flaps her wings, what'll they say then? She doesn't want anything to do with you, Boa. You sure of that, peasant, you too? No, but I saw it with my own eyes. What'll I tie her with? What animals, what animals, at least a chicken is small, it's more like a game, but a llama! And what if Curly buggers the fatboy? We were smoking in the latrines in the classroom building, keep your lights down. The Jaguar was on the toilet, straining, and it looked like he was being screwed. How about it, Jaguar, how about it? Shut up, they're cutting me, I've got to concentrate. And the beak? And suppose we buggered the fatboy, Curly said. Who? The one in the ninth, the fatboy. Haven't you ever pinched him? Oomph. It isn't a bad idea, but does he let you or doesn't he? They tell me Lañas buggers him when he's on guard duty. Oomph, at last. How about it, the bastard said. And who goes first, I don't want to do it now with all the noise she makes. Here's a piece of string for her beak. Don't let her go, peasant, or she'll fly away. Who's ready? Cava's got her by the beak, Curly tells her not to move her beak because she's going to get screwed anyway, and I tied up her feet. Let's draw lots. Who's got some matches? Cut the head off one of them and show me the rest, I'm too old to fall for any tricks. Curly'll probably win. Listen, does it make any difference whether he lets you? It doesn't to me. That little laugh like a sting. Okay, Curly, but just for the hell of it. And if he doesn't let you? Shut up, I can smell a non-com, it's a good thing he didn't come near, I'm a real he-man. And suppose we screwed the noncom? The Boa screws a dog, the sharper said, why not the fatboy, he's human at least. I saw him in the mess hall, he's on the shit list, he was bullying the eight Dogs at his table. No, he probably wouldn't let you. Who said I'm afraid, did somebody say I'm afraid? I could screw a whole section of fatboys, one after the other, and still be as good as new. We've got to have a plan, the Jaguar said, it'll make things easier. Who got the short match? The chicken was on the ground, gasping. That peasant Cava, can't they see what he's doing with his hand? He likes to play with himself, but it's dead, the Boa's the one who gets a hard-on even when he's marching. We've drawn lots, everything's ready, screw her or we'll screw you like the llamas in your village. Don't you know a story? What if we get the Poet here to tell us one of those stories that make your cock stand up? But that's horseshit, I can get a hard-on just by thinking about it, it's all a matter of will power. What if I get a dose? What's the matter, loverboy, what's got into you, peasant, don't you know the Boa is cleaner than your mother ever since he's been screwing Skimpy? Where did you get those crazy ideas, haven't they told you chickens are more sanitary than dogs? So we'll do it even if they catch us red-handed. And the patrol? Huarina's the Officer of the Guard, he's a slob, and on Saturday the patrol's a laugh. And if there's trouble? A meeting of the Circle: You're a convicted squealer, Cadet, but would you tell if they beat you up? Let's go, they're going to blow taps. And keep your lights down, damn it. Look, the bastard said, she stood up by herself, pass her over. Take her. Me? Yes, you. Are you sure chickens have holes? Maybe this blonde's a virgin. She's moving, look, it's probably a rooster, a queer one. Don't laugh or talk, please. Please. That shitty little laugh. Can't you see that peasant's hand? You're feeling her up, you bastard. I'm looking for the, don't rush me, I've found it. What'd he say? She's got a hole, shut up please, for Christ's sake don't laugh or the elephant's trunk'll go down. What an ape. Those peasants from the mountains, my brother said, they're bad ones, the worst there is. Traitors and cowards. Rotten to the core. Shut your beak, you dirty bitch! Lieutenant Gamboa, here's somebody screwing a chicken. It's almost ten o'clock, Curly said. It's after quarter past ten. Has anybody seen the guards? I'll screw one of them too. You'd screw anything, I think, you're real hot, just promise you won't screw your own dear mother. There weren't any others in the barracks confined to the grounds, but there were some in the second section, and we went out barefoot. I'm freezing to death, I'll probably catch a cold. I can tell you right now, if I hear a whistle I'll take off. Let's bend over going up the stairs, they can see us from the guardhouse. No shit? We went into the barracks slowly and the Jaguar said, who's the bastard who said there was only two of them confined to quarters, there's about ten of those midgets snoring there. Are you going to clear out? Who? You know which bed he's in, you go first, we don't want to screw the wrong one. It's the third one, can't you tell how it smells of a nice little fatboy? Look, her feathers are coming out, I think she's dying. Are you finished? Tell me, do you always come off so fast, or just with chickens? Look at her, the poor little whore, I think the peasant killed her. Me? She's suffocating, all her holes are blocked up. If she moves any more, she's just pretending she's dead. Do you think animals have any feelings? Do you think they've got souls? I mean, do they like it, the way women do? Sure, Skimpy does, just like a woman. Boa, you make me puke. The things that go on. Look, the chicken's getting up. She liked it and she wants more, what about that? Look at her, she's walking like a drunk. And are we really going to eat her now? Somebody's going to get preg-

nant, don't forget what the peasant left inside her. I don't
even know how to kill a chicken. Shut up, the fire'll get rid
of the germs. Grab her by the neck and swing her around
in the air. Keep her quiet, Boa, I'm going to show you, just
watch this. Yes, sir, you showed us all right, very nice foot-
work too. She's dead now but Jesus, what a mess. Jesus,
what a mess, who's going to eat her the way she's all dust
and dirt? Are you sure the fire'll get rid of the germs? Let's
go make a fire, but over there behind the wall, it'll hide it
better. Don't make any noise or I'll murder you. Come on,
climb onto him, idiot, he's stretched out, he's ready. Christ
how that midget can kick, how he kicked, what are you
waiting for, climb onto him, can't you see he's naked as a
snake? Look out, Boa, don't stop his mouth like that, he'll
smother. He keeps getting away, he's worse than the chicken,
Curly said, lie still or I'll kill you, I'm giving it to you, stop
kicking, what more do you want. Let's go, the midgets are
getting up, I told you so, damn it, the midgets are all getting
up, there's going to be bloodshed. The one that turned on
the lights had guts. The one that shouted, they're trying to
screw us, come on, let's get them, that one had guts too.
They rattled me with that business of the lights. Was that
why I let go of his mouth? Save me, fellows! The only time
I ever heard a scream like that was when my mother threw
a chair at my brother. And you midgets, who told you to get
up, who told you to turn on the lights? The brigadier? We're
not going to let you get away with it, you lousy queers! What
did you say, did you say what I think you did, you can't
talk like that to cadets, stand at attention. And you, you can
stop screaming, can't you see it was just a joke? Wait and
see, I'll take care of you midgets. And the Jaguar was still
laughing, I remember how he laughed while I was beating
up the midgets. Okay, we're going now, but listen to me
and don't forget what I'm telling you: either you keep your
traps shut or we'll screw the whole section, and not the way
you like. The trouble with these midgets is, they're all too

nervous, they don't know a joke when they see it. Should we duck down again on the stairs? Ugh, Curly said, chewing at a bone, it tastes of burnt feathers.

2

When the morning wind sprang up at La Perla, scattering the fog, pushing it toward the sea, and the grounds of the Leoncio Prado Military Academy grew clearer, like a smoke-filled house whose windows have just been opened, an anonymous soldier appeared in the doorway of the soldiers' barracks, yawning, and walked toward the barracks of the cadets. The bugle he carried swung back and forth with the movements of his body, and shone dully in the pale, dim light. When he reached the Third Year, he stopped in the exact center of the patio. He was hunched up inside his greenish uniform, and with the last remnants of the fog blurring his shape, he looked like a phantom. He stood motionless for a few moments, then slowly came to life, rubbing his hands and spitting. Then he blew his bugle. He heard the echo of his own notes, and a few seconds later the cursing of the Dogs, who swore at him for putting an end to their sleep. The bugler walked on to the barracks of the Fourth Year, escorted by those diminishing insults. A few of the sentries from the last watch had come out of the Fourth after hearing the reveille at the Third. They mocked him and insulted him; sometimes they threw stones at him. Then he went on to the Fifth. The bugler was wholly awake by now, and walked more briskly. There was no reaction at the Fifth: the veterans knew they had fifteen minutes between reveille and the whistle that called them to fall in, and they stayed in bed till half the time was gone. The bugler returned to his barracks, rubbing his hands and spitting again. He was not disturbed by the cursing of the

Dogs or the insults of the Fourth: he scarcely noticed
them. . .except on Saturdays. There were field exercises on
Saturdays, reveille was an hour earlier, and the buglers
dreaded that duty. At five o'clock it was still completely dark,
and the cadets, half-drunk with sleep and rage, bombarded
the bugler from the windows with anything they could lay
their hands on. Therefore the buglers violated the regulations on Saturdays: they blew reveille from the parade
ground, a safe distance from the patios, and they blew it as
rapidly as possible.

The cadets in the Fifth could only stay in their bunks
for two or three minutes on Saturdays, because they only
had eight minutes, not fifteen, to wash, dress, make their
bunks, and fall in. But this Saturday was an exception. The
field exercises had been canceled because the Fifth was
scheduled to take the chemistry exam. By the time the veterans heard their reveille, at six, the Dogs and the Fourth
were already marching out the front gate toward the open
fields between La Perla and Callao.

A few moments after reveille, Alberto thought: Today's
the day we get passes. Somebody said, "It's only four minutes
to six. We ought to kill that bugler." Then the barracks was
silent. He opened his eyes, and saw that a pale gray light
was filtering through the windows. The sun ought to shine
on Saturdays at least. The latrine door opened and Alberto
saw the pallid face of the Slave. The upper bunks kept cutting off his head as he came down the aisle. He had already
shaved. He got up before reveille to be the first to fall in,
Alberto told himself. He closed his eyes. When the Slave
stopped at his bunk and touched his shoulder, he half-
opened his eyes again. The Slave had a large head but it
topped a skeleton body that was swallowed up by his blue
pajamas.

"Lt. Gamboa's on duty today."

"I know," Alberto said. "I've still got time."

"All right," the Slave said. "I thought you were still asleep." He smiled vaguely and went away.

He wants to be a friend of mine, Alberto thought. He closed his eyes again and lay inert. The pavement along Diego Ferré is shining with the dew. The sidewalks along Porta and Ocharán are strewn with the leaves the night wind blew down. A natty young man is walking along, smoking a Chesterfield. I swear to God, I'm going to see the whores today.

"Seven minutes!" That was Vallano, bellowing from the doorway. And then the rush: the bunks creaked, the lockers squeaked and slammed, boot heels hammered the tiles, the cadets grunted as they grazed or bumped into each other. But the loudest noise was their cursing, which was like tongues of fire in a cloud of smoke. Their curses were not aimed at any definite target: they swore at such abstractions as God, the Officers, the Mothers of Others, with more music than meaning.

Alberto jumped out of his bunk and put on his socks and boots. His boots were still without laces, and he swore. By the time he got the laces in, most of the cadets had made their bunks and were dressing. "Slave!" Vallano shouted, "sing me something. I like to hear you while I'm washing." "Sentry," Arróspide roared, "they stole one of my laces!" "You're to blame." "You'll be confined to the grounds, you bastard." "It was the Slave," someone said, "I know, I saw him." "We'll have to report him to the captain," Vallano said, "we don't want crooks in the barracks." "Oh, my," a cracked voice yelled, "our poor little Negress is afraid of burglars," "Ay, ay," some of them sang. "Ay, ay, ay," the whole barracks howled. "You're all sons of bitches," Vallano said. He went out, slamming the door behind him. Alberto got dressed and ran to the latrine. The Jaguar was combing his hair at the next sink.

"I need fifty points for the chemistry exam," Alberto said with his mouth full of tooth paste. "How much?"

"They're going to flunk you, Poet." The Jaguar peered in the mirror and tried to smooth down his hair, but the stubborn blond spikes kept bobbing up behind the comb. "We haven't got the exam. We didn't go."

"You didn't get the exam?"

"No. We didn't even go."

Then they heard the whistle. The steady buzz that came from the barracks and latrines increased and suddenly stopped. The voice of Lt. Gamboa was like thunder out in the patio: "Brigadiers, write down the last three that fall in." The buzz started up again, in a lower tone. Alberto began to run. He had his comb and toothbrush in his pocket and he wrapped his towel around his waist under his jacket like a sash. The formation was half assembled. He bumped into the cadet in front of him and someone grabbed him from behind. Alberto held on to Vallano's belt, hopping up and down to avoid the kicks with which the newcomers tried to break up the clusters of cadets in order to find a place. "Don't muss me up, you bastard," Vallano said. Little by little the front ranks straightened out and the brigadiers—the cadet noncoms—began to count those present. In back, the disorder and struggling continued, with the latecomers trying to make themselves places by elbowing and muttering threats. Lt. Gamboa watched the formation from the edge of the parade ground. He was tall and heavily built. His cap was insolently cocked to one side. He turned his head back and forth very slowly, and his smile was contemptuous.

"Silence!" he shouted.

The cadets stopped murmuring. The lieutenant had his hands on his hips. When he dropped them to his side, they swung back and forth for a moment before becoming motionless. Then he began walking toward the battalion, his face hard and stern now, and very dark. Three of the army noncoms—Varúa, Morte, and Pezoa—followed him a few steps behind. Gamboa halted and glanced at his watch.

"Three minutes," he said. He gazed from one end of the

formation to the other, like a shepherd inspecting his flock. "The Dogs fall in in two and a half minutes."

There was a wave of stifled laughter throughout the battalion. Gamboa raised his eyebrows, and immediately there was silence again.

"I meant, the Third Year cadets."

Another wave of laughter, this time more daring. The cadets' faces remained serious, the laughter came from their bellies and died on their lips without changing their expressions. Gamboa put his hands on his hips. There was silence again, as sudden as the stab of a knife. The noncoms stared at him, hypnotized. "He's in a good mood," Vallano whispered.

"Brigadiers," Gamboa said, "check them by sections."

He accented the last word, drawing it out, while his eyes narrowed slightly. There was a sigh of relief from the tail end of the battalion. Gamboa took a step forward and looked down the rows of motionless cadets.

"And don't forget the last three," he added.

A low buzzing arose from the rear of the battalion. The brigadiers went through the ranks of their sections with pencils and slips of paper in their hands. The buzzing sounded like a swarm of flies trying to escape from a sheet of flypaper. Out of the corner of his eye Alberto could see who the three victims in the first section were. Urioste. Núñez. Revilla. And he could hear Revilla murmur, "Come on, Monkey, swap places with me. You're already on the shit list for another month. What difference will six more points make?" "Ten soles," the Monkey said. "I'm broke right now, but I'll pay you later." "Go fuck yourself."

"Who's talking there?" the lieutenant shouted. The muttering lessened but went on.

"Silence!" Gamboa roared. "Silence, goddamn it!"

This time he was obeyed. The brigadiers emerged from the ranks, stood at attention two yards from the noncoms, clicked their heels and saluted. After handing in the lists, they asked permission to return to their sections. The non-coms nodded or said, "Go on," and the brigadiers ran back to their places. Then the noncoms handed the lists to Gamboa. The lieutenant had his own way of returning a salute: his heels clicked like the crack of a pistol, and instead of bringing his hand up to his brow, he curled it over his right eye. The cadets stood rigid as they watched him take the lists. He glanced through them, dangled them, waved them about like a fan. What was he waiting for? He gave the battalion an amused look. Suddenly he grinned.

"Six points or a right angle?" he asked.

There was a wave of applause, and some of the cadets shouted, "Viva Gamboa!"

"Am I losing my mind or is somebody talking in the ranks?" the lieutenant said. The cadets were silent. Gamboa walked by the brigadiers, his hands on his hips.

"Bring the last three out here," he shouted. "On the double. By sections."

Urioste, Núñez, and Revilla ran out from their places at the rear. As they went by, Vallano said to them, "You're lucky it's Gamboa, you suckers." The three cadets stood at attention in front of the lieutenant. "Which do you want," Gamboa asked them, "a right angle or six points? Take your choice."

All three of them said, "A right angle." The lieutenant nodded and shrugged his shoulders. "I know them as if they were my own kids," he mumbled to himself as Urioste, Núñez, and Revilla smiled gratefully. "All right," Gamboa told them, "take the right-angle position."

The three cadets bent over like hinges, their upper bodies parallel with the ground. Gamboa studied them for a moment, then lowered Revilla's head a little with his elbow. "Cover your balls," he said. "With both hands."

He motioned to the noncom Pezoa, a small, muscular half-breed with a big, carnivorous jaw. Pezoa was an excellent soccer player and his kick had tremendous force. He measured the distance and swayed a little, and his foot flashed up and landed. Revilla let out a whimper. Gamboa motioned to the cadet to go back to his place.

"Bah!" he said. "You're getting soft, Pezoa. You didn't even budge him."

The noncom turned pale. His slanted eyes were fixed on Núñez. This time he put everything into it. Also, he kicked him with the toe of his boot. The cadet screamed as he fell forward, staggered on all fours for a couple of yards, and then collapsed. Pezoa glanced anxiously at Gamboa, who smiled at him. The cadets also smiled. Even Núñez, who had got up and was rubbing his buttocks with both hands, had a smile on his face. Pezoa took aim again. Urioste was the huskiest cadet in the first section, perhaps in the whole Academy. He spread his legs a little to balance himself better. The kick scarcely rocked him at all.

"Second section," Gamboa said. "The last three."

Then the cadets from the other sections were punished. The ones from the eighth, ninth and tenth were so small that the noncom's kicks sent them tumbling to the edge of the parade ground. Gamboa never forgot to ask each one if he preferred a right angle or six points. He told all of them, "Take your choice."

Alberto paid attention to the right angles for a while, but later he tried to remember the last chemistry classes. He could only recall a few vague formulas, a few scattered terms. I wonder if Vallano's done his studying? The Jaguar was standing beside him; he had taken someone else's place. "Jaguar," Alberto whispered, "give me at least twenty points. How much?" "You're crazy," the Jaguar said. "I already told you we didn't get the exam. So stop talking about it. For your own good."

"Fall out by sections," Gamboa told them.

The formation broke up and the cadets stampeded into the mess hall, jabbering and shouting as they crowded to

their places. Each table seated ten, with a cadet from the
Fifth at the head. When the cadets from the Third were at
their places the mess sergeant blew his whistle and they
stood at attention in front of their chairs. When he blew it
again they sat down. During other meals the loudspeakers
poured out military marches or Peruvian music—waltzes,
folk songs from the coast, folk songs from the Andes—but
during breakfast the only sound was the endless, chaotic
chatter of the cadets. "Things are going to change around
here, because if they don't, Cadet, are you going to eat
that whole slice of beef by yourself? you'd better leave us
a little of it, a hunk of gristle, Cadet, sure, they had it as
bad as we do, come on, Fernández, give us some more rice,
some more meat, some more Jello, Cadet, come on, don't
spit in the food, Cadet, you think I'm kidding, I don't look
tough for the fun of it, don't fart around with me, Dog, and
if my Dogs spit in my soup I'd get Arróspide and we'd make
them strip naked and we'd goose-step them until they
croaked, what did you say, do you want another serving,
who's going to make my bed, I am, Cadet, who's going to
give me a cigarette, I am, Cadet, who's going to buy me an
Inca Cola at La Perlita, I am, Cadet, who's going to kiss my
ass, tell me that."

Then the Fifth came in and sat down. Three-fourths of
the tables were empty and the mess hall looked larger than
it was. The open fields stretched out beyond the windows,
with the vicuña standing motionless in the tall grass, its
ears raised, its big, liquid eyes staring at nothing. "Maybe
you don't know it but I've seen you shoving in so you can
sit beside me. Maybe you don't know it but when Vallano
asked who was the waiter and everybody shouted the Slave
and I said why not your mothers, tell me why not and they
all sang Ay, ay, ay, I saw you put your hand down and
almost touch my knee." Eight high-pitched voices went on
singing effeminate ayes, and several of the cadets made
circles with their thumbs and forefingers, and held them out

toward Alberto. "You mean I like to bugger them?" he said. "And what'll you do if I drop my pants?" "*Ay, ay, ay.*" The Slave got up and filled their cups. They told him, "If you don't give us enough milk we'll cut your balls off." Alberto turned to Vallano: "Do you know any chemistry?"

"No."

"Whisper the answers to me. How much?"

Vallano looked at him suspiciously, and said, "Five letters. Good ones."

"And your mother," Alberto asked, "how's she doing?"

"Okay," Vallano said. "Let me know if you change your mind."

The Slave sat down again and reached out for a slice of bread. Arróspide batted his hand and the bread slid across the table and fell to the floor. Arróspide, roaring with laughter, bent over to pick it up. Suddenly he stopped laughing. When they could see his face again it was grim. He stood up, stretched out his arm, and grabbed Vallano by the collar. "You've got to be pretty damned stupid not to tell colors apart in broad daylight. Either that or you've got to have pretty shitty luck. It takes brains to be a crook, even if you're just stealing a bootlace or something. What would happen if Arróspide settled it with his fists, black or white, what would happen?" "I didn't notice it was black," Vallano said, taking the lace out of his boot. Arróspide accepted it calmly. "Good thing you gave it back," he said, "or I'd have beaten the hell out of you." The chorus exploded again in a rhythmical falsetto: *Ay, ay, ay.* "Bullshit," Vallano said. "You watch, I'm going to empty out your locker before the end of the year. What I need now is a lace. Sell me one, Cava, you're the peddler around here. Wake up, I'm talking to you, what's the matter with you." Cava looked up quickly from his empty cup and gazed at Vallano in dread. "What?" he asked. "What?" Alberto leaned over toward the Slave: "You sure you saw Cava last night?"

"Yes," the Slave said, "it was Cava."

"You'd better not tell anybody you saw him. Something's up. The Jaguar tried to tell me they didn't get the exam, but look at his face, the bastard."

The whistle blew and they jumped up and ran out to the field. Gamboa was waiting for them with his arms crossed on his chest and the whistle in his mouth. The vicuña loped away, terrified by the sudden stampede. Look, can't you see they're going to flunk me in chemistry on account of you, Golden Toes, can't you see I'm sick on account of you. Here's twenty soles, the Slave loaned them to me, if you want I'll write you some letters, don't be like that, don't get me nervous, don't make me flunk the chemistry exam, can't you see the Jaguar's got the answers, can't you see I'm worse off than Skimpy. The brigadiers made their count again and reported to the noncoms, who reported to Lt. Gamboa. It had started to drizzle. Alberto touched Vallano's leg with his boot. Vallano glanced at him out of the corner of his eye.

"I'll write you three letters."

"Four."

"Okay, four."

Vallano nodded, and ran his tongue over his lips to lick off the last crumbs of bread.

The first section's classroom was on the second floor of what was still called the New Building, although the dampness had already stained it and discolored it. The building next to it was the Assembly Hall, a big barn with crude benches where the cadets saw movies once a week. The drizzle had turned the parade ground into a bottomless mirror. The cadets trampled its shining surface with their boots. Their boots rose and fell to the blasts of the whistle. When they reached the foot of the stairs, the cadets broke ranks and charged up. Their muddy boots kept slipping on the stairs and the noncoms never stopped swearing. The classrooms looked out on one side over the cement patio where on any other day the cadets of the Fourth and the Dogs of the Third would have to march through a shower of spit and missiles from the Fifth. One day the Negro, Vallano, threw a piece of wood. There was a loud scream, and one of the Dogs raced across the patio like a meteor, covering his ear with both hands. A trickle of blood ran out between his fingers and made a dark stain on his jacket. The whole section was confined to the grounds for two weeks but the guilty person was never discovered. On the first day they were free Vallano bought two packs of cigarettes for each of the thirty cadets. "Jesus, that's a lot," the Negro grumbled. "One pack each'd be plenty." The Jaguar and his buddies warned him: "Two apiece or we'll hold a meeting of the Circle."

"Just twenty points," Vallano told Alberto. "Not a point more. I'm not going to risk my neck for just four letters."

"No," Alberto said, "at least thirty. And I'll show you what questions with my finger. Don't whisper the answers. Show me your exam."

"I'll whisper them." The desks held two students each. Alberto and Vallano were sitting in the last row behind Cava and the Boa, who were both so broad-shouldered that they made a good screen.

"Like the last time? You told me the wrong answers on purpose."

Vallano laughed. "Four letters," he said. "Two pages each."

Pezoa the noncom appeared in the doorway carrying a stack of exams. He looked at the cadets with his small, malevolent eyes, and from time to time he moistened the tips of his thin mustache with his tongue.

"Anyone who takes out a book," he said, "or looks at anyone else's exam, will automatically flunk. And besides that, six points. Brigadier, pass out the exam."

"The Rat."

Pezoa started and flushed, and his eyes looked like two slashes. He straightened his shirt with his babyish hand.

"The deal's off," Alberto said. "I didn't know we'd get the Rat. I'd rather copy from the book."

Arróspide passed out the exams. The noncom looked at his watch.

"Eight o'clock," he said. "You've got forty minutes."

"The Rat."

"There isn't a one of you that's a man!" Pezoa roared. "I'd like to see the face of that hero that keeps saying 'The Rat.'"

The desks came to life: they rose up a fraction of an inch and banged down on the floor, at first in disorder, then in rhythm, while a chorus of voices shouted, "The Rat! The Rat!"

"Shut up, you cowards!" the noncom bellowed.

Suddenly Lt. Gamboa and the chemistry teacher entered the room. The teacher was a slight, nervous-looking man, and next to Gamboa, who was tall and muscular, he seemed very insignificant in his civilian clothes, which were somewhat too large for him.

"What's going on, Pezoa?"

The noncom saluted. "Just a little horseplay, sir."

Everything stood still. There was absolute silence.

"Oh, really?" Gamboa said. "You go to the second section, Pezoa. I'll take care of these youngsters."

Pezoa saluted again and left. The chemistry teacher followed him. He seemed to be intimidated by so many uniforms.

"Vallano," Alberto whispered, "the deal's back on."

Without looking at him, the Negro shook his head and ran his finger across his throat. Arróspide had finished passing out the exams. The cadets bent their heads over the pages. Fifteen plus five, plus three, plus five, blank, plus three, blank, blank, plus three, no, blank, that's—what—thirty-one, right in the neck. If it'd end in the middle, if they'd call him out, if something'd happen so he'd have to leave in a hurry, Golden Toes.

Alberto answered the questions slowly, printing the words. Gamboa's heels clicked on the tile floor. Whenever a cadet raised his eyes from his exam, they always met the mocking eyes of the lieutenant, who said, "Do you want me to whisper you the answers? Keep your head down. The only people I let watch me are my wife and the maid."

When he had finished answering all the questions he could, Alberto glanced at Vallano. The Negro was scribbling furiously, biting his tongue. Then Alberto very cautiously looked around the room. Some of the cadets were only pretending to write, moving their pens a fraction of an inch above the paper. He reread the exam and answered two more questions by sheer guesswork. There was a distant, underground noise. The cadets stirred restlessly in their seats. The air grew denser: something invisible floated above those bent heads, a warm, impalpable something, a nebulosity, a diaphanous emotion, a dew. How to escape the lieutenant's watchfulness for just a few seconds?

Gamboa laughed at them. He stopped walking about and stood in the middle of the classroom. His arms were crossed, his muscles showed under his cream-colored shirt, and his eyes took in everything at a glance, as they did in the field exercises when he sent his company through the mud and had them charge through the scrub or the boulders with a mere flick of his hand or a short blast on his whistle: the cadets under his command felt proud when they saw the anger and frustration of the officers and cadets from the other companies, who always ended up by being ambushed, surrounded, trounced. Gamboa, with his helmet shining in the early light, would point his finger toward a tall adobe wall, calmly, casually, imperturbable in the face of the invisible enemy occupying the heights and the nearby defiles and even the stretch of beach beyond the cliffs, and shout: "Over the wall, you birds!" And the cadets of the first company would race forward like meteors, their fixed bayonets jabbing at the sky and their hearts filled with a tremendous rage as they trampled down the plants in the furrows—if only the plants were the heads of Chileans or Ecuadoreans, if only the blood would spurt out from under their boots, if only their enemies would die—until they came gasping and swearing to the foot of the adobe wall. Then they would sling their rifles, reach up their swollen hands, dig their nails into the cracks, flatten themselves against the wall, and slither up it somehow, keeping their eyes on the top, and then they would jump in a crouch, and land, hearing nothing except their own curses and the excited pounding of the blood in their temples and chests. But Gamboa would already be ahead of them, standing on top of a high rock, with hardly a scratch, sniffing the sea wind and calculating. The cadets, squatting or sprawling, kept their eyes fixed on him: life or death depended on his commands. Suddenly he would glare at them and they were not his birds any more, they were worms. "Spread out! You're all bunched together like sheep!" So the worms would stand up and move apart, with their old mended fatigues flapping in the wind, with the patches and seams looking like scabs and scars, and then get down in the mud again, hiding in the weeds but still looking at Gamboa with the same docile, pleading eyes they had turned up to him on the night he broke up the Circle.

They formed the Circle only forty-eight hours after they had taken off their civilian clothes and been scalped by the Academy barber and put on their crisp khaki uniforms and fallen in for the first time in the stadium to the commands of whistles and harsh voices. It was the last day of summer, and the sky over Lima, after burning like an ember for three months, was ash gray with clouds, as if this were the beginning of a long dark dream. They came from all parts of Peru. They had never seen each other before but they were all together now, lined up in front of the cement hulks whose insides they had not yet seen. The voice of Capt. Garrido informed them that their civilian lives had ended for three years, that they would all be made into men, that the true military spirit consisted of three simple things: obedience, courage, and hard work. But the Circle came later, after their first meal in the Academy, after they were free at last from the supervision of the officers and noncoms. As they left the mess hall they looked at the cadets of the Fourth and Fifth with suspicion, something less of curiosity, something even less of sympathy.

The Slave was coming down the mess hall stairs, alone, when his arm was gripped tightly and a voice murmured in his ear: "Come with us, Dog." He smiled and followed them meekly. Around him, a number of the classmates he had met that morning were also seized and hustled across the field to the Fourth Year barracks. There were no classes that day. The Dogs were at the mercy of the Fourth from lunch time until dinner. The Slave was not sure to what section he was taken, nor by whom. But the barracks was full of cigarette smoke and uniforms and he could hear shouts and laughter. He had hardly entered, the smile still on his lips, when he felt a blow on his shoulder. He fell to the floor, rolled over and lay there on his back. A foot was planted on his stomach. Ten faces looked down at him impassively, as if he were an insect, and he could not see the ceiling.

A voice said, "To start off, sing 'I'm a Dog' a hundred times in the rhythm of a Mexican ballad."

It was impossible. He was stunned, his eyes were bulging from their sockets, his throat was burning. The foot pressed a little harder on his stomach.

"He doesn't want to," the voice said. "The Dog doesn't want to sing."

And they opened their mouths and spit on him, not once but again and again, until he had to close his eyes. When the spitting stopped, the same anonymous voice, turning like a screw, repeated: "Sing 'I'm a Dog' a hundred times in the rhythm of a Mexican ballad."

This time he obeyed and his throat forced out the required words to the tune of "Rancho Grande." It was almost impossible: without the original words, the melody sometimes turned into hoarse screams. But apparently that made no difference, because they listened to him attentively.

"That's enough," the voice said. "Now, in the rhythm of a bolero."

And after that, a mambo and a waltz. Then they told him: "Get up."

He stood up and ran his hand across his face, then wiped it off on the seat of his pants. The voice said, "Did anybody tell you to clean your face? No, Dog, nobody told you to."

Their mouths opened again and he automatically closed his eyes until it stopped.

"These two gentlemen here are cadets," the voice said. "Stand at attention, Dog. That's good. These cadets have made a bet and you're going to be the judge."

The one on the right hit him first and the Slave felt a searing pain in his arm. The one on the left hit him an instant later.

"Now, then, what do you think? Which one hit you the hardest?"

"Both the same."

"So that means it was a tie," the voice said. "We'll have to break the tie."

A moment later the relentless voice asked him, "By the way, Dog, do your arms hurt you?"

"No," the Slave said.

It was true. He had lost the sense of his body, and of time also. His dazed mind was remembering the waveless sea off Puerto Eten, and he heard his mother tell him, "Be careful, Ricardito, you'll step on a sting ray," and she reached out her long, protecting arms to gather him in, under a pitiless sun.

"That's a lie," the voice said. "If they don't hurt you, Dog, why are you bawling?"

He thought they had finished. But they had only begun.

"Are you a dog or a human being?" the voice asked him.
"A dog, Cadet."

"So why are you standing up? Dogs go around on all fours."

He dropped down, and when he put his hands on the floor he felt a burning pain in his arms. There was another boy next to him, also on hands and knees.

"Correct," the voice said. "And when two dogs meet in the street, what do they do? Answer me, Dog, I'm talking to you."

The Slave was kicked in the buttocks, and he answered hurriedly, "I don't know, Cadet."

"They fight," the voice said. "They bark and they leap at each other. And they bite."

The Slave could not remember having seen the face of the boy who was being initiated with him. He must have come from one of the last sections because he was so small. His features were twisted with dread, and the voice had scarcely stopped speaking when he lunged forward, barking and frothing at the mouth, and suddenly the Slave felt a bite on his shoulder like that of a rabid dog. Then his whole body reacted, and as he barked and bit he felt certain that his skin was covered with thick fur, that his mouth was a pointed muzzle, that over his back his tail cracked like a whip.

"That's enough," the voice said. "You're the winner. But the midget fooled us. He isn't a male dog, he's a female. Do you know what a male and a female do when they meet in the street?"

"No, Cadet," the Slave said.

"They lick each other. First they sniff around and then they lick each other."

After that, they took him out of the barracks to the stadium and he could not remember if it was still daytime or if it was night. They stripped him and the voice ordered him to lie down and "swim" on his back around the soccer field. Later they took him into one of the barracks of the Fourth, where he made up a lot of bunks, sang and danced on a locker, imitated movie stars, polished many pairs of boots, cleaned a floor tile with his tongue, screwed a pillow, drank piss, but all that took place in a feverish dream and suddenly he found himself back in his own section, stretched out on his bunk, thinking: I swear I'll run away from here. Tomorrow morning. The barracks was silent. The boys looked at each other, and in spite of having been beaten and spit on, smeared and pissed on, they were solemn, even ceremonious. That same night, after the bugle played taps, the Circle was born.

They were all in their bunks but no one was asleep. The bugler had just left the patio. Then a silhouette left one of the bunks, moved down the barracks and went into the latrine. The leaves of the door swung back and forth behind him. A few moments later they could hear him retching and then vomiting, loudly, desperately. Almost all of them jumped out of their bunks and ran barefoot to the latrine. Vallano, who was tall and thin, was in the middle of that yellowish room, rubbing his stomach. Instead of going over to him, they watched his strained black face as he threw up again. Finally Vallano went over to a sink and rinsed out his mouth. Then they began to talk excitedly, all at once, cursing the cadets of the Fourth in the vilest language they knew.

"We can't let this keep on," Arróspide said. "We've got to do something." His white face stood out among the copper complexions of the others. He was in a rage and his fist shook in the air.

"Let's bring in the guy they call the Jaguar," Cava suggested.

It was the first time they had heard that name. "Who?" some of them asked. "Is he in our section?"

"Yes," Cava said. "He's still in his bunk. It's the first one next to the latrine."

"Why do we need the Jaguar?" Arróspide asked. "Aren't there enough of us already?"

"No," Cava said, "it isn't that. He's different. They haven't initiated him. I saw the whole thing. He didn't even give them time. They took him to the stadium along with me, out there behind the barracks. And he just laughed in their faces and said, 'You're going to initiate me, are you? We'll see, we'll see.' Then he laughed in their faces again. And there were ten of them."

"Then what?" Arróspide asked.

"They looked at him sort of surprised," Cava said. "There were ten of them, don't forget. But that was when they took us to the stadium. Out there, a lot of others gathered around us, twenty or more, a whole gang of cadets from the Fourth. And he still laughed in their faces. 'You're going to initiate me, are you?' he asked them. 'How nice, how nice.'"

"And?" Alberto said.

"'Are you a killer, Dog?' they asked him. And listen to this, he went and jumped them. And he was still laughing. I tell you there were ten or twenty of them, maybe even more, but they couldn't grab him. Some of them took out their belts and started swinging at him, but I swear by the Virgin they didn't get close to him, they were all too scared, and I saw a bunch of them fall down, just listen to this, some of them were grabbing their balls, some of them had bloody noses, and all the time he kept on laughing and shouting, 'You're going to initiate me, are you? How nice, how nice.'"

"Is that why you call him the Jaguar?" Arróspide asked.

"I didn't name him," Cava said. "He named himself. They had him surrounded and they'd forgot all about me. They were threatening him with their belts and he started to insult them and even their mothers. Then one of them said, 'We'll have to show this animal to Gambarina.' So they called over a great big cadet with a face like a bruiser. They said he was a weight-lifter."

"Why did they call him over?" Alberto asked.

"So they'd fight," Cava said. "They told him, 'Look, Dog, you think you're so brave, here's somebody your own size.' So he told them, 'They call me the Jaguar. Watch out when you call me a Dog.'"

"Did they laugh?" someone asked.

"No," Cava said. "They made room for them. And he was still laughing, even while he was fighting."

"Who won?" Arróspide asked.

"They didn't fight very long," Cava said. "I could see why they called him the Jaguar. He's quick, he's damned quick. He isn't too strong, but he's just like an eel. Gambarina strained a gut but he couldn't grab hold of him, and the Jaguar kept giving it to him with his head and his feet again and again, and Gambarina couldn't do a thing. So he said. 'We've had enough fun for today. I'm worn out.' But everybody could see he was all beat up."

"Then what?" Alberto asked.

"That's all," Cava said. "They let him go and started initiating me."

"Go get him," Arróspide said.

They were squatting in a circle. A few of them had lit cigarettes, which were passed from hand to hand. The latrine began to fill up with smoke. When the Jaguar came in, behind Cava, they all realized that Cava had been lying to them: the Jaguar's chin and cheekbones were bruised and so was his flat bulldog nose. He stood in the middle of the circle and looked at them from under his long blond lashes out of strange, violent blue eyes. The sneer on his lips seemed forced, like his insolent posture and the calculated slowness with which he studied them one by one. The same was true of his sudden, cutting laughter when it echoed in the room. But no one interrupted him. They waited, motionless, until he had finished examining them and laughing at them.

"They say the initiation lasts a whole month," Cava said. "We can't put up with this shit for all that time."

The Jaguar nodded. "That's right," he said. "We've got to defend ourselves. We'll get revenge on the Fourth, we'll really make them pay for their fun. The important thing is to remember their faces, and their names and sections if you can. We've got to go around in groups. We'll hold our meetings at night after taps. There's another thing: we've got to think up a name for our gang."

"The Falcons?" someone suggested timidly.

"No," the Jaguar said. "That sounds like kid stuff. We'll call ourselves the Circle."

Classes began the next morning. During recesses, the cadets from the Fourth bullied the Dogs by setting up duck-races: ten or fifteen Dogs, lined up in a row with their hands on their hips and their knees bent, waddled forward at the word of command, imitating the movements of a duck and quacking at the top of their voices. The losers had to form right angles. The cadets from the Fourth also frisked every one of the Dogs, taking away their money and cigarettes, and they mixed cocktails of gun grease, oil, and soap which the Dogs had to drink in one gulp, holding the glass in their teeth. The Circle began its counterattack two days later, shortly after breakfast. The three Years swarmed noisily out of the mess hall and spread across the field like a stain. Suddenly a hail of stones flew over their bare heads and a cadet from the Fourth rolled on the ground, moaning. After they fell in, they saw the wounded cadet being taken to the infirmary by his friends. On the following night, a sentry from the Fourth was attacked by masked shadows while he was sleeping on the grass. The bugler found him at daybreak: he had been stripped naked and tied up, his body was covered with bruises and weak from shivering in the cold. Others were stoned or beaten up. But the most daring stroke was an invasion of the kitchen to empty bags of shit in the soup kettles of the Fourth Year: this sent many of them to the infirmary with dysentery. The cadets of the Fourth were enraged by these anonymous reprisals, and carried on the initiations even more brutally. The Circle met every night, various proposals were discussed, and the Jaguar chose one of them, worked out the details, then gave his instructions. The month of automatic confinement to barracks passed quickly, in the midst of wild excitement. The tension created by the initiations and the actions of the Circle was increased by a new excitement: their first pass-day was approaching and their navy-blue uniforms were being made. The officers gave them an hour's lecture each day on the conduct of a uniformed cadet in public.

"A uniform attracts the girls like honey," Vallano said, rolling his eyes greedily.

It wasn't as bad as they said, it wasn't even as bad as I thought it was at the time, not counting what happened when Gamboa came into the latrine after taps, you can't compare that month with the other Sundays without passes. On Sundays, that month, the Third Year took over the Academy. There was a movie in the middle of the day and then their families arrived. The Dogs wandered around the parade ground, the field, the stadium and the patios, surrounded by doting relatives. A week before the first pass, they tried on their wool uniforms: navy-blue trousers, jackets with gilt buttons, white caps. Their hair grew out slowly and they were more and more eager for the pass-day to come. After the meetings of the Circle they talked about their plans for the first pass-day. And how did he know about it, was it just by chance or did somebody squeal, and what if Huarina'd been on duty, or Lt. Cobos? Yes, at least not so fast, it seems to me that if the Circle hadn't been discovered the section wouldn't've turned into such trash, we'd've been sitting pretty, not so fast. The Jaguar was standing up, talking about one of the cadets from the Fourth, a brigadier. The rest of them squatted as usual as they listened to him. They kept passing around their cigarettes. The smoke rose up, bumped against the ceiling, came back down and circulated through the room like an opaque, multiform monster. "But even if he did, Jaguar, it isn't something to kill a guy for," Vallano said, "It's all right to get revenge but not like that," Urioste said, "What really stinks about all this is he might end up by losing an eye," Pallasta said, "People get what they're looking for," the Jaguar said, but who knows what would've happened, and which came first, the bang on the door or the shout? Lt. Gamboa had either pushed open the double door with his hands or kicked it open, but the cadets went on squatting there, not hearing the noise at the door and Arróspide's shout, but watching the stale smoke flow out into the dark barracks through the open door. It was almost filled by the tall figure of Lt. Gamboa, who was holding the halves open with both hands. The cadets dropped their cigarettes, but since they were all barefoot they could not stamp them out. They all stood at attention in rigid, exaggerated postures. Gamboa stepped on the cigarettes and then counted the cadets. "Thirty-two," he said. "The whole section. Who's the brigadier?"

Arróspide stepped forward.

"Tell me what's going on here," Gamboa said in a quiet voice. "From the beginning. And don't leave anything out."

Arróspide glanced at the others out of the corner of his eye while the lieutenant waited as motionless as a tree. What about the way he complained to him? And then we were all his sons after we began complaining, and what a dirty deal, Lieutenant, you don't know the way they initiated us, don't men have the right to defend themselves, and what a dirty deal, Lieutenant, they beat us up, they really hurt us, they insulted our mothers, look at what happened to Montesinos, look at his ass from all those right angles, Lieutenant, and he was looking at the ceiling, what a dirty deal, without saying a word to us, except he said, just tell me the facts, never mind your remarks, speak one at a time, don't make such a racket, you'll wake up the other sections, and what a dirty deal, the regulations, he began reciting them, I ought to expel the whole bunch of you but the army is tolerant, it understands that you kids still don't know about military life and respect for your superiors and team spirit, but I don't want any more of this, Yes, Lieutenant, this time but it's the last time I'm not going to report you, Yes, Lieutenant, all I'm going to do is hold back your first pass, Yes, Lieutenant, let's see if you can learn to behave like men, Yes, Lieutenant, if it happens again there'll be a court-martial, Yes, Lieutenant, so memorize the regulations if you want a pass for the Saturday after next, now get some sleep, you guards get back to your posts, I'll be checking you in five minutes, Yes, Lieutenant.

The Circle never met again, though later the Jaguar used the same name for his own group. That first Saturday, the first section spread out along the rusty iron railing to watch the Dogs from the other sections, proud and excited, stream out into Costanera Avenue and dye it with their shining uniforms, their immaculate white caps, their gleaming leather satchels. They saw them gang up at the battered Malecón, with the sea rasping behind it, to wait for the Miraflores-Callao bus, or go down to Palmeras Avenue to get to Progreso Avenue, which cuts through a cluster of small farms and enters Lima by way of Breña, or, in the opposite direction, swings down in a wide, smooth curve to Bellavista and Callao. They watched them all disappear, and when the avenue was empty again, and wet with fog, they still stood there with their faces against the bars until they heard the bugle calling them to the mess hall. Then they walked away, slowly and silently, leaving behind them the statue of the hero, whose blind eyes had regarded the explosive joy of the departed and the gloom of the punished section as they disappeared among the lead-colored buildings.

That same afternoon, as they left the mess hall under the languid gaze of the vicuña, the first fight in the section broke out. I wouldn't have let him pick on me, neither would Cava or Arróspide, who would? Nobody, just him, because the Jaguar isn't God and everything would've been different if he'd talked back, or if he'd made a joke of it, or if he'd grabbed a rock or a stick, or even if he'd run away, but to start trembling, man, anything but that. They were still crowding down the stairs, and suddenly there was complete confusion and then two of them stumbled and fell down on the grass. As they sat up, thirty pairs of eyes watched them from the stairs as if from a grandstand. No one had a chance to break it up, or even to understand at first what had happened, because the Jaguar turned like a cornered cat and hit the other one square in the face without any warning and then jumped on top of him and hit him again and again on the head, in the face, on the shoulders. The cadets stared at those two unrelenting fists without even hearing how the other one said, "Excuse me, Jaguar, I didn't mean to push you, it was just an accident, honest it was." What he shouldn't have done was get onto his knees, he shouldn't have done that. And besides, when he put his palms together he looked like my mother during the novenas, or like a little kid getting first communion, you'd've thought the Jaguar was the Archbishop and the other one was confessing, I remember all about it, Rospigliosi said, and it made my stomach turn over, man. The Jaguar was on his feet, looking down contemptuously at the kneeling cadet, his fist still raised as if he were going to hit that livid face again. The rest of them were silent. "You make me sick," the Jaguar said. "You haven't got any guts or anything else. You're just a slave."

"Eight-thirty," Gamboa said. "Ten more minutes."

The whole class groaned and shifted in their seats. I'm going to smoke a cigarette in the latrine, Alberto thought as he signed his exam. At that same moment a little ball of paper hit his desk, rolled a few inches and came to a stop against his arm. He glanced all around before picking it up. When he raised his eyes again, Lt. Gamboa was smiling at him. I wonder if he noticed, Alberto thought. Just as he lowered his eyes the lieutenant said, "Cadet, would you like to give me that thing that just landed on your desk. The rest of you keep your mouths shut!"

Alberto stood up. Gamboa took the ball of paper without looking at it. He uncrumpled it and held it up to the light. As he read it, his eyes were like two grasshoppers, jumping back and forth between the paper and the desks.

"Do you know what this is, Cadet?" Gamboa asked.

"No, Sir."

"The answers to the exam, that's all. What about that? Do you know who sent you this present?"

"No, Sir."

"Your guardian angel," Gamboa said. "Do you know who he is?"

"No, Sir."

"Give me your exam and sit down." Gamboa tore it to shreds and put it on the desk. "Your guardian angel," he said, "has got exactly thirty seconds to stand up."

The cadets looked at each other.

"Fifteen seconds," Gamboa said. "I told you thirty."

"I did it, Sir," a weak voice told him.

Alberto turned to look: the Slave was on his feet, white in the face, deaf to the laughter of the others.

"Your name," Gamboa said.

"Ricardo Arana."

"You understand that each cadet has to answer the questions by himself?"

"Yes, Lieutenant."

"Very well," Gamboa said. "Then you also understand that I'll have to confine you to the grounds on Saturday and Sunday. That's how the army has to be. No favors to anybody, not even to the angels." He looked at his watch and added, "Time's up. Hand in your exams."

3

I was in Sáenz Peña and when I left I was going back to
Bellavista on foot. Sometimes I ran into Skinny Higueras,
who was one of my brother's friends before Perico was
drafted by the army. He always asked me, "What do you
hear from him?" "Nothing. He hasn't written since they sent
him into the jungle." "Where are you going in such a hurry?
Come on and talk for a while." I wanted to get back to Bellavista as soon as I could, but Higueras was older than I was
and he always did me the favor of treating me like someone
his own age. He took me into a bar and asked me, "What'll
you have?" "I don't know, it doesn't matter, whatever you
have." "Okay," Skinny said. "Waiter, two shots!" And then he
slapped me on the back: "Watch out you don't get drunk."
The pisco burned my throat and made my eyes water. "Suck
a piece of lime," he said, "it's smoother that way. And smoke
a cigarette." We talked about soccer, about my brother, about
my school. He told me a lot of things about Perico I didn't
know. I always thought he was easygoing but it turned out
he liked to fight, one night he even got into a knife fight over
a woman. And you'd never have guessed it but he was a
ladies' man. When Higueras told me how he'd knocked up
one of his girl friends and they almost made him marry her,
I couldn't say a word. "Yes," he said, "you've got a nephew
who must be about four years old by now. Doesn't that make
you feel old?" But I was only delayed for a short time, because I made up an excuse to leave him. When I got home I
felt very nervous and I was afraid my mother would get
suspicious. I took out my books and said, "I'm going to study
next door," and she didn't say anything. She barely moved
her head. Sometimes she didn't even do that. The house next
door was larger than ours, but it was also very old. Before I
rang the bell I rubbed my hands together till they were red,

but even so they were still sweaty. Sometimes Tere came to
the door. I always felt wonderful when I saw her. But usually
her aunt let me in. She was one of my mother's friends. She
didn't like me, they say that when I was a kid I pestered her
all the time. "Go study in the kitchen," she growled, "the
light's better there." We studied together while her aunt
cooked their dinner, and the room was full of the smell of
garlic and onions. Tere was always very neat, it was wonderful to see the neat covers on her books and notebooks and
her small, even handwriting. There were never any blots,
and she underlined all the headings in two colors. I told her,
"You're going to be a painter," to make her laugh. Because
she laughed every time I opened my mouth, in a way you
couldn't forget. It was a real honest laugh, a good loud one,
and she also clapped her hands. Sometimes I'd meet her
coming back from school and anybody could tell she was
different from the rest of the girls, her hair was never mussed
up and she never had ink spots on her fingers. What I liked
best about her was her face. Her legs were too thin and you
still couldn't see her breasts, or maybe you could, but I
don't believe I ever thought about her legs or even her
breasts, only about her face. If I was playing with myself at
night in bed and I suddenly thought about her, I felt
ashamed of myself and went to the toilet to piss. But I
thought all the time about kissing her. When I closed my
eyes and pictured her, I could see both of us already grown
up and married. We used to study together every afternoon
for at least two hours, sometimes longer, and I always lied,
I said, "I've still got lots to do," so we could stay in the
kitchen a little longer. I'd tell her, "Look, if you're getting
tired I'll go home," but she never got tired. That year they
gave me very high grades and all the teachers were good to
me, they held me up as an example, they asked me to go to
the blackboard and sometimes they made me a monitor, and
the guys from Sáenz Peña called me teacher's pet. I didn't
get along with my classmates, I'd talk with them during

school but I'd leave them as soon as we got out. I only spent time with Higueras. I'd see him on a corner of the plaza in Bellavista and the minute he spotted me he'd come over. During all that time the only thing I thought about was getting back by five o'clock and the only thing I hated was Sunday. We studied together through Saturday, but on Sunday Tere and her aunt went into Lima to visit relatives, and I'd spend the whole day in the house or I'd go to Potao to watch a soccer game. My mother never gave me any money and she was always complaining about what a small pension my father left her when he died. "And think of it," she'd say, "he served the government for thirty years." The money was just barely enough to pay the rent and the food bills. Before I began studying with Tere I used to go to the movies sometimes with a few of the guys from school, but I think that during that whole year I never went anywhere, not even to a soccer game or anything. The year after that I had some money, but I always felt bitter when I remembered how I used to study with Tere every afternoon.

But that movie deal was better than the chicken or the midget. Stop that, Skimpy, stop biting me. A lot better. And that was when we were in the Fourth Year, and even though it'd been a year since Gamboa broke up the big Circle, the Jaguar went on saying, "They'll all join up again someday and we four'll be the bosses." And it was even better than before, because when we were Dogs the Circle was only one section and this time it was as if the whole Year was in the Circle and we were the ones who were really running things, the Jaguar more than the rest of us. And then there was the time the Dog broke his finger and you could see the whole section was with us and backed us up. "Climb up the ladder, Dog," Curly said, "and make it snappy or I might get mad." How the Dog stared at us! "High places make me dizzy, Cadets." The Jaguar started laughing and Cava got mad. "Do you know who you're making fun of, Dog?" So he climbed up, but he must've been really scared. "Keep on, keep on, sonny," Curly told him. "And now sing," the Jaguar said, "but like a real singer, using your hands." He was hanging on like a monkey and the foot of the ladder rattled against the tiles. "But what if I fall, Cadets?" "So you fall," I told him. He straightened up, still shaking, and began to sing. "He'll crack his skull any minute now," Cava said, and the Jaguar was doubled up with laughter. But it wasn't much of a fall, I've jumped from higher places out in the field. Why did he have to grab at the washstand? "I think he's torn his finger off," the Jaguar said when he saw how the Dog's hand was streaming blood. "You're all confined to the grounds for a month or more," the captain said, "until the guilty parties step forward." The section didn't squeal and the Jaguar asked them, "Why don't you come back into the Circle if you're all such he-men?" The Dogs were all gutless, that was the trouble with them. Our battles with the Fifth were better than the initiations, even when I'm dead I won't forget that year, most of all what happened in the movies. The Jaguar set it up. He was right beside me and they almost broke my back. The Dogs were lucky, we hardly touched them that time, we were too busy with the guys from the Fifth. They say that revenge is sweet, and that's right, I've never enjoyed anything so much as that day in the stadium when I came face to face with one of the bastards that initiated me when I was a Dog. They almost expelled us, but it was worth it. That business between the Fourth and the Third, that's just a game, the real deal is between the Fourth and the Fifth. Who could forget the initiation they gave us? And that business of getting in between the Fifth and the Dogs in the movies, that was done on purpose, to get something started. The Jaguar also dreamed up that trick about our caps. When you saw somebody from the Fifth coming along, you let him get near you and when he was a yard away you'd raise your hand as if you were going to salute him, so he'd salute you and you'd just take off your cap. "Are you trying to make a fool out of me?" "No, Cadet, I'm just scratching my head, I've got an awful case of dandruff." It was a real war, you could tell that very clearly from the rope deal and from what happened in the movies. It was during the winter but it was hot in there, we almost smothered under that tin roof with over a thousand guys crammed together. I didn't see his face when we went in, I just heard his voice, but I bet he was a peasant. "What a mob," the Jaguar said, "my ass is too big for the space." He was at the end of the row and the Poet was dunning somebody: "Look, do you think I work for nothing, or just because you're so pretty?" It was dark by then and somebody told him, "Shut up or we'll shut you up." I'm pretty sure the Jaguar didn't put the bricks on his seat just so he'd block the view, he wanted to see better. I was bending over to light a match and when I heard the guy from the Fifth I dropped my cigarette and got down on my hands and knees to look for it and that's when it all started happening. "Look, Cadet, clear those bricks off your seat, I want to see the picture." "Are you speaking to me, Cadet?" I asked him. "No, the one next to you." "You mean me?" the Jaguar asked. "Who do you think I mean?" "Will you please shut your big mouth," the Jaguar said, "and let me watch these cowboys?" "You're not going to get rid of those bricks?" "I guess not," the Jaguar said. Then I got back in my seat without looking for the cigarette any more, I couldn't find it. Things were getting started now, so I tightened my belt a little. "You aren't going to obey me?" the cadet from the Fifth asked him. "No," the Jaguar said, "why should I?" He was having a good time baiting him. Then the ones in back started to whistle. The Poet began singing Ay, ay, ay and the rest of the section joined in. "Are you trying to make fun of me?" the guy from the Fifth demanded. "It looks that way, Cadet," the Jaguar said. It was going to take place in the dark, it was really going to be something to talk about, in the dark and right in the

Assembly Hall, something that'd never happened before. The Jaguar said later that he was the first one, but I saw what really happened, it was the other one or else a friend of his that stuck his oar in. And he must've been furious, he piled on the Jaguar without any warning and my ears hurt the way they were shouting. Everybody stood up and I saw some shadows on top of me and they started kicking me. I don't remember anything about the movie, it'd just begun. And what about the Poet, were they really beating him up or was he just shouting like that so they'd think he was a lunatic? And you could also hear Lt. Huarina shouting, "Lights, Sergeant, lights, are you deaf?" Then the Dogs started shouting, "Lights, lights!" without knowing what was going on, and they said the other two Years'll jump on us while the lights are out. The air was full of cigarettes, everybody wanted to get rid of them, we didn't want to get caught smoking, it's a miracle there wasn't a fire. What a chance, come on, gang, let'em have it, this is where we get our revenge. I don't know how the Jaguar got out of it alive. The shadows kept circling around me and my hands hurt me and so did my feet from all that fighting, I know I must've hit some of the guys from the Fourth also but how could you tell what you were doing in the darkness? "Sgt. Varúa, what's the matter with those goddamn lights," Huarina bellowed, "can't you tell these animals are killing each other?" There were fights everywhere, that's the honest truth, it's just lucky no one was really hurt. And when they turned the lights on, all you could hear were the whistles. Huarina wasn't in sight, but the lieutenants and noncoms of the Fifth and Third were shouting at us. "Clear the way, damn it, clear the way!" What a laugh, nobody'd let them through, and the bastards got mad and started swinging at anybody, I'll never forget how the Rat, that Pezoa, hit me so hard in the belly I couldn't breathe. Then I started looking around for the Jaguar, I told myself if they've beat him up they'll have to answer to me, but there he was, as fresh as a daisy, slugging away and dying of laughter, he had more lives than a cat. And afterward, what a lot of faking, everybody sticks together when it comes to screwing the officers and the noncoms, nothing's been going on, we're all buddies, I don't know a thing about it, and it was the same way with the Fifth, you've got to be fair to them about that. Finally they got the Dogs out, they were all scared to death, and then the Fifth. So then we were the only ones in the Assembly Hall and we started singing *Ay, ay, ay.* "I think I made him eat a couple of those bricks he was bitching about," the Jaguar said. And they all started saying, "The Fifth is really pissed off, we made fools out of them in front of the Dogs, they'll attack the Fourth tonight." The officers were running around like mice, asking us, "How did this mess begin? Start talking or you'll go to the guardhouse." We didn't even listen to them. They're going to come, they're going to come, we can't let them surprise us in the barracks, we'll go out and wait for them in the field. The Jaguar was on top of a locker and we all listened to him the way we used to when we were Dogs and the Circle met in the latrine to plan our revenge. We've got to defend ourselves, a man who's prepared is worth two that aren't, you guards go out to the parade ground and keep watch. The minute you see them coming, shout for us to come out. Get some things to throw, roll up some toilet paper and squeeze it in your hand, that way your punches'll have a kick like a mule, fasten razor blades on the tips of your boots like the spurs on the game-cocks at the Coliseum, fill your pockets with stones, don't forget to wear jockstraps, a man has to watch out for his balls more than his soul. Everybody obeyed him and Curly jumped up and down on the beds, it was like the Circle again except the whole Year was in on it, listen, they're getting ready in all the other barracks too. "Damn it, there aren't enough stones," the Poet said, "let's pull up a few tiles." And everybody swapped cigarettes and put their arms around each other. We got into bed with our uniforms on and some of us even with our boots on. Are they coming, are they coming yet? Skimpy, keep still, stop biting, damn you. Even the dog was excited, barking and jumping around, though usually she was so quiet, you'll have to go sleep with the vicuña, Skimpy, I've got to take care of these so the Fifth won't bang them up.

The house on the corner of Diego Ferré and Ocharán was fronted on both streets by a white wall about three feet high and thirty feet long. There was a lamppost at the edge of the sidewalk near the corner, and the post and the wall served as the goal for one of the teams, the team that won the toss. The losers had to make a goal fifty yards back on Ocharán by putting a rock or a pile of jackets at the edge of the sidewalk. But although the goals were only as wide as the sidewalk, the playing field included the whole street. The game they played was soccer. They wore sneakers, just as they did on the field at the Terraza Club, and they made sure the ball was not fully inflated, to prevent it from bouncing too high. For the most part they kept the ball on the ground, making very short passes and trying for goals from close up, without kicking hard. They marked the bounds with a piece of chalk but after a few minutes their sneakers and the ball erased the lines and there were hot arguments to decide whether a goal was legal. The game took place in an atmosphere of vigilance and dread. No matter how careful they were, there would always be the time when Pluto or one of the others would forget himself and kick the ball too hard or hit it with his head. It would fly over the wall of one of the houses along the playing field, land in the garden and squash the geraniums, and if it had real force behind it it would bang against a door or a window, that was the worst because it rattled the door or broke the windowpane, and when that happened the players gave the ball up for lost and shouted a warning and ran away. As they ran, Pluto would keep yelling, "They're after us, they're coming after us!" No one would turn his head to see if it was true, they would all run faster, shouting, "Hurry up, they're after us, they've called the cops!" That was the moment when Alberto, who was out in front, gasped, "The cliff, let's go down the cliff!" And they all followed him, saying, "Good, the cliff!" He could hear the labored breathing of his friends: Pluto's, irregular and animal-like; Tico's, short and steady; Babe's, farther and farther away because he was the slowest; Emilio's, the calm breathing of an athlete who measured his strength scientifically, breathing in through his nose and out through his mouth; and next to him, Paco's and Sorbino's, and that of the rest, a muffled sound that surrounded him and encouraged him to run faster down the second block of Diego Ferré to the corner of Colón and then to the right, keeping close to the wall to save distance on the turn. After that it was easier because Colón was downhill and the red bricks of the Malecón were only half a block away, and beyond them, merging with the horizon, the gray ocean whose shore they would soon reach. The other boys in the neighborhood always made fun of Alberto because whenever they were lying around on the small lawn at Pluto's house, discussing plans, Alberto always said, "Let's go down the cliff." Those trips were long and difficult. They crossed the brick wall at the end of Colón, then stood on a little jut of land while they figured out a way down, studying the steep drop with skilled and serious eyes, debating the best route, searching out the obstacles between their perch and the stony beach. Alberto was the most eager strategist. Without taking his eyes from the cliffside he described the route he favored in quick, short phrases, imitating the speech and gestures of a movie hero: "First, that rock down there, the one with the feathers on it, it's good and solid, then you've only got to jump about three feet, see there, then you go down along those black rocks, they're all flat, after that it's easier, you can slide all the way down the other side, and it'll take us to a beach we've never been on." If anyone objected—Emilio, for example, who liked to be the leader—Alberto defended his ideas passionately, and the group took sides. Their excited arguments warmed the damp mornings in Miraflores. Behind them, an uninterrupted line of cars passed along the Malecón. Sometimes a passenger thrust his head out of a window, and if it happened to be a boy their eyes were filled with envy. Alberto's point of view usually won out, because he fought so hard and so stubbornly in these arguments that the others became bored. They went down the cliff very cautiously, forgetting all about the disagreement, joined in a complete friendship that showed in their looks, their smiles, the words of encouragement they exchanged. Every time one of them got around an obstacle or made a dangerous leap, the others cheered him. Time went by slowly, full of tension. The closer they came to their objective, the more daring they became. They could hear, close to them now, that strange noise which reached their beds at night in Miraflores, and which here was a deafening roar of stones and water; they could smell the salt and clean sea shells; and then they were on the beach, a tiny fan between the cliff and the water's edge, where they all dropped in a heap, joking, kidding about the dangers of the descent, pretending to shove each other, keeping up a great racket. If the morning was not too cold, or if it was one of those afternoons when a lukewarm sun came out unexpectedly in the ashen sky, Alberto took off his shoes and socks, rolled up his pants above his knees, and jumped into the surf, while the others cheered him on with their shouts. He felt the cold water on his legs and the polished stones under his feet, and from there, holding up his pants-legs with one hand, he splashed his friends with the other. They ducked behind each other, then took off their socks and shoes and went out to drench him, and the grand battle began. Later, soaked to the skin, they returned to the beach, stretched out on the stones, and argued about the climb back up. It was difficult and exhausting. When they got back to the neighborhood they sprawled out on the lawn at Pluto's house, smoking the Viceroys they had bought at the corner store along with some peppermints to hide the smell of tobacco on their breath.

Sometimes, instead of playing soccer, or climbing down to the beach, or racing around the block on their bicycles, they went to see a movie. If it was Saturday they all went together to the matinee at the Excelsior or the Ricardo Palma, usually getting balcony seats. They sat in the front row, made lots of noise, threw lighted matches down on the people below, and argued about the scenes in the picture at the top of their voices. Sunday was different. In the morning they had to go to Mass at the Champagnat Academy in Miraflores; only Emilio and Alberto studied in Lima. They usually got together at ten in the morning in the main park, still dressed in their uniforms, and sat on the benches watching the people going into the church or starting arguments with boys from other neighborhoods. In the afternoon they went to the movies, this time downstairs, well-dressed, their hair combed, all of them half-suffocated by the ties and starched collars their parents made them wear. Some of them had to chaperon their sisters; the others followed them down Larco Avenue, calling them nursemaids and fairies. The girls in the neighborhood, who were as numerous as the boys, also formed a tightly-knit group that was bitterly hostile toward the boys. When the boys were together and spotted one of the girls, they ran up and surrounded her and pulled her hair till she cried, jeering at her brother when he complained, "She'll tell my old man and he'll punish me for not defending her." On the other hand, when one of the boys showed up alone, the girls stuck their tongues out at him and called him all sorts of names, and he had to put up with their insults, red-faced with embarrassment but keeping the same pace to show them he was not a coward who was afraid of mere women.

But they didn't come, it was the officers' fault, it must've been. We thought it was them and we jumped out of bed but the guards stopped us. "Quiet, it's the soldiers." They'd got the peasants up at midnight and they had them out on the parade grounds, armed to the teeth as if they were going into battle, and the lieutenants and noncoms were there too, it's a cinch they knew something was up. But they would've liked to come, we found out later they spent the night getting ready, they even made slings and ammonia bombs. How we yelled Motherfuckers! at the soldiers, they were furious and they pointed their bayonets at us. He'll never forget that deal, they say the colonel almost hit him, maybe he did hit him, "Huarina, you're a mess," we ruined him in front of the Minister, in front of the Ambassadors, they say he practically bawled. Everything would've ended like that if it hadn't been for the fiesta the next day, well done Colonel, what's this about exhibiting us like monkeys, armed drill in front of the archbishop and a lunch for everyone together, gymnastics and field events in front of the ministers and generals and a lunch for everyone together, a full-dress parade and speeches, and a lunch for everyone together in front of the ambassadors, well done, well done. We all knew something was going to happen, it was in the air, the Jaguar said, "We've got to win all the events in the stadium, we can't lose a single one, we've got to make a clean sweep, in the sack race, the foot races, everything." But there was hardly anything, it began with the tug of war, my arms still ache from pulling so hard, how they shouted, "Come on, Boa," "Harder, Boa," "Harder, harder," "Hooray, hooray." And in the morning, before breakfast, they came over to Urioste and the Jaguar and me and told us, "Pull till it kills you but don't give ground, do it for the section." The only one who didn't get wind of it was Huarina, the horse's ass. But the Rat could smell it, be careful you don't try any funny business in front of the colonel, and don't laugh in my face, I may be a little shrimp but I've won so many championships at Judo I can't keep track of them. Keep still, you bitch, stop biting me, Skimpy. And the place was crowded, you couldn't make out Gen. Mendoza among all those uniforms. The one with the most medals, and I'll die laughing if I remember the mike, the worst possible luck, what a kick we got out of it, I'm going to piss if I laugh any more, I'm going to split my guts if I keep remembering that mike. Who'd've thought it'd be so serious, but look at how the Fifth is, they're giving us dirty looks, they're moving their lips to tell us we're all motherfuckers. So we began telling them the same thing, easy, slower, Skimpy. Ready, Cadets? Pay attention to the whistle. "Armed drill without spoken commands," the mike said, "changes of step and direction, forward march." And then the gymnasts, I hope you've had a good bath, you cruddy bastards. One two three, step lively and salute. That midget is a damned good gymnast, he hasn't got hardly any muscles but he's real clever. We didn't see the colonel either but that didn't matter, I know him by heart, why do you smear on so much hair oil, don't talk to me about military bearing because I think about the colonel, if he loosens his belt his stomach plops to the ground and what a laugh, that face he puts on. I think the only things he likes are assemblies and parades, look at my boys, how trim they are, oompah, oompah, the circus will now begin, with my trained dogs, my trained fleas, my rope-walking elephants, oompah, oompah. If I had a squeaky voice like his I'd start chain-smoking to get hoarse, it isn't a military voice. I've never seen him in the field, I can't imagine him in a trench, but yes, sir, more and more shows, that third rank is crooked, Cadet, pay attention, officers, they're getting out of step, martial bearing and deportment, what a horse's ass, what a face he made about that rope business. They say the minister was sweating and he said to the colonel, "Have those sons of bitches gone crazy or what?" There we were, face to face, the Fifth and the Fourth, on opposite sides of the soccer field. How excited they were, they squirmed in their seats like snakes, with the Dogs on the other side, watching without understanding a thing, just

wait a minute and you're going to see something good.
Huarina walked back and forth near us and said, "Do you
think you can?" "You can confine me to the grounds for a
year if we don't win," the Jaguar told him, but I wasn't so
sure, they had some big brutes, Gambarina, Risueño,
Carnero, real big brutes. My arms ached even before, just
from my nerves. "Put the Jaguar in front," they shouted
from the stands, and "Boa, we're counting on you." The guys
in the section started singing *Ay, ay, ay* and Huarina laughed
until he realized it was to razz the Fifth and he began to
tear his hair, what are you doing, you animals, there's
General Mendoza up there, and the ambassador, and the
colonel, what are you doing, and the tears ran out of his
eyes. I have to laugh when I remember how the colonel said,
"You mustn't believe that tug of war is simply a matter of
muscles, it's also a matter of skill and intelligence, of coopera-
tion, it isn't easy to coordinate your efforts," that just kills
me. The fellows applauded us the way I've never heard
them, anybody with any heart in him got all excited. The
Fifth were already on the field in their black gym suits and
they got applauded too. One of the lieutenants marked the
line and you'd've thought we'd already started, the way the
cheering-section screamed: "Fourth! Fourth!" and "Here's
a cheer for the old Fourth Year!" "What are you shouting
for," the Jaguar asked me, "don't you know it'll tire you
out?" But it was all so exciting. "This is the day, hooray,
we're on our way, hoorah, so here's a cheer for the old
Fourth Year, rah, rah, rah!" "Okay," Huarina said, "let's go.
Put everything you've got into it, make a good name for the
Year." And he didn't even suspect what was coming. Run,
guys, the Jaguar out front, let's go, let's go, Urioste, let's go,
let's go, Boa, come on, come on, Torres, beat'em, beat'em,
Riofrío, Pestana, Cuevas, Zapata, let's go, let's go, we'll die
before we give up an inch. Run with your mouths closed,
we're near the stands, let's see if we can see General Mendoza, don't forget to raise your arms when Torres says three.

There's more people than it looked like, and all that brass, they must be the minister's aides, I'd like to get a good look at the ambassadors, how they're applauding and we haven't even started. That's it, now a half turn, the lieutenant must have the rope ready, I hope to God he's tied the knots right, look at the dirty looks the Fifth are giving us, don't scare me, I'm shaking already, halt. "Hooray, hoorah!" And then Gambarina came up a little closer, without paying any attention to the lieutenant who was straightening out the rope and counting the knots, and said, "You wise guys think you're going to show us up. Just watch out or you'll end up without any balls." "And how is your mother these days?" the Jaguar asked him. "I'll talk to you later," Gambarina said. "Stop horsing around," the lieutenant said, "team captains come forward, line up, start tugging when the whistle blows, the minute anybody crosses the line I'll blow it again and you stop. The first side that wins twice is the winner. And don't start squawking afterward, I never play favorites." Calisthenics, calisthenics, jump, keep your mouth closed, Jesus Christ how the cheering-section's yelling Boa, Boa, even louder than Jaguar or else I'm crazy, what are they waiting for, blow that whistle. "Ready, guys," the Jaguar said, "give it everything you've got." Then Gambarina let go of the rope and shook his fist at us, they were all worked up as if they were sure they couldn't lose. And what made us feel good was the way the rest of the Fourth cheered us, I could feel it in my arms and legs, come on, one, two, three, no, Jesus, oh Jesus, oh Jesus, four, five, the rope's twisting like an eel, I knew the goddamned knots weren't big enough, your hands keep, five, six, slipping, seven, fuck me if we aren't beating them, the sweat's blinding me, that's the way real he-men sweat, nine, come on, come on, just a little more, come on, come on, the whistle, I'll be fucked. The Fifth began shouting, "It was a trick, Lieutenant" and "We didn't cross the line, Lieutenant." Hooray, the guys from the Fourth are standing up cheering, they've taken their caps off, they're waving them, are they shouting Boa, they're singing, crying, screaming, long live Peru, death to the Fifth, don't scowl like that or I'll bust out laughing, hooray, hoorah. "Stop sniveling," the lieutenant said. "One to nothing, favor of the Fourth. Get ready for the second one." Come on, guys, what a cheering-section the Fourth has got, that's the right way to cheer, I can see you, Cava, you peasant, and you, Curly, keep shouting, it's good for our muscles, I'm sweating like a horse, damn this rope, keep still, Skimpy, stop biting me. What happened was, our feet slipped on the grass, just like roller skates, I thought something would bust inside me, I could tell my veins were standing out, who's letting up, don't conk out on us, who the hell's letting up, they grab the rope harder, they think about the Year, four, three, come on, what's the matter with the cheering-section, damn that Jaguar, they've tied us. But they got more tired than we did, they dropped to their knees or flopped onto their backs, sweating and gasping for breath. "Tied one to one," the lieutenant said. "And don't flop around like that, you look like old ladies." Then they began to insult us to make us afraid of them. "We'll get you after it's over." "You'd better start praying because we're going to screw you one and all." "Shut your traps or we'll take care of you right now." So the lieutenant bawled them out: "Watch out what you're saying, they can hear you in the stands, I'll get even with you later." Hooray! and how is your mother, we're talking to you and no one else. This time the cheers were faster and louder, they yelled until they were red in the face. Fourth, Fourth, zoom, boom; hooray, hoorah! One more match and we'd make them eat the dust. "They're going to jump us," the Jaguar said, "they don't care if the stands are packed full of generals, you watch. This is going to be something special. Didn't you see the way Gambarina was looking at me?" The insults from the cheering-section were rolling across the field, Huarina was galloping back and forth, the colonel and the minister heard the whole thing, the brigadiers were writing down four, five, ten names per section, one month two months confined to quarters. Come on, guys, bust your guts, we'll show who's who in the Leoncio Prado, we'll show who's got hair on their chests and balls like a bull, come on. We were all tugging when I saw that crowd coming, it was like a big black cloud with red dots, it came down from the stands where the Fifth was, a whole big crowd of them, "Here comes the Fifth," the Jaguar shouted, "take care of yourselves," then Gambarina let go of the rope and the others from the Fifth all stumbled and crossed the line, I shouted we won, the Jaguar and Gambarina were wrestling on the ground and Urioste and Zapata ran past me with their tongues hanging out, to slug the ones from the Fifth, the crowd got bigger and bigger, then Pallasta signaled to the stands where the Fourth was, come out here, can't you see they're after us, the lieutenant was trying to break up the fight between the Jaguar and Gambarina without seeing what was happening behind his back, "You bastards, the colonel's watching you," then another crowd came out, our own guys, the whole Fourth was like the Circle, where's Cava that half-breed, good, here's Curly, we're all together again and this time we're all bosses. And suddenly the squeaky voice of the colonel, you could hear it everywhere, officers, this is a disgrace, stop it at once, they're disgracing the Academy, and then I recognized the son of a bitch that initiated me, those big dark lips, how nice to meet you, we've got some unfinished business, I wish my brother could've seen me, he always hated those peasants from the Andes, those big open lips, those big scared eyes, all of a sudden they started whipping us, the officers and noncoms took off their belts and they even tell me some of the officers that were just guests came down out of the stands and took off their belts, they had a lot of nerve because they didn't belong to the Academy, I don't think I got hit with the leather, I got hit with the buckle, that's why my back hurts so much. "Obviously it was a plot,

General, but I assure you they'll be punished for it." "Plot?
Don't be an ass. Just stop them fighting, if you can." "Excuse
me, Colonel, but you ought to turn off the microphone."
Whistles and whips, all those lieutenants and I didn't see
them, my shoulders were burning they whipped me so hard,
the Jaguar and Gambarina were snarled up on the grass
like a pair of spiders. But it turned out all right, Skimpy,
stop biting me, you bitch. Then we lined up again and I felt
hot and tired, I hoped they'd give us a break, I wanted to lie
down on the grass and take a rest. Nobody said anything,
you wouldn't believe how quiet it was, we just stood there
gasping for breath, we didn't think about getting passes, just
about getting back to our bunks for a good long siesta. So
then they screwed us, the minister confined us to the grounds
until the end of the year, that made the Dogs happy but if
they didn't do anything why were they so scared, okay, go
on home but don't forget what you saw, and the officers were
even scareder, Huarina was white as a sheet, look in the
mirror and your face'll scare the hell out of you, Curly was
next to me, he whispered, "Is General Mendoza the fat one
with that dame in the blue dress? I thought he was infantry
but the bastard's artillery, look at his insignia." The colonel
almost swallowed the mike but he didn't know where to
begin so he squeaked, "Cadets!" and rested a while and
squeaked, "Cadets!" again even squeakier, look out, you
bitch, I'm going to laugh, we all stood there like ramrods
but scared shitless like the rest. Okay, Skimpy, you don't
believe me, nobody'd believe me, but honest the colonel
kept on squeaking, "Cadets! Cadets! Cadets!" and "We'll
settle all these problems among ourselves," and "I'd like to
address a few words to our distinguished guests, I beg your
pardon and I assure you this has never happened before and
will never happen again" and "We all hope this distinguished
lady will pardon us." I don't know who started it but we
clapped for about five minutes, anyway my hands got sore,
and she stood up and started throwing kisses, too bad she

was so far away, I couldn't tell if she was good looking or not or young or old. Stop scratching me, Skimpy. They say she was even crying. But then, "Third Year, dress uniforms. Fourth and Fifth, as you were." You poor little bitch, you wouldn't know why nobody made a move, not the officers, the noncoms, the brigadiers, the guests, not even the Dogs, you wouldn't know the devil really exists. And then she jumped and said, "Colonel!" and he said, "My dear lady," because she was the ambassador's wife, "I'm at a loss for words," "Sir, not into the mike," "I beg you, Colonel," how long did it last, Skimpy? Not long, everybody was looking at fatty and the mike and the woman, and the next time she spoke we knew she was a gringa. "As a personal favor to me, Colonel?" There was a silence, we all waited at attention, and then, "Cadets! Cadets! We'll forget this shameful incident, but don't let it happen again, you know the punishment you deserve and you deserve it thoroughly from the army point of view, but this gracious and distinguished lady," and he bowed to her, "is your champion." So the old fart let us go and they told me afterward Gamboa said, "Is this a goddamned nunnery, women giving the orders," and we were so grateful to her we gave a locomotive cheer, I wonder who invented it, it starts out slow, chug, one two three four five, chug, one two three four, chug, one two three, chug, one two, chug, one, chug, chug, chugchugchug, and over again to chugchugchug, and over again, and the ones from the Guadalupe were sore as hell at our cheers and our chugchugchugs during the athletic meet, we also had to give the ambassador's wife our hooray, hoorah, even the Dogs began applauding, the officers and noncoms didn't stop us, it went on, chugchugchug, they kept their eyes on the colonel, the ambassador's wife and the minister started leaving, the minister turned back and said you think you're all pretty smart but I'm going to mop up the floor with you, but then he started laughing, and Gen. Mendoza and the ambassadors and the officers and the guests too, chugchugchug, we're the best in the world, hooray, hoorah, chug-chugchug, the cadets of the Leoncio Prado one hundred percent, hooray for Peru, Cadets, someday our country will call for us and we'll be ready, stouthearted and lofty-minded, "Where's that Gambarina so I can give him a kiss?" the Jaguar said, "I want to know if he's still alive after the way I banged his head on the ground," the woman was bawling with gratitude for all the cheers, Skimpy, life in the Academy is hard and strict but it's got its compensation, too bad the Circle never got back to what it was, the devil always sticks his nose into anything good, I used to feel wonderful when the thirty of us got together in the latrine, so now we're going to get screwed on account of that peasant Cava, on account of a lousy pane of glass, for Christ's sakes stop biting me, Skimpy, you bitch.

He had also forgotten the days that followed, monotonous and humiliating days. He got up early, his body aching from lack of sleep, and wandered through the half-furnished rooms of that unfamiliar house. There was a sort of small storeroom up on the roof, with stacks of old magazines and newspapers, and he would spend whole mornings and afternoons distractedly leafing through them. He avoided his parents, and spoke to them only in monosyllables. "What do you think of your father?" his mother asked him one day. "I don't," he said, "I don't think a thing." And on another day: "Are you happy, Richi?" "No." The day after they arrived in Lima, his father came to his bed, smiling and offering his cheek to be kissed. "Good morning," Ricardo said without moving. A shadow crossed his father's face. The battle began that same day. Ricardo stayed in bed until he heard his father close the outside door. When he saw him at lunch time, he mumbled, "Good afternoon," and ran up to the storeroom. Sometimes they took him out for a ride after lunch. Ricardo sat alone in the back seat of the car, pretending to take an enormous interest in the parks, avenues, and plazas. He never opened his mouth, but kept his ears open to everything his father and mother were saying. Sometimes the meaning of certain allusions escaped him, and on those nights his sleeplessness was like a fever. He was always on guard. If they spoke to him unexpectedly he said: "Huh?" or "What?" One night he heard them talking about him in the next room. "He's hardly eight years old," his mother said. "He'll get used to you." "He's had more than enough time," his father said, and his voice was different: flat and curt. "But he didn't know you before," his mother protested. "It's just a matter of time." "You haven't brought him up right," his father said. "It's your fault he's the way he is. He acts like a girl." Then their voices sank to a murmur. A few days later he was seriously frightened: his parents began to talk in riddles and their whole manner was strangely different. He spied on them even more carefully, not missing the slightest glance or gesture. But he could not solve the mystery by himself. One morning while she was hugging him his mother asked, "What if you had a baby sister?" He thought: If I kill myself, it'll be their fault, and they'll both go to Hell. He was growing more and more impatient, because it was the end of summer and in the autumn they were going to send him to school and he would be out of the house most of the day. One afternoon, after thinking for a long time up in the storeroom, he went to his mother and asked her, "Can't you send me to a boarding school?" He had tried to speak in what he thought was a natural voice, but his mother's eyes filled with tears. He thrust his hands into his pockets and said, "I don't like to study very much. Remember what Aunt Adelina said in Chiclayo. And that would make papa mad. In a boarding school they *make* you study." His mother looked at him intently and he felt confused. "But who'd keep your mamma company?" "She would," Ricardo answered without hesitation. "Who?" "My baby sister." The anxiety vanished from his mother's face; there was only a look of weariness in her eyes. "You won't have any sister," she said. "I forgot to tell you." He spent the rest of the day brooding about his mistake, and it was torture to realize how he had betrayed himself. That night, in bed, but with his eyes wide open in the dark, he saw a way of making up for his blunder: he would keep his words to them to the absolute minimum, he would spend as much time as possible in the storeroom, he would. . . Then his thoughts were interrupted by the sound of an angry voice, and suddenly his room was rocked by a thunderous voice using words he had never heard before. It terrified him. At moments, among his father's shouts and insults, he could hear his mother's weak, pleading cries. There was silence for a moment, then the sound of a loud slap, and by the time his mother had screamed, "Richi!" he had already leaped out of bed. He ran to the door, opened it, and burst into the other room shouting, "Don't hit my mamma!" He could see his mother in her nightgown, her face was dim in the shaded light, he heard her murmur something, and then a great white silhouette loomed up in front of him. He's naked, he thought, and he was terrified again. His father hit him with his open hand and he fell down without uttering a sound. He got up again immediately but everything was spinning around him. He wanted to say that nobody had ever hit him before, he wouldn't be hit, but before he could say it his father hit him again and he fell down on the floor. He was dazed but he could see his mother jump off the bed and his father stop her and throw her back onto it, and then he saw him coming toward him, still bellowing, and he felt himself hoisted in the air and he was back in his own room, his own bed, and the man who looked white in the darkness hit him in the face again, and he could see how the man got between himself and his mother when she came to the door, and how he dragged her away as if she were a rag doll, slamming the door behind him. Then he sank down and down in a turbulent nightmare.

4

He got off the bus at the Alcanfores stop and walked with long strides down the three blocks to his house. As he crossed one of the streets he passed a group of small boys. A sarcastic voice asked him, "Are you selling chocolates?" The others all laughed. Years before, he and the other boys in the neighborhood also used to shout "Chocolates for sale!" at the cadets from the Military Academy. The sky was leaden gray but the weather was not cold. The Alcanfores Inn looked deserted. His mother opened the door for him and kissed him.

"You're late," she said. "Why, Alberto?"

"The Callao streetcars are always crammed full, mamma. And they only go by once every half hour."

His mother had taken his bag and cap and she followed him to his room. It was a small house, all on one floor, and shining clean. Alberto took off his jacket and tie and threw them on a chair. His mother picked them up and folded them carefully.

"Do you want lunch right now?"

"I'd like to take a shower first."

"Have you missed me?"

"Yes, mamma, a lot."

Alberto took off his shirt. Before he took off his trousers he put on his bathrobe: his mother had not seen him naked since he had become a cadet.

"I'll clean and press your uniform. It's awfully dusty."

"I know," Alberto said. He put on his slippers, opened a bureau drawer and took out a shirt, underwear, socks. Then he took a pair of gleaming black shoes out of the bedside stand.

"I polished them this morning," his mother said.

"You're going to ruin your hands. You shouldn't have done it, mamma."

"Who cares about my hands?" his mother sighed. "Now that he's deserted me. . ."

"We had a real tough exam this morning," Alberto said, interrupting her. "I didn't do very well."

"Oh?" his mother murmured. "Don't you want me to fill the tub for you?"

"No. I'm going to take a shower."

"All right. I'll go and fix our lunch."

She turned away and walked as far as the door.

"Mamma."

She stopped in the doorway. She was a small woman, with very white hair and sunken, lifeless eyes. She was not wearing any make-up and her hair was disheveled. She had on a faded apron over her skirt. Alberto remembered the time, not too long ago, when his mother used to spend hours in front of her mirror, rubbing face cream into her wrinkles, lining her eyes, powdering her face. She went to the beauty shop every afternoon, and when she was going out somewhere, selecting a dress to wear would bring on an attack of nerves. She had changed completely after his father left her.

"Have you seen my father?"

She sighed again and her cheeks reddened. "Imagine it, he was here just this Thursday," she said. "I opened the door without knowing who it was. He hasn't got the least bit of shame, Alberto. You can't guess what he's like. He wanted you to go see him. He offered me money again. He wants to torture me to death." She raised her eyes and lowered her voice: "You've just got to accept it, my son."

"I'm going to take a shower," he said. "I'm filthy."

He walked past his mother, patting her head and thinking, We'll never have a centavo. He spent a long time in the shower. After soaping himself thoroughly, he scrubbed his body with both hands and turned the water back and forth from hot to cold. As if I were trying to sober up, he thought. Then he got dressed. It was the same as on other Saturdays:

his civilian clothes felt strange at first, too soft, his skin missed the harsh touch of khaki. His mother was waiting for him in the dining room. They ate lunch in silence. Each time he finished a piece of bread, his mother anxiously passed him the bread basket.

"Are you going out?"

"Yes, mamma. I've got to do an errand for a buddy who's confined to the grounds. I'll be back right away."

His mother blinked at him several times and Alberto was afraid she would start weeping.

"I never see you at all," she said. "When you go out you spend the whole day away from the house. Don't you ever think of your mother?"

"I'll only be gone for an hour, mamma," Alberto said uncomfortably. "Maybe even less."

He had been hungry when they sat down at the table, but the meal seemed endless and tasteless. Every week he dreamed about his pass, but the moment he got home he felt irritable: his mother's overwhelming attentions were as hard to put up with as the Academy. Also, there was something new to get used to. Before, she sent him out of the house on any pretext whatsoever, in order to gossip with the flock of women friends who came to play canasta every afternoon. But now she clung only to him, begging him to give her all his free time, and Alberto spent hours listening to her complain about her tragic fate. And she always worked herself into a state where she called on God and prayed at the top of her voice. That was another difference. She had often forgotten to go to Mass at all, and Alberto had frequently caught her sniggering with her cronies about the priests and the pious hypocrites. Now she went to church almost every day, and she even had a spiritual adviser, a Jesuit she referred to as "a holy man." She also went to novenas, and one Saturday Alberto found a life of St. Rosa of Lima on his bedside stand. His mother gathered up the dishes and brushed the crumbs off the table with her hand.

"I'll be back by five," he said.

"Berto," she said, "I'll buy some cookies for our tea."

The woman was fat and greasy and dirty. Her lank hair kept falling over her eyes and she kept pushing it back with her left hand and then scratching her head. She had a square of cardboard in her other hand, using it to fan the reluctant fire. The charcoal got damp at night and when it was lighted it smoked. The kitchen walls were black with soot and the woman's face was thoroughly smudged. "I'm going to go blind," she muttered. The smoke and the sparks made her eyes water, and her eyelids were always swollen.

"What did you say?" Teresa asked from the next room.

"Nothing," the woman growled, bending over the pot. The soup had still not come to a boil.

"What?" the girl asked.

"Are you deaf? I said I'm going to go blind."

"Do you want me to help you?"

"You don't know how," the woman said gruffly. She stirred the pot with one hand and picked her nose with the other. "You don't know how to do anything. You can't cook, you can't sew, you can't do a thing. Poor little you."

Teresa refused to reply. She had just come back from work and was cleaning up the house. Her aunt did the housework on weekdays, but on Saturdays and Sundays Teresa did it. It was not a hard job, because the house only had two rooms besides the kitchen: a bedroom, and another room that served as dining room, living room and sewing room. The house was old and rickety, and almost without furniture. "Go see your aunt and uncle this afternoon," the woman said. "Let's hope they won't be as stingy as they were last month."

A few bubbles had finally started rising to the surface, and the woman's eyes brightened a little.

"I'll go see them tomorrow," Teresa said. "I can't go today."

"You can't?" The woman waved the piece of cardboard she used as a fan.

"No. I've got a date."

The piece of cardboard stopped dead and the woman raised her head. Her surprise lasted for several seconds. Then she went back to fanning the fire.

"A date?"

"Yes." The girl had stopped sweeping and she held the broom a few inches off the floor. "I've been invited to the movies."

"The movies? Who?"

The soup was at a full boil now but the woman seemed to have forgotten about it. She turned toward the next room, waiting for Teresa's answer, worried and motionless, her hair down over her forehead.

"Who invited you?" she insisted, and began to fan her face.

"The boy on the corner," Teresa said, resting the broom on the floor.

"Which corner?"

"The brick house. The two-story one. His name's Arana."

"Is that their name? Arana?"

"Yes."

"Is he the one that wears a uniform?" the woman asked.

"Yes. He's from the Military Academy. He gets a pass today. He's calling for me at six."

The woman went over to Teresa. Her bulging eyes were wide open. "He's from a good family," she said. "Well-dressed. They've even got a car."

"Yes," Teresa said. "A blue one."

"Have you ever been in it?" the woman asked her harshly.

"No. I've only talked with him once, two weeks ago. He was going to come last Sunday but then he couldn't. He sent me a letter."

The woman suddenly turned around and lumbered into the kitchen. The fire had gone out again, but the soup was still boiling.

"You're almost eighteen," she said, pushing her hair back. "It's time you realized it. I'll go blind and we'll starve to death if you don't get around to doing something. You can't let that boy get away. You're lucky he's noticed you. At your age I was already pregnant. Why did the good Lord have to give me children if He was just going to take them away from me? Bah!"

"I know, Aunt," Teresa said.

As she went on with her sweeping she looked down at her high-heeled gray shoes. They were dirty and worn-out. What if Arana took her to a high-class theater?

"Is he a soldier?" the woman asked.

"No. He's a cadet at the Leoncio Prado. It's an academy like the rest, but it's run by the army."

"The Academy?" The woman snorted indignantly. "I thought he was a man. Bah! You don't care if I'm getting old. All you want is for me to die so you'll be rid of me once and for all."

Alberto was tying his tie. That clean-shaven face, that well-combed head of hair, that bright white shirt, that light-colored tie, that trim gray jacket, that handkerchief peeking out of his breast pocket, that scrubbed and elegant person reflected in the bathroom mirror, was all that really himself?

"You're a good boy," his mother said from the living room. Then, sadly: "You look just like your father."

Alberto came out of the bathroom and leaned over to kiss her. His mother offered him her forehead. She only came up to his shoulders and he thought how fragile she was. Her hair was almost white. She doesn't dye it any more, he thought. She looks a hundred years old.

"Here he is!" his mother said.

And a moment later the doorbell rang. "Don't answer it,"

his mother said when Alberto started toward the door, but she made no move to stop him.

"Hello, papa," Alberto said.

His father was a short, heavily-built man, going somewhat bald. He was dressed in an impeccable blue suit, and when Alberto kissed his cheek he could smell a sharp perfume. His father smiled, patted him on the back, and glanced around the room. His mother was standing in the little hall that led to the bathroom, looking completely resigned: her head was bowed, her eyes were half-closed, her hands were folded on her skirt, and her neck was thrust forward a little as if to be helpful to the executioner.

"Good morning, Carmela."

"What did you come back for?" his mother asked without moving.

His father closed the door without the slightest embarrassment, tossed his leather brief case on a chair and then sat down, still smiling, still casual, and motioned to Alberto to sit down beside him. Alberto looked at his mother; she had not moved.

"Carmela, come here, girl," his father said in a breezy voice. "Let's have a little chat. We can talk in front of Alberto, he's a man now."

Alberto felt pleased. His father, unlike his mother, seemed younger, healthier, stronger. There was something irrepressible in his voice, his expressions, his gestures. Was that because he was happy?

"There's nothing to talk about," his mother said. "Absolutely nothing."

"Come, now," his father said. "We're civilized people. We can settle the whole thing if you'll just calm down."

"You monster! You devil!" his mother screamed. She shook her fists at him, and her usually meek face was red and contorted and her eyes were flashing. "Get out of here! This is my house! I pay the rent myself!"

His father clapped his hands over his ears, grinning. Alberto looked at his wristwatch. His mother had begun weeping and her body was racked with sobs. She made no attempt to wipe away the tears that coursed down her cheeks.

"Carmela, calm down," his father said. "I don't want a fight. Let's try to be sensible. You can't go on like this. It's ridiculous. You've got to get out of this dump, hire some servants, start living again. You can't let yourself go to pieces. Think of your son."

"Get out!" she screamed. "This is a decent home. You haven't got any right to disgrace it. Go on, go back to your loose women. We don't want anything to do with you. And you can keep your money too. I've got more than enough to educate my son."

"Nonsense. You're living like a beggar," his father said. "Don't you have any self-respect? Why in the name of God won't you let me give you an income?"

"Alberto!" his mother shrieked. "Don't let him insult me! He isn't satisfied to disgrace me in front of all Lima. Now he wants to kill me. Do something, Alberto!"

"Please, papa," Alberto said dully, "please don't fight."

"Keep quiet," his father said, looking very solemn and superior. "You're too young. Some day you'll understand. Life isn't so simple."

Alberto wanted to laugh. He remembered the day he saw his father in downtown Lima with a beautiful blonde. His father saw him too, and looked away. That night he went to his son's room with the same pompous expression on his face and told him the very same thing.

"Carmela," his father went on, "I'd like to make you a proposition. Listen to me for a moment."

His mother froze into her tragic attitude again, but Alberto could see that she was looking at his father with a calculating expression in her eyes.

"What you're really worried about," his father said, "is the gossip. I can understand that. It's important to keep up appearances."

"You cynic!" his mother cried, then bowed her head again. "Don't interrupt me, girl. If you want, we can live together again. We'll rent a decent house in Miraflores. Perhaps we can even get the one we used to have in Diego Ferré. Or we can live in San Antonio or wherever you want. The one thing is, I insist on having complete freedom. I want to live my own life." He was speaking calmly, with that bright sparkle in his eyes that had surprised Alberto. "And of course we'll have to stop having scenes. We don't come from good families for nothing."

His mother was weeping noisily by now, and between her sobs she screeched insults at his father, calling him an adulterer, a degenerate, a bundle of filth. Alberto said, "Excuse me, papa. I've got to go out on an errand. Will you let me leave?"

His father seemed disconcerted for a moment, but then he smiled amiably and nodded his head. "Yes, son, of course. I'll try to convince your mother. It's the best way out. And don't worry about it. Study hard, you've got a fine future ahead of you. I've already told you I'll send you to the United States next year if you do a good job on your exams."

"*I'll* take care of my poor son's future!" his mother shouted.

Alberto kissed his parents and went out quickly, closing the door behind him.

Teresa had finished washing the dishes. Her aunt was resting in the bedroom. The girl picked up a towel and a bar of soap and tiptoed out of the house. The house next door was old and narrow, with faded yellow walls. She knocked on the door. A slim, cheerful girl opened it for her.

"Hello, Tere."

"Hello, Rosa. Can I take a bath?"

"Come in."

They went down a dark hallway. Its walls were covered with photographs clipped from magazines and newspapers: movie stars and soccer players.

"Look at this one," Rosa said. "They gave it to me this morning. It's Glenn Ford. Have you ever seen any of his movies?"

"No. But I'd like to."

The dining room was at the end of the hallway. Rosa's parents were eating in complete silence. The chair that the wife was sitting in had lost its back. The husband raised his eyes from the newspaper beside his plate and looked at Teresa.

"Ah, Teresita," he said, getting up.

"Hello," she said.

He was growing old; he was pot-bellied and bow-legged, with sleepy-looking eyes. He grinned and reached out a hand to the girl's face in a friendly way, but Teresa stepped back and his hand wavered in the air and then dropped.

"I want to take a bath, Señora," Teresa said to the wife. "All right?"

"Yes," the woman said curtly. "It'll be a sol. Have you got it?"

Teresa stretched out her hand. The coin was dull and lifeless from long usage.

"Make it snappy," the woman said. "There isn't much water."

The bathroom was a dim nook only a yard square with some slimy, worn-out boards on the tile floor. The shower was a pipe on the wall. Teresa closed the door and hung the towel on the handle, making sure it covered the keyhole. Then she undressed. She was slender, with a graceful figure and very dark skin. She turned on the water. It was cold again. As she soaped herself, she heard the wife shout, "Get away from there, you filthy old goat!" The husband's footsteps went away and she could hear the couple arguing. She got dressed and went out. The husband was sitting at the table, and when he saw Teresa he winked at her. The wife scowled: "You're getting the floor wet."

"I'm going home now," Teresa said. "Thank you, Señora."

"So long, Teresa," the husband said. "Come back whenever you want to."

Rosa went to the door with her. In the hallway Teresa whispered, "Do me a favor, Rosita. Lend me your blue ribbon. The one you were wearing Saturday. I'll bring it back tonight if you want."

Rosa nodded and put a finger to her lips. She tiptoed down the hallway, vanished for a few moments, and came tiptoeing back.

"Here," she said, with the look of a happy conspirator. "but what do you want it for? Where're you going?"

"I've got a date," Teresa said. "He's taking me to the movies."

Her eyes were shining with joy.

A light drizzle swayed the leaves on the trees along Alcanfores Street. Alberto went into the corner store, bought a pack of cigarettes, and walked down to Larco Avenue. A lot of cars were going by, some of them almost new, with bright-colored tops that contrasted with the gray of the buildings and the sky. There were also a great many pedestrians, and he watched a tall, slinky girl in black tights until she vanished in the crowd. The express was late as usual. Then Alberto noticed a couple of boys grinning at him. It was a few seconds before he recognized them. He turned pink and said, "Hi!" and they came running over with open arms.

"Where've you been all this while?" one of them asked him. He was wearing a sporty suit, and his hair was combed up in a peak like the comb of a rooster. "Is it really you?" he asked Alberto.

"We thought you didn't live in Miraflores any more," the other one said. He was short and heavy, and was wearing loafers. "You haven't been around to the neighborhood for years."

"Well, I'm living in Alcanfores now," Alberto said. "I'm

going to the Leoncio Prado. I only get out on weekends."

"You mean the Military Academy?" the one with the hair-do asked him. "It must be a real bitch. What'd you do to get sent there?"

"It's not too bad. Not after you get used to it."

The express was full when it arrived, and they had to stand up and hold onto the overhead rail. Alberto thought about the people he saw on Saturdays on the La Perla buses or the Lima-Callao streetcars: loud ties, if any, and a smell of sweat and dirt. But on the express: clean clothes, dignified faces, smiles.

"And your car?" Alberto asked.

"Mine?" the one in loafers said. "It's my father's. He won't let me use it any more. I had an accident."

"What, you didn't know?" the other one said excitedly. "You didn't hear about the race on the Malecón?"

"No, I didn't hear a thing."

"Where've you been living, man? This Tico is a real fiend." The other gave a satisfied smile. "He made a bet with that crazy Julio—the guy that lived on Francia Street, you remember him—for a race on the Malecón to La Quebrada. And it'd been raining, the pair of idiots. I was co-pilot for this one here. The highway patrol caught Julio, but we got away. We'd just come from a party, so you can imagine."

"But the accident?" Alberto asked.

"That was after. Tico decided it'd be a good idea to drive backward for a while. He hit a post. Can you see this scar? And Tico didn't even get scratched. It isn't fair, the luck he's got."

Tico smiled broadly, gleefully.

"He's a fiend, all right," Alberto said. "How's everything in the neighborhood?"

"Fine," Tico said. "We don't get together during the week the way we used to, the girls are taking exams and they're only around on Saturdays and Sundays. Things have changed, their parents let them go out with us, to parties or the movies. Their old ladies are getting civilized, they even let them have steady boy friends. Did you know Pluto's going around with Helena?"

"You're going around with Helena?" Alberto asked.

"It'll be a month tomorrow," Pluto said, blushing.

"And they let her go out with you?"

"Of course they do, man. Sometimes her mother invites me to lunch. You used to really like her, right?"

"Me?" Alberto said. "No."

"Sure you did!" Pluto said. "You were nuts about her. Don't you remember the time we were teaching you how to dance at Emilio's house? We told you you'd have to tell her how you felt."

"Those were the days," Tico said.

"Hey, now," Pluto said, looking toward the back of the express. "Do you gentlemen see what I see?"

He shoved his way to the back seats. Tico and Alberto followed him. The girl was aware of them and turned her head to look out the window at the trees along the avenue. She was plump and pretty. Her nose was wriggling like a rabbit's. It was almost pressed up against the window, and her breath clouded the glass.

"Hello, my love," Pluto said.

"Don't molest my sweetheart," Tico said, "or I'll kill you."

"It doesn't matter," Pluto said. "I'd gladly die for her." He spread his arms like an orator. "I love her!"

Tico and Pluto laughed loudly. The girl went on looking at the trees.

"Don't mind him, my darling," Tico said. "He's just a savage. Pluto, ask the señorita to excuse you."

"You're right," Pluto said. "I'm a savage and I regret it. Please forgive me. Tell me you forgive me or I'll make a scene."

"Have a heart," Tico said.

Alberto was also looking out the window. The trees were moist, the pavement shining. There was a steady stream of cars coming from the other direction. The express had already passed through Orrantia and its big, multicolored houses. Now the houses were small and drab.

"This is disgraceful," a woman said. "Leave the poor girl alone!"

Tico and Pluto went on laughing. The girl stopped looking at the avenue for a moment and glanced around her with the quick, bright eyes of a squirrel. A smile crossed her face and vanished.

"With the greatest pleasure, Señora," Tico said. Then turning to the girl again: "Please excuse us, Señorita."

"This is my stop," Alberto said, shaking hands. "I'll be seeing you."

"Come on with us," Tico said. "We'll go to the movies. We can get a girl for you. She's really okay."

"No, I can't," Alberto said. "I've got a date."

"In Lince?" Pluto asked him with a malicious grin. "So you've got something going, you half-breed! Well, I hope you make it. And don't get lost again, come around to the neighborhood, everybody still remembers you."

I knew she'd be ugly, he thought when he first saw her in the doorway. And he hurriedly said, "Good afternoon. Is Teresa in?"

"I'm Teresa."

"I've got a message from Arana. Ricardo Arana."

"Come in," the girl said in a shy voice. "Sit down."

Alberto sat down gingerly on the edge of the chair, wondering if it might not collapse. There was a gap in the curtains that separated the rooms, and he could see the end of a bed and a woman's large, dark feet.

"Arana didn't get a pass," Alberto said. "It was just bad luck. They confined him to the grounds this morning. He told me he had a date with you and he asked me to come and excuse him."

"They confined him?" the girl asked. Her face clearly

revealed her disappointment. She had her hair tied up at the back of her neck with a blue ribbon. I wonder if he's ever kissed her, Alberto thought.

"That's something that happens to everybody," he said. "It's all in your luck. He'll come and see you next Saturday."

"Who is it?" a grumpy voice demanded. Alberto looked over, and the feet had vanished. A moment later a greasy face peered out between the curtains. Alberto stood up.

"It's a friend of Arana's," Teresa said. "His name is. . ."

Alberto told them his name. The hand he had to shake was fat, limp, sweaty, clammy. The woman gave him a theatrical smile and started talking so fast there was no chance of interrupting. Her prattle sounded to him like a caricature of all the polite jargon he had heard since childhood, spiced with fine, superfluous adjectives and with here a Don, there a Señor, and she asked him innumerable questions without waiting for answers. He felt trapped in a web of words, in an echoing labyrinth.

"Sit down, sit down," the woman said, waving toward the chair and bowing to him over her vast bosom, "don't put yourself out on my account, just feel right at home, it's a poor home but a decent one, you know what I mean, I've earned my daily bread my whole life long with the sweat of my brow, I'm a seamstress and I've been able to give Teresita a good education, she's my niece, you know, the poor thing's an orphan, she owes everything to me, sit down, Señor Alberto."

"Arana was confined to the grounds," Teresa said. She avoided looking at Alberto or her aunt. "This señor brought me the message."

Señor? Alberto thought. He tried to see the girl's eyes but she was looking down at the floor. The woman stiffened and dropped her arms but there was still the trace of a frozen smile on her thick lips, her flat nose, and the pouches under her eyes.

"Poor thing," she said. "Poor boy, how his mother'll

suffer, I've had children myself so I know what a mother's grief is, my children died, that's the way God is and there's no use trying to understand, but he'll get out next week, life is hard for all of us, I know it only too well, you youngsters shouldn't think about it, tell me, where are you going to take Teresita?"

"Aunt," the girl said with a gesture of impatience, "he came to give me a message. He isn't. . ."

"Don't worry about me," the woman added, generous, understanding, self-sacrificing. "You young people are happier when you're alone together, I was young once too and now I'm old, that's life, but you'll have your troubles soon enough, the older you get the worse it is, did you know I'm going blind?"

"Aunt," the girl said. "Please. . ."

"If you'll let us," Alberto said, "we could go to a movie. That is, if it's all right with you."

The girl had lowered her eyes again. She was silent and could not tell what to do with her hands.

"Bring her back early," the aunt said. "Young people shouldn't stay out late, Don Alberto." She turned to Teresa. "Come with me a minute. Excuse us, Señor."

She took Teresa by the arm and led her into the other room. The woman's words reached his ears in fragments, as if partly blown away by a high wind. He could make out isolated words, but he could not put them together. Still, he could understand obscurely that the girl refused to go out with him, and that the aunt, without replying to that, was creating a grand, all-inclusive portrait of him, or rather, of the ideal being he represented in her eyes: she saw him as rich, elegant, enviable, a man of the world.

The curtains parted again. Alberto smiled. The girl was rubbing her hands, disgusted and even shyer than before.

"You can go out," the woman said. "I take very good care of her, I want you to know. I don't let her go out with just anybody. She's a good worker, though you wouldn't think it to see how thin she is. I'm happy you're going to enjoy yourselves for a while."

The girl went to the door and stood aside for Alberto to go out first. The drizzle had stopped, but the air smelled damp and the sidewalk and the street were glistening and slippery. Alberto walked beside Teresa on the outside of the sidewalk. He took out his cigarettes and lit one. He glanced at her from the corner of his eye: she was upset, and walked with short quick steps, looking straight ahead. They reached the corner without having spoken. Teresa stopped.

"You can leave me here," she said. "I know a girl, a friend of mine, who lives on the next block. Thanks for everything."

"No," Alberto said. "Why?"

"You'll have to excuse my aunt," Teresa said. She was looking at him now, and seemed calmer. "She's very kind, she'll do everything she can so I can go out on a date."

"Yes," Alberto said, "she's very nice, very friendly."

"But she talks a lot," Teresa said, and laughed.

She isn't pretty but she's got beautiful teeth, Alberto thought. How did the Slave get to be her boy friend?

"Will Arana be mad if you go out with me?"

"He isn't my boy friend," she said. "This is the first time we had a date. He didn't tell you?"

"No."

They were still at the corner. They could see a few people at a distance on the streets around them. It began drizzling again, and a fine mist drifted down on them. They were silent for a moment. Alberto dropped his cigarette and stamped it out.

"Well," Teresa said, reaching out her hand, "good-by."

"No," Alberto said. "You can visit your friend some other time. Let's go to the movies."

Her face grew very serious. "Don't invite me because you think you ought to. Really. Haven't you got something you have to do?"

"Even if I did, I'd invite you," Alberto said. "But honestly, I don't."

"All right," she said. She stretched out her hand, palm up, and looked at the sky. Alberto could see that her eyes were gleaming.

"It's raining."

"Just barely."

"Let's take the express."

They walked down to Arequipa Avenue. Alberto lit another cigarette.

"You just put one out," Teresa said. "Do you smoke a lot?"

"No. Only when I'm on pass."

"Don't they let you smoke in the Academy?"

"Strictly forbidden. But of course we smoke anyway, in secret."

As they approached the avenue the houses were larger, the streets wider. Groups of people went by. Some boys in shirt sleeves shouted something at Teresa. Alberto turned around to go back, but she stopped him.

"Don't pay any attention to them," she said. "They're always saying silly things."

"They shouldn't bother a girl when she's with a fellow," Alberto said. "That's an insult."

"You cadets from the Leoncio Prado, you all like to fight."

He reddened with pleasure. Vallano was right: the cadets really impressed the girls. Not those in Miraflores, but those in Lince. He started talking about the Academy, the rivalries among the Years, the field exercises, the vicuña, the dog Skimpy. Teresa listened attentively, and showed how she liked his stories. Then she told him she worked in a downtown office and that earlier she had studied typing and shorthand in a secretarial school. They got on the express at the Raimondi Academy stop and got off at the San Martín Plaza. Pluto and Tico were there under the arcades. They looked them up and down, and Tico grinned at Alberto and winked his eye.

"Aren't you going to the movies?"

"They stood us up," Pluto said.

They said good-by. Alberto could hear them whispering behind him. He felt as if the dirty looks of the whole neighborhood were falling on him like a cloudburst.

"What movie would you like to see?" he asked.

"I don't know," she said. "Any one you want."

Alberto bought a newspaper and read out the movie ads in a loud, affected voice. Teresa laughed and the people walking through the arcades turned to look at them. They decided to go to the Metro. Alberto bought two tickets for downstairs. If Arana only knew how I'm spending the money he loaned me, he thought. And now I can't go see Golden Toes. He smiled at Teresa and she smiled back at him. It was still early and the theater was almost empty. Alberto grew very talkative: since he was not intimidated by this girl, he could make good use of all the smart phrases and wisecracks and puns he had heard so often in the neighborhood.

"The Metro's awfully pretty," she said. "Very elegant."

"You haven't been in here before?"

"No. I hardly ever go to the downtown theaters. I get out of work late, at six-thirty."

"Don't you like the movies?"

"Yes, lots! I go every Sunday. But I go to a neighborhood theater near my house."

The picture was in color, with a great many dance numbers. The head dancer was also a comedian. He mixed people's names up, he took pratfalls, he made faces, he rolled his eyes. You can tell he's a queer from a mile off, Alberto thought. He turned to look at Teresa. She was completely absorbed by what was happening on the screen: her mouth was half open and there was a hungry stare in her eyes. Later, when they were outside, she described the whole movie as if Alberto had not seen any part of it. She chattered about the actresses' dresses and their jewelry, and

when she recalled the comedy episodes her laughter was
very bright and innocent.

"You have a good memory," he said. "How can you remember all that?"

"I told you, I'm crazy about the movies. When I'm seeing
a good movie I forget everything else. It's like I'm in
another world."

"Yes," Alberto said, "I could tell. You looked as if you
were hypnotized."

They got on the express and sat down side by side. The
San Martín Plaza was full of people who had come out from
the first showing of the movies and were walking around
under the street lights. There was a tangle of cars on all
sides of the square. As they approached the Raimondi stop,
Alberto pushed the button.

"You don't have to go with me," she said. "I can get
home alone. I've already taken up enough of your time."

He objected, and insisted on going with her. The street
that ran into the middle of Lince was dark. A few couples
went by. Others were standing together in the shadows, and
stopped murmuring or kissing when someone passed them.

"You really didn't have anything to do?" Teresa asked.

"No, honest."

"I don't believe you."

"But it's true. Why don't you believe me?"

She hesitated. Finally she said, "You haven't got a girl
friend?"

"No," he said. "No, I don't."

"I know you're lying. But you must have had lots of
them."

"Not lots," Alberto said. "Just a few. And have you had
a lot of boy friends?"

"Me? Not one."

Should I ask her to be my girl friend right now? Alberto
wondered. "That's not true," he said. "You must have had
dozens."

Arequipa Avenue with its double line of cars was far away now. The street was narrow and the shadows were even deeper. The drops of water that had gathered on the leaves and branches during the afternoon drizzle were gently dripping from the trees onto the sidewalk.

"Is that because you haven't wanted to?"

"What do you mean?"

"Why you haven't had any boy friends." He paused for a moment. "A pretty girl can have as many as she wants."

"Oh," Teresa said. "But I'm not pretty. Don't you think I know it?"

Alberto objected strongly, and said, "You're one of the prettiest girls I've ever seen."

Teresa turned to look at him. "Now you're making fun of me," she murmured.

I'm an imbecile, Alberto thought. He heard Teresa's little steps beside him, two for each one of his, and he glanced over at her. She had her head bent a little, her arms crossed on her breast, her mouth closed. The blue ribbon looked black, and was lost against her black hair; it stood out when they passed under a street light, then disappeared in the darkness again. They walked to the door of her house without speaking.

"Thank you," Teresa said. "Thanks for everything."

They shook hands. "See you soon." Alberto turned away, walked a few feet, and came back.

"Teresa."

She had raised her hand to knock on the door. She looked around, startled.

"Have you got anything to do tomorrow?" he asked.

"Tomorrow?"

"Yes. I'd like to take you to the movies. How about it?"

"I haven't got anything to do. Thanks very much."

"I'll come by for you at five," he said.

Before she went into the house, Teresa watched Alberto until he vanished from sight.

When his mother opened the door, Alberto immediately began to make his excuses. Her eyes were filled with reproach and she was sighing loudly. They went in and sat down in the living room. His mother was silent and resentful. Alberto felt infinitely bored.

"I'm sorry," he told her once again. "Don't be cross, mamma. Honest, I did everything I could to get away early, but they wouldn't let me go. I'm feeling kind of tired. Is it all right if I go to bed now?"

There was no reply. She was still looking at him accusingly, and he wondered, When will it start? It was not long, for suddenly she put her face in her hands and started weeping quietly. Alberto stroked her hair. She asked him why he made her suffer so. He swore he loved her above everything else in the world. She said he was a hypocrite, just like his father. Between her sobs and her appeals to God she told him how she had bought cakes and cookies at the store around the corner, how she had picked out the very best they had, how their tea had got cold on the table, how her loneliness and her tragic grief had been sent to her by the Lord in Heaven to test her moral fortitude and her spirit of self-sacrifice. Alberto raised her head with both hands and leaned over to kiss her brow. He was thinking: Here's another week gone by and I still haven't been to see Golden Toes. Then his mother was calmer, and asked him to try to eat the dinner she herself had prepared for him with her own two hands. Alberto agreed, and while he was eating a bowl of vegetable soup she embraced him and said, "You're the only hope I've got in the whole wide world." She told him that his father had left the house after about an hour, that he had made all sorts of proposals—a trip somewhere, a pretended reconciliation, a divorce, an amicable separation—and that she had turned down all of them without hesitating an instant.

Then they went back to the living room and Alberto asked her if he could smoke. She nodded, but when she saw him light his cigarette she burst into tears and began talking about how time flies, how little boys grow up so fast, how life is ephemeral. She reminisced about her childhood, the family trips to Europe, her friends at school, her good looks, her suitors, the many young men she turned down to marry this man whose only purpose now was to destroy her. Then, lowering her voice, and putting on her most tragic expression, she began talking about his father. She repeated again and again, "He wasn't like this when I met him," and she described how good he was at sports, all the tennis tournaments he won, his fine manners, their honeymoon in Brazil, the midnight walks they used to take, hand in hand, on the beach at Ipanema. "But he got into bad company," she said. "Lima's the most corrupt city in the world. But I'll save his soul with my prayers." Alberto listened to her in silence, thinking about Golden Toes, another week without seeing her, and he wondered what the Slave would say when he found out he took Teresa to the movies, and he thought about Pluto and Helena, and the Military Academy, and the neighborhood he had not visited for three years. At last, his mother yawned. He stood up, said good night to her, and went to his room. While he was undressing he noticed an envelope on the stand beside his bed, with his name printed in big letters. He opened it and took out a fifty-sol bill.

"He left that for you," his mother said from the doorway. She sighed. "It's the only thing I accepted from him. My poor little boy, there's no reason you should have to suffer too!"

He threw his arms around his mother, lifted her off the floor, and whirled her around, saying, "Just you wait, mamma, it'll all come out all right, I promise you I'll do everything you want me to." She smiled happily and said, "We don't need anybody else." In the midst of their patting and hugging, he asked her permission to go out.

"Just a few minutes," he said. "I want some fresh air."

Her smile died, but she agreed. He put on his tie and

jacket again, ran his comb through his hair, and left. His mother called out to him from the front window: "Don't forget to say your prayers before you go to bed."

Vallano was the first one to mention her nickname in the barracks. One Sunday at midnight, when the cadets had taken off their dress uniforms and were smoking the cigarettes they had got past the officer of the guard by hiding them in their caps, Vallano started talking to himself in an undertone about a woman in the fourth block of Huatica Street. His eyes rolled in their sockets like two magnetized steel balls, and he sounded very excited.

"Shut up, you clown," the Jaguar said. "Cut it out."

But he went on talking while he was making his bunk. Cava, who was already in bed, asked him, "What did you say she's called?"

"Golden Toes."

"Must be a new one," Arróspide said. "I know everybody in the fourth block and I don't remember that name."

On the following Sunday, Cava and the Jaguar and Arróspide were also talking about her. They kept nudging each other and laughing. "Didn't I tell you?" Vallano asked them proudly. "Just follow my advice." A week later, half of the section knew her and the name of Golden Toes began to ring in Alberto's ears like a popular song. The vague but suggestive references he heard them make aroused his imagination. In his dreams, her name took on strange, voluptuous, contradictory meanings: the woman was always the same and yet different, a presence that vanished when he was about to touch her or uncover her face, provoking the most extravagant impulses or submerging him in a tenderness so profound that he felt he would die of impatience.

Alberto talked about Golden Toes as much as anyone else in the section. No one suspected that he knew about Huatica Street and its environs only by hearsay, because he repeated anecdotes he had been told and invented all kinds of lurid stories. But he could not overcome a certain inner discontent. The more he talked about sexual adventures to his friends, who either laughed or shamelessly thrust their hands into their pockets, the more certain he was that he would never go to bed with a woman except in his dreams, and this depressed him so much that he swore he would go to Huatica Street on his very next pass, even if he had to steal twenty soles, even if he got syphilis.

He got off at the corner of Wilson and the 28th of July. I'm fifteen but I look older, he thought. I haven't got any reason to be nervous. He lit a cigarette, then threw it away after only two puffs. As he went down the 28th of July, the avenue grew more and more crowded, and after he crossed the tracks of the Lima-Chorrillos streetcar he found himself in the midst of a swarm of workers, housemaids, mestizos with lank hair, mixed Chinese who walked as if they were dancing, copper-colored Indians, smiling half-breeds. He could tell he was in the Victoria district by the smell of native food and drink that filled the air, an almost visible smell of fried porkskin and pisco, of ham rolls and sweat, of beer and dirty feet.

As he crossed the Victoria Plaza, which was huge and crowded, the stone Inca that loomed against the sky reminded him of the hero's statue at the Academy, and also of what Vallano said once: "Manco Cápac is a pimp, he's pointing the way to Huatica Street." The crowd forced him to walk slowly, and he almost suffocated. The lights on the avenue seemed deliberately weak and far apart, thus accentuating the profiles of the men who walked by looking in the windows of the identical little houses lined up along the sidewalks. At the corner of Huatica and the 28th of July, Alberto heard a chorus of abuse from inside a restaurant run by a Japanese dwarf. He saw a group of men and women arguing viciously around a bottle-covered table. He lingered a few moments on the corner. He had his hands in his pockets and he stole glances at the people around him. Some of the men were glassy-eyed, others seemed deliriously happy.

He straightened his jacket and went into the fourth block, the narrowest. There was an attempt at a superior smile on his lips but his eyes were full of anxiety. He only had to walk a few yards; he knew by heart that Golden Toes lived in the second house. There were three men at the door of it, one behind another. Alberto peered in the window: there was a tiny sitting room lighted by a red bulb, with a chair, a yellowed and unrecognizable photograph on the wall, and a small bench under the window. She must be short, he thought, disappointed. A hand took him by the shoulder.

"Hey, there, kiddie," the man said, his breath reeking with onions, "are you blind or just a wise guy?"

The street lights only lit up the middle of the street and the dim glow of the red bulb scarcely reached the window. Alberto could not see the man's face. Suddenly he was aware that the crowd of men in the block kept close to the walls, where they were almost in darkness. The street itself was empty.

"Well?" the man said. "Answer me."

"What's the matter?" Alberto asked him.

"I don't really give a shit," the man said, "but I'm not a sucker. Nobody shoves his finger in my mouth, get me? Or anyplace else."

"Okay," Alberto said, "but what do you want?"

"Go get at the end of the line. Don't try to be smart."

"All right," Alberto said. "You don't have to get sore."

He turned away from the window and the man let him go. He went to the end of the line and leaned against the wall, smoking four cigarettes one after the other. The man in front of him went in and came out again almost at once. As he walked away he was muttering something about the high cost of living. Then Alberto heard a woman's voice on the other side of the door: "Come on in."

He crossed the empty sitting room. The pane of glass in

the inside door had been painted over. I'm not scared, he told himself. I'm a man. He opened the door. The room was as small as the other. It also had a red bulb, but it seemed brighter, cruder. The room was full of bric-a-brac and for a moment Alberto felt lost. He glanced around without letting his eyes rest on anything, and when he looked at the woman stretched out on the bed her face was only a blur and he noticed only the vague dark patterns that decorated her bathrobe, mere shadows that could have been either flowers or birds. Suddenly he felt calm again. The woman sat up, and yes, it was true, she was short: her feet barely grazed the floor. Her dyed hair was black at the roots under a disorderly heap of blonde curls. Her face was heavily made up. She was smiling at him. He looked down and saw two pearly fish, lively, earthy, meaty, "good enough to eat in one bite, without any butter" as Vallano said, and completely foreign to that plump body from which they dangled, and to that formless, fatuous mouth, and to those dead eyes that were studying him.

"You're from the Leoncio Prado," she said.

"Yes."

"First section of the Fifth."

"Yes," Alberto said.

The woman cackled. "That's eight of them today," she said. "And last week, Christ knows how many. I must be you guys' mascot."

"This is the first time I've come here," Alberto said, blushing. "I. . ."

He was interrupted by another cackle, this one noisier than the first. "I'm not superstitious," she said, still laughing. "I don't work for free and I've been around enough so I don't fall for that line. Every day there's somebody who's here for the very first time, I like their nerve."

"It isn't that," Alberto said. "I've got some money."

"Now that's what I *do* like," she said. "Put it on the dresser. And snap it up, General, I ain't got all night."

Alberto undressed, folding each item of his clothing. She

watched him indifferently. When he was naked, she lay back on the bed and mechanically opened her bathrobe. She was naked except for a drooping rose-colored brassiere. She's a real blonde, Alberto thought. He dropped down beside her and she put her arms around him and squeezed. He could feel her belly moving under his, seeking a better adjustment, a closer fit. Then she raised her legs and bent her knees, and he felt those fish rest gently on his hips for a moment, move up to the small of his back, move down over his buttocks and thighs, move slowly up and down, up and down. A few moments later her hands moved down from his shoulders to his waist, back up to his shoulders, up and down, in the same rhythm as her feet. She had her mouth next to his ear and he could hear her whispering, then sighing, then swearing. And then her hands and feet stopped moving.

"Are we going to take a siesta, or what?" she asked.

"Don't get mad," Alberto mumbled. "I don't know what's happened to me."

"Well, *I* know," she said. "You jack off."

He tried to laugh convincingly, and made a filthy remark. The woman cackled again and pushed him to one side. She sat up in the bed and looked at him with the hardest eyes Alberto had ever seen.

"Maybe you're a virgin after all," she said. "Lie down."

Alberto stretched out on the bed. He saw Golden Toes kneeling beside him, the light was behind her and it reddened her pale skin and darkened her hair, he thought of her as a statue in a museum, a wax figure, a performer he had seen at the circus, he was not paying attention to her hands, he could not pay attention to her busy hands or her cloying voice as she called him an idiot and a pervert, and then the objects and the symbols disappeared and all that was left was the red light enveloping him, that and a vast anxiety.

There was a flood tide of white military caps under the clock at the San Martín Plaza, because that was the last stop for the streetcar to Callao. As the cadets poured in, the newsboys and civil guards and cab drivers and loungers out in front of the Bolívar Hotel and the Romano Bar were all completely silent, watching them intently. The cadets arrived in groups, from all directions, some of them from the local bars. They held up traffic, insulted the drivers who asked to get by, insulted the women who were daring enough to walk through the plaza, and ran back and forth shouting jokes and obscenities. As the streetcars arrived, the cadets ganged into them and the civilians let themselves be shoved to the back of the line. The Dogs swore under their breath when they were about to get on the streetcar and felt a hand on their neck and heard a voice say: "Cadets first, then Dogs."

"It's ten-thirty," Vallano said. "I hope the last bus hasn't left."

"It's only ten-twenty," Arróspide said. "We've got plenty of time."

The streetcar was crowded, and both of them had to stand up. On Sundays the Academy buses went to Bellavista to look for the cadets.

"Do you see what I see?" Vallano asked. "Two Dogs. They've got their arms over their shoulders to hide their insignias, the wise guys."

"Excuse me," Arróspide said as he bulled his way to the seats where the two Dogs were. The streetcar had already gone by the 2nd of May and was passing through the invisible little Indian farms.

"Well, well, Cadets," Vallano said.

The two boys pretended they were not aware they had been spoken to. Arróspide tapped one of them on the head.

"We're tired," Vallano said. "Get up."

The two cadets obeyed him.

"What did you do yesterday?" Arróspide asked.

"Not too much," Vallano said. "There was a fiesta on Saturday that ended up as a wake. It was somebody's birthday, I think. When I showed up there was a hell of a fight going on. The wife opened the door for me and screamed, 'Get a doctor and a priest!' so I left like a shot. It was quite some rumpus. Oh, yes, I went to Huatica Street. By the way, I've got something to tell the section about the Poet."

"What?" Arróspide asked.

"I'll tell you when we're all together. It's a honey of a story."

But he could not keep it until they got to the barracks. The last bus from the Academy was going down Palmeras Avenue toward the cliffs of La Perla. Vallano, who was sitting on his bag, said, "Hey, this looks like the section's private bus. We're almost all here."

"That's right, little Negress," the Jaguar said. "Watch out, we might rape you."

"You know something?" Vallano said.

"What?" the Jaguar asked him. "Have they raped you already?"

"Listen to me," Vallano said. "It's about the Poet."

"What's the matter?" Alberto asked. He was squeezed into a back corner.

"Oh, so you're here. All the worse for you. I went to see Golden Toes on Saturday night and she told me you paid her to jack you off."

"Bah!" the Jaguar said. "I'd've done it for you free."

There was some polite, reluctant laughter.

"When Golden Toes and Vallano are in bed it must be something like coffee with milk," Arróspide said.

"And with the Poet on top of them it'd be a Negro sandwich, a hotdog," the Jaguar added.

"Everybody out!" the noncom Pezoa shouted. The bus had stopped at the gate to the Academy and all the cadets jumped out. As he was about to enter, Alberto remembered he had not hidden his cigarettes. He took a step backward, and at that moment he noticed there were only two soldiers in the doorway of the guardhouse. He was even more surprised to see there were no officers around.

"Have the lieutenants dropped dead?" Vallano asked.

"I hope God hears your prayer," Arróspide said.

Alberto went into the barracks. It was in darkness, but the open door to the latrine let out a thin light by which the cadets undressed at their lockers.

"Fernández," someone said.

"Hi," Alberto said. "What's the matter?"

The Slave was standing beside him in his pajamas, his face twisted and strange.

"You haven't heard?"

"No. What's up?"

"They know the chemistry exam was stolen. There was a broken window. The colonel was here yesterday. He was shouting at the officers in the mess hall and they've all gone wild. And those of us who were on guard Friday night. . ."

"Yes," Alberto said, "what?"

"Confined to the grounds until they know who did it."

"Shit!" Alberto said. "Goddamn him!"

5

One day I thought, I've never been alone with her. Why don't I go and wait for her when she gets out of school? But I didn't have the nerve. What was I going to say to her? And where would I get the money for the fare? Tere went to have lunch on weekdays with some relatives who lived near her school in Lima. I'd thought of going to the school at noon to walk her to her relatives' house so we could be together a little while. The year before, a guy gave me fifteen reales to pass out handbills, but you couldn't do it in half a second. I spent hours wondering how to get the money. Then I thought of asking Skinny Higueras to lend me a sol. He always invited me to have a cup of coffee or a shot of pisco and a cigarette, so a sol couldn't mean very much to him. That same afternoon, when I met him in the plaza in Bellavista, I asked him for it. "Why, sure, man," he told me, "that's what friends are for." I promised him I'd pay it back on my birthday, and he laughed and said, "Of course. Pay me when you can. Here." When I had the sol in my pocket I felt so happy that I couldn't sleep that night and the next day I kept yawning in my classes every few minutes. Three days later I told my mother, "I'm going to have lunch in Chucuito. I've got a friend there." I asked the teacher at school to let me leave half an hour early, and since I was one of the best students he said it was all right.

The streetcar was almost empty, so I couldn't sneak in free, but they only charged me half fare. I got out at the 2nd of May Plaza. One time when we were going down Alfonso Ugarte Avenue to visit my godfather, my mother told me, "See that big building, that's where Teresita goes to school." I never forgot it and I knew if I saw it again I'd recognize it, but I could never find Alfonso Ugarte Avenue and I remember I was on Colmena and when I realized it I ran back and that was when I found that big black building near the Bolognesi Plaza. They were just getting out, there was a crowd of students, big and little, and I felt too embarrassed. I turned around and went down to the corner and stood in the entrance to a store, half hiding behind the window while I watched for her. It was winter but I was sweating. When I finally saw her at a distance, the first thing I did was go into the store because I lost my nerve. But then I came out again and saw her walking away toward the Bolognesi Plaza. She was all alone, but even so I didn't go up to her. When she was out of sight I went back to the 2nd of May and got on the streetcar swearing at myself. I still had fifty centavos but I didn't buy anything to eat. I was in a bad mood all day and when we studied together in the afternoon I hardly said anything. She asked me what was wrong and I only blushed.

The next day it occurred to me during class that I ought

to go there again and wait for her, so I went to the teacher and asked him if I could leave early again. "All right," he said, "but I want you to tell your mother that if you keep leaving early it will interfere with your studies." I knew the way now, so I got to her school before it let out. When they finally appeared, I was feeling the same as I did the day before, but this time I said to myself, I'm going to go up to her, I'm going to go up to her. She was one of the last ones out, and she was all alone. I waited until she was a little way off and then I started walking along behind her. I walked faster when she got to the Bolognesi Plaza, then I caught up with her. I said, "Hi, Tere." She was somewhat surprised, I could tell it from her eyes, but she said, "Hi, what are you doing here?" in a very natural way, and I didn't know what to invent so I just said, "I got out of school before you did and I thought I'd come and meet you. Why do you ask?" "Nothing," she said, "I was just wondering." I asked her if she was going to her relatives' house and she said she was. "And you?" she added. "I don't know," I said. "If you don't mind, I'll walk you there." "Good," she said, "it isn't very far." Her aunt and uncle lived on Arica Avenue. We hardly said anything on the way. She answered everything I said but without looking at me. When we got to the corner she said, "My aunt and uncle live in the next block, you'd better leave me here." I smiled at her and she reached out her hand. "So long," I said. "Are we going to study this afternoon?" "Yes, of course," she said, "I've got an awful lot of work to do." And then, a moment later: "Thanks for coming."

"La Perlita" was at the far end of the field, between the mess hall and the classroom building, against the back wall of the Academy. It was a small concrete building with a big open window that served as a counter. Day and night you could see the frightening face of the half-breed Paulino: slanted Japanese eyes, thick Negro lips, copper-colored Indian skin, high cheekbones, lank black hair. At the counter Paulino sold coffee and hot chocolate and soft drinks, cookies and pastries and candies; in the back, which is to say the enclosed but almost roofless hide-out against the back wall, the ideal place to jump over before the patrols began, he sold pisco and cigarettes at double the regular price. Paulino slept on a straw mattress next to the wall, and at night the ants walked around on his body as if it were a village square. Under the mattress there was a board covering the hole Paulino had dug with his hands as a hiding place for the packs of cigarettes and bottles of pisco he sold to the cadets.

On Saturdays and Sundays after lunch, the cadets who had been confined to the grounds went out to the hide-out, arriving in small groups so as not to arouse suspicion. They sprawled around on the ground, waiting for Paulino to open his cache, and passed the time by squashing the ants with flat stones. The half-breed was both generous and malicious: he would give them cigarettes and pisco on credit but first they had to beg for it and entertain him. Paulino's hide-out was so small it could not hold more than twenty cadets. When there were no places left, the latecomers sat in the field and threw stones at the vicuña until some of the others came out. Those from the Third rarely had a chance to get in on these parties because the cadets from the Fourth and Fifth either chased them away or used them as lookouts. The parties lasted for hours, beginning at lunch and ending at dinner time. On Sundays the cadets who were confined to the grounds found it somewhat easier to accept the fact they could not go out on pass, but on Saturdays they were still hopeful and made all kinds of plans for getting out through some convincing lie to the Officer of the Day or some reckless stunt such as jumping over the front wall in broad daylight. But only one or two of the dozens who were confined each week managed to get out. The rest of them wandered through the empty patios of the Academy, buried themselves in their bunks, stared with vacant eyes as they tried to over-

come their deadly boredom by imagining they were outside.
Those who had money went to Paulino's hide-out to smoke,
drink pisco, and be eaten by the ants.

Mass was said on Sunday mornings after breakfast. The
chaplain of the Academy was a blond, cheerful priest who
delivered patriotic sermons in which he spoke of the immaculate lives of the great and their love for God and Peru,
and sang the praises of discipline and order, and compared
the military with the missionaries, the heroes with the
martyrs, and the army with the church. The cadets admired
the chaplain because they considered him an honest man:
they had often seen him in street clothes barging around in
the worst parts of Callao with alcohol on his breath and a
lewd look in his eyes.

He had also forgotten that on the next morning he had
lain in bed with his eyes closed for a long time after he
woke up. When the door opened he felt the same terror run
through him. He held his breath. He was sure it was his
father coming to beat him. But it was his mother. Her expression was very serious, and she looked at him intently.
"Where is he?" he asked. "He's gone, it's after ten." He took
a deep breath and sat up. The room was full of light. He
could hear the noises from the street, the clattering streetcar, the auto horns. He felt weak, as if he were convalescing
from a long and dangerous illness. He hoped his mother
would say something about what had happened. But no: she
simply walked here and there, pretending to straighten up
the room, moving a chair, fiddling with the curtain. "Let's
go back to Chiclayo," he said. His mother went over to him
and began to caress him. Her long fingers stroked his hair,
then moved down to his shoulder: it was a warm, satisfying
feeling, and it reminded him of earlier days. And the voice
he heard now was the same tender voice he had known in
his earliest childhood. He ignored what she was trying to
tell him, the words were superfluous, the tenderness was all

in their music. But his mother told him, "We can't ever go back to Chiclayo. You've got to live with your papa from now on." He turned to look at her, sure she would break down with remorse, but his mother was perfectly calm, was even smiling. "I'd rather live with Aunt Adelina than with him!" he shouted. His mother, without changing her expression, attempted to calm him. "The trouble is," she said in a quiet voice, "you didn't know him before, and he didn't know you. But everything's going to change. You'll see. When you get to know each other, you'll love him and he'll love you, the way it is in every family." "But he hit me last night," he said hoarsely. "He punched me, as if I was big. I don't want to live with him." His mother continued to stroke his head, but now that touch was not a caress to him but an intolerable pressure. "He's got a bad disposition," his mother said, "but he's really got a good heart. You have to know how to treat him. You're a little to blame too. You don't do anything to try and win him over. He's very angry about what happened last night. You're still too little, you don't understand. You'll see I'm right, you'll understand later on. When he comes back today, ask him to forgive you for having gone into the room. You have to make up to him. It's the only way of keeping him happy." He could feel his heart throbbing heavily, like one of those big toads that infested the orchard at the house in Chiclayo and that looked like a gland with eyes, like a bellows filling and emptying. Then he understood: She's on his side, she's his accomplice. He decided to be as cautious as possible now that he could not trust his mother. At noon, when he heard the outside door open, he went downstairs to meet his father. Without looking at him he said, "Excuse me about last night."

"What else did she tell you?" the Slave asked.

"Nothing," Alberto said. "You've been repeating the same question all week. Can't you talk about anything else?"

"I'm sorry," the Slave said. "But today's Saturday. She's going to think I'm a liar."

"Why should she think that? You've written to her. And besides, what do you care what she thinks?"

"I'm really in love with her," the Slave said. "I don't want her to get the wrong idea about me."

"Take my advice and think about something else," Alberto said. "You can't tell how long you'll be confined to the grounds. Maybe for weeks. It isn't smart to keep thinking about a woman."

"I'm not like you," the Slave said humbly. "I don't have any will power. I'd like to forget her but all I do is think about her. If I don't get a pass next Saturday I'll go crazy. Listen, did she ask you anything about me?"

"Damn it," Alberto said, "I only saw her for five minutes in the doorway of her house. How many times do I have to tell you I didn't talk about anything with her? I didn't even have a chance to get a good look at her face."

"Then why don't you want to write her a letter for me?"

"Because I don't," Alberto said. "I don't feel like it."

"That's kind of funny," the Slave said, "because you write letters for everybody else. Why not for me?"

"I've never met the other girls," Alberto said. "And besides, I don't want to write letters. I don't need the money. Why would I need it if I'm going to be locked in here for God knows how many weeks?"

"Next Saturday I'm going to get out somehow," the Slave said. "Even if I have to jump over the wall."

"Okay," Alberto said. "But let's go to Paulino's. I'm fed up and I want to get drunk."

"You go," the Slave said. "I'm going to stay in the barracks."

"Are you afraid?"

"No. But I don't like them to make fun of me."

"Nobody's going to make fun of you," Alberto said, "we're just going to get drunk. Just sock the first guy that makes a wisecrack and that's that. Come on, let's get going."

The barracks had slowly been emptying. After lunch, the ten cadets in the section who were confined to the grounds had stretched out on their bunks to smoke. Then the Boa persuaded some of them to go to "La Perlita." A while later, Vallano and a few of the rest went to join a card game that had been started by some of the cadets in the second section. Alberto and the Slave stood up, closed their lockers and went out. The patios, the parade ground and the field were all deserted. They walked toward "La Perlita," their hands in their pockets, without speaking. It was a gray, windless day. Suddenly they heard a laugh. A few yards off in the weeds they discovered a cadet with his cap down over his eyes.

"You didn't see me, Cadets," he said with a grin. "I could've killed both of you."

"Don't you know enough to salute your superiors?" Alberto asked. "Attention, goddamn it!"

The boy leaped to his feet and saluted. His expression was very solemn.

"Are there many guys at Paulino's?" Alberto asked.

"Not too many, Cadet. Maybe ten."

"You can lie down again," the Slave said.

"Do you smoke, Dog?" Alberto asked.

"Yes, Cadet. But I haven't got any cigarettes. Frisk me if you want. I haven't had a pass for two weeks."

"Poor little you," Alberto said. "I bleed for you. Here." He took a pack of cigarettes out of his pocket and held it out. The boy looked at him suspiciously and was afraid to reach out his hand.

"Take two," Alberto said. "That's to show you we're okay."

The Slave was watching them absently. The cadet reached out very timidly without shifting his glance from Alberto's face. He took two cigarettes, and smiled.

"Thanks, Cadets," he said. "You really are okay."

"Don't mention it," Alberto said. "But one good turn deserves another. Come around tonight and make up my bed. I'm in the first section."

"Yes, Cadet."

"Let's go," the Slave said.

The entrance to Paulino's hide-out was a tin door leaning against the wall. It was not fastened, and a strong wind could blow it down. Alberto and the Slave went over to it after making sure there were no officers around. From outside they could hear laughter and the Boa's raucous voice. Alberto was on tiptoe, signaling to the Slave to keep silent. He put his hands on the door and shoved. There was a metallic crash and in the opening they could see a dozen terrified faces.

"You're all under arrest," Alberto said. "Drunkards, fairies, degenerates, jack-offs, everybody goes to the guardhouse."

They stood in the doorway. The Slave was right behind Alberto, with a meek, submissive expression on his face. A quick, monkey-like figure jumped up from among the cadets sprawling on the ground and ran over to Alberto. "Come on in, damn it," he said. "Hurry up, hurry up, they can see you. And never mind your gags, Poet, some day you're going to get us all screwed."

"Don't talk like that to me, you damned half-breed," Alberto said as he went in. The cadets all turned to look at Paulino's frowning face. His big, swollen lips opened up like a clam.

"What's the matter, whitey?" he asked. "Do you want me to bow to you, or what?"

"Or what?" Alberto asked, flopping down on the ground. The Slave lay down next to him. Paulino began shaking with laughter. His lips gaped open for a moment and revealed his jagged teeth and the holes among them.

"So you've brought your little whore," he said. "And what'll you do if we rape her?"

"Good idea!" the Boa yelled. "Let's all fuck the Slave!"

"Why not this monkey Paulino?" Alberto said. "He's a lot sexier."

"You're just trying to pick a fight," Paulino said, shrugging his shoulders. He lay down next to the Boa. Someone had put

the door back in place. Alberto found a bottle of pisco among
the crowd of bodies. He stretched out his hand for it but
Paulino grabbed it.

"It's fifteen centavos a slug."

"You crook," Alberto said. He took out his wallet and gave
him a five-sol bill. "Okay, ten slugs."

"Just for you," Paulino asked, "or including the little
woman?"

"For both of us."

The Boa laughed loudly. The bottle went from hand to
hand. Paulino kept track of the slugs, and if anyone drank
more than his share, he snatched the bottle away from him.
When the Slave took a swallow he coughed and his eyes
filled with tears. "These two've been together every minute
for a whole week," the Boa said, pointing at Alberto and the
Slave. "I'd like to know what's going on."

"Okay," one of the cadets said, resting his head on the
Boa's shoulder, "but what about the bet?"

Paulino became extremely excited. He laughed, he patted
everyone, he said, "Let's start, let's start," and the cadets
took advantage of his excitement to steal extra swallows of
pisco. In a few minutes the bottle was empty. Alberto, his
head on his arms, looked over at the Slave: there was a small
red ant on his cheek and apparently he was not aware of it.
His eyes had a moist gleam and his face was flushed. And
now the half-breed'll fish out some money or a bottle or a
pack of cigarettes, and then there'll be a pestilence, a pool of
shit, and I'll open my pants, and you'll open your pants, and
he'll open his pants, and the half-breed'll start trembling,
we'll all start trembling, I wish Gamboa could stick his head
in and smell the smell there'll be. Paulino was squatting
down, digging in the ground with his fingers. A little later
he stood up again, holding a small sack. When he moved it,
there was a clinking of coins. His whole face revealed his
tremendous excitement: his nostrils were dilated, his wide-
open purplish lips were thrust forward as if in search of prey,

his temples throbbed, his forehead and cheeks were streaming with sweat. And then he'll sit down, he'll start panting
like a dog, the spit'll run down his chin, his hands'll go crazy,
his voice'll crack, get your filthy hand off me, he'll dance
around, he'll whistle and sing and shout, he'll roll around on
the ants, his hair'll fall over his eyes, get your hand away
or I'll cut your balls off, he'll sprawl on the ground, he'll bury
his head in the dirt and the weeds, he'll cry, his hands and
his body'll be still, they'll go dead.

"Here's ten soles in fifty centavo pieces," Paulino said.
"And there's another bottle of pisco for whoever's second.
But he'll have to give everybody a drink."

Alberto had put his head between his arms. He explored
a miniature dark world, but his ears rang with that loud
excitement: laughter, Paulino's frantic breathing, the sound
of bodies stretching or moving about. Then he turned over
on his back. Above his head he could see a piece of tin and
a piece of the gray sky, both of them the same size. The
Slave was lying beside him. His pallor was not only in his
face but also in his neck and hands, and the blue veins
showed through his white skin.

"Come on, Fernández," the Slave whispered. "Let's get
out of here."

"No," Alberto said. "I want to win that bag of money."

The Boa was laughing wildly now. By turning his head
a little, Alberto could see the Boa's large boots, his thick
legs, his naked belly sticking out between the tails of his
khaki shirt and his unbuttoned pants, his bull neck, his
lightless eyes. Some of the cadets lowered their pants,
others merely opened their flies. Paulino dashed around in
the circle of bodies with drool running from his lips. He
was jingling the bag of coins with one hand and waving the
bottle of pisco with the other. "The Boa wants them to
bring him Skimpy," someone said, but no one laughed.
Alberto unbuttoned his pants very slowly, his eyes half-
closed, and tried to remember the face and body of Golden

Toes, but the image was fleeting and when it vanished it was replaced by another, that of a dark-skinned girl, which also vanished but returned, and he could see her hands, her sensitive mouth, and the drizzle was falling on her, moistening her clothes, and the red light at Huatica Street was shining in the depths of those dark eyes and he said shit and then the fleshy white thighs of Golden Toes returned and vanished again and Arequipa Avenue was crowded with cars going by the Raimondi Academy stop where he and the girl had waited.

"And you, what are you waiting for?" Paulino asked indignantly. The Slave had stretched out and was lying motionless with his head on his hands. The half-breed was standing over him, and he looked enormous. "Fuck him," the Boa shouted. "Fuck the Poet's sweetheart. If the Poet makes a move, I'll break his neck." Alberto looked at the ground: he could see some black dots but he could not find a stone. His body stiffened and he clenched his fists. Paulino had bent over, with his knees spread out on either side of the Slave's legs.

"If you touch him, I'll break your jaw," Alberto said.

"He's in love with the Slave," the Boa said, but his voice showed he had lost interest in Paulino and Alberto. It was a weak voice now, muted and distant. The half-breed grinned and opened his mouth, and his tongue wiped away the mass of foam on his lips. "I'm not going to do anything to him," he said. "It's just that he's so slow. I want to help him."

The Slave was motionless, looking up at the bit of roofing while Paulino unfastened his belt and unbuttoned his pants. Alberto turned his head away and looked up: the tin was white, the sky was gray, and he could hear music, the dialogue of the red ants in their subterranean labyrinths, labyrinths with red lights, with a reddish glow in which everything seemed dark including the skin of that woman who was devoured by fire from the tips of her adorable

THE TIME OF THE HERO 127

little feet to the roots of her dyed hair, there was a large
stain on the wall, the cadenced rocking motions of that boy
kept time like a pendulum, anchoring the hide-out to the
ground, keeping it from rising in the wind and falling into
the reddish spiral of Huatica Street, onto those thighs of milk
and honey, the girl walking in the drizzle with light, quick,
graceful steps, but this time the volcanic flow was here,
definitively here in some part of his soul, and it began to
grow, to spread its tentacles through the secret passages of
his body, driving the girl from his memory, his blood, and
secreting a perfume, a liquor, a form below his belly that his
hands were caressing now, and suddenly something burning
and enslaving arose and he could see, hear, feel the pleasure
that was advancing, smoking, unfolding in a tangle of bones,
muscles, nerves, toward infinity, toward the paradise the
red ants could never enter, but then he was distracted because Paulino was panting so loudly, was flopping on the
ground somewhere nearby, and the Boa was muttering
broken phrases. He could feel the ground under his shoulders
again, and when he turned to look, his eyes felt as if they had
been pierced by needles. Paulino was beside the Boa, who
let him stroke his body, completely ignoring him. The half-
breed was gasping for breath, was uttering little cries. The
Boa had his eyes shut, his body was writhing. And now the
smell begins, we'll empty the bottle in seconds, we'll start
singing, and somebody'll crack some jokes and the half-
breed'll get sad, and my mouth'll feel dry, and when I smoke
I'll want to vomit, and I'll feel like going to sleep, and then
the hangover, and some day I'll get TB because Dr. Guerra
said jacking off is as bad for you as screwing a woman seven
times in a row.

The Boa was shouting now, but he ignored him: he was
a tiny being asleep in the convoluted heart of a rose-colored
shell, where no wind, no fire, no water could penetrate his
refuge. Then he came back to reality. The Boa had the half-
breed down on the ground and was hitting him, shouting,

"You bit me, you goddamned half-breed, I'm going to kill you, you peasant!" Some of the others had sat up and were watching with languid eyes. Paulino made no attempt to defend himself and after a moment the Boa let him go. The half-breed stood up, wiped his mouth, then reached down for the bag of coins and the bottle of pisco. He handed the money to the Boa.

"I finished second," Cárdenas said.

Paulino went toward him with the bottle, but Villa, who was next to Alberto, stopped him. "That's a lie," he said. "It wasn't him."

"Who was it, then?" Paulino asked.

"The Slave."

The Boa stopped counting the money and his little eyes switched to the Slave, who was still on his back, his arms stretched out at his sides.

"Who'd've guessed it," the Boa said. "He's got a cock like a real man's."

"And you've got one like a burro's," Alberto said. "Button your pants, you freak of nature."

The Boa roared with laughter and started to prance around the hide-out, jumping over the sprawled bodies with his penis in his hands, chanting, "I piss on everybody, I fuck everybody, I'm not called the Boa for nothing, I can kill a woman with one shot." The others cleaned themselves and adjusted their clothes. The Slave had opened his bottle of pisco, and after taking a long swallow and spitting, he passed it to Alberto. Everyone drank and smoked. Paulino was sitting in a corner, with a drawn, melancholy expression. And now we'll leave and wash our hands and later they'll blow the whistle and we'll fall in and march to the mess hall, one, two, one, two, and we'll eat and leave the mess hall and go to the barracks and someone'll shout, a contest, and someone'll say we already had one at Paulino's and the Boa won, and he'll say the Slave was there too, the Poet brought him along and wouldn't let us screw him and he even came

out second in the contest, and they'll blow taps and we'll
sleep and then tomorrow and Monday and how many weeks?

Emilio slapped him on the shoulder and said, "There she
is." Alberto raised his head. Helena was leaning over the rail
of the lobby. She looked at him and smiled. Emilio nudged
him and repeated, "There she is. Go ahead, go ahead." "Shut
up, man," Alberto whispered, "can't you see she's with Ana?"
A dark-skinned girl had appeared beside the redhead as she
leaned over the rail: it was Ana, Emilio's sister. "Don't worry
about her," Emilio said. "I'll handle her. Let's go." Alberto
nodded and they went up the stairs of the Terrazas Club.
The lobby was full of young people, and there was music
coming from the rooms on the other side of the club. "But
don't get near us, for any reason at all," Alberto murmured
as they climbed the stairs. "And don't let your sister interrupt
us. Follow us, if you want, but keep a good way off." As they
drew near them, the two girls laughed. Helena looked older.
She was slender, sweet looking, radiant, and at first glance
there was nothing to suggest boldness. But the boys in the
neighborhood knew her. When the other girls were accosted
in the street, they started crying, or lowered their eyes and
looked embarrassed, or trembled with fright, but Helena
stood up to her assailants, she defied them with burning
eyes, like a little wild animal, and her strong clear voice
hurled back sarcasm for sarcasm, or else she took the initiative and called the boys by their most offensive nicknames
and even threatened them, her face proud, her body tense
and straight as she waved her fists at them, holding off the
whole ring of boys, breaking through it, and marching away
with a look of triumph. But that was before. Some time ago
—no one could remember exactly what month, what season
of the year (perhaps during the July vacation when Tico's
parents gave him a birthday party)—the hostile atmosphere
that existed between the boys and girls began to disappear.
The boys no longer waited for a girl to go by so that they

could scare her or make fun of her; instead, they were pleased when one of them came in sight and felt a timid, stammering sort of cordiality. And on the other hand, when the girls were on the balcony at Laura's or Ana's house and one of the boys went by, they stopped talking in their ordinary voices, whispered mysteriously in each other's ears, and greeted him by his correct name, and besides feeling flattered he could sense the excitement his presence had aroused in them. When the boys were lounging in the garden at Emilio's house they talked about different things than formerly. No one mentioned soccer games any more, or foot races, or trips down the cliff to the beach. They smoked almost incessantly (not choking now) as they tried to figure out the best way of getting in to see the For Adults Only movies, or discussed the possibilities of another party. Would their parents let them play the record-player and dance? Would it last as long as the last one, that ended at midnight? And each of them described his meetings and conversations with the various girls of the neighborhood. The parents of all of them, boys and girls, had now taken on a vast importance. Some, like Ana's father and Laura's mother, enjoyed a unanimous esteem, because they greeted the boys pleasantly, allowed them to talk with their daughters, asked them about their studies. Others, like Tico's father and Helena's mother (strict, possessive), intimidated them and chased them away.

"Are you going to the matinee?" Alberto asked.

They were walking by themselves along the Malecón. He could hear the footsteps of Emilio and Ana behind him. Helena nodded and said, "Yes, to the Leuro." Alberto decided to wait: it would be easier to ask her in the darkness of the theater. Tico had explored the ground for him a few days earlier, and Helena had said, "You never can tell. But I might agree to go around with him if he asks me in the right way." It was a clear summer morning, with a bright sun in a blue sky over the nearby ocean, and he felt optimistic: the omens were all favorable. He was never unsure of himself with the girls in the neighborhood, he could crack clever jokes for them or talk to them seriously, but Helena made conversation difficult. She argued about everything, contested the most innocent statement, never talked for the sheer fun of it, and expressed her opinions in as cutting a manner as she could. Once, Alberto told her he had been late for Mass but had got there before the Credo at least. "That's not worth a thing," she said. "If you die tonight, you'll go straight down to Hell." On another occasion, Ana and Helena watched one of the soccer games from the balcony. Afterward, Alberto asked her, "What did you think of the game?" And she answered, "You play very badly." But the week before, in the Miraflores Park, when a group of boys and girls had gotten together and were strolling around, Alberto walked next to Helena and she treated him in a friendly manner. The others turned to look at them, and said, "What a good-looking couple."

They had left the Malecón and were walking along Juan Fanning toward Helena's house. Alberto could not hear the footsteps of Emilio and Ana now. "Will we see each other at the movies?" he asked her. "Are you going to the Leuro too?" Helena asked him with wide-eyed innocence. "Yes," he said, "I am." "Good, then perhaps we'll see each other." On the corner near her house, she held out her hand. Colón Street, which crossed Diego Ferré in the heart of the neighborhood, was completely empty: the boys were down on the beach or at the Terrazas swimming pool. "You're really going to the Leuro, aren't you?" Alberto asked. "Yes," she said, "unless something happens." "What could happen?" "I don't know," she said very seriously. "An earthquake or something." "I've got something to tell you at the movies," Alberto said. He looked her in the eyes, and she blinked at him and seemed astonished. "You've got something to tell me? What?" "I'll tell you at the movies." "Why not right now? It's better to get things out of the way as soon as possi-

ble." He tried not to blush. "You already know what I'm going to tell you," he said. "No," she said, apparently even
more astonished. "I can't begin to guess what it could be."
"If you want, I'll tell you right now," Alberto said. "That's
better," she said. "Take a chance."

And now we'll leave and later they'll blow the whistle and
we'll fall in and march to the mess hall, one, two, one, two,
and we'll eat surrounded by empty tables and we'll go out
into the empty patio and we'll go into the empty barracks
and someone'll shout, a contest, and I'll say, we already had
one at the half-breed's and the Boa won, the Boa always
wins, the Boa's going to win next Saturday too, and they'll
blow taps and we'll sleep and it'll be Sunday and then
Monday and the ones that got out on pass they'll come back
and we'll buy cigarettes from them and I'll pay for them with
letters or stories. Alberto and the Slave were stretched out
on two neighboring bunks in the deserted barracks. The Boa
and the others who were confined to the grounds had just left
for "La Perlita." Alberto was smoking a cigarette butt.

"It could last till the end of the year," the Slave said.

"What could?"

"This confinement."

"What the fuck do you keep talking about it for? Shut up
or go to sleep. You're not the only one who's confined."

"I know, but maybe we won't get out till the end of the
year."

"That's right," Alberto said. "Unless they find out it was
Cava. But how can they find out?"

"It isn't fair," the Slave said. "That peasant goes out on
pass every Saturday, without any worries. And we're stuck
in here when he's the one that's to blame."

"Life is *so* cruel," Alberto said. "There ain't no justice."

"But it's a month today since I got a pass," the Slave said.
"I've never been confined this long."

"You ought to be getting used to it."

"Teresa doesn't answer me," the Slave said. "I've sent her two letters."

"What the shit do you care?" Alberto said. "The world is full of women."

"But I like this one. I'm not interested in the others. Can't you tell?"

"Of course I can. And it means you're screwed."

"Do you know how I got to know her?"

"No. How would I know that?"

"I saw her go by my house every day. I'd watch her from the window and sometimes I'd say hello to her."

"Did you jack off thinking about her?"

"No. I just liked to see her."

"How romantic."

"One day I went out a little before she came by and I waited for her at the corner."

"Did you pinch her?"

"I went up to her and offered to shake hands."

"And what did you tell her?"

"My name. And I asked her what hers was. And I said, 'I'm pleased to meet you.'"

"You're an imbecile. And what did she say?"

"She told me her name."

"Have you ever kissed her?"

"No. I haven't even gone out with her."

"You're a damned liar. Come on, swear you've never kissed her."

"What's the matter?"

"Nothing. I don't like people to lie to me."

"Why should I lie to you? Don't you think I wanted to kiss her? But I've only been with her three or four times, on the corner. I can't go see her on account of this damned Academy. Probably she's got somebody else for a boy friend by now."

"Who?"

"How would I know? Somebody. She's very pretty."

"Not so very. I'd've said she was sort of ugly."

"Well, I think she's pretty."

"You're a babe in arms. What I like a woman for is to fuck her."

"I really think I'm in love with this girl."

"Stop, you're making me weep with emotion."

"If she'll wait for me until I finish my studies, I'll marry her."

"I bet she'll cheat on you. But never mind, I'll be a witness for you if you like."

"Why do you say that?"

"You just look like a guy whose wife'd cheat on him."

"Probably she didn't get my two letters."

"Probably."

"Why didn't you want to write to her for me? You've written several letters this week."

"Because I didn't feel like it."

"What've you got against me? What're you mad about?"

"This confinement's got me in a bad mood. Or do you think you're the only one who's sick of not getting out?"

"Why did you come to the Leoncio Prado?"

Alberto laughed. "To save the family honor."

"Can't you ever be serious?"

"I'm being serious right now, Slave. My father said I was trampling on the family traditions. So he put me in here to straighten me out."

"Why didn't you just flunk the entrance exams?"

"On account of a girl. She was just stringing me along, you know what I mean? I got into this pigpen on account of a girl and my family."

"Were you in love with the girl?"

"I liked her."

"Was she pretty?"

"Yes."

"What was her name? What happened?"

"Helena. And nothing happened. Besides, I don't like to talk about my personal affairs."

"But I tell you all about mine."

"That's because you like to. Don't tell me a thing if you don't want to."

"Have you got any cigarettes?"

"No. Let's go get some."

"I haven't got a centavo."

"I've got two soles. Get up and we'll go to Paulino's."

"I'm fed up with 'La Perlita.' The Boa and the half-breed make me sick to my stomach."

"Okay, stay here, then. I'm going to go."

Alberto stood up. The Slave watched him put on his cap and tighten his tie.

"Want me to tell you something?" the Slave said. "I know you're going to make fun of me, but that's all right."

"What is it?"

"You're the only friend I've got. Before this I didn't have any friends at all, just acquaintances. I mean outside. In here I didn't even have acquaintances. You're the only person I like to be with."

"That sounds like the way a fairy says he's in love with somebody."

The Slave smiled. "You're an animal," he said. "But you're a good guy."

Alberto left. At the doorway, he said, "If I get hold of some cigarettes I'll bring you one."

The patio was damp. It had rained while they were talking in the barracks, but Alberto had not noticed. Far off, he could see a cadet sitting among the weeds. Was it the same one who was the lookout the Saturday before? And now I'll go in to Paulino's, and we'll have a contest and the Boa'll win and there'll be that smell and then we'll leave and go through the empty patio into the barracks and someone'll say, a contest, and I'll say, we were at the half-breed's and the Boa won, he'll win next Saturday too, and they'll blow taps and we'll sleep and Sunday'll come and Monday and how many weeks?

6

He could bear the loneliness and the humiliation that he had known since he was a child and that only wounded his spirit. What was horrible was this imprisonment, this vast exterior solitude that he had not chosen, that had been imposed on him like a strait jacket. He was standing in front of the lieutenant's door, but he had still not raised his hand to knock. Nevertheless, he knew he was going to do it; he had delayed three weeks in making up his mind, but now he was neither troubled nor afraid. It was his hand that was betraying him: it hung at his side, motionless, limp, dead. It was not the first time. At the Salesian Academy they called him a sissy; he was so timid that everything frightened him. The other boys surrounded him during recess and shouted, "Go on, sissy, cry!" He backed up until his shoulders were against the wall. Their faces were close to his, their voices were loud, their mouths were like fierce muzzles ready to snap at him. He started to cry. One day he told himself, I've got to do something. In the middle of a class he challenged the bravest boy in the Year to a fight. By now, he had forgotten his name and his face, even his way of fighting. When they squared off in the empty lot, surrounded by a circle of eager spectators, he was not afraid that time either, was not even excited: all he felt was a complete discouragement and resignation. His body would not return or dodge the blows. He had to wait until the other was tired of hitting him. It was to punish and transform this cowardly body of his that he had forced himself to enter the Leoncio Prado and to put up with those twenty-four long months. Now he had lost hope. He would never be like the Jaguar, who dominated others through violence, nor even like Alberto, who was quick-witted and could put on an act so that the others would not victimize him. As for himself, they had known at once what he was like: defenseless, weak, a slave. Freedom was the only thing he wanted now, to handle his loneliness in his own way, to take her to see a movie, to be alone with her somewhere, anywhere. He raised his hand and knocked on the door three times.

Had Lt. Huarina been asleep? His swollen eyes looked like two enormous wounds in his round face. His hair was disheveled and he seemed to be looking at him through a mist.

"I'd like to talk with you, Lieutenant."

In the world of the officers, Lt. Huarina was like himself in the world of the cadets: a misfit. He was small and weak, his voice when he gave commands made everyone laugh, the noncoms were contemptuous of him and handed him their reports without coming to attention. His company was the worst organized, Capt. Garrido reprimanded him in public, and the cadets drew caricatures of him on the walls, showing him in knee pants, masturbating. It was said that he owned a small store in Los Barrios Altos where his wife sold candy and cookies. Why had he attended the Military School?

"What is it?"

"Can't I come in? It's something important, Sir."

"If you want to talk with me you'll have to go through the proper channels."

The cadets were not the only ones who imitated Lt. Gamboa, because Huarina assumed the same strict attitude when referring to the regulations. But with those delicate hands and that ridiculous mustache—a little black smudge under his nose—how could he deceive anyone?

"I don't want the others to know, Lieutenant. It's really serious."

The lieutenant stepped aside and he went in. The bed was rumpled, and the Slave thought that a cell in a monastery would be something like this: bare, mournful, a little sinister. There was an ash tray on the floor near the bed. It was full of cigarette butts, and one of them was still smolder-ing.

"What is it?" Huarina repeated.

"It's about the pane of glass."

"Name and section," Huarina said quickly.

"Cadet Ricardo Arana, Fifth Year, first section."

"What about the glass?"

His tongue was the coward now, it refused to move, it was dry, it felt like a rough stone. Was he afraid? The Circle had always been hostile toward him. And after the Jaguar, Cava was the worst: he took away his cigarettes and his money, and once he had urinated on him while he was sleeping. To a certain extent he felt justified, because every-one in the Academy respected revenge. But still, something deep in his heart was accusing him. I'm not just betraying the Circle, he thought, I'm betraying the whole Year, all of the cadets.

"Well, go ahead," Huarina said crossly. "Or did you just come in to get a look at me? Don't you know me yet?"

"It was Cava," the Slave said. He lowered his eyes. "Can I have a pass this Saturday?"

"What?" the lieutenant said. Huarina had not understood, he could still invent something and get out of it.

"It was Cava that broke the glass," he said. "He stole the chemistry exam. I saw him going to the classroom building. Will the confinement be lifted?"

"No," the lieutenant said. "We'll see about that later. First, repeat what you just said."

Huarina's face had grown rounder and there were creases in his cheeks near the corners of his lips, which had opened and were trembling a little. His eyes gleamed with satisfac-tion. The Slave felt calm. The Academy, the pass, the future no longer meant anything. He told himself that Lt. Huarina did not look grateful. That was natural, after all, because he lived in a different world. Perhaps he even despised him.

"Write it down," Huarina said. "Right now. Here's a pencil and paper."

"What do you want me to write, Lieutenant?"

"I'll dictate it. 'I saw Cadet'—what's his name?—'Cava, such-and-such section'—now the date and the time—'approaching the classroom building for the purpose of taking illegal possession of the chemistry exam.' Write clearly. 'I make this statement at the request of Lt. Remigio Huarina, who discovered the perpetrator of the theft and also my participation. . .'"

"But Lieutenant, I didn't. . ."

"'. . .my involuntary participation in the affair as a witness.' Sign it. Then print your name in block letters. Big ones."

"I didn't see him steal it," the Slave said. "I just saw him going toward the classrooms. I haven't had a pass for four weeks, Lieutenant."

"Don't worry. I'll take care of everything. Don't be afraid."

"I'm not afraid!" the Slave shouted, and the officer raised his eyes, astonished. "I haven't had a pass for four weeks, Lieutenant. This Saturday it'll be five."

Huarina nodded. "Sign this paper," he said. "I'll give you a pass so you can go out today after class. Come back in at eleven."

The Slave signed it. The lieutenant read the paper again, his eyes dancing in their sockets. He moved his lips as he read it.

"What'll they do to him?" the Slave asked. It was a stupid question and he knew it, but he had to say something. The lieutenant was carefully holding the paper with the tips of his fingers to keep from wrinkling it.

"Have you spoken to Lieutenant Gamboa about this?" For a moment the animation vanished from his smooth, round face, and he waited for the Slave's answer with a look of alarm. It would have been simple to spoil Huarina's happiness, to wreck his triumph. He only had to say yes.

"No, Lieutenant. Not to anybody."

"Good. Don't say a word," the lieutenant said. "Wait for

my instructions. Come see me after class, in dress uniform. I'll take you past the guards."

"Yes, Lieutenant." The Slave hesitated before adding: "I wouldn't want the other cadets to know that I. . ."

"A man has to accept the responsibility for his actions," Huarina said in a stern voice. "That's the first thing they teach you in the army."

"Yes, Lieutenant. But if they found out I reported him. . ."

"I know," Huarina said, reading the statement for the fourth time. "They'd butcher you. But you don't have to worry. The officers' meetings are always secret."

Maybe they'll expel me too, the Slave thought. He left Huarina's quarters. He was positive that no one had seen him, because after lunch the cadets stretched out on their bunks or on the grass in the stadium. He could see the vicuña out in the open field: slender, motionless, sniffing the breeze. It must be very unhappy, he thought. He was surprised: he ought to be feeling elated or terrified, some physical reaction should be reminding him of what he had just done. He used to believe that after a murderer had committed his crime he went about in a daze as if he had been hypnotized. But his only feeling was of indifference. He thought, I'll have six hours outside. I'll go and see her but I can't tell her anything about what's happened. If only there were somebody he could talk to, somebody who would understand or at least listen to him! How could he trust Alberto? He had refused to write to Teresa for him, and during the last few days he was angry at him all the time when they were alone—because he defended him when there were others around—as if he had some grievance against him. I can't trust anybody, he thought. Why are they all against me?

His hands trembled slightly, but that was the only reaction his body made when he pushed open the door to the barracks and saw Cava standing by his locker. If he sees me he'll know I've just screwed him, he thought.

"What's the matter?" Alberto asked.

"Nothing. Why?"

"You're white as a sheet. Go over to the infirmary, they'll take you in for sure."

"I'm all right."

"That doesn't matter," Alberto said. "What more do you want when you're confined? I wish I could look half that pale. You eat better in the infirmary and you can get some rest."

"But you lose your pass," the Slave said.

"What pass? We're going to be in here a long time. Though there's a rumor everybody might get a pass next Sunday. It's the colonel's birthday. That's what they say, anyway. What are you laughing about?"

"Nothing."

How could Alberto talk so calmly about their confinement? How could he get used to the idea of not getting out?

"Unless you want to jump over the wall," Alberto said. "But it's easier from the infirmary. There isn't any supervision at night. You have to let yourself down on the Costanera side and you can slip through the bars like nothing."

"They don't jump over the wall very much now," the Slave said. "Ever since they started the patrol."

"It was easier before," Alberto said. "But a lot of them still do it. That half-breed Urioste went out Monday and came back at four in the morning."

After all, why not go to the infirmary? Why go outside? Doctor, I've got spots in front of my eyes, I've got a headache, I've got palpitations, I have cold sweats, I'm a coward. Whenever they were confined the cadets tried to get admitted to the infirmary. You could spend the whole day in your pajamas, doing nothing, and there was always plenty of food. But the Academy doctor and the attendants were becoming stricter. A fever was no longer enough: they knew that if you put banana peels on your forehead for a couple of hours, your temperature would go up to about 102. And gonorrhea was out ever since they discovered the trick Curly and the Jaguar used: they had shown up at the infirmary with their penises smeared with condensed milk. The Jaguar also invented the breath-holding trick. You held your breath until there were tears in your eyes, several times in a row, just before you were examined, and your heart sped up and began to pound like a drum. The attendant would say, "Admitted with symptoms of tachycardia."

"I've never jumped over the wall," the Slave said.

"I'm not surprised," Alberto said. "I did it a few times last year. One time we went to a fiesta in La Punta with Arróspide and we didn't get back until just before reveille. Things were better then."

"Poet," Vallano shouted, "did you go to La Salle Academy?"

"Yes," Alberto said. "Why?"

"Curly says everybody that goes to La Salle is a fairy. Is that right?"

"No," Alberto said. "All wrong. There weren't any Negroes at La Salle."

Curly laughed. "You're screwed," he said to Vallano. "The Poet's got you screwed."

"I may be a Negro but I'm more of a man than any of you," Vallano said. "And if somebody wants me to prove it, come on over."

"My my, how you scare me!" someone said. "Oh mamma, help!"

"Ay, ay, ay," Curly sang.

"Slave," the Jaguar shouted. "Go ahead and make him prove it. Then tell us if the Negro is as much of a man as he says."

"Oh mamma, help!"

"You too!" Vallano roared. "If you've got any guts, come on over, I'm ready."

"What's up?" the Boa asked in a hoarse voice. He had just awakened.

"Boa, the Negro says you're a queer," Alberto said.

"He said it's obvious you're a queer."

"That's exactly what he said."

"He's been talking about you for more than an hour."

"They're all liars," Vallano said. "Do you think I talk about people behind their back?"

Everybody laughed.

"They're kidding you," Vallano added. "Can't you tell?" He raised his voice. "Next time you crack a joke like that, I'll beat the shit out of you, Poet. I'm warning you. You damn near got me in a fight with the boy."

"My my my," Alberto said. "Did you hear that, Boa? He called you a boy."

"You trying to start something, Negro?" the Boa asked.

"No, of course not," Vallano said. "You're my friend."

"Then don't call me a boy."

"Poet, I swear I'm going to beat the shit out of you."

"Barking Negroes never bite," the Jaguar said.

The Slave thought, Deep down, they're all friends. They insult each other, they argue all the time, but deep down they have a lot of fun together. I'm the only one here they look at as a stranger.

"Her legs were plump, smooth and white. They were so luscious they made you want to bite into them." Alberto studied what he had just written, attempting to calculate its erotic possibilities. It seemed promising. He was lying on the floor in the sunlight that filtered through the grimy windows of the summerhouse. His head was supported on one hand, his other hand was holding a pencil over a half-filled sheet of paper. There were other pages, some of them covered with writing, strewn around on the dusty floor among the cigarette butts and burned matches. The summerhouse had been built at the same time as the Academy, in a small garden containing a fishpond. The pond was always empty and green with moss, and clouds of mosquitoes hovered over it. No one, not even the colonel, knew the purpose of the summerhouse, which stood about six feet off the ground on four concrete pillars and was reached by a narrow winding staircase. Probably none of the officers or cadets had entered the summerhouse until the Jaguar managed to open the locked door with a special skeleton key which almost the whole section helped him to make. This had given the lonely summerhouse a function: it served as a hideout for those who wanted to take a siesta instead of going to class. "The bedroom trembled as if there were an earthquake. The woman moaned and tore her hair, saying, 'Enough, enough,' but the man would not let go of her. His nervous hand went on exploring her body, scratching her, penetrating her. When the woman grew silent and lay as if dead, the man burst out laughing. His laughter sounded like the howl of a wild animal." He held the pencil between his teeth and reread the whole page. Then he added a final sentence: "The woman thought the last bites were the best of all, and she was happy to know the man would come back again the next day." Alberto leafed through the pages he had written: four stories in less than two hours. He felt he had done well. There were still a few minutes before they would blow the whistle announcing the end of class. He turned over on his back, rested his head on the floor, and lay there with his body completely lax. The sun shone on his face now, but it was so weak that he kept his eyes open.

The sun had come out during the lunch hour. The mess-hall was suddenly brighter and the usual chaotic murmur stopped dead as fifteen hundred heads turned to look out at the field. The grass looked golden, and the surrounding buildings threw shadows. It was the first time the sun had come out in October since Alberto had entered the Academy. He immediately thought, I'll go to the summerhouse and write. When they fell in, he whispered to the Slave, "If there's a roll call, answer for me." They reached the class-rooms, and he took advantage of the officer's carelessness to

duck into one of the washrooms. He waited until the cadets
had entered the classrooms, then slipped out and went to
the summerhouse. He had written his four-page stories with
hardly a pause, but during the last one he began to feel
drowsy and was tempted to drop the pencil and let his mind
wander. He had run out of cigarettes days ago and he tried
to smoke the twisted butts he found in the summerhouse, but
he scarcely took two puffs: the tobacco was brittle with age
and the dust he breathed in made him cough.

Read it again, Vallano, read that last part again, come on,
read it again, Negro, and my poor abandoned mother thinking about her son here surrounded by so many half-breeds,
but in those days she wouldn't've been upset about it, not
even there in the midst of us listening to *Eleodora's Pleasures,* read it again, Vallano, we'd gone out on our first pass
and we were back in again, you were the smartest, you
brought Eleodora in your suitcase, all I brought back was
some food, if only I'd known. The cadets were sitting on
their bunks, intent, silent, hanging on Vallano's lips as he
read to them in an excited voice. Sometimes he stopped
reading and waited, without raising his eyes from the book.
At once there was a whole storm of protests. Read it again,
Vallano, I'm getting a good idea for passing the time and
making a few centavos, and my mother praying to God and
the saints, Saturday and Sunday, he'll drag all of us down
the road to perdition, my father's bewitched by the
Eleodoras. After reading the yellowish pages of the little
book three or four times, Vallano put it into a pocket of his
jacket and gave a scornful look at the others, who were all
watching him enviously. At last one of them got up the courage to say, "Lend it to me." Five, ten, fifteen cadets besieged
him, shouting, "Come on, lend it to me, Negro." Vallano
grinned, opening his wide mouth; his eyes danced with glee,
his nose twitched, he had taken a triumphal stance, the
whole barracks was around him, pleading with him, praising
him. He merely insulted them: "You jack-offs, you repulsive

bastards, why don't you go read the Bible or *Don Quixote?*" They flattered him, they told him: "Negro, you're sharp, you really are." Suddenly Vallano realized he could take advantage of the situation. "I'll rent it," he said. Then they pushed him and threatened him, one of them spit on him, another one called him a selfish son of a bitch. Vallano laughed uproariously, stretched out on his bunk, and took *Eleodora's Pleasures* out of his pocket; he held it up in front of his eyes, which were glittering with malice, and pretended to read it, moving his lips lasciviously. Five cigarettes, ten cigarettes, Vallano, Negro, lend me Eleodora, I want to jack-off, oh mamma I knew the Boa'd be first from the way he scratched Skimpy while the Negro was reading, she howled and then kept quiet, I thought of a wonderful idea for passing the time and making a few centavos, I had a raft of ideas and the only thing I needed was an opportunity. Alberto saw that the noncom was coming directly toward their row, and out of the corner of his eye he could see that Curly was still absorbed in reading: he had the book fastened to the jacket of the cadet in front of him. He must have been straining his eyes to read it, because the print was very small. Alberto could not warn him that danger was coming: the noncom never took his eyes off him and was approaching as stealthily as a cat stalking its prey. It was impossible to move his elbow or his foot without being seen. The noncom crouched and then leaped on Curly, who let out a scream, and grabbed *Eleodora's Pleasures* with a cat-like swipe. But he shouldn't've trampled on it and burned it, he shouldn't've left our house to go chasing whores, he shouldn't've abandoned my mother, we shouldn't've left the big house on Diego Ferré with its garden and all, I shouldn't've known the neighborhood or Helena, he shouldn't've confined Curly for two weeks, I shouldn't've begun to write stories, I shouldn't've left Miraflores, I shouldn't've got to know Teresa and I shouldn't've fallen in love with her. Vallano laughed about it, but he could not

hide his depression, his homesickness, his bitterness. Sometimes he grew serious and said, "Damn it, I was really in
love with Eleodora. Curly, it's your fault I've lost the
woman I love." The cadets sang *Ay, ay, ay* and swayed like
rumba dancers, they pinched Vallano on the cheeks and the
buttocks, and the Jaguar leaped at the Slave, picked him up
bodily while the others watched in silence, and threw him
against Vallano, saying, "You can have this whore as a gift."
The Slave got up, straightened his clothes, and began to
move away. The Boa caught him under the shoulders and
lifted him up. The effort made his veins bulge and his neck
swell out. He held him in the air for only a few seconds and
then let him fall like a rag. The Slave limped out of the
barracks. "Damn it," Vallano said, "I tell you I'm dying of
grief." And then I said I'll write you a better story than
Eleodora for half a pack of cigarettes and that morning I
knew what'd happened it was mental telepathy or the hand
of God, what's my father doing, mamma, and Vallano said
honest? here's paper and a pencil and I hope the angels
inspire you, and she said courage, my son, we've suffered a
terrible misfortune, he's beyond hope, he's abandoned us,
and I began writing and the whole section got around me
the way they did around the Negro when he was reading.
Alberto wrote a sentence in an unsteady hand, and half a
dozen heads tried to read it over his shoulder. He stopped,
raised his pencil, raised his head and read it aloud to them.
They congratulated him, and a few of them made some sug-
gestions which he rejected. As he went on, he became more
daring: the coarse words gave way to grand erotic allegories,
but the actions were few and repetitious: preliminary
caresses, normal love, anal and oral and manual love, ec-
stasy, convulsions, battles without quarter between bristling
organs, and again the preliminary caresses, et cetera. When
he finished writing it—ten pages in a notebook, on both
sides of the page—Alberto had a flash of inspiration and
announced the title: *The Sins of the Flesh*. He read the

story to them in an excited voice. The barracks listened to him with something like awe, and now and then they laughed appreciatively. When he finished, they applauded him and clapped him on the back. Someone said, "Fernández, you're a poet." "That's right," someone else said, "he's a real poet." And that same day the Boa came over to me with a mysterious look on his face while we were washing up and told me write another story like that and I'll buy it from you, you're a good guy, Boa, a great jack-off, you were my first customer and I'll always remember you, you got sore at first when I told you fifty centavos a page, but you resigned yourself to your fate and we changed houses and that was when I left the neighborhood and my friends and Miraflores itself and began my career as a writer, I've earned good money in spite of all the deadbeats.

It was a Sunday in the middle of June. Alberto was sitting on the grass watching the cadets who strolled around the parade ground with their relatives. A few yards away there was another boy from the Third, but from a different section. He had a letter in his hands and was reading and rereading it with a troubled expression. "Are you on barracks detail?" Alberto asked him. The boy nodded and pointed to his arm band. "That's worse than being confined," Alberto said. "I know," the other said. And later we walked over to the sixth section and lay down and smoked Inca cigarettes and he told me where he was from and he said my father sent me here to the Military Academy because I was in love with a girl from a bad family and then he showed me her picture and he told me that as soon as he got out of the Academy he was going to marry her, and that same day she stopped using make-up and wearing jewelry and seeing her friends and playing canasta and every Saturday when I went home on pass she looked older.

"But don't you like her as much any more?" Alberto asked him. "Why do you look like that when you talk about her?"

The boy lowered his voice, speaking as if to himself. "I don't know how to write to her," he said.

"Why not?" Alberto asked.

"I don't know. I just don't. She's very intelligent. She writes me wonderful letters."

"It's easy to write a letter," Alberto said. "Easiest thing in the world."

"Not for me. It's easy to know what you want to say, but not to say it."

"Bah!" Alberto said. "I could write ten love letters in an hour."

And I wrote a few letters for him and the girl answered them and he bought me a cola and some cigarettes at "La Perlita," and one day he took me to see a cadet in the eighth section and he asked me can you write him a letter to the girl he's got in Iquitos and so I asked her do you want me to go see him and talk to him and she told me there's nothing we can do except pray to God and she began going to Mass and novenas and giving me advice Alberto you've got to be more religious you've got to love God with all your heart so that when you grow up you won't fall into temptation like your father and I told him okay but you'll have to pay me.

Alberto thought, that was more than two years ago. How time flies. He closed his eyes and he could see Teresa's face. Suddenly he was filled with anxiety. This was the first time he had been confined without caring too much about losing his pass. She uses cheap paper, he thought, and her handwriting is terrible. I've read better letters than hers. He had read them a number of times, always on the sly. He kept them inside his cap, like the cigarettes he sneaked into the Academy on Sundays. The first week, after receiving a letter from Teresa, he was eager to reply at once, but after writing the date he felt uncertain and disturbed. All the words and phrases he could think of seemed artificial and useless. He tore up several beginnings and finally decided to answer her with a few simple lines: "We're confined to the grounds on account of some trouble here. I don't know when I'll get a pass. I was very pleased to get your letter. I think about you all the time and the first thing I'll do when I get a pass is to go and see you." The Slave followed him everywhere, offered him cigarettes and fruit and sandwiches, talked to him confidentially. He always tried to be next to him in the mess hall, in formations, in the movies. Alberto thought of that pallid face, that meek expression, that innocent smile, and he hated him. Every time he saw the Slave coming up to him he felt sick to his stomach. One way or another the conversation always got around to Teresa, and Alberto had to cover up by pretending to be completely cynical, or by acting friendly and giving him wise advice: "Don't ask her to be your girl friend in a letter, man. You've got to ask her to her face, so you can tell what she's really thinking. The first time you get a pass, go to her house and ask her." And the Slave always listened solemnly and agreed without any argument. I'll tell him as soon as we get a pass, Alberto thought, as soon as we're outside the Academy gates. He's already so bitter I don't want to make it worse than I have to. I'll tell him I'm sorry but the girl likes me and I'll knock your teeth out if you go to see her. Then I'll take her out to the Necochea Park. The park was at the end of the Malecón, above the steep ocher cliffs against which the sea around Miraflores pounded so noisily; from the very edge of it, in winter, you could make out a ghostly scene through the rifts in the fog: an empty beach with immense and solitary rocks. We'll sit on the last bench, he thought, next to the log railing. The sun had warmed his face and body, and he kept his eyes closed to prevent the image from vanishing.

When he woke up, the sun had disappeared again and the light was a dim gray. His back ached and his head felt heavy: he should have known better than to go to sleep on a wooden floor. He was still drowsy, he wanted to stay there, he blinked his eyes, he wished he had a cigarette, just one. Then he sat up and looked out. The garden was empty, the classrooms looked deserted. What time was it? They blew the whistle for going to the mess hall at six-thirty. He looked all around, very cautiously, but the Academy was dead. He climbed down out of the summerhouse and walked through the garden and hurried past the buildings without seeing anyone at all. Finally, when he came to the parade ground, he saw a group of cadets chasing the vicuña, and he knew that the cadets were walking two by two in the patios, wrapped up in their big green coats, and that a vast racket was spilling out of the barracks. He wanted a cigarette desperately. When he got to the patio of the Fifth he turned around and went to the guardhouse. It was Wednesday, he could expect some letters. The doorway was blocked with cadets. "Let me in," he said, "the Officer of the Day sent for me."

No one moved. "Get in line," someone said.

"I'm not waiting for letters," Alberto said. "The lieutenant wants to see me."

"Fuck you. Get in line."

Alberto waited. Whenever a cadet came out, the line surged forward and they struggled to enter first. He reached the door, and to kill time he read the notice that was posted on it. "Fifth Year. Officer of the Guard: Lt. Pedro Pitaluga. N.C.O: Joaquín Morte. Cadets on active service: 360. Cadets committed to the infirmary: 8. Special order: Confinement of the guards on duty Sept. 13th is suspended." It was signed by the captain. He reread the last part of it several times and then began shouting, and the noncom on duty, Pezoa, said, "Who's shooting off all that shit out there, silence, goddamn it, silence!"

Alberto ran to the barracks, his heart bursting with impatience. He met Arróspide in the doorway. "We aren't confined any more," he said. "The captain must've gone crazy."

"No," Arróspide said. "Haven't you heard? Somebody ratted. Cava's in the guardhouse."

"What? You mean they squealed on him? Who did it?"

"That's what we're going to find out," Arróspide said.

Alberto went into the barracks. As on all important occasions, the atmosphere had changed, and the clump of his boots sounded strange in the tense silence. Many pairs of eyes followed him from the bunks. He went to his own bunk and gave a look around: the Jaguar, Curly and the Boa were all absent. Vallano was reading a comic book on the next bunk.

"Do they know who it was?" Alberto asked.

"It'll get out," Vallano said. "They can't expel Cava without it getting out."

"Where are the others?"

Vallano nodded toward the latrine.

"What are they doing?"

"It's a meeting. I don't know what they're doing."

Alberto got up and went over to the Slave's bunk. It was empty. He pushed open one half of the latrine door. He could tell that the whole section was watching him. They were hunched in a corner, the three of them, with the Jaguar in the middle. They glared at him.

"What do you want?" the Jaguar asked.

"To take a leak," Alberto said. "I believe it's allowed."

"No," the Jaguar said. "Get out."

Alberto turned back into the barracks and went over to the Slave's bunk again.

"Where is he?"

"Who?" Vallano asked without raising his eyes from the comic book.

"The Slave."

"He got a pass."

"What?"

"He left after class."

"With a pass? Are you sure?"

"How else would they let him out? His mother's sick, I think."

That squealer, that liar, I might've known from that face of his, why did he get a pass, maybe his mother really is dying, if I go in the latrine and say Jaguar the Slave's the squealer, you can't do anything right now because he's out on pass, he made everybody believe his mother's sick, but don't worry, it won't be long, let me join the Circle, I want to get revenge for that peasant Cava too. But Cava's face had vanished into a mist that also obscured the Circle and the rest of the barracks. It lessened the anger and contempt that had overwhelmed him a moment before, but in its turn the mist dissolved and he saw that pale face with its sorry attempt at a smile. Alberto went to his bunk and lay down. He searched his pockets but only found a few shreds of tobacco. He swore. Vallano raised his eyes from his comic book and looked at him for a moment. Alberto put an arm over his face. He felt a tremendous anxiety and his nerves prickled under his skin. He had a vague fear that someone would somehow detect the hell that was inside of him, and to hide it he yawned noisily. I'm an idiot, he thought. He'll wake me up tonight and I know what kind of a look he'll have, I can see him as if he were here, as if he were here, as if he were telling me you double-crosser you invited her to the movies and you wrote to her and she wrote back and you never told me anything about it and you let me talk about her all the time, that's why you let, why you didn't want, why you said, but no, he won't have time to open his mouth or wake me up because I'll jump him before he touches me, before he gets to my bed, I'll knock him down and I'll keep on punching him and I'll yell get up everybody I've got the shit-assed squealer that told on Cava. But these thoughts became tangled with others and he was oppressed by the continuing silence in the barracks. When he opened his eyes he could make out, through the narrow slit between his shirtsleeve and his face, a few fragments of the barracks windows, the ceiling, the almost black sky, the glow from the lights around the parade ground. He could be there right now, he could be getting off the bus and walking through those streets at Lince, he could be with her already, he could be asking her to be his girl friend, with that disgusting

battalion had already fallen in. He stopped running and walked quickly but naturally. He saluted the officer in charge as he went by. The officer returned the salute automatically. When he reached the safety of the stadium, far away from the barracks, he felt a profound relief. He skirted the soldiers' quarters, where he could hear them talking and swearing, and ran along the boundary wall to the corner. The bricks and adobes that had served for other escapes were still lying there. He dropped to the ground and looked back very cautiously toward the barracks, which were separated from him by the rectangular green expanse of the soccer field. He could see almost nothing but he could hear the sound of whistles: the battalions were marching to the mess hall. He could not see anyone near the soldiers' quarters either. Without standing up he gathered a few of the bricks and piled them against the foot of the wall. What if he was not strong enough to hoist himself up? He had always jumped over the wall on the other side of the grounds, next to "La Perlita." He took a last look around him, jumped to his feet, climbed up on the bricks and raised his arms.

The surface of the wall was uneven. Alberto pulled himself up until his eyes were above the top of the wall. He could see the empty fields, almost in darkness now, and beyond them the neat row of palm trees that lined Progreso Avenue. A few seconds later he slipped back, and could only see the wall, but his hands still gripped the top. That's right, I swear to God you're going to pay me for it, Slave, you're going to pay me in front of her, if I fall and break a leg they'll call my house and if my father comes I'll tell him what happened, they're expelling me for jumping over the wall but you left our house to go chasing your whores, that's worse. His knees and feet clung to the rough surface of the wall, they braced themselves in the cracks, they fumbled their way upward. When he reached the top, he hunched there like a monkey just long enough to pick out a bit of level ground. Then he jumped, landed and rolled over, closed his eyes, rubbed his head and his knees, sat up, got up on his feet. He began to run across a plowed field, trampling on the seedlings. His feet sank into the soft earth and he could feel the shoots pricking his ankles. Some of them broke under his boots. And what a fool, anybody could see me, could tell who I am from my cap and my insignia, that's a cadet, he's running away, like my father, and what if I went to see Golden Toes, but mamma please that's enough, after all you're old now and you've still got your religion, but those two are going to pay for all this, along with that old witch of an aunt, that madame, that lousy seamstress, that gabby bitch. There was no one at the bus stop. The bus arrived at the same time he did and he had to jump on while it was in motion. Once again he felt a profound calmness. He was squeezed in among a crowd of people. He could not see anything from the windows because the night had fallen, but he knew the bus was traveling past the empty fields, the small farms, a factory or two, a slum section with tin and cardboard shacks, the bull ring. And he went in, he said hello to her with that cowardly smile, she said hello sit down, that old witch came out and started gabbing and calling him señor and then she went out and left them alone, and he said I've come here to, in order to, I mean that I, don't you know that I, the thing is that I, that I sent word with—er—Alberto, oh yes he took me to the movies but that's all and yes I did write to him but I'm really crazy about you and then they kissed or they're kissing or they'll be kissing, mouth to mouth, dear God let them be kissing when I get there, let them be stark naked dear God. He got off at Alfonso Ugarte and walked toward the Bolognesi Plaza, weaving among the clerks and officials who were coming out of the cafés or standing in groups on the corners. He crossed the four lanes of traffic and reached the plaza. There was another bronze hero in the center of it, collapsing in the shadows, riddled with Chilean bullets. Pledge allegiance to the flag of the fatherland, to the blood of our heroes, and we were scrambling down the cliff to the beach when Pluto said look up there and I saw Helena, so we swore allegiance and the Minister blew his nose and then scratched it, and my poor mother, no more canasta, no more fiestas or suppers or trips, papa take me to the soccer game, no, that's a game for Negroes, my boy, next year I'll get you into the Yacht Club, into a crew, but then he went out chasing the girls, girls like Teresa. He walked along Colón, which was as empty as if it were a street in another world, as anachronistic as its square nineteenth-century houses, occupied now by people who could only pretend to be upper class: lighted signs on the housefronts, an absence of traffic, dilapidated benches and statues. Then he got on the Miraflores express, which was as bright and gleaming as the inside of a refrigerator. The people around him were silent and unsmiling. He got off at the Raimondi Academy stop and walked through the gloomy streets of Lince: a few little stores, dim street lights, dark houses. So you've never gone out on a date, what're you trying to tell me, but after all with that face God gave you, yes the Metro is very nice, don't tell me, we'll see if the Slave takes you to the downtown matinees, I'll take you to a park, to the beach, to the United States, I'll take you to Chosica on Sundays, so that's what you had in mind, so mamma I've got to tell you something, I fell in love with this little broad and she cheated on me the way my father cheated on you, but before we get married, before I ask her, before everything, what can you tell me? He had reached the corner of the street where Teresa lived and was pressed against the wall so that the shadows would hide him. He looked all around, but the streets were deserted. They were moving furniture in the house behind him: someone was pushing a dresser into place or out of place, slowly, methodically. He ran his hand over his hair, smoothing it down, fingering the part in it to be sure it was straight. He took out his handkerchief and wiped his forehead and his lips. He straightened his shirt.

He raised one foot and polished his shoe against his pantleg, then did the same with the other one. I'll go in, I'll shake hands with him, I'll be all smiles, I can only stay a moment, excuse me, Teresa, give me my two letters, please, here are yours, be quiet, Slave, you and I'll talk later, man to man, we don't want to fight in front of her, or aren't you a man? Alberto was opposite the door, at the foot of the three concrete steps. He listened but he could not hear anything. Yet he was sure they were in there: the door was outlined by a thread of light, and an instant before he had felt an almost ethereal touch, as of a hand seeking support. And I'll come by for you in my new convertible, with my silk shirt, my filter-tip cigarettes, my leather jacket, my hat with its bright red feather, I'll honk the horn, I'll tell them to get in, I just came back from the United States yesterday, let's go for a ride, let's go out to my house in Orrantia, I'd like you to meet my wife, she's an American who used to be a movie star, we got married in Hollywood the same day I graduated from the Academy, come on, Slave, get in, come on, Teresa, get in, would you like me to turn on the radio?

Alberto knocked twice on the door, more loudly the second time. After a moment he saw a woman's figure in the open doorway, a silhouette without features. The light from inside only showed her head and shoulders. "Who is it?" she asked. Alberto did not answer. Then she moved aside, and the light struck him in the face.

"Hello, Teresa," he said. "I'd like to talk with you for a minute. It's very important. And please tell him to come here."

"Why, hello, Alberto," she said. "I didn't recognize you. Come in, come in. You scared me!"

He went in and glanced quickly, suspiciously around the empty room. The curtains that closed off the other room were still swaying back and forth. He could see an unmade bed, with a smaller one on the other side of the room; both of them were empty. He smiled and turned around. Teresa was closing the door, and Alberto noticed that before she left it she patted her hair and smoothed her skirt. Then she faced him. Suddenly he realized that the face he had pictured so many times in the Academy was not as soft, as gentle, as the face he was seeing now, the face he had seen at the Metro, or at the door when she said goodbye, a timid face, with such timid eyes that she would not look at him. She was smiling but ill at ease: she folded her hands, unfolded them, dropped them, folded them again.

"I ran away from the Academy," he said. He blushed and lowered his eyes.

"You ran away?" Her lips were still open but that was all she said. She looked at him anxiously and reached out her hands. "What happened? Please tell me. But sit down. Nobody's here. My aunt went out."

Alberto stared at her. "But what about the Slave?"

"Who?"

"Ricardo Arana."

"Oh," she said. She was calm, she was smiling again. "You mean the boy that lives on the corner."

"He didn't come see you?"

"Me? No. Why should he?"

"Tell me the truth!" Alberto shouted. "Why do you lie to me? I mean that. . ." He broke off, mumbled something, stopped.

Teresa looked at him and shook her head. She was still unsure of her hands but there was something new in her eyes, a look of—was it?—suspicion. "Why do you ask me that?" Her voice was very low and smooth, and a bit ironic.

"The Slave got a pass. I thought he'd come here to see you. He told them his mother was sick."

"But why would he come here?"

"Because he loves you."

This time, Teresa blushed. "I didn't know," she said. "I hardly know him. But. . ."

"That's why I jumped over the wall," Alberto said. He was

silent for a moment. Then he said, "All right, I was jealous. I'm in love with you too."

7

She always looked so neat, so clean, that I thought, Why don't the rest of them look like that? And it wasn't just changing her clothes, it wasn't that, because what clothes did she have? When we were studying together and she got ink on her hands, she pushed her books aside and went to wash her hands. And if a page she was writing got even a little blot on it, she tore it up and started over. "But you're losing a lot of time," I told her. "The best thing is to erase it. Use a razor blade and you won't be able to tell the difference." She shook her head. It was the only thing that made her angry. Her temples began to throb—slowly, like a heart—under her black hair, and she pursed her lips. But when she came back from the bathroom she was smiling again. Her school uniform was a blue skirt and a white blouse. Sometimes I saw her coming back from school and I thought, Not a wrinkle, not a speck. She also had a plaid dress that covered her shoulders and fastened at the neck with a ribbon. It was sleeveless, and she wore a reddish-brown jacket over it. She only buttoned the top button, and when she walked, the ends of the jacket flapped in the breeze, and how nice she looked. That was the dress she wore on Sundays when she went to visit her relatives. Sundays were the worst days. I got up early and went to the Bellavista Plaza. I sat on a bench or looked at the movie posters, but I always kept an eye on the house, nobody could leave without my seeing them. On weekdays Tere went to buy bread at Tilau's bakery, which was next to the movie theater. I told her, "What luck, we're always running into each other." If the bakery was crowded, Tere waited outside and I pushed my way in. Tilau always waited on me first because we were friends. One day, when Tere and I went in together, Tilau said, "Ah, here come the sweethearts. The same as usual? Two hot *chancay* for each one?" The other customers laughed, Tere blushed, and I said, "Come on, Tilau, lay off the jokes and wait on us." But the bakery was closed on Sundays. I watched them from a bench or the entrance to the Bellavista movie theater. They waited for the bus that went along Costanera. Sometimes I put on an act: I stuck my hands in my pockets and walked past them kicking a stone or a bottle cap along in front of me, and without stopping I said, "Good morning, Señora, hi, there, Tere," and then went into my house or to Sáenz Peña.

She also wore her plaid dress and her jacket on Monday nights, because her aunt took her to the Bellavista theater, the ladies' section. I'd ask my mother to lend me a magazine, then I'd go to the plaza to wait till the movie let out and I could see her go by with her aunt, talking about the picture.

On the other days she wore a maroon skirt. It was old and rather faded. Sometimes I saw her aunt mending the skirt and she really did a good job, you could hardly see the stitches, she wasn't a seamstress for nothing. If Tere mended it herself, she kept her uniform on after school and put a newspaper on the chair so her uniform wouldn't get soiled. She wore a white blouse with her maroon skirt: it had three buttons but she only fastened the bottom two, so it showed her long dark throat. In the wintertime she wore her jacket over the blouse, without fastening any of the jacket buttons. I thought, What a knack for keeping well dressed. She only had two pairs of shoes and there wasn't very much she could do about them. At school she wore a pair of black shoes with laces, that sort of looked like men's shoes. But she had such small feet you didn't think about that. They were always brightly polished, without any dust or spots on them. I'm sure she took them off and polished them as soon as she got home, because I'd see her go in her house with the black shoes on and then a little later, when I went in to study with her, she'd be wearing her white shoes, with the black ones in the doorway to the kitchen, shining like mirrors. I don't think she put shoe polish on them every day, but at least she wiped them off with a rag.

Her white shoes were old. When she forgot herself, when she crossed her legs and had one foot in the air, I could see the bottoms were worn out, and one time she stubbed her toe against the leg of the table and let out a cry, and her aunt came over and took off her shoe and began to massage her foot, and I could see there was a piece of cardboard doubled up inside her shoe. I said to myself, She's got a hole in her shoe. One day I watched her clean her white shoes. She went over them very carefully with a piece of chalk, as carefully as she always did her homework. They looked like new then, but only for a moment, because as soon as she brushed against something the chalk rubbed off and you could see the stains. I thought, if she just had enough chalk, her shoes could look new all the time. She could carry a piece of chalk in her handbag and as soon as they got dirty she could take the chalk out and fix them. There was a bookstore in front of my school and one afternoon I went in and asked them how much for a box of chalk. The big one cost six soles, the little one was four fifty. I didn't know it cost that much. I was embarrassed to ask Skinny Higueras to lend me more money because I still hadn't paid him back the sol. We were friendlier than ever now, even though we only saw each other off and on in that same cheap bar. He told me jokes, asked me about my schoolwork, gave me cigarettes, taught me how to make smoke rings and how to hold in the smoke and let it out through my nose. Finally I got up the courage to ask him to lend me four fifty. "Of course, man," he said, "whatever you want," and he handed it to me without even asking me what it was for. I ran to the bookstore and bought the box of chalk. I was thinking of telling her,

"I've brought you a present, Tere," and when I went to her house I was still thinking of saying it. But as soon as I saw her I changed my mind and just said, "They gave me this at school but I haven't got any use for it. Would you like it?" And she told me, "Yes, of course, let me have it."

I don't believe in the devil but sometimes the Jaguar makes me wonder. He says he doesn't believe in anything, but that's a lie, a mere sham. You could tell it when he hit Arróspide for saying something bad about Saint Rosa. "My mother was very fond of Saint Rosa and if you say things about her it's like saying things about my mother." A mere sham. The devil must have a face like the Jaguar's, the same kind of smile, the same sharp horns. "They're coming to get Cava," he said, "they've found out all about it." He started laughing, and Curly and I couldn't think of anything to say. Then the soldiers came. How did he guess? I always dream that I go up behind him and knock him cold and then keep pounding him while he's on the floor, biff, bang, pow, and let's see what he does when he comes to. Curly must be thinking the same sort of thing. "The Jaguar's an animal, Boa," he told me this afternoon, "the worst there is. Did you see how he guessed about the peasant, and the way he laughed?" If I'd been the one that got screwed, he'd've pissed his pants laughing about it. He almost went crazy afterward but not on account of the peasant, just himself. "They did this to me, but they don't know who they're messing with." But Cava was the one who was in the guardhouse, and my hair stood on end because what if the dice'd picked me for the job? I'd like to see them screw the Jaguar, I wonder how he'd look, nobody ever screws him, that's the worst of it, he guesses everything ahead of time. They say animals can sense things from the smell, they just take a sniff and there it is, they can tell what's going to happen. My mother says, "The day we had the earthquake in 1940

I knew something was going to happen because all of a sudden the dogs in the neighborhood went crazy, they ran around and howled as if they could see the devil himself. A little while later the earthquake started." It's the same with the Jaguar. He put on one of those faces of his and said, "Somebody's gone and squealed. I swear by the Virgin that's what's happened." And that was before Huarina and Morte came in, before we even heard their footsteps or anything. What a dirty shame, none of the officers could've seen the peasant do it, none of the noncoms either, if they'd seen him they'd've kicked him out three weeks ago, it makes me sick, it had to be some squealer of a cadet. A Dog, maybe, or somebody from the Fourth. The guys in the Fourth are Dogs too, bigger and smarter but still Dogs. We were never Dogs, not really, because the Circle made them respect us, hard as it was. When we were in the Fourth, would anybody from the Fifth dare to tell us to make their beds? I'll knock you on your ass, I'll spit on you, hey Jaguar, Curly, Cava, come and help me, my hands ache from punching this asshole from the Fifth. They didn't even bother the midgets in the tenth section, all on account of the Jaguar, he was the only one that didn't let himself get initiated, he set the example, a real honest-to-God man, but so what? So we had some good times, better than anything that's happened since, but I wouldn't want to go back, I'd rather get out, and I hope we don't get screwed on account of all this, I'll kill that peasant Cava if he gets scared and drags us into it. "I'll bet anything on him," Curly said, "he won't let out a word no matter what they do to him." It'd be just my luck to get screwed right before final exams, on account of a lousy pane of glass. No, I wouldn't want to be a Dog again and take it for another three years, not after knowing what it's like, no, not after knowing all about it. Some of the Dogs say, I'm going to be a soldier, I'm going to be an aviator, I'm going to be a sailor. All the light-skinned ones want to be sailors. Okay, just wait a few months and we'll see.

The room looked out on a wide garden full of many colorful flowers. The window was open all the way, and they could smell the wet grass. Babe put on the same record for the fourth time and said, "Get up, don't be such a fool, it's for your own good." Alberto had collapsed into an easy chair, exhausted. Pluto and Emilio had come to watch the lessons, and spent the whole time cracking jokes, making insinuations, mentioning Helena's name. In a few moments he would see himself in the tall mirror, swaying very solemnly in Babe's arms, his body as stiff as before, and Pluto would say, "There you go, you're dancing like a robot again."

He stood up. Emilio had lit a cigarette and was sharing drags with Pluto. Alberto looked over at them: they were sitting on the sofa, arguing whether English or American tobacco was better. He ignored them. "Let's go," Babe said. "This time, you lead." They started dancing again, slowly at first, trying very carefully to follow the rhythm of that creole waltz, one step to the right, one step to the left, turn this way, turn that way. "You're doing better," Babe said, "but you've got to do it a little faster, with the music. Listen, tum-tum, tum-tum, turn, tum-tum, tum-tum, turn." Alberto was feeling more relaxed, more at ease: he stopped thinking about the steps and his feet no longer collided with Babe's.

"You're doing all right," Babe said, "but don't dance so stiffly. It isn't just a question of moving your feet. When you turn you've got to bend a little, like this. Watch me." Babe showed him how, a forced smile on his white face. He turned on his heel, and when he finished the turn his smile had disappeared. "It's just a trick, like changing steps or doing figures, but you'll learn all that later. Right now you've got to learn how to lead your partner correctly. Don't be afraid, she'll know how to follow you. Put your hand behind her shoulder good and solid. Let me lead you for a moment so you'll see. Do you get it? And you squeeze her hand with your left, and about halfway through the dance, if you think she's willing, you slip your fingers between hers, and you

bring her closer, little by little, pulling her toward you with
your right, but slowly, gently. That's why you've got to have
your hand in the right place from the very beginning, not
just your finger tips, your whole hand, the way I showed
you, just under her shoulder. Later on, you can start sliding
it, but you pretend it's an accident, as if your hand slides
down by itself each time you turn. If the girl starts to pull
away or tighten up, then quick, talk about something, keep
talking and laughing, but never slack up with your hand.
And take lots and lots of turns, but make sure they're in the
same direction. If you spin to the right you won't get dizzy,
you can spin fifty times in a row, but she'll be spinning to
the left and she'll get dizzy right away. You'll see: once
you've whirled her around a few times she'll be leaning her
head against you to steady herself. Then you can slide your
hand down to her waist without being afraid. And you can
even put your cheek against hers. Do you understand?"

The waltz had ended and the record-player kept up a
monotonous scratching. Babe turned it off.

"He knows all the angles," Emilio said, pointing to Babe.
"He's as slick as they come."

"We're all set now," Pluto said. "Alberto knows how to
dance. So let's play some Happy Neighborhood."

The old name for the neighborhood, which had gone out
of use because it also referred to the red-light district on
Huatica Street, was revived for the new kind of casino that
Tico had invented months before at the Terrazas Club. The
whole deck was dealt out to four players, with the dealer
naming the wild cards, and it was played by partners. Since
then it was the only card game played in the neighborhood.

"But he's only learned the waltz and the bolero," Babe
said. "He's still got to learn the mambo."

"Not now," Alberto said. "We'll go on some other time."

When they went into Emilio's house at two o'clock in the
afternoon, Alberto was full of enthusiasm, and wisecracked

along with the rest. But four hours of lessons had worn him out. Only Babe was still full of life; the others were bored.

"Whatever you want," Babe said. "But remember, the party's tomorrow."

Alberto stretched. It's true, he told himself. And to make it worse, it's at Ana's house. They'll play mambos all night. Ana, like Babe, was a star dancer: she did figures, she invented new steps, her eyes sparkled with pleasure when the others stopped dancing to watch her. Will I spend the whole evening sitting in a corner while the others dance with Helena? I wish it'd be just for the neighborhood.

For some time the neighborhood had ceased to be an island, a walled fortress. Outsiders—boys from Miraflores (from the 28th of July, Francia Street, Reducto, La Quebrada), boys from San Isidro and even from Barranco—had suddenly appeared in the neighborhood. They were after the girls, and talked with them in the doorways of their houses, ignoring or defying the resentment of the neighborhood boys. Also, they were older, and sometimes they even threatened them on their home ground. The girls were to blame, because they encouraged these invasions. Sara, Pluto's cousin, had become the girl friend of a boy from San Isidro. Sometimes he brought along a couple of his friends, and Ana and Laura chatted with them. The outsiders came most often on days when there were parties. They appeared as if by magic. They hung around outside from the very beginning, joking with the mother, flattering her. If they were not successful in getting her to invite them in, they stayed outside with their noses pressed to the windows, eagerly watching the couples as they danced. They made gestures, faces, jokes, they used every trick they could think of to attract the attention of the girls and make them feel sorry for them. Sometimes one of the girls, one who had fewer dances, asked the hostess to let an outsider come in. That started it: in a few minutes the room was full of outsiders, who ended up by taking over the record-player and the girls. Ana was especially disloyal, her feeling for the neighborhood was very weak if she had any at all. She was more interested in the outsiders than she was in the boys who lived near her. If she had not invited the outsiders herself, she found a way of getting them in.

"Yes," Alberto said, "you're right. Teach me the mambo."

"Okay," Babe said, "but first let me smoke a cigarette. You can dance with Pluto till I finish."

Emilio yawned and nudged Pluto with his elbow. "Get up and show your stuff, you're the king of the mambo." Pluto laughed. He had a splendid laugh that shook his whole body.

"Yes or no?" Alberto asked peevishly.

"Don't get sore," Pluto said. "I'm coming."

He stood up and went over to put on a record. Babe had lit a cigarette and was tapping his foot to the rhythm of some song he remembered.

"Listen," Emilio said, "there's something I don't understand. You were the first one that started dancing, I mean during the first parties in the neighborhood when we began to go around with the girls. Have you forgotten?"

"That wasn't dancing," Alberto said. "It was just hopping around."

"We all started out the same way," Emilio said. "But then we learned how."

"But he stopped going to dances for a long time," Pluto said. "Don't you remember?"

"That's right," Alberto said. "That's what messed me up."

"It looked as if you wanted to become a priest," Pluto said. He had finished picking out a record and was turning it over and over in his hands. "You hardly even left the house."

"Bah," Alberto said. "It wasn't my fault. My mother wouldn't let me."

"And now?"

"Now she does. Things are getting better between her and my father."

"I don't get it," Babe said. "Where does he come into it?"

"His father's a Don Juan," Pluto said. "Didn't you know? Haven't you seen him when he comes back at night, how he wipes his mouth with his handkerchief before he goes inside?"

"Yes," Emilio said. "We saw him once in La Herradura. He had a real beautiful dame with him in his car. He's a lady-killer, all right."

"He's a good looker," Pluto said. "And a sharp dresser."

Alberto nodded with a pleased expression.

"But what's that got to do with their not letting you go to parties?" Babe asked.

"When my father starts running wild," Alberto said, "my mother keeps me in so I won't be like him when I'm older. She's afraid I'll be another skirt-chaser, a heller."

"Great," Babe said. "She's all right."

"My father likes the women too," Emilio said. "Sometimes he doesn't come home at all, and his handkerchiefs always have lipstick on them. But my mother doesn't care. She laughs and says, 'You old tomcat.' Ana's the only one who bawls him out."

"Look," Pluto said, "when are we going to dance?"

"Wait a minute, man," Emilio said. "Let's talk a little. We'll get more than enough dancing at the party."

"Every time we talk about the party," Babe said, "Alberto turns pale. Don't be such a fool, man. This time Helena's going to say she'll go around with you. I'll bet you anything you want."

"Do you think so?" Alberto asked.

"He's head over heels in love," Emilio said. "I've never seen anybody so far gone. I could never do what he did."

"What did I do?" Alberto asked.

"You asked her twenty times."

"Just three," Alberto said. "What are you exaggerating for?"

"I think he's right," Babe said. "If he likes her, he should keep after her until she agrees. He can take it out on her afterward."

"But haven't you got any pride?" Emilio asked. "When a girl turns me down I go for another one right away."

"She's going to listen to you this time," Babe said to Alberto. "The other day we were talking at Laura's house and Helena asked about you. You should've seen her blush when Tico asked her, 'Do you miss him?' "

"Honest?" Alberto asked.

"Head over heels in love," Emilio said. "Look at the way his eyes shine."

"What's probably the matter is you're not asking her the right way," Babe said. "You've got to make an impression on her. Do you know what you're going to say?"

"More or less," Alberto said. "At least I've got an idea."

"That's important," Babe said. "The best thing is to have your whole speech ready in advance."

"It all depends," Pluto said. "I'd rather make it up as I go along. When I first meet a girl I feel nervous but as soon as I start talking I get a million ideas. The sound of my voice inspires me."

"No," Emilio said, "Babe's right. I get everything ready too. If you do that, all you have to worry about is how you're going to say it, how you're going to look at her, when you're going to take her hand."

"You've got to have it all in your head," Babe said. "If you get a chance, try it out in front of your mirror."

"Yes," Alberto said. He hesitated for a moment. "What do *you* say?"

"It's not always the same," Babe said. "It depends on the girl." Emilio nodded in agreement. "You can't ask Helena straight out if she'll be your girl friend. First you've got to soften her up."

"Maybe that's why she turned me down," Alberto said. "The last time, I just asked her all of a sudden if she'd like to be my sweetheart."

"You were an idiot," Emilio said. "And besides, you asked her in the morning. And out in the street. You must've been crazy."

"I asked a girl during Mass once," Pluto said, "and it worked out fine."

"No," Emilio said. He turned to Alberto. "Look, get her to dance with you tomorrow. Wait till they play a bolero. Don't ask her during a mambo. It's got to be more romantic."

"Don't worry about that," Babe said. "When you're all ready, give me a signal and I'll put on Leo Marini's 'I Love You.'"

"That's my bolero!" Pluto cried. "Every time I've asked a girl while we were dancing to 'I Love You,' she's told me yes. It never fails."

"All right," Alberto said, "I'll give you a signal."

"Get her to dance with you and don't let her get away," Emilio said. "Steer her to a corner without her noticing it. That's so the other couples won't hear you. Then whisper in her ear, 'Helenita, you're driving me crazy.'"

"You imbecile!" Pluto shouted. "Do you want her to turn him down all over again?"

"Why?" Emilio said. "I always start out that way."

"No," Babe said, "that's too crude, too clumsy. First you have to look very serious and tell her, 'Helena, I've got something very important to say to you. I like you a lot. In fact, I'm in love with you. Do you want to go around with me?'"

"And if she doesn't say anything," Pluto added, "ask her, 'Helenita, don't you care for me at all?'"

"And then you squeeze her hand," Babe said. "Slowly, with lots of tenderness."

"Don't look so pale, man," Emilio said, giving Alberto a pat on the back. "Don't worry, this time she'll say yes."

"That's right," Babe said. "You'll see."

"And after you ask her," Pluto said, "we'll gather around and sing 'Here Are Two Sweethearts.' I'll see to that, I give you my word."

Alberto smiled.

"But right now you've got to learn the mambo," Babe said. "Go on, your partner's waiting for you."

Pluto was holding his arms out theatrically.

Cava said he was going to be a soldier, but not in the infantry, in the artillery. He hasn't talked about it lately but he must've been thinking about it. Those peasants are stubborn, when they get an idea in their head it stays there. Almost all the soldiers are peasants. I don't think anybody from the coast would think of being a soldier. Cava's got the face of a peasant and a soldier, and now they've screwed him out of everything, the Academy, his army career, that's what must hurt the most. The peasants have bad luck, something's always happening to them. Just on account of some dirty squealer that we'll probably never find, they're going to rip off his insignia in front of everybody, I can see it, how it's going to be, and it gives me the shivers to think that if my number'd come up I'd be the one in the guardhouse. But I wouldn't've broken the glass, you have to be stupid to do that. The peasants are kind of stupid. It must've been because he was scared, though that peasant Cava isn't any coward. But this once he got scared, it's the only way to explain it. Besides his bad luck. All the peasants have bad luck, the worst things are always happening to them. It's good luck not to be born a peasant. And the hard part is, he wasn't expecting it, nobody was, he was feeling fine, he kept baiting that fairy Fontana, you always have a good time in French class, he's a real character, that Fontana. The peasant said, Fontana's all sort of: he's sort of short, sort of blond, and sort of like a man. His eyes are bluer than the Jaguar's, but they've got a different look in them, half serious, half mocking. They say he isn't a Frenchman, he's a Peruvian trying to pass as a Frenchman, and that means he's a son of a bitch. I don't know anything worse than betraying your country. But it's probably a lie, because where do they get all

these things they tell about Fontana? Every day there's
something new. Maybe he isn't even queer, but where did
he get that high voice, and those gestures that make you
want to pinch his cheeks? If it's true he's trying to pass as a
Frenchman, I'm glad I've given him a bad time. I'm glad
they all give him a bad time. And I'll keep it up until the
last day of classes. Señor Fontana, how do you say "pile of
shit" in French? Sometimes you have to feel sorry for him,
he isn't a bad guy, just kind of odd. He started crying one
day, I think on account of the razor blades. Everybody
brought a razor blade to class and stuck it in a crack in his
desk and the Jaguar said you make them play by just pluck-
ing them with your finger. Fontana kept opening and closing
his mouth but all you could hear was zoom, zoom, zoom.
We didn't laugh, so as not to lose the rhythm, and the fairy
went on opening and closing his mouth, zoom, zoom, zoom,
louder and louder, everybody together, let's see who gets
tired first. We kept it up for three quarters of an hour, maybe
more. Who's going to win, who's going to be the first to give
up? Fontana pretended nothing was happening, he opened
and closed his mouth like a deaf and dumb person, and the
concert got prettier all the time. Finally he closed his eyes,
and when he opened them again he was crying. He's a fairy.
But he still kept trying to talk, he didn't give up. Zoom,
zoom, zoom. Then he left the classroom and everybody said,
"He's gone to call the lieutenant, we're going to get screwed
for sure," but the good thing about it was he just went away.
They bait him every day and he never calls the officers. He
must be afraid they'll hit him, the best thing is not to look
like a coward. Sometimes it almost seems as if he likes to
have them bait him. Fairies are sure odd. But he's a good
guy, he never flunks anyone in the exams. It's his own fault
they bait him. What's he doing in a school for he-men with
that voice of his and those fairy gestures? The peasant makes
it rough for him all the time, he really despises him. He
starts in on him the minute he comes in the classroom. How

do you say "fairy" in French, teacher? Do you like to polish the knob? You must be very artistic, teacher, why don't you sing us something in French in that lovely voice of yours? Teacher, your eyes are exactly like Rita Hayworth's. And the fairy always replied, he always answered, but in French. Look, teacher, don't be a wise guy, don't insult us, I challenge you to a boxing match, Jaguar don't be discourteous. The thing is, they've got him screwed, we've got him under our thumb. One day we spit all over him while he was writing on the blackboard, he was all covered with slime, Cava said "How repulsive, he ought to take a bath before he comes to class." But that time he did call the lieutenant, that was the only time, what a fool he made of himself, that's why he never called the officers again, Gamboa's really something, we all found out what he's made of. He looked him up and down, what suspense, nobody even breathed. And what would you like me to do, Señor? You're in charge here in the classroom. It's very easy to make them respect you. Watch. Then he looked at us for a moment and said Attention! Goddamn, in less than a second we were on our feet. Kneel down! Goddamn, in less than a second we were on the floor. Duck-walk in your places! and we all began duck-walking. It lasted more than ten minutes, I think. I felt as if somebody'd pounded my knees with a crowbar, one, two, one, two, very serious, like ducks, till Gamboa said Halt! Does anybody want to have it out with me, man to man? Not even the flies moved. Fontana looked at him and couldn't believe it. You'll have to make them respect you yourself, Señor, they don't appreciate good manners, you have to get tough with them. After he left, we started saying "You little queer" without moving our lips. That's what Cava was doing this afternoon, he's sort of a ventriloquist, he doesn't move his lips at all but his voice comes out good and clear, even if you're watching him you can't believe it. While Cava was doing that, the Jaguar said, "They're coming to get Cava, they've found out all about it." He started laughing and Cava looked all around, so did Curly and I, what's the matter. Just then Huarina appeared in the doorway and said, "Cava, come with us. Excuse me, Señor Fontana, but it's an important matter." The peasant's a good guy, he got up and went out without looking at us and the Jaguar said, "They don't know who they're messing with," and he began to curse Cava, that shitty peasant, he got screwed because he's so stupid, it was all about the peasant, as if it was his fault they were going to expel him.

He had forgotten the tiny, identical acts that made up his life in the days following his discovery that he could not trust his mother either; but he had not forgotten the discouragement, the bitterness, the resentment and the fear with which his heart was filled. The worst thing was to have to pretend. Earlier, he waited for his father to leave the house before getting out of bed. But one morning someone pulled the sheets off him while he was still asleep. He felt cold, and opened his eyes to the clear light of the dawn. Then his heart stood still: his father was looking down at him with the same fire in his eyes as on that night. He heard him say, "How old are you?"

"Ten."

"Are you a man? Answer me."

"Yes," he stammered.

"Get out of that bed, then," the voice said. "Women are the only ones who spend the day in bed, they're lazy but they've got a right to be because they're women. They've brought you up like a little girl. But I'm going to make a man out of you."

He got out of bed and began to dress, but in his terrified haste he tried to put on the wrong shoe, he buttoned his shirt up wrong, he could not find his belt, his hands trembled so much that he could not tie his shoelaces.

"From now on, when I come down to breakfast I want to

see you at the table waiting for me. With your hands and face washed and your hair combed. Do you hear me?"

He ate breakfast with him after that, changing his tactics to suit whatever mood his father was in. If he saw that he was smiling, with calm eyes and a smooth forehead, he asked him questions that would flatter him, listened to him with the profoundest attention, nodded his head, opened his eyes wide, asked him if he would like him to wash the car. On the other hand, if he saw that his father's expression was stern, if his greeting went unanswered, he kept silent and listened to his threats with bowed head, as if repentant. There was less tension at lunch because his mother ate with them and diverted his father's attention. His parents talked to each other and he could get through the meal unnoticed. The torment ended in the evening. His father came home late, and he was able to eat before he arrived. From seven o'clock on, he would tag after his mother, complaining that he was tired, he felt sleepy, he had a headache. Then he would gobble his food and run up to his room. Sometimes he was still undressing when he heard his father parking the car. He would turn out the light and hide under the covers. An hour later he would get up, finish undressing in the dark, put on his pajamas and get into bed again.

Now and then he went out for a walk in the morning. Salaverry Avenue was deserted at ten o'clock, but occasionally a half-filled streetcar went rumbling by. He walked down to Brazil Avenue and stopped at the corner. He never crossed over, because his mother had told him not to. He watched the cars disappearing in the distance, in the direction of the center of town, and he thought of the Bolognesi Plaza at the end of the avenue, remembering it from the day his parents took him out for a drive: the noisy swarm of cars and buses, the crowded walks, the mirror-like tops of the automobiles reflecting the brilliant lines and letters of the electric signs. Lima frightened him, it was too big, you could lose yourself in it and never find your way home; the people on the street were total strangers. In Chiclayo he had gone out for walks alone: the people he met patted his head and called him by his name, and he smiled at them. He had seen them many times, in his house, in the main plaza, at Mass on Sundays, on the beach at Eten.

Then he walked down to the end of Brazil Avenue and sat on one of the benches in that little semicircular park on the edge of the cliffs, above the ash-gray sea. The parks in Chiclayo—there were only a few of them, he knew them all by memory—were also old like this one, but the benches did not have this rust, this moss, this sadness that made you feel so lonely under the gray sky as you listened to the melancholy mumble of the ocean. Sometimes, while he was sitting with his back to the sea, looking down Brazil Avenue and remembering the highway from the north that had brought him to Lima, he wanted to cry, to cry out. He recalled his Aunt Adelina coming back from the store and asking him with a smile in her eyes, "Can't you guess what I found?" and taking out a package of caramels or a piece of chocolate, which he grabbed from her hand. He recalled the sun, the white light that bathed the streets all year long, keeping them warm and pleasant; he recalled the excitement of Sundays, the trips to Eten, the hot yellow sand, the clear blue sky. He looked up: gray clouds everywhere, without a single break in them. He went back to his house, walking slowly, dragging his feet like an old man. He thought: When I grow up I'll go back to Chiclayo. And I'll never come to Lima again.

8

Lt. Gamboa opened his eyes. The only light that came in through the window of his room was the dim glow of the far-off lights of the parade ground; the sky was black. A few seconds later his alarm clock went off. He got up, rubbed his eyes, and collected his towel, soap, razor, and toothbrush. The hallway and the washroom were in darkness, and there was no sound from the nearby room: as usual, he was the first one up. Fifteen minutes later, back in his room, he heard the other alarm clocks go off. The dawn was beginning now: far away, behind the yellow glow of the lights, a dim blue light grew steadily stronger. He put on his field uniform without hurrying, and then left his room. Instead of crossing by the barracks of the cadets, he went to the guardhouse through the open field. It was rather cold and he had not put on his jacket. The soldiers on guard saluted him and he returned their salute. The lieutenant on duty, Pedro Pitaluga, was dozing hunched over in a chair, his head in his hands.

"Attention!" Gamboa barked.

Pitaluga jumped up, his eyes still closed. Gamboa laughed.

"Don't horse around, man," Pitaluga said as he sat down again. He scratched his head. "I thought it was the Piranha. I'm dead tired. What time is it?"

"Almost five. You've still got forty minutes to go. That's not so long. Why do you try to sleep? It's the worst thing you can do."

"I know," Pitaluga said, yawning. "I've violated the regulations."

"Yes," Gamboa said with a grin. "But that isn't why I said it. If you try to sleep sitting up, you feel terrible afterward. The best thing is to do something. That way, the time goes by without your even noticing it."

"Do what? Talk with the soldiers? Yes, Lieutenant, no, Lieutenant. Brilliant conversation. And the next thing you know, they're asking you for a furlough."

"I always study when I'm Officer of the Guard. It's the best time. I can't study during the day."

"Sure," Pitaluga said, "you're the model officer. By the way, what got you up so early?"

"Today's Saturday. Don't you remember?"

"Field exercises," Pitaluga said. He offered a cigarette to

Gamboa but he refused it. "One thing about this duty, I get out of the exercises."

Gamboa remembered their years at the Military School. Pitaluga was in the same section with him. He was a poor student but an excellent marksman. Once, during the annual maneuvers, he waded into the swollen river, dragging his horse behind him. The water came up to his shoulders, and the horse neighed with terror. The others begged him to come back, but Pitaluga managed to overcome the current and reach the other side, soaking wet and happy. Their captain congratulated him in front of everybody, telling him, "You're a real man." But now Pitaluga was always complaining about his duties, especially the field exercises. He was like the soldiers and cadets, all he thought about was getting a pass. The others had a good excuse: they were only in the army for the time being. Most of the soldiers had been dragged out of their mountain villages by force and put into the ranks; as for the cadets, most of them were in the Academy because their families wanted to get rid of them for a while. But Pitaluga had chosen his career. And he was not the only one: every two weeks Huarina invented some new illness for his wife in order to get a pass; Martínez drank in secret while he was Officer of the Guard, and everyone knew his thermos of "coffee" was full of pisco. Why not ask for a discharge? Pitaluga was getting fat, he never studied, he was always dead drunk when he came back from a pass. He'll be a lieutenant for years and years, Gamboa said to himself. But then he thought: Unless he's got political connections. Gamboa loved the military life for exactly the same reasons that the others hated it: discipline, rank, field exercises.

"I'm going to use the telephone."

"At this time of the morning?"

"Yes," Gamboa said. "My wife is up by now. She's leaving at six."

Pitaluga made a vague gesture, then put his head in his

hands again, like a turtle drawing into its shell. Gamboa's voice at the telephone was low and gentle, he asked a number of questions, mentioned pills against nausea and the cold, insisted on a telegram, repeated "Are you all right?" several times, and murmured a brief good-by. Pitaluga dropped his arms to his sides, and his head dangled like a bell. Then he blinked a few times and smiled without enthusiasm. "You sound like a honeymooner," he said. "You talk to her as if you just got married yesterday."

"We've been married three months," Gamboa said.

"I got married a year ago. And I'll be damned if I want to talk to her. She's a terror, just like her mother. If I called her up at this hour, she'd scream her head off, she'd call me everything she could think of."

Gamboa smiled. "My wife's very young," he said. "She's only eighteen. We're going to have a baby."

"I'm sorry," Pitaluga said. "I didn't know. You've got to take precautions."

"I want to have a son."

"Of course," Pitaluga said. "I can tell that. So you can make a soldier out of him."

Gamboa looked surprised. "I don't know if I'd like him to be a soldier," he muttered. He looked Pitaluga up and down. "In any case, I wouldn't want him to be a soldier like you."

Pitaluga stood up. "What kind of a crack is that?" he asked bitterly.

"Bah," Gamboa said. "Forget it."

He turned and left the guardhouse. The sentries saluted him again. One of them had his cap down over his ear. Gamboa was on the point of bawling him out for it, but then he stopped: there was no use having any hard feelings with Pitaluga, who had buried his head in his hands again. This time, Pitaluga could not doze off. He swore, and then shouted to one of the soldiers to bring him a cup of coffee.

When Gamboa reached the patio of the Fifth, the bugler had already sounded reveille at the Third and the Fourth and was about to sound it in front of the barracks of the last Year. He saw Gamboa, lowered the bugle from his lips, came to attention and saluted. The soldiers and cadets at the Academy all knew that Gamboa was the only officer there who returned the salutes of those under him in a correct military fashion. The others merely gave them a nod, some-times not even that. Gamboa folded his arms and waited for the reveille to end. He looked at his watch. There were a few cadet sentries in the doorways of the barracks. He looked them over one by one. When they found themselves in front of him, the cadets put on their caps and straightened their ties, then came to attention and saluted. Then they turned and disappeared into the barracks. The usual racket had begun. A moment later Pezoa came running up.

"Good morning, Lieutenant."

"Good morning. What's the matter?"

"Nothing, Lieutenant," the noncom said. "Why, Lieuten-ant?"

"You ought to be in the patio when the bugler gets here. It's your duty to go through the barracks and hurry them up. Don't you know that?"

"Yes, Lieutenant."

"Then what are you doing here? Get into the barracks. If the Year doesn't fall in in seven minutes, I'll hold you responsible."

"Yes, Lieutenant."

Pezoa went into the first sections on the run. Gamboa remained standing in the center of the patio, glancing now and then at his watch. He could hear the confused welter of sounds that poured out from all around the patio and con-verged on him as the guy-ropes of a circus tent converge on the center pole. He could sense, without entering the bar-racks, all the emotions the cadets were feeling and express-ing: their anger at being awakened so early, their exaspera-tion at having so little time to make their bunks and get dressed, the impatience and excitement of those who liked to shoot and play soldier, the disgust of those who would go out and flounder around in the fields without caring what they did, just doing it because they had to, and the suppressed happiness of those who would come back from the field exercises to take a shower, change into their blue and black dress uniforms, and go out on pass.

At seven past five Gamboa blew a long blast on his whistle. He could hear curses and protests, but at almost the same moment the barracks doors burst open and spilled out a dark green mass of cadets, who pushed and shoved and swore as they hurried to fall in, still adjusting their uniforms as they ran, but only using one hand because they were holding up their rifles with the other. The day had not yet fully dawned, that second Saturday in October; it was the same as other dawns, other Saturdays, other days of field exercises. Suddenly Gamboa heard a loud metallic crash and then a curse.

"Whoever dropped that rifle, come here!" he shouted.

The racket stopped abruptly. All the cadets looked straight ahead with their rifles at their sides. Pezoa tiptoed over to the lieutenant and stood at his side.

"I said, whoever dropped that rifle, come here!"

The silence was broken by the sound of boots on the concrete. The eyes of the whole battalion turned toward Gamboa. The lieutenant glared at the cadet for a moment, then said, "Your name."

The boy stammered his name, company, and section.

"Inspect his rifle, Pezoa," the lieutenant said.

The noncom rushed up to the cadet, seized his rifle, and inspected it ceremoniously: he looked it all over, turned it this way and that, opened and closed the bolt, checked the sights, tested the trigger.

"Scratches on the stock, Sir," he said. "And it isn't properly oiled."

"How long have you been in the Academy, Cadet?"

"Three years, Sir."

"And you still don't know how to take care of your rifle?

You should never let it fall on the ground. It's better to crack your skull than to drop your rifle. A soldier's gun is as important to him as his balls. You protect your balls, don't you, Cadet?"

"Yes, Lieutenant."

"Good," Gamboa said. "You should take the same care of your rifle. Go back to your section. Pezoa, mark him down for six points."

The noncom took out his notebook and wrote in it, after wetting the point of the pencil with his tongue.

Gamboa gave the order to march. After the last section of the Fifth had entered the mess hall, he went to the officers' mess. He was the first one there. A few minutes later the lieutenants and captains began to arrive. The officers of the Fifth—Huarina, Pitaluga and Calzada—sat down next to Gamboa.

"Snap it up, Indian," Pitaluga said. "You should serve an officer the minute he comes in." The soldier who was waiting on them murmured an apology, but Gamboa was not listening: the sound of an airplane cut through the dawn and the lieutenant's eyes explored the damp gray sky. Then he lowered them and looked at the open field. The fifteen hundred rifles of the cadets were stacked in groups of four, each of the four supporting the others by the muzzle. The vicuña wandered aimlessly among the straight rows of pyramids, sniffing at them.

"Have they decided anything at the officers meetings?" Calzada asked. He was the heaviest of the four. He was chewing a piece of bread and he talked with his mouth full.

"Yesterday," Huarina said. "It ended late, after ten o'clock. The colonel was furious."

"He's always furious," Pitaluga said. "On account of what he finds out or what he doesn't find out." He nudged Huarina. "But you shouldn't kick. You've been lucky this time. You've got something that's going to look good on your service record."

"Yes," Huarina said. "It wasn't easy."

"When are they going to strip off his insignia?" Calzada asked. "That'll be fun to watch."

"Monday at eleven."

"They're born delinquents," Pitaluga said. "They never learn. Don't they know what's what? It's a plain case of breaking and entering. We've expelled half a dozen cadets just since I've been here."

"They don't come to the Academy because they want to," Gamboa said. "That's the trouble."

"You're right," Calzada said. "They think like civilians."

"Sometimes they think we're priests," Huarina said. "One cadet even wanted me to hear confession, he wanted me to give him advice. Believe it or not."

"Half of them are sent here so they won't turn out to be gangsters," Gamboa said. "And the other half, so they won't turn out to be fairies. It's their parents' fault."

"You'd think the Academy was a reform school," Pitaluga said, pounding his fist on the table. "Everything's done half-way in Peru, and that's why everything goes wrong. The soldiers we get are filthy, they're crawling with lice, and they're all thieves. But you can beat some civilization into them. After a year in the army, the only thing Indian about an Indian is his looks. But it's the opposite with the cadets, they go from bad to worse. The ones in the Fifth are even worse than the Dogs."

"Spare the rod and spoil the child," Calzada said. "It's a damned shame we aren't allowed to beat them up. If you even raise your hand they put in a complaint, and then there's a great big stink."

"Here comes the Piranha," Huarina murmured.

The four lieutenants stood up. Captain Garrido greeted them with a nod. He was a tall man, with a pallid face, somewhat greenish about the cheekbones. They called him the Piranha because, like that savage fish of the Amazon basin, his double row of enormous gleaming teeth protruded beyond his lips, and his jaws were always working. He handed a sheet of paper to each of them.

"Instructions for the field exercises," he said. "The Fifth goes out beyond the plowed fields to the open ground on the other side of the hill. You'll have to hurry. It'll take us almost an hour just to get there."

"Shall we have them fall in or do you want us to wait for you, Captain?" Gamboa asked.

"Go ahead," Garrido said. "I'll catch up with you."

The four lieutenants left together. When they reached the field, they spread out in a straight line. Then they blew their whistles. The uproar in the mess hall grew louder and a moment later the cadets came pouring out. They grabbed their rifles, ran to the parade ground, and fell in by sections.

A little later the battalion went out through the main gate of the Academy, between the rigid sentries, into Costanera Avenue. The pavement was clean and shining. The cadets, three abreast, widened the formation in such a way that the lateral columns were on either side of the avenue and the middle column in the center of it. When the battalion reached Palmeras Avenue, Gamboa ordered a turn toward Bellavista. As they went down the slope, under the great curved leaves of the trees, the cadets could see an indistinct mass at the far end: the buildings of the Naval Arsenal and the port of Callao. At each side there were the tall old houses of La Perla with their vine-covered walls, their rusted bars protecting gardens of all sizes. By the time the battalion was approaching Progreso Avenue, the morning had begun to come alive: barefooted women with baskets and sacks of vegetables stopped to watch the cadets; a pack of dogs ran along beside the battalion, leaping and barking; sick-looking, dirty little boys escorted it the way dolphins escort a ship at sea.

The battalion halted at Progreso Avenue, where there was a steady stream of cars and buses. At a signal from Gamboa, the noncoms Morte and Pezoa stood in the middle of the avenue, stopping the flow of traffic while the battalion crossed. Some of the drivers were annoyed and honked their horns, and the cadets insulted them. Gamboa, at the head of the battalion, raised his hand and signaled that instead of going in the direction of the port they were to turn off into the level fields, skirting a field of newly-sprouted cotton. When the whole battalion was out on the weed-covered ground, Gamboa called to the noncoms.

"See that hill?" He pointed his finger at a dim mound on the far side of the cotton field.

"Yes, Lieutenant," Morte and Pezoa said.

"That's the objective. Pezoa, go on ahead with half a dozen cadets. Inspect it thoroughly, and if there's anyone out there, tell them to go away. Don't let anybody stay on the hill or even near it. Is that clear?"

Pezoa nodded and went over to the first section. "I want six volunteers," he said.

No one stepped forward: the cadets looked everywhere except straight ahead. Gamboa walked up beside Pezoa. "The first six, fall out," he said. "Go with the noncom."

Pezoa began running across the cotton field, raising and lowering his right arm, with his fist clenched, to signal that the cadets should follow him on the double. Gamboa walked back a few steps to join the other lieutenants.

"I've sent Pezoa ahead to clear the terrain."

"Good," Calzada said. "I don't think we'll have any problems. My outfit stays on this side."

"I have to attack from the north," Huarina said. "I'm always the one that gets screwed, I've still got to walk two and a half miles."

"An hour to get to the top isn't any too much," Gamboa said. "We'll have to make them climb fast."

"I hope the targets are okay," Calzada said. "Last month the wind blew them away and we were aiming at the clouds."

"Don't worry," Gamboa said. "They aren't cardboard this

time, they're cloth, a yard in diameter. The soldiers put them up yesterday. Don't start firing till you get within two hundred yards."

"Very well, General," Calzada said. "And what else are you going to teach us?"

"There's no use wasting ammunition," Gamboa said. "Anyway, your company won't make a single hit."

"Do you want to bet on that, General?" Calzada asked.

"Fifty soles."

"I'll hold the money," Huarina said.

"Okay," Calzada said. "Look out, here comes the Piranha."

The captain came up to them. "Well, what are you waiting for?"

"We're all ready," Calzada said. "We were waiting for you, Captain."

"Do you know your positions?"

"Yes, Sir."

"And have you sent somebody to make sure the terrain is clear of civilians?"

"Yes, Captain. Pezoa and six cadets."

"Good. Let's synchronize our watches," the captain said. "We start at nine. Begin firing at nine thirty. Stop firing as soon as the assault begins. Understand?"

"Yes, Captain."

"They should all be at the summit by ten. There's room for everybody. Take your companies to their positions on the double, to get them warmed up."

The lieutenants moved off, but the captain remained where he was. He could hear the officers issuing their commands. Gamboa's voice was the strongest, the most energetic. A little later, he was alone. The battalion had split up into three companies, which went out in different directions to surround the hill. The cadets were still chattering as they ran, but the captain could only make out a few stray phrases in the hubbub. The lieutenants were at the heads of their companies, the noncoms on the flanks. Capt. Garrido raised his field glasses to his eyes. The targets came into focus: they were located halfway up the hill, about five yards apart. They were perfect circles. He would have liked to fire at them too, but that was for the cadets now. For him, the field exercises were merely a bore, he had nothing to do except observe them. He opened a pack of cigarettes and tapped one out. He had to strike several matches before he got it lit, because of the strong wind. Then he walked quickly after the first company. It was interesting to watch Gamboa in action, since he took the exercises so seriously.

When he reached the base of the hill, Gamboa realized that the cadets were genuinely tired. Some of them were running with open mouths and purple faces, and all of them had their eyes fixed on him. He could see the anguish with which they waited for the command to halt. But he did not give the command. He glanced up at the white circles of the targets, the bare ocher slopes that dropped down toward the cotton field, and higher up, above the targets, the wide, bulging crest of the hill. And he kept on running, first along the base of the hill, then through the open field, racing as fast as he could, struggling not to open his mouth although he felt that his heart and lungs were crying out for a great mouthful of air. The veins in his neck were swollen and his whole body was drenched with sweat. He gave a last look backward, to see if they had got to within a thousand yards of the objective. Then he closed his eyes and managed to run even faster, taking longer strides and flailing the air with his arms. He reached the scrub that grew on the barren land outside the cotton field, next to the irrigation ditch which the instructions indicated as the limits of the first company's position. He stopped there, and only then allowed himself to open his mouth and breathe deeply. Before turning around, he wiped the sweat from his face so that the cadets would not realize that he too was exhausted. The first to reach the position were the noncoms and Arróspide. Then the rest of them came up, in complete disorder: the columns had disappeared, leaving only clusters, scattered bunches. A little later the three sections regrouped, forming a horseshoe around Gamboa. He could hear the brute panting of the hundred and twenty cadets, who had rested their rifles on the ground.

"Brigadiers, front and center!" Gamboa said. Arróspide and two other cadets stepped forward. "Company, at ease!"

The lieutenant walked a few steps away, followed by the noncoms and the three brigadiers. Then he squatted down and scratched lines and crosses on the ground as he explained the details of the various stages of the attack. "Do you understand the placement of the troops?" Gamboa asked, and his five subordinates nodded. "Good. The combat groups will begin fanning out as soon as the order to advance is given. And fanning out doesn't mean ganging up like sheep, it means keeping apart but in a skirmish line. Understand? Good. Our company attacks the south front, the one we're facing. See it?"

The noncoms and brigadiers looked up at the hill and nodded.

"What are the instructions for the advance, Sir?" Morte asked. The brigadiers turned to look at him and the noncom flushed.

"I'm coming to that," Gamboa said. "Forward ten yards at a time. Periodic advance. The cadets will run ten yards as fast as they can, then hit the dirt. . .and if anybody digs his rifle in the dirt, I'll kick his ass from here to the guardhouse. When everybody in the first line is down on the ground, I'll blow the whistle again and the second line will fire. Just one round. Understand? As soon as they've fired, they'll run forward ten yards and hit the dirt. The third line will fire and run forward. Then we'll repeat it from the beginning. All the movements should be done at my commands. We'll keep it up till we're a hundred yards from the objective. Then the sections should close in a little so as to keep out of the terrain where the other companies are.

The final attack will be made by the three sections at once. The hill should be almost clear by then, with only a few enemy positions left."

"How long do we have to take the objective?" Morte asked.

"An hour," Gamboa said. "But that's my problem. You non-coms and brigadiers have to watch out that your men don't spread out too much or get too close together. And don't let anybody lag behind. Also, keep in contact with me, in case I need you."

"Do we brigadiers go first or last?" Arróspide asked.

"Brigadiers in the first line, noncoms at the rear. Any more questions? Good. Go brief the squad leaders. We'll be starting in fifteen minutes."

The noncoms and brigadiers went off on the double. Gamboa saw Capt. Garrido coming and was about to stand up, but the Piranha motioned that he should remain squatting. Both of them watched the cadets, who had broken up into groups of twelve. They tightened their belts, knotted their bootlaces more securely, pulled down their caps, wiped the dust off their rifles, checked their slings.

"They like this," the captain said. "The morons. Just look at them. You'd think they were going to a dance."

"I know," Gamboa said. "They believe in war."

"If they ever had to fight a real battle," the captain said, "they'd all be cowards or deserters. But lucky for them, the only shooting we ever do is on maneuvers. I don't think Peru will ever have an honest-to-God war."

"But Captain," Gamboa said, "we're surrounded by enemies. You know yourself that Ecuador and Colombia are just waiting for the right moment to take a piece of the jungle away from us. And we still haven't got even with Chile for Arica and Tarapacá."

"That's just talk," the captain said. "Nowadays everything gets settled by the big powers. I was in the campaign against Ecuador in '41. We could've gone all the way to

Quito, but no, the big powers had to butt in and find a diplomatic solution. The nerve of them! The civilians end up deciding everything. It doesn't mean a damned thing to be a soldier in Peru any more."

"It used to be different," Gamboa said.

Pezoa and the six cadets came running back. The captain called to him. "Have you covered the whole hill?"

"Yes, Captain. It's completely clear."

"It's almost nine, Captain," Gamboa said. "I'm going to begin."

"Go ahead," the captain said. And he added, with a sudden gust of peevishness, "Give those lazy bastards a good workout."

Gamboa returned to the company. He looked them over, from one end to the other, as if he were estimating their hidden possibilities, the limits of their endurance, the extent of their courage. His head was tilted back a little. The wind fluttered his combat shirt and the wisps of black hair that stuck out from under his cap.

"Goddamn it, spread out!" he shouted. "Do you want to get yourselves butchered? There should be at least five yards between each man. Do you think you're going to Mass?"

The squad leaders left their places and shouted to the cadets to separate. The three lines grew longer and sparser.

"It's going to be a zigzag advance," Gamboa said. He spoke in a loud voice so that they could hear him at both ends of the lines. "You were taught about that in the Third. So make sure you don't advance one behind the other. This isn't a parade. And if anybody doesn't hit the dirt when I give the command, or gets ahead or behind against my orders, he's a corpse. And the corpses won't get a pass on Saturday or Sunday. Is that clear?"

He turned toward Capt. Garrido, but the captain seemed distracted: he was gazing off at the horizon with wandering eyes. Gamboa raised the whistle to his lips. There was a brief stirring in the lines.

"First attack line, ready for action! L...
lead, noncoms in the rear."

He looked at his watch again. It was exactly
He gave a long blast on his whistle. The s...
startled the captain and hurt his ears. He realize...
a few moments he had forgotten all about the exerc...
he felt rather guilty. He walked over into the scrub ...
the company to follow the action.

Before the sound of the whistle died, Capt. Garrido co...
see the first attack line surge forward in three groups. Th...
cadets ran at top speed, fanning out like the tail of a peacock.
They ran bent over, following the brigadiers, carrying their
rifles upright in their right hands, the muzzle pointing at the
sky, the butt a few inches from the ground. Then there was
a second blast on the whistle, shorter than the first but
sharper and further off—Gamboa had run off to one side to
control the movements—and suddenly the line vanished
among the weeds as if felled by a whirlwind. The captain
was reminded of the tin soldiers in a shooting gallery when
the BB's knocked them over. Then he could hear Gamboa
roaring: "Why did that group get ahead? Rospigliosi, you
horse's ass, do you want to get shot? Keep your rifles out of
the dirt!" The whistle blew again, and the line sprang up
out of the weeds and advanced on the run. A moment later,
at another blast from the whistle, it vanished again, and
Gamboa's voice was lost in the distance. The captain could
hear loud curses and unfamiliar names, could see the first
line advancing, then his attention was distracted by the
other two lines. The cadets had forgotten that the captain
was nearby: they were shouting to each other, making fun
of those who had gone ahead with Gamboa. "That Negro
Vallano flops like a frog, he must have rubber bones. And
that shitty Slave, he's afraid he'll scratch his face."

Suddenly Gamboa appeared before the captain, shouting:
"Second attack line, ready for action!" The squad leaders
raised their right hands, the thirty-six cadets stood tense and

tionless. Capt. Garrido looked at Gamboa. His face was
lm but he was clenching his fists and his eyes were bright
nd restless: they jumped everywhere, glittering, glowering,
miling. The second line rushed forward, the cadets grew
smaller, the lieutenant ran beside them with his whistle in
his hand.

Now the captain could see two lines spread out in the
field, alternately dropping down and leaping up. They gave
a semblance of life to that inanimate landscape. But he could
not see whether the cadets hit the ground in the prescribed
manner: left knee, left hip, left elbow, with the rifle against
their ribs instead of in the dirt. Nor whether the combat
groups were keeping together. Nor whether the brigadiers
were still out in front, like spearheads, but without losing
contact with the lieutenant. And then Gamboa reappeared,
his face as calm as before but with fire in his eyes. He blew
his whistle and the last line ran toward the hill, followed by
the noncoms. There were three lines advancing now, further
and further away, and the captain was left alone in the
spiny scrub. He stayed there for several minutes, thinking
how slow, how sluggish the cadets were, compared to the
soldiers or the graduates of the Military School.

Then he walked on behind the company, using his field-
glasses. From a distance, the operation looked like a simul-
taneous advance and retreat: when the first line hit the
ground, the second charged past them and took the lead,
and then the third line replaced the second. On the next
advance, the three lines returned to their original order, and
seconds later they merged into a single line. Gamboa waved
his hands and shouted, he seemed to be aiming and shooting
at certain cadets with his finger. Capt. Garrido could not
hear him but he could guess what he was saying.

And suddenly the captain heard the firing. He looked at
his watch. Right, he thought. Exactly nine-thirty. He raised
his field glasses, and saw that the first line had reached the
prescribed position. Then he looked up at the targets but

could not make out the hits. He ran forward abou
yards and raised his glasses again. This time he cou
that the targets had a dozen perforations. The soldiers
better, he thought, but these cadets are going to be reser\
officers when they graduate. It's scandalous. He kept moving
ahead, without taking the glasses from his eyes. The lines
continued to advance ten yards at a time. The second line
fired, and the echo had scarcely died when the whistle
ordered the front and rear lines to advance. The cadets
looked very small against the horizon as they ran and then
threw themselves down. Another whistle blast and another
line fired. After each round of firing the captain inspected
the targets and estimated the hits. As the company neared
the hill, their shooting was more accurate: the targets were
riddled by now. He looked at the faces of the cadets who
were firing. They were red, infantile, beardless faces, one
eye closed and the other fixed on the sight. The recoil
jarred those young bodies, but although their shoulders hurt
already, they would have to leap up, run forward, hit the
ground and fire again, surrounded by an atmosphere of
violence that was only a simulacrum. Capt. Garrido knew
that war was not like that.

A moment later he noticed a green silhouette, and he
would have stepped on it if he had not swerved in time; he
also saw a rifle with its muzzle buried in the ground, against
all the instructions for the care of weapons. He could not
guess the meaning of that fallen body and gun. He leaned
over. The boy's face was distorted with pain and his mouth
and eyes were wide open. The bullet had struck him in the
head. A little stream of blood ran down his neck.

The captain dropped the field glasses he was carrying in
his hand. He picked up the cadet, putting one arm under
his shoulders and the other under his legs, and began running headlong toward the hill, shouting, "Lieutenant
Gamboa, Lieutenant Gamboa!" But he had to run a number
of yards before they could hear him. The first company—

identical green beetles clambering up the slope toward the targets—was too absorbed in Gamboa's commands and the effort of climbing to look behind. The captain tried to locate the lieutenant's light-colored uniform or one of the noncoms. Suddenly the beetles stopped and turned around, and the captain realized he was being watched by dozens of cadets. "Gamboa, noncoms!" he shouted. "Come here, hurry!" The cadets were running down the hill toward him and he felt foolish with that boy in his arms. I've got a dog's luck, he thought. The colonel's going to put this on my record.

Gamboa was the first to reach him. He stared at the cadet in astonishment and bent over to look closer, but the captain shouted, "Quick, get him to the infirmary! As quick as you can!"

The two noncoms, Morte and Pezoa, picked up the body and started racing across the field. They were followed by the captain, the lieutenant, and the cadets. The cadets came running up from all directions to take a shocked look at that face as it bobbed up and down: a pale, emaciated face which all of them recognized.

"Faster," the captain said, "faster."

Suddenly Gamboa grabbed the cadet away from the noncoms, hoisted him onto his shoulders, and ran ahead. In only a few seconds he was already several yards away.

"Cadets," the captain shouted, "stop the first car that comes by!"

The cadets left the noncoms and cut across the field on the run. The captain remained behind, with Morte and Pezoa.

"Is he from the first company?" he asked.

"Yes, Captain," Pezoa said. "The first section."

"What's his name?"

"Ricardo Arana, Captain." He hesitated for an instant, then added: "They call him the Slave."

PART TWO

I'm twenty years old. Don't let anyone tell me it is the most beautiful period of life.

—PAUL NIZAN

1

I feel sorry for poor Skimpy, last night she kept howling and howling. I wrapped her up in my blanket, and even put my pillow on her, but you could still hear the noise she was making. Every little while she seemed to be choking and suffocating, and her howling was terrible, it woke up the whole barracks. It wouldn't've made so much difference before, but now they're all so nervous they started to swear and shout insults and tell me, "Get her out of here or else," and I had to talk tough with some of them from my bunk. By midnight it was just too much. I was as sleepy as the rest and Skimpy kept howling louder and louder. Finally some of them got up and came over to my bunk with boots in their hands. I didn't want to have a fight with the whole section, now that we're all so upset anyway. So I pulled her out of my bunk and carried her down to the patio and left her there, but the minute I turned my back I could tell she was following me and I had to bawl her out. "Shut up, you bitch, and stay where I put you." But Skimpy kept following me, with her bad leg held up so it wouldn't touch the ground, and it was pitiful to see how hard she tried to catch up with me. Then I picked her up again and carried her out to the field, I put her down in the weeds and scratched her neck for a while, then I came back and this time she didn't follow me. But I didn't sleep well, in fact I didn't sleep at all. Just when I'd be falling asleep, bang, my eyes'd open by themselves and I'd start thinking about the poor dog, and besides that I started sneezing because I didn't put on my shoes when I took her out to the patio, also my pajamas are full of holes and I think there must've been a cold wind, maybe it was even raining. Poor Skimpy, freezing out there, and she always feels the cold so much. Lots of times I've made her angry at night because I turn over and she gets uncovered. She growls a little and pulls at the blanket with her teeth until she's covered up again, or she burrows down to the foot of the bed so she can feel the warmth from my feet. Dogs are very faithful, more so than relatives, no doubt about that. Skimpy is a mongrel, a mixture of every kind of dog, but she's got a heart of gold. I don't remember when she came to the Academy. I'm sure nobody brought her here, she was going by one day and decided to come in and look around. She liked it, so she stayed. I think she was already in the Academy when we arrived. Maybe she was even born here, she may be a native of the Leoncio Prado. When I first noticed her she was very small, she kept coming into the section all the time, beginning with the days of the initiation, she seemed to think it was her home, if anybody from the Fourth came in she rushed at his feet and barked and tried to bite him. And she was stubborn, they'd send her flying with a kick but she'd get up and charge again, still barking and showing her teeth, the little teeth of a half-grown pup. She's full-grown now, she must be over three years old, that's old for a dog because they don't live too long, especially if they're mongrels and don't get much to eat. I don't remember ever seeing Skimpy eat very much. Sometimes I toss scraps to her, they're the best meal she gets. She doesn't eat grass, she only chews it for the juice and then spits it out. She'll take a mouthful of grass and chew it for hours and hours like an Indian chewing coca. She was always around in the section and some of them said she had fleas and they ran her out, but Skimpy always came back, they chased her away a hundred times but a few minutes later the door began creaking a little and you could see her muzzle down at the bottom next to the floor. We had to laugh at how stubborn she was, and sometimes we let her in and played with her. I don't know who thought of calling her Skimpy. Nobody ever knows where nicknames come from. When they started calling me the Boa, I laughed at first but then I got mad and asked everybody, who made it up, but they just said What's-his-name and now I can't get rid of that nickname, they even use it in the neighborhood. I think it must've been Vallano. He was always telling me, "Give us a demonstration, piss over your belt," or "Show us that cock of yours that hangs down to your knees." But I'm not sure it was Vallano after all.

Alberto felt someone grasp his arm. He could not recognize the cadet's face, but nevertheless the boy was smiling at him as if they knew each other. A shorter cadet was standing behind him. He could not see them clearly: it was only six in the afternoon, but the fog had already come in from the sea. They were in the patio of the Fifth, near the parade ground. Groups of cadets were passing back and forth.

"Wait a minute, Poet," the boy said. "You know all kinds of things, is it true that ovary means the same as balls, only feminine?"

"Let go," Alberto said. "I'm in a hurry."

"Don't be like that. It won't take a minute. We've got a bet on."

"About a song," the smaller one said, coming forward. "A Bolivian song. He's half Bolivian and he knows some songs from there. Strange kinds of songs. Go ahead, sing it for him so he can see."

"I told you to let go," Alberto said. "I haven't got time."

But instead of releasing him, the cadet gripped him harder; then he sang:

> With what sharp pangs
> My ovary is torn,
> Because of the little one
> Soon to be born.

The smaller cadet laughed.

"Are you going to let go?"

"No. First tell me if they're the same."

"That isn't fair," the smaller one said. "You're telling him what to say."

"Yes, they're the same," Alberto shouted and yanked himself free. As he walked away, the two boys remained where they were, arguing. He hurried toward the officers' quarters, skirted them, and was only ten yards from the infirmary. But he could hardly distinguish its outline, and the doors and windows were all hidden by the fog. There was no one in the entry, nor in the little guard room. He went up to the second floor, taking the stairs two at a time. There was a man in a white apron near the doorway. He had a newspaper in his hands but he was not reading it; he was staring at the wall with a sinister look.

"Get out of here, Cadet," he said, straightening up. "It's off limits."

"I want to see Cadet Arana."

"No," the man growled. "Nobody can see Cadet Arana. Nobody."

"But it's important," Alberto said. "Please. Or let me talk to the doctor on duty."

"I'm the doctor on duty."

"You're lying. You're an attendant. I want to talk with the doctor."

"I don't like your attitude," the man said. He had let the newspaper fall to the floor.

"If you won't call the doctor, I'm going in to look for him," Alberto said. "I'm going in whether you like it or not."

"What's the matter with you, Cadet? Are you crazy?"

"You bastard, call the doctor!" Alberto shouted. "Goddamn it, call the doctor!"

"This Academy's nothing but a bunch of savages," the man said. He got up and went down the corridor. The walls had been painted white, perhaps recently, but the dampness had already stained them with big gray patches. A few moments later the attendant returned with a tall, thin man with glasses.

"What do you want, Cadet?"

"I want to see Cadet Arana, Doctor."

"You can't," the doctor said with a helpless gesture. "Didn't the soldier tell you you can't come up here? They could punish you for this."

"I came here three times yesterday," Alberto said. "The soldier wouldn't let me in. But he isn't here today. Please, Doctor, let me see him, even if it's just for a minute."

"I'm very sorry, but it isn't up to me. You know what the rules are like. Cadet Arana can't have any visitors, nobody can see him. Is he a relative of yours?"

"No," Alberto said. "But I've got to talk with him. It's very important."

The doctor put his hand on his shoulder and looked at him sympathetically. "Cadet Arana can't talk with anyone. He's still unconscious. But don't worry, he'll be all right. Now get out of here, please. Don't make me call an officer."

"Can I see him if I bring an order from the captain?"

"No," the doctor said. "Only with an order from the colonel."

I waited for her three or four times a week outside her school, but she didn't always come past me. My mother got used to eating lunch alone, though I don't know if she really believed I was going to a friend's house. But anyway it was better for her not to have me there, because that way she spent less on food. Sometimes when I did come home for lunch she'd give me a disgusted look and ask me, "Aren't you going to Chucuito today?" What I really wanted was to wait for her every day, but they wouldn't let me out early at the 2nd of May school. It was easy to sneak away on Mondays, we had physical education on Mondays and after recess I'd just hide behind a pillar until the class went away with the instructor, Señor Zapata, and then I'd walk out the front gate. Señor Zapata was a boxing champion in his day, but after he got old he didn't like to work and never even called the roll. He'd take us out to the playing field and say, "All right, get up a soccer game, it's good exercise for your legs. But don't go too far away." Then he'd sit down on the grass and read a magazine. I couldn't get out early on Tuesdays because the mathematics teacher knew all of us by name, but on Wednesdays it was easy again because we had art and music and the teacher, Señor Cigüeña, lived on the moon or somewhere—anyway, he didn't live in this world. I could get out the back way during the eleven o'clock recess and catch a streetcar half a block from the school.

Skinny Higueras kept on giving me money. He always waited for me in the Bellavista Plaza, and invited me to have a drink and a cigarette while he talked about my brother, about girls, about everything. "You're a man now," he told me, "one hundred percent." Sometimes he gave me money before I asked him for it. He didn't give me very much, fifty centavos or a sol, but it was enough for the fare. I'd go to the 2nd of May Plaza, walk down Alfonso Ugarte Avenue to her school, and wait for her as usual in the corner store. Sometimes she came over to me and said, "You got out early again today?" and then she started talking about something else and so did I. She's very intelligent, I thought, she changes the subject so I won't feel embarrassed. We walked toward her relatives' house, about eight blocks away, and I always made sure we walked slowly, either by taking short steps or by stopping to look in the store windows, but it never took us longer than half an hour. We talked about the same things: what happened in our schools that morning, what we'd be studying that afternoon, what the exams'd be like and whether we'd pass them. I knew all the girls in her class by their names and she knew the names and nicknames of my friends and my teachers; she also knew the jokes about all the best-known students at the 2nd of May.

One day I thought of telling her, "Last night I dreamed we grew up and got married." I felt sure she'd ask me a lot of questions, so I made up all sorts of answers that'd keep the conversation going. The next day, while we were walking down Arica Avenue, I suddenly told her, "You know, last night I dreamed that. . ." "What about? What did you dream?" she asked me. And I only said, "I dreamed that both of us passed our exams." "I just hope your dream comes true," she said.

While I was with her we always came across some of the students from the La Salle in their light brown uniforms, and that was another topic of conversation. "They're fairies," I told her. "They'd look sick at the 2nd of May. Look at their white faces, you'd think they came from the Academy of the Marian Brothers in Callao, that's where they play soccer like little girls, if they get kicked they start yelling for their mothers, just look at their faces." She laughed and I went on talking about them, but finally I couldn't think of anything else to say and I told myself, We're almost there. The thing that really made me nervous was the idea that she'd get bored at hearing me talk about the same things all the time, but then I remembered how she kept repeating things and I didn't get bored. Like when she'd tell me twice or even three times about the picture she and her aunt saw on Monday. We were talking about the movies when I finally got up the courage to tell her something serious. She asked me if I'd seen some picture, I forget which one. I said no, and she asked me, "Don't you ever go to the movies?" "Now and then," I told her, "but last year I used to go every week. With a couple of friends from the 2nd of May. We could get in free at the Sáenz Peña on Wednesdays because one of my friends had a cousin who was a city cop and when he was on duty there he let us go up to the balcony without any tickets. We waited till the lights went out, then we went downstairs and got better seats. We just had to jump over the rail." "But didn't they catch you?" she asked me. "Sure they did," I said, "but they couldn't kick us out. I told you my friend's cousin was a cop." She asked me, "Why don't you go with them any more?" "They go on Thursdays now," I said, "because the cop's day on duty there was changed." "And you don't go with them?" she asked me, and without even thinking I said, "I'd rather go to your house and be with you." Then I realized what I'd said and I stopped talking. It got worse, too, because she gave me a very serious look, and I thought, Now I've made her mad. So I said, "Maybe I'll go with them one of these weeks. To tell the truth, though, I don't care very much about the movies." Then I began to talk about something else, but I couldn't stop thinking about the look I'd seen on her face, a look that was different from any I'd seen before, as if she'd guessed everything I was thinking but didn't dare say to her.

One day Skinny Higueras gave me a sol and a half. "So you can buy cigarettes," he told me, "or get drunk if you're having girl trouble." The next day I was walking with her along Arica Avenue, near the Brenda movie theater, and we happened to stop in front of a bakeshop window. There were some chocolate pastries on display, and she said, "How delicious they look!" I remembered the money I had in my pocket, and I've hardly ever felt so happy. I said, "Wait here, I've got a sol, I'm going to buy one of those," and she said, "No, don't waste your money, I was only joking," but I went in and asked the clerk for one of those pastries. I was so excited I didn't even wait for my change, but the clerk was honest, he caught up with me and said, "You forgot your change. Here." When I gave her the pastry, she told me, "But it isn't all for me. We'll go halves." I didn't want to and I tried to convince her I didn't feel hungry, but she insisted and finally she told me, "At least take a bite," then she reached out and put it to my mouth. I took a bite and she laughed. "You've got it all over your face," she said, "what an idiot I am, it's my fault, I'll clean it off." She raised her other hand and brought it up to my face. I stood still and

my smile froze when I felt her touching me, I didn't dare
breathe when she ran her fingers over my mouth, my lips
would've moved and she would've realized I wanted to kiss
her hand. "There," she said, and we went on walking toward
La Salle without saying a word, I was dazed by what had
just happened and I was sure she'd gone slow when she ran
her fingers over my mouth, or that she'd done it several
times, and I told myself, Perhaps she did it on purpose.

Besides, it wasn't Skimpy that brought the fleas in. I think
she got the fleas from the Academy, that is, from the
peasants. One time those bastards Curly and the Jaguar went
and put a whole bunch of lice on the poor thing. The Jaguar
came back from someplace or other, probably one of the
pigsties in the first block on Huatica Street, with some
enormous lice on him. He picked them off and had them
walking around on the floor of the latrine, they were big as
ants, and Curly said, "Why don't we put them on somebody?" and Skimpy was there watching, that's the kind of
luck she has. So they put them on her. Curly held her by
the neck when she started kicking and the Jaguar put them
on with both hands. Then they both got excited and the
Jaguar shouted, "I've still got tons of them, who'll we initiate?" and Curly shouted, "The Slave!" I went with them.
He was asleep. I remember how I grabbed his head and
covered his eyes, and Curly held his legs. The Jaguar put
the lice in his hair, and I said, "Be careful, damn it, you're
getting them on my sleeves." If I'd known that what's
happened to the guy was going to happen, I don't think
I'd've grabbed his head that time, and I wouldn't've bullied
him so much. But I don't think he had any trouble getting rid
of the lice. It was Skimpy they almost ate alive. She lost almost all of her hair and she kept rubbing herself against the
walls, she looked like one of those mangy dogs you see in the
slums, her whole body was one big sore. It must've hurt a
lot, she never stopped rubbing herself against the walls,

especially the barracks walls because they're rough cement. Her back looked like the Peruvian flag, red and white, white and red, plaster and blood. So then the Jaguar said, "If we put some pepper on her, she'll start talking like a human being," and he told me, "Boa, go swipe some peppers from the kitchen." I went there and one of the cooks gave me several hot peppers. We ground them up with a stone on the tile floor, and the peasant Cava said, "Faster, faster." Then the Jaguar said, "Grab her and hold her, I'm going to cure her." He was right, she almost did talk. She jumped all around and squirmed like a snake and Christ what howls she let out. The noncom Morte was startled by the noise and came in to see what was happening, and when he saw the way Skimpy was jumping around he laughed till he had tears in his eyes and he said, "What crazy bastards, what crazy bastards." But the funny thing is, it cured her just like that, her hair grew out, I think she even gained a little weight. I'm sure she thought I helped put the pepper on her to cure her, animals aren't very intelligent and God knows how she got that idea into her head. But from that day on, she followed me around all the time. She'd get between my feet during drill so I could hardly march, and she'd lie under my chair in the mess hall and wag her tail if I threw her some scraps. She'd wait for me outside the door of the classroom building, and when she saw me come out for recess she'd greet me by nuzzling my legs. At night she'd climb up on my bed and try to lap my face. I used to have fun hitting her. She'd go away but she'd always come back again, sizing me up with her eyes, are you going to hit me this time or not, I'll get a little closer, I'd better move back, are you going to kick me this time, she was really smart. And everybody began making fun of me, they said, "You're sleeping with her, you animal," but that was a lie because I still didn't even have any idea of screwing a dog. At first I got mad at the way she always tagged after me, but sometimes I'd scratch her head, without thinking anything about it, and I found out how much she enjoyed it. She'd get on top of me at night and keep moving around and I couldn't get to sleep, so I'd put my hand on the back of her neck and scratch her a little. Then she'd keep still. When they heard her moving around, everybody made fun of me, "That's enough, Boa, leave the poor thing alone, you're going to strangle her," come here, you bitch, this is what you want, isn't it, I'll scratch your head and your belly. Then she'd lie there as still as stone, but I could feel how she was trembling with happiness, and if I stopped scratching her for even a second she jumped up and even in the darkness I could see she'd opened her mouth and was showing me those white teeth of hers. I don't know why dogs have such white teeth but they all do, I've never seen a dog with a black tooth and I don't remember hearing of a dog that lost a tooth or that got a cavity and had to have the tooth pulled out. That's a funny thing about dogs, and another one is, they don't sleep. I thought it was only Skimpy that didn't sleep, but later somebody told me all dogs are the same, they stay awake all night. At first it used to make me nervous, it even scared me a little, the moment I opened my eyes I'd see her there looking at me and sometimes I couldn't get to sleep because I was thinking about how she spent the night beside me without closing her eyes. It'd make anybody nervous to realize he was being spied on, even if it was only by a dog that didn't understand anything. Though sometimes she seemed to understand.

Alberto turned around and walked down the stairs. A middle-aged man was coming up them. His face was haggard and his eyes were filled with anxiety.

"Señor," Alberto said.

The man had already passed him. He stopped and turned to look at him.

"Excuse me," Alberto said, "but are you a relative of Cadet Ricardo Arana?"

The man looked at him closely, as if attempting to place him. "I'm his father," he said. "Why?"

Alberto walked back up a couple of steps. Their eyes were on the same level. Arana's father was still peering at him intently. There were dark circles under his eyes, revealing his worry and his lack of sleep.

"Can you tell me how Arana is?" Alberto asked.

"I can't see him," the man said in a hoarse voice. "They won't let anybody in. Not even his own parents. They haven't got any right to do that. Are you a friend of his?"

"We're in the same section," Alberto said. "They wouldn't let me in either."

The man nodded. He seemed completely crushed. He had not shaved for several days, his shirt collar was wrinkled and soiled, and his tie had slipped to one side. The knot in his tie was ridiculously small.

"I could only catch a glimpse of him," he said. "From the doorway. They shouldn't do that to us."

"How is he?" Alberto asked. "What did the doctor tell you?"

The man raised his hand and ran the back of it across his lips. "I don't know," he said. "They've operated on him twice. His mother's almost crazy. I can't figure out how it could happen. And just when he was going to graduate. Only God can save him now. His mother's praying in the chapel. The doctor says he might let us see him tonight."

"He'll be okay," Alberto said. "The Academy's doctors are the best there are, Señor."

"Yes," the man said, "yes, I know. The captain tells us the chances are very good. He's a very friendly sort of person. I think his name is Garrido. He even brought us the colonel's very best wishes." He brushed his mouth with his hand again, then fished in his pockets and brought out a pack of cigarettes. He offered one to Alberto, who refused it with a thank you. Then he fished in his pockets again but could not find any matches.

"Wait a minute," Alberto said, "I'll go get you a light."

"I'll go with you," the man said. "I don't have to sit here two days in a row with nobody to talk to. I'm a nervous wreck. I hope to God it all comes out all right."

They left the infirmary. There was a soldier on guard in the little room near the entrance. He looked surprised when he saw Alberto, and leaned forward in his chair, but then decided not to say anything. Outside, it was dark by now. Alberto led the way across the open field in the direction of "La Perlita." They could see the lights in the distant barracks. There was no sound whatsoever.

"Were you with him when it happened?" the man asked.

"Yes," Alberto said. "But not close to him. I was at the other end of the line. It was the captain who found him. While we were climbing the hill."

"It isn't fair," the man said. "It isn't a just punishment. We're decent people. We go to Mass every Sunday. We've never done anything wrong. His mother spends all her time working for her charities. Why did God punish us like this?"

"We feel pretty bad in the section," Alberto said. "All of us." After a long pause, he added, "We think a lot of him. He's a real buddy."

"I know," the man said. "He's all right. But only on account of me. I've had to be pretty strict with him now and then. For his own good, you know. It hasn't been easy to make a man out of him. He's my only son. Everything I do is for him, for his future. Won't you tell me something about him? I mean, here at the Academy. Ricardo doesn't talk very much. He never tells us anything. But sometimes I don't think he's been happy."

"Well. . .it's kind of rough," Alberto said. "You have to get used to it. Nobody's happy at the start."

"But it did him good," the man said, almost passionately. "It did him good, it changed him, it made a man out of him. Nobody can say it didn't! Nobody!" Then, in a calmer voice, "You don't know what he was like when he was little. But the Academy gave him some guts, gave him a spine. And anyway, if he wanted to quit he just had to tell me. I asked him to go to the Academy and he agreed. It isn't my fault. I just did what I thought was best. For him, I mean."

"It's all right, Señor," Alberto said. "Don't get upset. He's going to get better."

"His mother thinks I'm to blame," the man said, ignoring what Alberto told him. "That's a woman for you. They aren't fair, they don't understand. But I've got a clear conscience, absolutely clear. I wanted him to be a man. A somebody. Do you think I was wrong?"

"I don't know," Alberto said, confused. "I mean, no. But the main thing is for Arana to get better."

"I'm all nerves," the man said. "Don't mind what I say. Sometimes I lose control."

They arrived at "La Perlita." Paulino was behind the counter, his head resting on his hand. He looked at Alberto as if he were seeing him for the first time.

"A box of matches," Alberto said.

Paulino glanced suspiciously at Arana's father. "I'm all out," he said.

"Not for me," Alberto said. "For the señor."

Without a word, Paulino reached under the counter and brought out a box of matches. The man had to use three of them to light his cigarette. In the brief flashes, Alberto could see how his hands were trembling.

"A cup of coffee," the man said. He turned to Alberto. "What would you like?"

"I haven't got any coffee," Paulino said in a bored voice. "There's cola if you want."

"All right," the man said. "A cola. Anything."

He had forgotten that calm morning: it was sunless, but there was no rain. He got off the Lima–San Miguel streetcar at the stop near the Brazil movie theater. It was where

he always got off. He preferred to walk those ten unneces-
sary blocks, even in the rain, to increase the distance that
separated him from the inevitable meeting. It was the last
time he would make the trip: exams had ended the week
before, they had just handed out the grades, the school was
dead and would not come to life again for three months. His
schoolmates were happy at the thought of the vacation, but
he felt afraid. The school was his only refuge. The summer
would drown him in a dangerous inertia, at the mercy of his
parents.

Instead of turning onto Salaverry Avenue, he continued
along Brazil Avenue to the park. He sat down on a bench,
thrust his hands into his pockets, hunched over a little and
remained there motionless. He felt old. His life was monotonous, without any incentives, a heavy burden. In class, his
schoolmates cut up the moment the teacher turned his back.
They played practical jokes, threw spitballs, grinned at
each other. He studied them, very serious and uncomfortable. Why couldn't he be like them, live without worries,
make friends, have relatives who cared about him? He
closed his eyes and sat there for a long time, thinking about
Chiclayo, about his Aunt Adelina, about the happy impatience with which he had waited for the coming of
summer when he was little. Then he stood up and headed
for his house with lagging steps.

A block before he got there, his heart turned over: the
blue car was parked in front of the house. Had he lost track
of the time? He asked a passing stranger what time it was.
It was only eleven o'clock. His father never came home before one. He walked faster. As he reached the doorway he
could hear his parents' voices. They were arguing. I'll tell
them a streetcar got derailed, he thought as he rang the
doorbell, I'll say I had to walk from Old Magdalena.

His father opened the door for him. He was smiling, and
there was not the least sign of anger in his eyes. To his
amazement, his father gave him a cordial slap on the arm

and said, almost joyfully, "Ah, so you're here at last. Your mother and I were just talking about you. Come in, come in."

He felt calmer then and his face immediately broke into that stupid, helpless, impersonal smile that constituted his best defense. His mother was in the living room. She embraced him tenderly and he felt ill at ease: her effusiveness could change his father's good humor. During the last few months he had been forced to act as a judge or witness in the family squabbles. It was humiliating, horrible. He had to answer yes to all the belligerent questions his father hurled at him, although they were made up of grave accusations against his mother: waste, carelessness, incompetence, whoring. What would he have to testify about this time?

"Look," his father said amiably. "On the table. There's something I brought for you."

He turned his eyes. The cover of the pamphlet showed the blurred front of a large building, and below it there was a sentence in capital letters: "The Leoncio Prado Academy is not just a gateway to a military career." He picked it up and began to glance through it with a stunned expression on his face. It had pictures of soccer fields, a gleaming swimming pool, a mess hall, and some empty barracks, all of them clean and orderly. The center spread was a color photograph showing a formation of perfect ranks marching past a reviewing stand.

"Doesn't it look great?" his father asked. His voice was still cordial, but he knew that voice so well by now that he could detect the slight change of tone in it, a change that suggested a warning.

"Yes," he said quickly, "it looks great."

"Of course it does!" his father said. He paused for a moment, then turned to his wife. "You see? I told you he'd be the first one to agree."

"I don't like it," she said in a weak voice. And without looking at her son she added, "If you want to go there, do what you think is best. But don't ask me for my opinion. I'm not in favor of your going to a military school."

He looked up. "To be a cadet in a military school?" His eyes were shining. "But that'd be great, mamma, I'd like that a lot."

"Ah, these women," his father said. "They're all alike. Stupid and sentimental. They never understand anything. Go ahead, son, explain to this woman that the best thing you could do is to go to a military school."

"He doesn't even know what it's like," she murmured.

"Yes, I do," he said excitedly. "It's the best thing for me. I've always told you I wanted to be a cadet. My father's right."

"Look, son," his father said, "your mother thinks you're a dumbbell who can't make up his own mind. Now do you see all the harm she's done you?"

"It'll be wonderful," the boy said. "Wonderful."

"All right," his mother said. "If we can't discuss it, I'll just keep my mouth shut. But I want you to know I don't like it."

"I didn't ask your opinion," her husband said. "I'll settle these matters myself. I was simply telling you what I've decided."

She stood up and left the room. His father calmed down at once. "You've got two months to get ready," he said. "The entrance exams aren't going to be easy, but you're not an imbecile, you can pass them without any trouble. Isn't that right?"

"I'll study hard. I'll do everything I can to get in."

"That's the way," his father said. "I'll enroll you in the Leoncio Prado and I'll buy you the sample exams. I suppose it'll cost me a lot of money, but it's worth it. It's for your own good. They'll make a man out of you. They'll give you a strong body, a strong personality. I wish to God I'd had someone to worry about my future the way I do about yours."

"Yes. Thank you. Thank you very much. . ." And after
hesitating a moment, he added for the first time, "Papa."

"You can go to the movies after lunch," his father said.
"I'll advance you ten soles on your allowance."

Skimpy feels unhappy on Saturdays. Before, it was different. She went out with us on the field exercises, racing
around and jumping and barking when she heard the shots
whistling over her head, she was everywhere at once, she
got more excited than she ever did on other days. But after
she became my pet she wasn't the same. She began acting
strange on Saturdays, she stuck to me like a leech, walking
right beside me, licking me and glancing up with her big
wet eyes. I noticed a good while ago that when I come in
from the field exercises and go to take a shower, or after I
finish showering and come back into the barracks to put on
my dress uniform, she crawls under my bunk and starts
whining very softly, she knows I'm going out on pass. And
she's still whining when we fall in, and she follows me with
her head bowed down, you'd think she was a soul in torment.
She stops at the main gate of the Academy and raises her
head to look at me, and even when I'm a good way off,
even when I'm as far as Palmeras Avenue, I know she's still
there at the gate, looking down the road, waiting. I don't
know why but she never tries to follow me out of the
Academy, though nobody's ever told her to stay in, I guess
it's some sort of idea she's got, like a penance or something,
that's a queer thing too. And when I come back on Sunday
night, she's always there at the gate, excited, whining, running back and forth among the cadets as they enter, sniffing
at everybody, and I know she can tell me from a distance
because I can hear her running over to me, barking and
wagging her tail, and the minute she reaches me she jumps
up and down and her whole body quivers with joy. She's a
faithful dog and I'm sorry now that I hurt her. I haven't
always treated her right, lots of times I've made her suffer

just because I was feeling bad or wanted to have some fun. But Skimpy never got mad at me, it seemed as if she even enjoyed it, perhaps she thought I was showing her how much I liked her. "Jump, Skimpy, come on, don't be afraid," and the poor dog, up there on the locker, kept growling and barking and shivering, she was scared to be up there. "Come on, jump, Skimpy." But she wouldn't jump until I gave her a little push from behind, then she jumped to the floor with her hair standing on end. But it was only a joke, I didn't feel sorry for her and she didn't really mind doing it, even though it hurt her when she landed. What I did to her today was different, it wasn't any joke, I did it on purpose. But it was only partly my fault. Too many things've happened all of a sudden. That poor peasant Cava, what they did to him was enough to make anybody nervous, and then the Slave with a bullet in his head, no wonder we're all on edge. Besides all that, they shouldn't've made us wear our dark blue uniforms, not in this summer heat, we all sweated like pigs and felt sick to our stomachs. When'll they bring him out, what'll he look like, he's got to look different after all that time in the guardhouse, he must've lost weight, they've probably had him on bread and water, locked up all the time except when the officers grilled him, standing at attention in front of the colonel and the rest, I can almost hear the questions and the shouting, they must've thrown the book at him. He's a peasant, but so what, he took it like a man, he didn't say a word about anybody else, he told them the blame was all his: I did it, I stole the chemistry exam, nobody helped me, nobody knew about it, I broke the windowpane myself, it cut my hands, look at the scabs I've got. Then back to the guardhouse again, to wait for a soldier to hand in a meal through the peephole, I know what kind of meal it was, the same as they give to the soldiers. And to think what his father'll do when he goes back to the mountains and says, "They expelled me." His father must be really brutal, all the peasants are brutal, I had a friend at school who came from Puno and sometimes he came back to school with great big welts where his father hit him with a belt. That poor peasant Cava, he's had a bad time, I really feel sorry for him. I know I won't see him again. That's the way it is, we've been together for three whole years, almost, and now he'll go back to the mountains and won't ever study again, he'll just stay up there with the Indians and the llamas, he'll just be a stupid field hand. That's the worst thing about this Academy, if they expel you the time you spent here doesn't count, the bastards know how to screw you coming and going. The peasant's had some bad times all right, and the whole section thought the way I did when they had us standing in our blue uniforms out in the patio with the sun beating down on us. We waited and waited but nothing happened. Finally the lieutenants arrived in their flashiest uniforms, then the major who's in charge of the soldiers, then the colonel himself. What a horse's ass. So we all stood at attention. The lieutenants saluted him, we shivered in our boots, and he started yapping at us. We didn't even dare cough, but it wasn't only that, they scared us but we also felt sad, especially those of us in the section, we knew we'd be seeing a guy who'd lived with us such a long time, a guy we'd seen dressed and undressed, a guy who'd turned out to be okay, who'd done so many things with us, you'd need to have a heart of stone not to feel sad about it. The colonel talked to us in that fairy voice of his, he was white with anger and he said awful things about the peasant, the section, the Year, everybody, and I began to realize that Skimpy was chewing at my shoes. Go away, Skimpy, get out of here, you mangy bitch, go chew the colonel's shoelaces, don't take advantage of me now. And I couldn't even give her a kick so she'd go away, Lt. Huarina and the noncom Morte were standing at attention less than a yard away from me and they'd know it if I even took a deep breath, stop that, you bitch, don't take advantage of me, but I never saw her so stubborn, she worked and worked at my shoelace until it broke and I could feel how my foot was loose inside my shoe. She was having a grand time, why don't you go away, Skimpy, you're to blame for everything. Instead of keeping still she began to chew at my other shoe, as if she understood I couldn't move a fraction of an inch, couldn't say anything, couldn't even give her a dirty look. Then they brought out the peasant Cava. He was between two soldiers, as if they were taking him out to shoot him, and his face was very pale. I could feel my stomach churning, and something bitter rose up in my throat. The peasant looked yellowish, he was marching between the two soldiers and they were peasants too, all three had the same appearance, they looked like triplets except Cava's face was yellowish. They came across the parade ground and everybody watched them. They turned and started marking time in front of the battalion, a few yards from the colonel and the lieutenants. I wondered why they went on marking time, then I realized the soldiers didn't know what to do in front of the officers and nobody remembered to give them the command to halt. Finally Gamboa stepped forward and made a gesture with his hand and the three of them halted. The soldiers moved back and left Cava there in front of us all alone and he didn't dare look at anybody, don't take it so hard, buddy, the Circle's with you, someday we'll get revenge for you. I told myself, now he'll start crying, don't cry, peasant, don't give those shits that satisfaction, stand up straight, don't tremble, show them what a man is. Just be calm, it won't take long, smile a little if you can, you'll see how it burns them up. I had a feeling the whole section was a volcano just waiting to erupt. The colonel was talking again, squeaking things at the peasant to lower his morale, you have to have a twisted mind to make a guy suffer any more after they'd already punished him so much. The colonel gave him advice we could all hear, he told him to let this teach him a lesson, he even talked about the life of Leoncio Prado, how the hero said to the Chileans when they were going to execute him, "I wish to command the firing squad myself," what a stupid fart. Then the bugle sounded and the Piranha went up to the peasant with his jaws working the way they do, and I thought, I'm going to cry with rage, and that damned Skimpy kept worrying my shoe and the cuff of my pants, I'll get even with you, you bitch, you're going to be sorry. Don't break down now, peasant, this next part's the worst but then you can get out of here, no more officers, no more confinements, no more guard duty. The peasant stayed motionless but he kept on getting paler, his skin's dark but his face was turning white, even from a distance you could see how his chin was trembling. But he didn't break down. He didn't step back or start crying when the Piranha ripped the insignias off his cap and his lapels, then the emblem off his breast pocket, he left him in rags, and the bugle sounded again and the two soldiers got on either side of him and marched him away. The peasant could hardly lift up his feet. They crossed the parade ground and I had to twist my eyes to see them as they went away. The poor guy couldn't keep in step, he just stumbled along, and every now and then he'd look down, I guess to see the way they wrecked his uniform. The soldiers lifted their feet smartly to make the colonel notice them. Then the wall hid them and I thought, you wait, Skimpy, keep on chewing my pants, your turn comes next, I'm going to pay you back, and they still didn't tell us to fall out because the colonel was talking about the heroes again. You must be outside by now, peasant, waiting for the bus, looking at the Academy for the last time, don't forget about us, and even if you do, the Circle's still here to get even for you. And you aren't a cadet any more, just another civilian, you can walk up to a lieutenant or a captain without saluting him, you don't have to step out of his way or give him your seat. Come on, Skimpy, why don't you jump up and bite my tie or my nose, do anything you want, make yourself right at home. The heat was terrible and the colonel kept on talking.

When Alberto left his house it was already beginning to grow dark, even though it was only six o'clock. He had taken at least half an hour to get ready, polishing his shoes, combing his hair, knotting his tie. He had even used his father's razor to shave off the thin fuzz on his upper lip and below his sideburns. He walked down to the corner of Ocharán and Juan Fanning, then whistled. A moment later Emilio appeared at the window. He too was all dressed up.

"It's six," Alberto said. "Hurry up."

"Two minutes."

Alberto looked at his watch, inspected the crease in his trousers, rearranged the handkerchief in his breast pocket, and stole a look at his reflection in a windowpane. The pomade had done its job, not a hair was out of place.

Emilio came out the side door. "The living room's full of people," he told Alberto. "There was a luncheon. God, it was awful. Everybody's drunk now, the house smells of whisky from top to bottom. My father's so drunk he won't listen to me. I tried to get my allowance but he wouldn't stop clowning."

"I've got some money," Alberto said. "Do you want me to lend you part of it?"

"If we go someplace, I'll need it. But if we stay in the park, never mind. Look, what do you have to do to get your allowance? Hasn't your old man seen your report card?"

"Not yet. Just my mother. But when he sees it, he's going to blow up. It's the first time they've flunked me in three courses. I'll have to study all summer. I'll hardly get out to the beach at all. But I'd rather not think about it. And anyway, he might not get mad. They're having a big fight at home."

"What happened?"

"My father didn't come home last night. He showed up this morning, all shaved and showered. He's really something."

"He's a killer, all right," Emilio agreed. "He's got rafts of women. What'd your mother say?"

"She threw an ash tray at him. Then she started wailing at the top of her voice. The whole neighborhood must've heard her."

They walked down Juan Fanning toward Larco. When they passed the little store where the Japanese sold fruit juices, he waved his hand to them; a few years before, they used to go there after the soccer games. The street lights had just come on, but the sidewalks were still shadowy because the leaves and branches of the trees blocked off the light. As they crossed Colón they both looked at Laura's house. The neighborhood girls usually gathered there before going to Salazar Park, but they had not arrived yet and the living room windows were dark.

"Maybe they went to Matilde's house," Emilio said. "Pluto and Babe went there after lunch." He chuckled. "That Babe must be out of his mind to go to Quinta de los Pinos, and on a Sunday, too. If Matilde's parents hadn't been around, those bullies would've given him a real beating. And Pluto too, even though he didn't have anything to do with it."

Alberto laughed. "He's crazy about her," he said. "Head over heels in love."

Quinta de los Pinos was a long way from the neighborhood, on the other side of Larco Avenue, beyond the main park, near the streetcar tracks to Chorrillos. A few years earlier, Quinta was enemy territory, but things had changed and the neighborhoods no longer had impassable boundaries. The outsiders strolled along Colón, Ocharán and Porta, visited the girls, courted them, went to their parties, took them to the movies. As a result, the neighborhood boys had to find girl friends in other places. At the beginning, they went in groups of eight or ten to explore the closest neighborhoods in Miraflores, such as the 28th of July and Francia Street; then the more distant ones, such as Angamos and Grau Avenue. (This last was where Susuki, the rear admiral's daughter, lived.) Some of them found girl friends in these other neighborhoods, and became part of them, though with-

out renouncing their loyalty to Diego Ferré. In a few of the
neighborhoods they ran into opposition: ridicule and sarcasm from the boys, rebuffs from the girls. But in Quinta de
los Pinos the hostility of the local boys turned into violence.
When Babe started going around with Matilde, they attacked him one night and doused him with buckets of water.
Nevertheless, Babe kept on going there and other boys from
the neighborhood went with him, because Matilde was not
the only girl in Quinta without a boy friend: there were
also Graciela and Molly.

"Look, there they are," Emilio said.

"No. Are you blind? That's the García girls."

They were on Larco Avenue, about twenty yards from the
park. The traffic moved slowly toward the park, turned on
itself in front of the esplanade, disappeared in the mass of
parked cars, and emerged, in lesser numbers, on the other
side; then it turned and went down Larco Avenue in the
opposite direction. Some of the cars had their radios on, and
Alberto and Emilio could hear dance music and a torrent
of young voices and laughter. The sidewalks where Larco
bordered Salazar Park were crowded. But none of this caught
their attention. The magnet that attracted the teen-agers of
Miraflores to Salazar Park had been at work for a long time.
They were not strangers in that crowd, they were part of it:
well-dressed, clean-smelling, happy, at home. They looked
around them and saw smiling faces, heard voices speaking a
language that was their own. These were the same faces they
had seen a thousand times around the swimming pool at the
Terrazas Club, on the Miraflores beach, in the Herradura,
at the Regatta Club, in the Ricardo Palma and Leuro and
Monte Carlo movie theaters; the same faces they saw at the
Saturday night parties. But they were not only familiar with
the looks and mannerisms of the young people who were
arriving like them for their dates in Salazar Park: they also
knew all about their lives, their problems, and ambitions.
They knew that Tony was unhappy, even though his father

gave him a sports car for Christmas, because Anita Men-
dizábal, the girl he was in love with, was a sly little flirt,
everybody in Miraflores could see it in her green eyes behind
the shadow of her long silken lashes. They knew that Vicky
and Manolo, who had just gone by them hand in hand, had
not been going together for very long, a week or ten days.
They knew that Paquito suffered because he was the laugh-
ingstock of Miraflores, what with his boils and his hunched
back. They knew that Sonia was leaving the next day for a
foreign country, perhaps for a long time, because her father
had been appointed ambassador, and that she was unhappy
about leaving her school and her friends and her riding
lessons. Moreover, Alberto and Emilio knew that they were
bound to that crowd by mutual ties: the others knew all
about both of them. In their absence, the others discussed
their romantic successes or failures, analyzed their love
affairs, talked them over when making out a list of those to
be invited to a party. In fact, Vicky and Manolo had been
talking about Alberto at the very moment they passed them.
"Did you see Alberto? Helena finally said she'd go around
with him, after turning him down five times. That was just
last week. And now she's going to break it off. Poor Alberto."

The park was full. Alberto and Emilio walked along the
low fence that enclosed the smooth green squares of grass.
There was a pool in the center, with red and golden fish and
a yellow-brown monument. Their expressions had changed:
they parted their lips, their eyes glowed and wandered, and
their smiles were exactly like all the smiles they saw. There
were several groups of outsiders leaning against the wall of
the Malecón, watching the crowd as it circled around the
squares. It was divided into two lines, moving in opposite
directions. The couples greeted each other with a nod that
did not alter their fixed half-smiles, a quick mechanical
motion that was more a sign of recognition than a greeting,
a sort of password. Alberto and Emilio took two turns around
the park, observing their friends, their acquaintances, and

the outsiders that had come from Lima and Magdalena and Chorrillos to look at the girls, who must have reminded them of movie stars. The outsiders tossed phrases toward the crowd, fishhooks they dangled among the shoals of girls.

"They haven't come yet," Emilio said. "What time is it?"

"Seven. But probably they're here and we just haven't seen them. Laura told me this morning they were coming no matter what. She said she was going to get Helena."

"She's stood you up. It wouldn't be the first time. Helena seems to love to do you dirt."

"Not now," Alberto said. "That was before. Now that she's going with me, it's different."

They took a few more turns, anxiously looking all around but without discovering them. They did see several couples from the neighborhood: Babe and Matilde, Tico and Graciela, Pluto and Molly.

"Something's happened," Alberto said. "They ought to be here by now."

"If they show up, you can go meet them alone," Emilio said in a peevish voice. "I don't stand for this sort of thing. I've got a little pride."

"Probably it isn't their fault. Their parents wouldn't let them out, or . . ."

"Baloney. When a girl wants to get out, she gets out, even if the world comes to an end."

They continued walking, silent, smoking one cigarette after another. A half hour later, Pluto signaled to them. "There they are," he said, pointing to the corner. "What are you waiting for?" Alberto hurried off in that direction, pushing his way through the couples. Emilio followed him, muttering under his breath. The girls were not alone, of course: a circle of outsiders surrounded them. "Excuse me," Alberto said, and the boys moved away without putting up any argument. A few moments later, Emilio and Laura, Alberto and Helena, were strolling slowly around the squares, hand in hand.

"I was afraid you weren't coming."

"I couldn't get out sooner. My mother was alone and I had to wait till my sister came back from the movies. And I can't stay very long. I've got to be home by eight."

"By eight? But it's already seven-thirty."

"No, not yet, it's only a quarter past."

"That's just about the same."

"What's the matter? Are you in a bad mood?"

"No. But try to understand my situation, Helena. It's pretty awful."

"What's pretty awful? I don't know what you're getting at."

"I mean the situation between you and me. We're hardly ever together."

"You see? I told you this was going to happen. That's why I didn't want to go around with you."

"But that hasn't got anything to do with it. If we're going together, it's only natural we should see each other a little. Before you became my girl friend, they used to let you go out like the other girls. But now they shut you in as if you were a baby. I think Inés is to blame."

"Don't say anything against my sister. I don't like people to talk about my family."

"I'm not talking about your family, but your sister isn't any too likable. I know she hates me."

"You? She doesn't even know your last name."

"That's what you think. Every time I see her at the Terrazas Club I say hello and she doesn't answer, but then I catch her watching me on the sly."

"Perhaps you're in love with her."

"Will you please stop needling me? What's the matter?"

"Nothing."

Alberto squeezed her hand and looked into her eyes. She seemed very serious. "Try to understand me, Helena. Why are you acting like this?"

"Like what?" she asked him curtly.

"I don't know. It's just that sometimes I think you don't like to be with me, and I'm more and more in love with you every day. That's why I get so desperate when I don't see you."

"I warned you at the beginning. Don't try to blame it on me."

"I've been following you around for over two years. And every time you turned me down, I thought: 'But someday she'll pay attention to me, and then I'll forget all this.' But now it's even worse. At least I used to see you all the time."

"Do you want to know something? I don't like you to speak to me like that."

"You don't like me to speak to you how?"

"I mean, saying what you did. You ought to have some pride. You shouldn't beg."

"I'm not begging. I'm telling you the truth. Aren't you my girl friend? Why do you want me to be proud?"

"I'm not saying it for my sake, only for yours."

"I'm the way I am. I can't change now."

"Oh? So that's that."

He squeezed her hand again and tried to meet her eyes, but this time she avoided his look. She seemed even more serious.

"Let's not fight," Alberto said. "We see each other so little."

"I've got to tell you something," she said.

"All right. What?"

"I've been thinking."

"About what, Helena?"

"I've been thinking it would be much better if we were simply friends."

"Friends? Are you trying to pick a fight? On account of what I told you? Don't be silly, Helena. Just forget everything I've told you."

"No, it isn't that. I was thinking about it before. We ought to go back to the way we were. We're very different, you know."

"I don't care about that. I'm in love with you, no matter how you are."

"But I'm not in love with you. I've thought it all over, and I'm not."

"Oh," Alberto said. "Well, all right, then."

They continued to walk slowly around, forgetting they were still holding hands. They went on for another twenty yards, without speaking, without looking at each other. As they went by the pool, she loosened her fingers in his hand, but gently, as if she were just making a suggestion. He understood and let go. But they kept on walking together, completely around the park, looking at the couples who came in the opposite direction and nodding to their acquaintances. When they reached Larco Avenue, they stopped and turned face to face.

"You've really thought it over?" Alberto asked.

"Yes," she said. "Yes, I believe I have."

"In that case, there's nothing to say."

She nodded, and smiled for an instant, but then she was serious again. He reached out to shake hands. She took his hand and said, "But we'll go on being friends, won't we?" There was a note of relief in her voice.

"Of course," he said. "Of course we will."

Alberto walked away, through the labyrinth of parked cars. When he reached Diego Ferré, he found it was empty, and he walked down the middle of the street. As he reached Colón he heard somebody running up behind him. A voice called his name. He turned around. It was Babe.

"What're you doing here?" Alberto asked. "And where's Matilde?"

"She left. She had to be home early." He patted Alberto on the shoulder. There was a friendly, even brotherly, expression on his face. "I'm sorry about Helena," he said. "But you're better off. That girl isn't right for you."

"How did you know? We just got through fighting."

"I knew last night. We all did. But nobody wanted to tell you ahead of time."

"Never mind the double talk. Say what you mean."

"You won't get sore at me?"

"No, man, tell me."

"Well. . .look, Helena's in love with Richard."

"Richard?"

"You know, the guy from San Isidro."

"Who told you?"

"Nobody. But everybody knows. They were at Nati's last night."

"You mean the party at Nati's house? Don't lie to me. Helena didn't go."

"Yes, she did. That's what we didn't want to tell you."

"She told me she wasn't going."

"Sure she did. Believe me, she isn't right for you."

"But you really saw her?"

"We all saw her. And she danced with Richard the whole time. Ana went over and asked her, 'Have you broken up with Alberto?' and she said, 'No, but I'll get rid of him to-morrow.' Don't get sore at me for telling you."

"Bah," Alberto said. "I don't give a damn. I was getting tired of her anyway."

"Fine!" Babe said, patting his shoulder again. "That's just what I wanted to hear. Go out and get yourself another girl friend. That's the best way to even things up." He thought for a moment, then smiled. "Say, what about Nati? She's terrific! And right now she hasn't got a boy friend."

"Well, maybe," Alberto said. "It isn't a bad idea."

They walked down the second block of Diego Ferré, and Alberto said good night at the door of his house. Babe patted his shoulder once more, to show that he understood. Alberto went directly upstairs to his room. The light was on, and his father was standing in the middle of the room with the report card in his hand. His mother was sitting on the bed, looking more worried than usual.

"Hello," Alberto said.

"Hello, son," his father said. He looked as dapper as ever. A dark suit, a clean shave, a fresh haircut, everything right.

He tried to appear stern, but his look softened as he took in his son's gleaming shoes, his neat tie, the snow-white handkerchief in his breast pocket, his well-kept hands, the cuffs of his shirt, the crease in his trousers. He examined him with a restless, ambiguous, complacent look, and then his expression recovered its assumed hardness.

"I left early," Alberto said. "I've got a headache."

"You must be coming down with a cold," his mother said. "You'd better go straight to bed, Albertito."

"But first we're going to have a little talk, young man," his father said, shaking the report card at him. "I've just finished looking at this."

"I didn't do too well in some subjects," Alberto said. "But the important thing is, I got through the year."

"Be quiet," his father said. "Don't talk like a fool. This has never happened in my family. I've never been more ashamed. Do you know how long we've taken first place in school, in the University, everywhere? For two hundred years! If your grandfather could see this report card, he'd die on the spot."

"And what about *my* family?" his wife asked him. "They were somebodies too. My father was in the Cabinet twice!"

"But that's all over with," he went on, ignoring her. "It's scandalous. I'm not going to let you drag my name in the mud. Tomorrow morning you begin studying with a private tutor to get ready for the entrance exams."

"What entrance exams?" Alberto asked.

"For the Leoncio Prado. It'll do you good."

"The Military Academy?" Alberto looked at him incredulously.

"I'm not so very sure about that Academy," his mother said. "He might get sick. It's awfully damp in La Perla."

"And you don't mind sending me to a school full of half-breeds?" Alberto asked.

"No," his father said. "It's the only way to straighten you out. You can get your own way with the priests, but not with the military. Besides, we've always been very democratic in my family. And in any case, a gentleman is a gentleman wherever he is. Go to bed now, and tomorrow you start studying. Good night."

"Where are you going?" his wife asked him, alarmed.

"I've got a very urgent appointment. But don't worry. I'll be home early."

"What a life I have," she sighed, lowering her head.

But when we fell out I put on a little act. Come here, Skimpy, come here, old girl, what a good dog you are, come here. And she came to me. It was all her fault, for trusting me, if she'd run away from me it wouldn't've happened. I'm sorry about it now, but when I went to the mess hall I was still furious, I didn't give a damn that she was out there on the grass with her leg all twisted to hell. I'm almost sure she's going to end up a cripple. It would've been better if she'd bled, that kind of injury heals, the skin closes up and there's nothing left but a scar. But she didn't bleed. She didn't bark either. The truth is, I held her muzzle with one hand while I twisted her leg with the other, the way that poor peasant Cava twisted the chicken's neck. It hurt her, I could tell from her eyes it was hurting her, take that, you bitch, you'll learn not to bother me when I'm in a formation, don't forget I'm your master, not your half-breed servant, don't chew my shoes when there're officers out front. She trembled, but silently, and it wasn't until I let her go that I realized what I'd done to her, she couldn't stand up, she collapsed and her leg was crooked, she got up and fell down, got up and fell down, and she began to howl softly and I felt like punishing her some more. But in the afternoon I felt sorry for her when I came back from the classroom building and saw her lying motionless on the grass in the same place I left her in the morning. I told her, "Come here, you good-for-nothing mongrel, come here and beg my pardon." She got up and fell down, got up and fell down, and finally she managed to hobble over to me on three legs, and what howls she let out, it must've hurt an awful lot. I've wrecked her, she's going to be a cripple the rest of her life. I really felt bad about it, I picked her up and tried to straighten her leg but that just made her shriek, I told myself there's something broken, better not to touch it. Skimpy doesn't carry grudges, she still lapped my hand and rested in my arms, and I scratched her neck and her belly. But as soon as I put her down to make her walk she collapsed again or only took a couple of hops, it was hard for her to keep her balance on only three legs, and she was howling again, I could tell how her leg hurt her whenever she tried to walk. The peasant Cava never liked Skimpy, he detested her. Sometimes I caught him throwing stones at her, or giving her a kick when he thought I wasn't looking. The peasants are all hypocrites and sneaks, and Cava was all peasant that way. My brother always says if you want to know if somebody's a peasant, look him in the eyes, you'll see he can't take it, he'll look away. My brother knows all about them, he used to be a truck driver. When I was little I wanted to be a truck driver like him. He went up into the mountains, as far as Ayacucho, twice a week, and came back the next day, this was for years, and I don't remember a single time when he didn't come back cursing the peasants. He'd have some drinks up there and then there'd be trouble. He said he was drunk when they jumped him that time, and it must be the truth, I can't believe they could've made such a mess of him if he'd been sober. One day I'll go up to Huancayo, I know who they were, I'll pay them back for what they did to him. "Look," the policeman said, "does the Valdivieso family live here?" "Yes," I said, "if you mean the family of Ricardo Valdivieso," and I remember my mother dragged me out of the way by the hair, she was startled, she looked suspiciously at the cop and said, "There's lots of Ricardo Valdiviesos in the world, we don't have to take the blame for what other people do, we're poor but honest, Señor, you don't want to pay attention to what the baby says." But I was ten years old, I wasn't any baby.

The cop laughed and said, "It isn't that Ricardo Valdivieso did anything, it's what they did to him. He's in a ward at the Public Aid, all sliced up. They knifed him from head to foot and he said to tell his family." "Go see how much money I've got left in that jar," my mother told me, "we'll have to take him some oranges." We were happy to buy the fruit for him, but we couldn't even give it to him, he was bandaged all over, you couldn't see anything but his eyes. The same policeman chatted with us there, he said, "What a brute! Do you know where he got knifed, Señora? In Huancayo. And do you know where he was picked up? Near Chosica. What a brute! He got into his truck and started for Lima as fast as he could. When they found him near Chosica, off the road, he'd fallen asleep on the steering wheel, more on account of the liquor than his wounds. And if you could see how that truck was, all sticky inside from the blood that poured out of the brute along the way. Excuse me for saying it, Señora, but I've never seen a brute like this one. Do you know what the doctor told him? He said, 'You're still drunk, man, you haven't come from Huancayo, not in that condition, you'd've died before you got half way here, they slashed you thirty times.' " And my mother said, "Yes, Señor, his father was the same, one time they brought him home half dead, he could hardly talk but he made me go out and buy him some more pisco, and he couldn't raise his arms so I had to hold the bottle to his lips myself, you can see what kind of a family it is. Ricardo turned out like his father, worse luck. Someday he'll go away like his father and we'll never know where he is or what he's doing. But the father of this one"—and she pointed to me—"was the quiet type, a homebody, just the opposite of the other. He came straight home from work, and at the end of the week he handed me his whole pay envelope, I gave him enough money for his cigarettes and his bus fare and I kept the rest. He was completely different from the other one, Señor, he hardly ever drank at all. But my oldest son, the one in the bandages, he had some kind of a grudge against him, and he gave him some very bad times. When Ricardo was late getting home, this was before he was full grown, my poor partner started shivering, he knew this brute was going to come in drunk and shout, 'Where is he, where's that guy that says he's my step-father? I want to have a little talk with him.' And my poor partner hid in the kitchen until Ricardo found him and chased him all around the house. It got so bad that *he* left me too. But at least he had a good reason." The cop almost died laughing and my brother Ricardo stirred in the bed. He was furious because he couldn't open his mouth to tell his mother to shut up and not put him in such a bad light. My mother gave the cop an orange and we took the rest of them home with us. And when Ricardo got well he told me, "Always watch out for the peasants, they're the sneakiest people in the world. They never stand up in front of you, they always do everything on the sly, behind your back. They waited till I was good and drunk, on the pisco they offered me themselves, before they jumped me. And now that I've lost my job, I can't go back to Huancayo and get even with them." That's why I've always hated the peasants. There weren't very many of them at my school, maybe two or three, and they'd learned to behave like us. But how sick I felt when I saw all the peasants they've got here at the Academy. There's more of them than there is of us from the coast. You'd think everybody in the Andes came down here, we've got peasants from Ayacucho, Puno, Cuzco, Huancayo, every damned one a complete peasant like poor Cava. We've got other ones besides him in the section but he was the one you could pick out the easiest. What hair! I don't understand how a man can have such stiff hair. I know he was ashamed of it. He tried to plaster it down, he bought God knows what kind of hair grease and smeared it on his head so his hair wouldn't stand up, his arm used to ache from rubbing in the rancid pig fat or whatever it was and from so much combing. And just when it looked like he had it all flat and smooth, pop! a hair stood up, and another, and fifty, and a thousand, especially next to his ears, that's where the peasants have hair like needles, also on the back of the head. Cava almost went crazy because they made so much fun about his hair and that stuff he used on it, I never smelled anything so rotten. I'll never forget the way they kidded him the time he came out with his hair slicked down and they all got around him and started counting, one, two, three, four, as loud as they could, and before we got to ten a few hairs were already standing up, his face turned green and the hairs kept popping up one after the other and before we counted fifty it looked like he was wearing a spiked helmet. That's what bothers the peasants the most, their hair, but Cava's the worst off, I never saw hair like that on anybody, you can hardly see his forehead, it grows right up from his eyebrows, it must be uncomfortable, like a wig, I know how I'd feel if I didn't have any forehead. One time they found him shaving his forehead with a razor, I think it was Vallano that found him, he ran into the barracks and said, "Come on, that peasant Cava's shaving the hair off his forehead, it's something worth seeing." We all ran to the washroom in the classroom building, because he'd gone over there so nobody'd catch him, and there was the peasant with shaving cream on his forehead instead of his cheeks, being extra careful with the razor so he wouldn't cut himself, and what fun we made of him. He got so mad at us he almost went out of his mind, that was the time he started a fight with the Negro Vallano, right there in the washroom. But the Negro was stronger than he was, he gave him an awful beating, and the Jaguar said, "Look, you're so anxious to get rid of your hair, we want to help you." I don't think he did right, the peasant was in the Circle, but the Jaguar never loses a chance to screw somebody. And the Negro Vallano was still full of life despite the fight, he was the first one to grab the peasant, then I did, and when we had a good hold on him the Jaguar started using the lather that was still on the brush, he lathered his forehead and about half of his head, then he began shaving him. Stay still, peasant, the razor's going to cut your scalp if you keep moving your head. The peasant flexed his muscles under my arms, but he couldn't move, all he could do was look daggers at the Jaguar. And the Jaguar went on scraping and scraping, he shaved off half his hair, what a laugh we got. Then the peasant stayed still and the Jaguar wiped off the lather with all that hair in it and suddenly he clapped his hand over the peasant's mouth. "Eat it, peasant, don't be so fussy, it's delicious, eat it." And how we laughed when he got up and ran to look at himself in the mirror. And I don't think I've ever laughed so hard in all my life as I did when I saw Cava walking ahead of us across the parade ground with half of his head shaved and the other half with that stiff black hair of his. The Poet saw him and started jumping up and down. "Here's the last of the Mohicans," he shouted, "we'd better call out the troops," and everybody came over and the peasant was surrounded by cadets, all of them laughing and pointing at him, and when he got to the patio two of the noncoms saw him and started laughing as hard as the cadets and the only thing the peasant could do was smile. Later, when we fell in, Lt. Huarina said, "What's the matter with you crazy shits, what are you laughing about? Brigadiers, come here." The brigadiers said, "It's nothing, Sir, all are present and accounted for," but one of the noncoms said, "There's a cadet in the first section with half his hair shaved off," and Huarina said, "Front and center, Cadet." We couldn't help laughing out loud when the peasant Cava came to attention in front of Huarina, the lieutenant told him, "Take off your cap," and he took it off. "Silence," Huarina shouted, "you're at attention, stop that laughing!" But we could see how his lips turned up at the corners when he looked at Cava's head. "What's been going on?" "Nothing, Lieutenant." "What do you mean, nothing, do you think the Academy is a circus?" "No, Lieutenant." "Then why's your head like that?" "I shaved it on account of the hot weather, Sir." Huarina laughed and said, "You're a cute little whore but this Academy isn't a whorehouse, go to the barbershop and get the rest of it cut off, you're confined until you look decent again." The poor peasant, he wasn't a bad guy, after that we got along fine. I didn't like him at the start, just because he was a peasant, I remembered what they did to my brother Ricardo, and I used to give him a bad time. When the Circle had a meeting and we rolled the dice to see who'd go and get even with somebody in the Fourth, if it turned out to be Cava I said we'd better pick somebody else, they'll catch him and then they'll murder us. And the peasant didn't say a word. Later, when they broke up the Circle and the Jaguar said, "The Circle's all finished but we can start another one if you want to, just with the four of us," I said yes but without any peasants, the peasants are cowards, and the Jaguar said, "We'll take care of that right now, we've got to be able to trust each other." He called Cava over and said, "The Boa tells us you're a coward, he doesn't want you in the Circle, you'll have to show him he's wrong." The peasant said all right. That evening the four of us went out to the stadium, taking off our insignias so we could get past the Fourth and Fifth, if they knew we were Dogs they'd grab us and make us work in their barracks. We reached the stadium without any trouble and the Jaguar said, "Okay, go ahead and fight, but don't shout or anything, the Fourth and Fifth're in their barracks, the sons of bitches'll hear you." And Curly said, "They'd better take off their shirts, they might get torn and there's a clothing inspection tomorrow." So we took off our shirts and the Jaguar said, "Start whenever you want." I was sure the peasant couldn't beat me, but I didn't know he could take so much punishment. That's another thing about the peasants, they can really take a lot. It's hard to believe, they're so short, but they really can. And Cava's as short as the rest of them, but he's solid as a rock. He hasn't got a body like us, he's almost square, and when you hit him it's as if he doesn't feel it, he can take almost anything. But he's a real brute, a real peasant, he grabbed my throat and my waist, it was hard to get loose, I pounded his back and his head and pushed him away but he came charging in again, just like a bull, he could really take it and then some. And it was pitiful to see how clumsy he was. I knew about that, the peasants don't know how to use their feet. The place they really know how is in Callao, they're better with their feet than they are with their hands, but it isn't so easy, you jump at the other guy's face with both of your feet. The peasants just use their two hands, they don't even know how to butt like the coast people, though God knows their heads are hard enough. I think the guys from Callao are the best fighters in the whole world. The Jaguar says he's from Bellavista but I don't believe it, he's from Callao, and anyway they aren't far apart. I've never seen anybody so quick with his feet, also with his head. He doesn't use his hands when he's fighting, he just kicks and butts, I've never wanted to fight with the Jaguar. "Let's quit, peasant," I told him, and he said, "All right if you want to, but don't call me a coward." "Put your shirts on," Curly said, "and wipe your faces, somebody's coming, I think it's the noncoms." But it wasn't the noncoms, it was some cadets from the Fifth. Five of them. "Why haven't you got your caps on?" one of them asked us. "You're Dogs, or else you're from the Fourth, don't try to lie to us." And another one said, "Attention, Dogs! Come on, let's get their money and their cigarettes!" But I was so tired I didn't do anything when that character frisked me. Then the guy that was frisking Curly said, "Hey, look at this, he's loaded," and the Jaguar smiled the way he does, watch out, he said, "You think you're somebody just because you're in the Fifth," and one of them asked, "What's that Dog saying?" We couldn't see their faces because it was too dark. Then another one asked the Jaguar, "Would you care to repeat what you just said, Dog?" and the Jaguar said, "If you weren't in the Fifth, Cadet, you wouldn't dare steal our money and our cigarettes." The cadets laughed and said, "You're a real tough one, aren't you?" and the Jaguar said, "That's right, I'm as tough as they come, and I don't think you'd have the guts to put your hands in my pockets if we were out in the street." "Listen to him, listen to him," another one said, "did you hear what I did?" And another one said, "If you want, Cadet, I'll take off my insignias and I'll still put my hands where I like." "No, Cadet," the Jaguar said, "I don't think you've got the guts." "Well, we'll soon find out," the cadet said. He took off his jacket, and a few moments later the Jaguar had him down on the ground, beating the shit out of him, the guy said, "What're you waiting for, help me," so the rest of them piled onto the Jaguar. Curly said, "I can't let them get away with anything like that." I jumped onto the pile, what a crazy sort of fight, nobody could see anybody else, sometimes I felt as if I got hit by a rock and I figured that must be the Jaguar with his kicking. We kept at it till the whistle blew and then we all got up and started running. We were quite a mess, we took off our shirts in the barracks and all four of us were bruised and swollen, we almost died laughing. The whole section came crowding into the latrine, asking us what happened, and the Poet rubbed tooth paste on our faces to take down the swelling. A little later, the Jaguar said, "That was like an initiation for the new Circle." And after a while I went over to poor Cava's bunk and told him, "Look, we're friends from now on." And he just said, "Of course we are."

They drank their colas in silence. Paulino watched them with his evil eyes. Arana's father merely sipped from the bottle, and sometimes he sat with it halfway to his mouth, his eyes completely blank. Then he came to, shook his head, and took another sip. Alberto had to force himself to drink his cola, the gas upset his stomach. He avoided talking because he was afraid the man would start confiding in him again.

His eyes wandered everywhere. He could not see the vicuña, probably it was in the stadium. It always went as far away as it could when the cadets had free time, but when they were in the classrooms it sauntered around in the field. Arana's father paid for the colas and gave Paulino a tip. The classroom building was invisible because the lights around the parade ground had not been turned on yet and the fog was even thicker.

"Did he suffer much?" the man asked. "I mean on Saturday, when they brought him in."

"No, Señor. He wasn't conscious. They got him into a car on Progreso Avenue and took him straight to the infirmary."

"They didn't let us know till Saturday afternoon," the man said in a tired voice. "It was about five o'clock. They didn't give him a pass for about a month. His mother wanted to come out here to see him. They always punished him for one thing or another. Captain Garrido called us on the phone. It was pretty hard to take, believe me. We came as fast as we could, we almost had an accident on Costanera. And they wouldn't even let us get near him. That wouldn't happen in a hospital."

"You can take him to a hospital if you want. They can't stop you."

"I know. But the doctor says he can't be moved. His condition's serious, no doubt about it, why try to fool ourselves any more. And his mother's going crazy. She keeps talking about what happened on Friday. It isn't fair, but that's the way women are. They twist things all around. I know I've been strict with the boy, but only for his own good. And what happened on Friday was nothing, absolutely nothing. But she throws it in my face every ten minutes."

"Arana didn't say a word about it," Alberto said. "Even though he tells me all his problems."

"Believe me, it was absolutely nothing. He came home

for a few hours, on some sort of a pass, I don't know how he got it, and he'd hardly arrived when he wanted to leave the house again. That wasn't very considerate, was it?—coming home and then running out again. So I told him to stay with his mother, she was upset on account of his not getting any passes. And that's all there was to it. A mere nothing. But now she keeps telling me I crucified him. Do you think that's fair?"

"Your wife must be nervous," Alberto said. "That's natural enough. A thing like. . ."

"You're right," the man said. "But she refuses to rest. She spent the whole day in the infirmary, waiting for the doctor. And all for nothing. He hardly even talks to us. 'Just be patient, folks, we're doing all we can, we'll keep you informed.' But the captain must have a kind heart, he tries to cheer us up, but put yourself in our place. It doesn't seem possible that an accident like this could happen after three years of training."

"You can't tell," Alberto said. "I mean. . ."

"The captain explained the whole thing. I know all about it. You can say what you want about the army but at least they're frank, they call a spade a spade, they don't talk in circles."

"Did he tell you all the details?"

"Of course," the man said. "That's the way he is. But it made my hair stand on end. It seems the rifle jumped or something when my son pulled the trigger. Didn't they tell you about that? I think it's partly the Academy's fault. What kind of training do they give you?"

"The captain told you he fired the shot himself?"

"Well, he sort of skipped over that," the man said, "but even so, he shouldn't've said anything, my wife was there, you know how sensitive women are. But that's how it is in the army, they speak out. I wanted my son to be like that. And do you know what the captain told us? He told us that a soldier has to pay dearly for his mistakes. He said the rifle was examined by experts, it was in perfect condition, so the boy was to blame. I don't know. It may have been an accident. It's hard to tell. The army knows more about these things than I do, it's part of their job. Besides, what difference does it make now?"

"That's what the captain told you?"

"Yes." The man thought for a moment, then looked at Alberto. "Why?"

"Nothing. We didn't even see it. We were climbing the hill."

"Excuse me," Paulino said, "but I've got to close."

"Let's go back to the infirmary," the man said. "They might let me see him, at least for a couple of minutes."

They stood up, and Paulino nodded good-by. They went back across the field. Arana's father walked with his hands clasped behind him. He had raised the lapels of his coat. The Slave never talked to me about him, Alberto thought. Or about his mother either.

"Can I ask you a favor?" he said. "I'd like to see Arana for a moment. I don't mean now. Tomorrow, or the day after, when he's better. You could get me in by telling them I'm a relative or a friend of the family."

"Yes," the man said. "I'll see what I can do. I'll speak with Captain Garrido. He seems very accommodating. A little bit strict, like all the army men. But after all, he has to be."

"I know," Alberto said. "They're all like that."

"Let me tell you something," the man said. "My son resents me very much. I'm sure of it. I'm going to have a talk with him, and if he's got any brains at all he'll understand that everything I did was for his own good. I'll make him see that the ones to blame are his mother and that crazy old Adelina."

"She's his aunt, isn't she?" Alberto asked.

"Yes," the man said, furious now. "She's out of her mind. She brought him up like a girl. She gave him dolls to play with, she even curled his hair. They can't fool me, I've seen some pictures they took of him in Chiclayo. Just think of it, my own son with his hair curled, and wearing skirts. They took advantage of the fact I wasn't there. But I put an end to all that."

"Do you travel a lot, Señor?"

"No," the man said in a harsh voice. "I've never been out of Lima. I don't like to travel. But when I got him back they'd already spoiled him, he was just a good-for-nothing. Do you blame me for wanting to make a man out of him? Is that something I ought to be ashamed of?"

"I'm sure he'll get well right away," Alberto said. "I'm sure of it."

"But perhaps I *have* been a little too severe," the man went on. "Because I cared for him so much. I did what I thought was best. His mother and that crazy Adelina can't understand. Would you like some advice? When you have a son, keep him away from his mother. There's nothing like a woman to ruin a boy for life."

"Yes," Alberto said. "Well, here we are."

"What's going on?" the man asked. "Why are they running?"

"It's the whistle. To fall in. I've got to go."

"I'll see you later," the man said. "And thanks for keeping me company."

Alberto started running. He caught up with one of the cadets. It was Urioste.

"It isn't seven yet," Alberto said.

"The Slave just died," Urioste said. "We're on our way to report it."

2

That year my birthday came on a holiday. My mother told me, "You'd better visit your godfather early, sometimes he goes out to the countryside." And she gave me a sol for the fare. I went to my godfather's house, he lived a long way off, out by the bridge, and when I got there he wasn't in. His wife came to the door. She's never liked us, and she gave me a sour look and said, "My husband isn't here. And I don't think he'll be back till tonight, so there's no use waiting for him." I went back to Bellavista very disappointed, I'd had the idea my godfather was going to give me five soles the way he did every year. I'd thought of buying Tere another box of chalk, but this time giving it to her as a real gift, and also a hundred-page notebook, her algebra notebook was filled up. Or I'd ask her to go to the movies, along with her aunt of course. I did some reckoning, with five soles I'd have enough for three downstairs seats and still have a little left over. When I got home, my mother said, "Your godfather's very disagreeable, just like that wife of his. I'm sure he told her to tell you he wasn't in." And I figured she was right. Then my mother said, "Oh, yes, Tere wants to see you. She came looking for you." "She did?" I said. "That's strange. I wonder what she wants." And I really didn't know why she'd come looking for me, it was the first time she'd done it and I suspected something, though not what actually happened. She's heard it's my birthday, I thought, she wants to say Happy Birthday to me. I was at her house in two jumps. I knocked, and her aunt opened the door. I greeted her but she hardly even looked at me, she just turned around and went back to the kitchen. The aunt always treated me like that, as if I were nothing at all. I stood in the open door for a moment, not quite daring to enter. Then Tere appeared, with a different sort of smile on her face. "Hello," she said, "come in." I only said, "Hello," and smiled as best I could. "Come on," she told me, "let's go to my room." I followed her, very curious and without saying anything. In her room, she opened a drawer and came over to me with a package. "Here," she said. "For your birthday." "How did you know the day?" I asked her. She said, "I've known since last year." I didn't know what to do with the package, it was pretty big. Finally I decided to open it. All

I had to do was unwrap it, it wasn't tied. The paper was brown like the paper they used in the bakeshop on the corner and I thought she probably made a special request for it. I took out a sleeveless sweater, almost the same color as the paper, and I knew she'd thought about that, she had good taste and she wanted to have the wrapping the same color as the sweater. I dropped the paper on the floor and looked at the sweater, I told her, "But it's wonderful. Thanks a million. It's really wonderful." Tere nodded, she seemed even happier than I was. "I knitted it at school," she said, "during our sewing classes. I made them believe it was for my brother." And she laughed. What she told me meant she'd planned the gift for a long time and was thinking about me when I wasn't with her, and giving me a gift meant she considered me as something more than just a friend. I kept on saying, "Thank you, thank you," and she laughed again and asked me, "Do you like it? Honestly? But try it on." I put it on and it was a little short, but I pulled it down so quickly she didn't notice, she was so happy she praised her own work, "It fits you, it fits you perfectly, and I didn't even know your right size, I had to guess." I took the sweater off and began wrapping it, but I couldn't do it very well and she said, "Let go, what a mess you're making of it, let me do it." She wrapped it up again without a single wrinkle, then she said, "I've got to give you a birthday embrace." She embraced me and I embraced her; for a few seconds I could feel her body against mine, and her hair brushed my face. Then I heard her cheerful laughter again. "Aren't you happy?" she asked me. "Why are you looking like that?" So I forced myself to laugh.

Lt. Gamboa was the first to enter. He had taken off his cap in the hall, and instead of saluting he merely came to attention and clicked his heels. The colonel was sitting at his desk; behind him, beyond the large window, Gamboa could sense the presence of the swirling fog, the main gate of the Academy, the road that passed it, the ocean. A few moments later they heard footsteps. Gamboa moved away from the door and then stood at attention again. Capt. Garrido and Lt. Huarina came in. Like Gamboa, they had placed their caps under their belts, between the first and second loops. The colonel remained seated at his desk without looking up. The room was elegant and spotless, the furniture carefully polished. Capt. Garrido turned to Gamboa, the muscles of his jaws working hard.

"And the other lieutenants?"

"I don't know, Captain. I told them to be here."

In a few moments, Calzada and Pitaluga came in. The colonel stood up. He was much shorter than the other officers, and extremely fat. His hair was almost white and he was wearing glasses. His gray eyes looked sunken and suspicious behind the lenses. He stared at the officers one by one. They were all at attention.

"At ease," the colonel said. "Sit down."

The lieutenants waited until Capt. Garrido picked out a seat. There were a number of leather-covered chairs arranged in a circle. The captain sat down in the one next to the floor lamp. The lieutenants sat down on either side of him. The colonel came up close to them. The officers all looked at him, bending forward a little, attentive, serious, respectful.

"Is everything all set?" the colonel asked.

"Yes, Sir," the captain said. "They're in the chapel right now. Some of the relatives are here for the wake. The first section is serving as the honor guard. The second replaces them at midnight. Then the others. Also, they delivered the wreaths."

"All of them?"

"Yes, Colonel. I put your card on the largest one myself. They also delivered the one from the officers and the one from the Parents' League. And a wreath for each Year. The relatives sent wreaths and flowers too."

"Have you talked with the president of the League about the funeral?"

"Yes, Sir. Twice. He said the whole executive committee was going to attend."

"Did he ask you any questions?" The colonel was frowning. "That Juanes is always poking his nose into everything. What did you tell him?"

"I didn't give him any details. I simply told him a cadet had died, without going into the circumstances. And I told him we ordered a wreath in the name of the League and they had to pay for it out of their own funds."

"You wait, they'll be around asking questions," the colonel said, clenching his fist. "Everybody's going to ask questions. You've always got schemers and busybodies in a case like this. It'll go all the way up to the Ministry!"

The captain and the lieutenants listened to him without blinking. The colonel had raised his voice and his last words were shouted.

"It's going to be very bad publicity," he added. "The Academy has plenty of enemies, and this is their big chance. They can take advantage of a stupid thing like this to smear us with a thousand lies. Especially me. We'll have to do everything we possibly can to protect ourselves. That's why I called this meeting."

The officers nodded, looking even more solemn.

"Who is Officer of the Day tomorrow?"

"I am, Colonel," Pitaluga said.

"All right. You'll read an Order of the Day at the first formation. Now listen closely. 'The officers and the student body deeply lament the accident which has cost the life of this cadet.' That's the way it should sound. Be sure to emphasize that it was due to his own negligence. Don't leave the slightest doubt about that. Then you can go on to say it should serve as a lesson and a warning, we're going to be stricter in enforcing the regulations, so forth and so on. Write it out this evening and bring it to me when you're finished.

I'll go over it myself to be sure it's right. Which one of you is the lieutenant in charge of the cadet's company?"

"I am, Colonel," Gamboa said.

"Get the sections together before the funeral. Give them a little talk. Tell them we're all very sorry about what happened but you can't make mistakes in the army without paying for them. And there's no place for sentimentality, that would be criminal, we've got to be good soldiers. Also, I want you to stay on after the others leave. This whole thing has got to be discussed. But first, I'd like to know about the funeral. Have you talked with the family, Garrido?"

"Yes, Sir. They agreed to have the funeral at six in the afternoon. I talked with his father. His mother is completely broken up. She . . ."

"Only the Fifth Year should attend," the colonel interrupted. "And tell the cadets to be careful what they say. We don't want to wash our dirty linen in public. The day after tomorrow I'll talk to them in the assembly hall. If even one of them makes some stupid remark, there could be a terrible scandal. The Minister would blow up if he heard about it, and there's plenty of people to tell him, you know how I'm surrounded by enemies. All right, here's what we'll do. Huarina, you're in charge of the transportation. Tell the Military School to send us some buses. Make sure they get to the right places. Afterward, make sure they get back where they belong. Do you understand?"

"Yes, Colonel."

"Pitaluga, you take care of the chapel. Be especially nice with the relatives. I'll go and talk with them myself in a little while. And tell the cadets in the honor guard to watch what they're doing. I don't intend to put up with any nonsense, it's got to be smooth from start to finish. I'm holding you directly responsible. I want the Fifth Year to give the impression that they're deeply affected by the death of this cadet. It might help us out a good deal."

"Excuse me, Colonel," Gamboa said, "but you don't have

to worry about that. It's been a real shock to all the cadets in my company."

"What?" The colonel looked stunned. "Tell me why."

"They're young, Sir," Gamboa said. "A few of them are seventeen. The rest are only sixteen. They've lived with him for almost three years. Naturally they're shocked."

"But *why?*" the colonel insisted. "What are they saying, what are they doing? How do you know they're shocked?"

"They don't sleep, Sir. I've checked the barracks at night. The cadets are in their bunks but they aren't asleep. They're talking about Arana."

"After the lights are out?"

"Yes, Colonel. Long after."

"Gamboa, you know that's against the regulations!" The colonel was shouting again.

"I made them stop it, Sir. They weren't noisy, they were almost whispering to each other. I've told the noncoms to keep an ear out."

"No wonder we have accidents like this!" The colonel waved his little white fists in the air. "You officers don't teach them discipline! Do you hear me, *discipline!*" He paused, then turned to Calzada, Pitaluga and Huarina. "You can leave," he said. "But remember, be careful, careful, careful!"

The three lieutenants stood up, clicked their heels, and left the room. The colonel sat down for a moment in Huarina's place, then stood up again and began to pace back and forth.

"Okay," he said, with an abrupt halt, "now tell me the truth. What happened?"

Capt. Garrido looked at Gamboa and nodded. The lieutenant turned to the colonel. "All the details I know are in my report," he said. "I was commanding the advance from the other side, the right flank. I didn't know anything was wrong until we'd almost reached the top of the hill. Then I saw Capt. Garrido carrying the cadet."

"And what about the noncoms?" the colonel asked. "Why weren't they there? Deaf, dumb, and blind as usual, eh?"

"They were at the rear, Colonel," Gamboa said. "According to the training instructions. So they didn't see any more than I did." He paused. "That was in my report."

"Impossible!" the colonel shouted. "It's absolutely impossible!" He waved his hands again, then fastened them on his belt, attempting to control himself. "Look, don't play stupid," he said. "Don't try to tell me that nobody saw it. He must have shouted or screamed or something. There were cadets all around him, weren't there? The obvious. . ."

"No, Sir," Gamboa said, breaking in. "The cadets were spread out across the field. They weren't side by side. And when I blew the whistle they all ran forward as hard as they could. I think the cadet was wounded when they started firing. If he did scream, nobody would hear it over the firing. And you have to consider the weeds, Sir. They're tall enough to hide anyone who's down on the ground. The cadets that came on from the rear didn't happen to see him. I've questioned the whole company."

The colonel turned to Capt. Garrido. "What about you? Daydreaming like him?"

"I was directing the attack from the rear, Sir," Garrido said, blinking. His jaws ground out the words like a pair of millstones. "The cadets advanced in lines. The cadet must have been wounded when his line advanced. And with a wound like that, he couldn't get up when the whistle blew again, so he stayed there in the weeds. He must have been out of position. That would explain why the other line didn't see him."

"Fine, fine," the colonel said. "But now, tell me what you think."

The captain and Gamboa looked at each other. There was an awkward silence which neither of them dared to break. At last the captain said, in a low voice, "Perhaps he shot himself with his own rifle. I mean, perhaps he really did.

When he hit the ground. He might have caught the trigger on some part of his uniform."

"No," the colonel said. "I've been talking with the doctor. There isn't any question about it, he got shot from behind. In the back of the neck. You're an old soldier, you know very well that guns don't go off by themselves. It's a good enough story to give to the family, it'll get us out from under, at least for the time being. But you're the ones to blame." The captain and the lieutenant shifted in their chairs. "Tell me about the firing."

"It was according to the instructions," Gamboa said. "They advanced under cover, one line covering another. The firing was carefully timed all the way through. I didn't give the order to fire until I was sure the advance troops were flat on the ground. I couldn't see everything from up front, of course, but it seemed to be going like clockwork. I don't feel I did anything wrong, Sir."

"And we've been running the same exercises for five years," the captain said. "The Fifth Year has gone through it at least a dozen times since they've been here at the Academy. They've also been out on maneuvers, under worse conditions. I set up the exercises according to the program I was given. I've never given a single order that wasn't in the book."

"So what?" the colonel asked. "All I want to know is, how did he get killed? Who made a mistake? Goddamn it, this isn't an army post!" He shook his pale fists again. "If a soldier gets shot, you bury him and that's the end of it. But these are students, sons from good families, it wouldn't take anything at all to create a scandal. And what if the cadet happened to be a general's son?"

"I have a theory, Sir," Gamboa said. The captain looked at him enviously. "This afternoon I inspected all their rifles. Most of them are old and unsafe, Colonel, as I'm sure you know. Some have got their sights out of line, some have got defective bores. These things wouldn't be enough by them-

selves, of course, but it's possible a cadet might get his sight
even further out of line, without realizing it. And if the bore
was defective too, the shot could go wild. So if Cadet Arana
was out of position, and exposed to the firing. . . But that's
just a theory, Colonel."

"Yes," the colonel said. He appeared calmer now, as if
something had been settled. "The bullet didn't fall from the
blue. It was fired by somebody in the rear line. But we can't
have these accidents here! Take all the rifles to the armory
tomorrow morning. Tell them they've got to replace the ones
that are worn out. Captain, I want a rifle inspection in the
other companies too. But not right away. We'd better wait
a few days. And don't make a big noise about it. In fact, I
don't want a word of it to leak out. The Academy's prestige
is at stake, and the army's as well. Fortunately the doctors
have been very cooperative. They're going to make a strictly
medical report, without any theorizing. The sensible thing
is to keep up the idea that it was an error by the cadet himself. If you hear any rumors or arguments, nip them in the
bud. Do you understand what I've said?"

"Colonel," the captain said, "please let me make an observation. Personally I believe this theory is much more likely."

"What theory? That he shot himself?"

"Yes, Sir. I'll go so far as to say flatly that the shot was
fired from the cadet's own rifle. Remember, Sir, they were
shooting at targets several yards above their heads. It's impossible to believe that a bullet could go that wild. The
cadet must have pulled the trigger by accident when he fell
on his rifle. I've often observed that the cadets hit the ground
very awkwardly. There's a technique, but they don't seem to
know it. And besides that, Cadet Arana never distinguished
himself in anything soldierly."

"It's possible, I suppose," the colonel said. He was very
calm now. "Yes, of course it's possible. Anything's possible.
What are you laughing at, Gamboa?"

"I'm not laughing, Sir. Excuse me, but I'm not."

"I hope you're right." The colonel patted his stomach, then smiled for the first time. "And let this be a lesson. The Fifth Year has given us altogether too much trouble. Especially that first section. Just a few days ago we had to expel a cadet for stealing exams. And now this. Be more careful in the future. I'm not threatening you. Don't get the wrong idea. But I've got a job to do. So have you. And we've got to do it like soldiers. Like Peruvians. Without questions or qualms. Very well, Señores, that's all."

Capt. Garrido and Lt. Gamboa stood up and left the room. The colonel watched them gravely until the door closed. Then he scratched his belly.

One afternoon after I got out of school, Skinny Higueras said, "Look, let's go to some other place, I don't want to go back to that bar." I told him it didn't matter and he took me to a bar on Sáenz Peña Avenue. It was dark and very dirty. After you passed the counter there was a small door that let you in to the main room. Skinny talked with the waiter for a couple of minutes. They seemed to be old friends. Then he ordered two shots, and when we finished them he looked at me very seriously and asked me if I was as much of a he-man as my brother. "I don't know," I said. "I guess so. Why?" "You owe me about twenty soles by now," he told me. "Isn't that right?" I almost started shaking, I'd forgot how much money I owed him and I thought, Now he's going to ask me to pay him and I haven't got it. But then he said, "I'm not trying to collect. Don't get me wrong. But look, you're a man now, you've got to have money. I can lend it to you when you need it, but first I've got to get it. Do you want to help me?" I asked him what I'd have to do. "Well, it's sort of risky," he said. "If you're scared, forget about it. I've cased the house, I know they aren't there right now. And they're filthy rich, they could fill a whole room with soles, the way Atahualpa filled that room with gold for Pizarro, you remember the story." "Stealing, you mean?" I asked him. "Yes," Skinny said. "But I don't like that particular word. They're rotten with money, I tell you, and what've *we* got? Nothing. So? Are you scared to help me? I'm not trying to force you into it, but where do you think your brother got his money from? And your part's going to be easy, you know I'm your friend." "No, I don't want to," I said. "I'm sorry, but I don't want to." It wasn't because it scared me, but he took me by surprise, I never even guessed that Skinny Higueras and my brother were both crooks. Then Skinny changed the subject, he ordered two more shots, gave me a cigarette, and told me the latest jokes. He was like that, he always had something new, and he could really tell a spicy story, he'd change his voice and make all sorts of faces. Then he'd laugh, opening his mouth so wide you could see his back teeth and his tonsils. I listened to what he was saying, and tried to laugh in the right places, but he must've known I was thinking about something else because all of a sudden he asked, "What's the matter? You don't like the idea? If you don't, then just forget it." I said, "But what if they catch you some day?" "The cops are all too stupid," he told me, "and besides, they're the worst crooks of all. And even if they do catch me, so what? That's life." I wanted to keep on talking about it, so I asked him, "If they catch you, how long'll you stay in jail?" "I don't know," he said. "It all depends on how much money I've got on me." And he told me about the time my brother got caught breaking into a house in La Perla. A cop was going by and he took out his pistol and aimed it at my brother and said, "We're going to the station, walk five yards ahead of me, don't try anything or I'll let you have it, you dirty crook." But my brother laughed in his face and said, "Are you drunk or something? I'm sneaking in here because the cook's waiting for me in her bed. If you don't believe it, just frisk me, you'll see." The cop hesitated for a moment, and then got curious. He went up to him and stuck his pistol right in his eye and began frisking him. "Don't move an inch," he told him, "or I'll shoot. If it doesn't kill you, at least it'll wreck your eye, so keep still." When his hand came out of my brother's pocket it was full of bills. My brother laughed again and said, "I told you I didn't need to steal anything. Look, you're a half-breed and I'm a half-breed, that means we're brothers. Keep the money and let me go. I'll see the cook some other time." The cop said, "I'm going to take a leak, over there behind the wall. If I find you here when I come back, I'll run you in for attempted bribery." Then Skinny told me about the time they both almost got caught on Jesús María. The cops saw them coming out of a house and one of the cops started blowing his whistle and they ran across the roofs. Finally they jumped down into a garden and my brother twisted his ankle. He said, "Keep running, I can't go on," but Skinny didn't want to get away alone so he dragged him into a sort of culvert. God knows how long they stayed there, hardly daring to breathe. Then they grabbed a taxi and went to Callao.

After that, I didn't see Skinny Higueras for quite a few days, and I thought, They must've caught him. But I saw him about a week later in the Bellavista Plaza and we went to the same bar to have a drink and to smoke and talk. He didn't mention that subject again for days in a row. I studied with Tere every afternoon, but I didn't go to meet her when she got out of school because I didn't have any money. I remember the Sunday I went out to see my godfather, without telling my mother I was going. It took me over three hours to get there, I had to cross the whole of Lima on foot. Before I knocked on the door I looked in the window to see if he was home, I was afraid if his wife came to the door again it'd be just like the last time, she'd tell me he wasn't there. I couldn't see anything so I knocked anyway. His wife didn't come to the door, it was one of his little daughters. I remember she didn't have any front teeth. She told me her father was up in the mountains and wouldn't be back for ten days. So I couldn't buy a notebook for Tere, but then some school friends loaned me the money and I bought it anyway. The worst thing was, I couldn't go wait for Tere at her school, I didn't have the fare, and one afternoon when we were studying together and her aunt went into the other room for a minute, she said, "You've never come back to wait for me at noon." I turned red. "I was thinking of going tomorrow," I told her. "You always get out at twelve, don't you?" That evening I went to the Bellavista Plaza to look for Skinny Higueras but I couldn't find him. It occurred to me he might be in that bar on Sáenz Peña, so I went there. The bar was crowded and full of smoke and there were some drunkards singing and shouting. When the waiter saw me come in, he said, "Get out of here, we don't serve kids." "I've got to see Skinny Higueras," I told him, "it's very important." Then the waiter recognized me and pointed to the door at the back. The main room was even more crowded, and the smoke was so thick you could hardly see a thing. There were women sitting at the tables or on the customers' laps. The men were pawing them and kissing them. One of the women grabbed my cheek and said, "Hello, there, sonny, what're *you* doing *here*?" I said, "Shut up, you whore." She only laughed at that, but the drunk who had his arm around her said, "I'm going to push your face in, you've insulted this lady." Just then, Skinny came over. He took the drunk by the arm and sat him down again. "This is my cousin," he told him, "anybody that tries to touch him has got to deal with me first." "Okay, Skinny," the man said, "but tell him not to call my women whores. He ought to learn better manners. He should respect his elders." Skinny put a hand on my shoulder and led me over to a table where three men were sitting. I didn't know a single one of them. Two of them were creoles, the other was a peasant. Skinny introduced me as a friend of his and ordered me a drink. I told him I wanted to talk with him alone. We went to the men's room and when we got there I said, "I need some money. Be a good guy and lend me two soles." He laughed and gave them to me. Then he asked, "Do you remember what we were talking about the other day?" I nodded. "Good," he said. "Then I want you to do me a favor too. I need you. We're friends, we've got to help each other. And it's just for this once. Okay?" "Yes," I said, "but only this once. And if it takes care of everything I owe you." "That's a deal," he said. "And unless something goes wrong, you won't be sorry." We went back to the table and Skinny said to the other three, "Señores, allow me to introduce you to our new partner." The three of them laughed and slapped me on the back. Then a couple of women came over to the table and one of them started pestering Skinny, she wanted to give him a kiss, and the peasant said, "Leave him alone. If you want to kiss somebody, why don't you pick on the boy here?" "I'd love to," she said, and kissed me on the mouth, and everybody laughed and joked. Then Skinny pushed her away. "All right," he told me, "now get out. And don't come back here. Wait for me tomorrow night in the Bellavista Plaza. Around eight o'clock. I'll meet you in front of the movie theater." I left the bar and went home, trying not to think about anything except how I could go and wait for Tere the next day. But I was all worked up about the things Skinny told me, I kept thinking about what could go wrong. If we got caught, they'd send me to the reform school because I was a minor. And Tere would hear all about it, one way or another. And she'd never want to see me again.

It was worse than if the chapel had been completely dark. The shifting half-light exaggerated every movement, cast weird shadows on the walls or the stone floor, and showed everyone's face so dimly, so gloomily, that it almost made them look hostile or even sinister. There was also that constant, plaintive murmuring behind them: a woman's voice repeating one single word, in the same tone, with the syllables running together. It made them more and more nervous, they would rather have heard her scream, or cry out to God and the Virgin, or sob and tear her hair. But ever since they came in with the noncom Pezoa, who lined them up in two columns along the chapel walls, on either side of the coffin, and gave them the order, "Right shoulder, arms!" they had heard nothing but that endless monotone. At last they began to make out other sounds and voices, which meant that people were arriving for the wake. They could not look at their watches: they were all standing at attention, half a yard apart, silent and motionless. The most they could do was to glance sidewise at the coffin, but all they could see was its polished black surface and the wreaths of white flowers. None of the persons in the front part of the chapel had gone up to the coffin. Probably they had gone up to it before the honor guard arrived, and were busy now attempting to console the mother. The Academy's chaplain, looking unusually serious, wandered toward the altar several times, but he always went back to the door, no doubt to be on hand as the groups of mourners arrived. Then he wandered through the aisles again, his eyes lowered, his cheerful young face contracted into a suitable expression; but no matter how often he passed the coffin, he never once stopped beside it, or even looked. The cadets in the honor guard had already been there a good while and their arms were starting to ache from the weight of their rifles. Also, it was growing hot: the chapel was small, every candle on the altar had been lighted, and they were wearing their wool uniforms. They sweated but they all stood rigid, their heels together, their left hands at their thighs, their right hands under the butts of their rifles, their bodies stiffly erect.

They had not been so serious earlier, however. Urioste had pushed open the barracks' door with his fists and told them the news—"The Slave's dead!" he gasped—and they could see how flushed his face was, how his lips trembled, how the sweat dripped from his forehead and his cheeks; behind him, they could see the Poet's ashen face and staring eyes.

But even then there were jokes. As soon as the door slammed shut again, Curly said, "He's probably gone straight down to hell, what a shame." And some of the others laughed. But their laughter was not as fierce and raucous as usual: instead of being the savage howls that greeted any announcement, it was brief, impersonal, perfunctory, almost defensive. And when Alberto shouted, "If anybody cracks another joke I'll kill him, you motherfucking bastards!" no one said a word. The cadets remained on their bunks or in front of their lockers, gazing at the moldering walls, the dark red floor tiles, the starless sky beyond the windows, the double doors of the latrine. They were silent for a number of minutes, hardly even glancing at each other. Then they went on straightening up their lockers, making their bunks, reading their comic books, mending their field uniforms. Little by little they began talking again, but not about the customary topics: there was no more joking, no more snarling, no more filth. And at first they even spoke in whispers, as they did after lights out, using short, careful sentences and avoiding any mention of the Slave. They asked each other for black thread, bits of cloth, cigarettes, class notes, writing paper, copies of exams. Later, they talked all around the subject, being cautious not to refer to their real concern. They asked each other questions—"What time did it happen?"—or made indirect comments—"Lt. Huarina said they were going to operate on him again," "He probably died on the operating table," "I wonder if they'll let us go to the funeral." At last, they began to talk openly about what had taken place. "To get it when you're still so young, that's pretty tough." "He should've died out there in the fields." "It's hell to take three days to die." "And with only two months to go, what rotten luck." There were indirect tributes, variations on several themes, and long intervals of silence. Some of the cadets remained silent, agreeing with a nod of their heads. When they heard the whistle they left the barracks without the usual hubbub, and took their places without any pushing or arguing; then they straightened their lines as precisely as possible, and came to attention before the brigadiers gave the command. They hardly spoke a word during supper: in that huge mess hall they could sense that the eyes of hundreds of cadets were turned toward them, and sometimes they could overhear remarks from the tables where the Dogs were sitting: "They're from the first, that was his section." A few of the Dogs even pointed toward them. They chewed their food mechanically, without tasting anything, and on the way out they answered with a grunt or a curse when the cadets from the other Years or sections became inquisitive enough to ask them questions. Afterward, in the barracks, the whole section gathered around Arróspide, and the Negro Vallano said what everyone was thinking: "Go tell the lieutenant we want to stand guard." He looked at the others and added, "At least, that's what *I* want to do. He was in our section, we owe it to him." No one cracked a joke at him; some of them nodded, others said, "Sure," "Of course we do," "Sure, go tell him." The brigadier went to speak with the lieutenant. When he came back, he said that they were to put on their dress uniforms, including their gloves, and to be sure their shoes were polished, and to fall in in half an hour with their rifles and bayonets but without their white belts. Everyone insisted that Arróspide had to speak with the lieutenant again, to tell him they wanted to stand guard all night, but when he returned again he reported that the lieutenant had refused permission. And now they were there —had been there for over an hour—in the shadowy dimness of the chapel, listening to the woman's ceaseless complaint and glancing now and then at the coffin. It rested alone in the center of the chapel, and it looked as if it were empty.

But no, he was there inside it. They knew this for certain when Lt. Pitaluga came into chapel, announced by the squeaking of his shoes. The sound drew their attention away from the mother's lament, and they were fascinated when they saw he was actually going up to the coffin. They watched him as he halted just before stepping on a wreath, bent his head a little to see more clearly, and stood motionless for almost a minute. Then they felt cold shivers run down their spines when he raised his hand, took off his cap, crossed himself hurriedly, and straightened up. His face looked swollen and his eyes were completely blank. He turned around and disappeared toward the back of the chapel. As he left their range of vision, as his footsteps died out, they were aware again of the mother's unending murmur.

Pitaluga returned almost at once. He walked along both lines of cadets, repeating in a low voice that they could put their rifles down and stand at rest. The cadets took advantage of this opportunity: they rubbed their aching shoulders and they moved a little closer together, slowly, almost imperceptibly. The lines closed up with such a grave, respectful silence that the movement increased the solemnity instead of disturbing it. Then they heard Pitaluga talking, and they understood immediately that he was talking to the mother. He must have been trying hard to speak in a low voice, and perhaps he was embarrassed because he could not. His voice was hoarse, even harsh, at the very best; and he also believed firmly in the idea that virility and a strong voice are inseparable. Therefore, they could make out at least part of what he was saying, especially the name of Arana—which they hardly recognized at first because they had known him as the Slave. Apparently the woman was not paying any attention: she never once stopped lamenting, and the lieutenant would give up for a brief while, then try again.

"What's Pitaluga telling her?" Arróspide asked, speaking through his closed teeth without moving his lips. He was at the head of one of the lines. Vallano, who was next to him, repeated the question, so did the Boa, and it was passed on to the other end of the line. The last cadet, the one nearest the bench where Pitaluga and the woman were, said, "He's talking about the Slave." And he went on to repeat the phrases he heard, without adding or subtracting anything; he even mimicked the lieutenant's voice. But it was not difficult to parrot that monologue: "An outstanding cadet, held in high esteem by all the officers and noncoms, very popular with his classmates, a brilliant and hardworking student, everyone deplores this tragic loss, the silence in the barracks, the sorrow, he was orderly, martial, upright in every way, always the first to line up, he would have made an excellent officer, loyal, brave, he looked for danger in the field exercises, we could trust him to carry out the most difficult missions without questions or complaints, but accidents like this can always happen, life is uncertain, we have to control our grief, the officers and teachers and cadets all share the family's loss, the colonel himself will be here to express his deeply felt condolences, the cadet will be buried with military honors, his classmates will be present in their dress uniforms, with their rifles and bayonets, the fatherland has lost one of its finest sons, but patience and resignation, his memory will be a part of the Academy's traditions, alive in the hearts of succeeding classes, the family has nothing to worry about, the Academy is assuming the responsibility for all the funeral expenses, the wreaths were ordered almost immediately after this misfortune, the one from the colonel is the largest." By this improvised means of transmission the cadets were able to follow Lt. Pitaluga's words, while still hearing the woman's interminable murmur. Occasionally, masculine voices interrupted Pitaluga for a moment or two.

Then the colonel arrived. They could recognize his short, quick, pigeon-toed steps. Pitaluga and the other men stopped talking, and the mother's complaining grew softer, more distant. The cadets came to attention without waiting for the command. They did not shoulder their rifles again, but they brought their heels together, stiffened their bodies, and looked straight ahead. A few moments later they heard the

colonel's thin little voice. He spoke much more quietly than
Pitaluga, and since they were also at attention now, the
human telephone line could not operate: only those who
were nearest the benches heard what he said. None of the
cadets could see him, even out of the corners of their eyes,
but they remembered how he looked in front of the microphone at assemblies, complacent, arrogant, puffed up with
his own importance, raising his hands to show that he was
not using a prepared text. No doubt he was talking once
again about spiritual values and how military life creates a
sound mind in a sound body and how discipline is the basis
of good order. They could picture him very clearly in their
minds: he was wearing his most grave and ceremonious expression; his soft little hands fluttered back and forth, up and
down, in front of the woman's reddened eyes, or alighted
for a moment on the belt around his stately paunch; he had
spread his legs to balance the weight of his body. And they
could guess the lessons he would drive home, the examples
he would evoke, that parade of illustrious heroes, the
martyrs of the War for Independence and the War with
Chile, the valiant immortal soldiers who had so generously
shed their blood during every peril to the fatherland. When
the colonel finished, the woman had stopped murmuring. It
was so great a surprise that the whole chapel seemed different, and some of the cadets glanced at each other uncomfortably. The silence was brief, however, because the colonel
and Lt. Pitaluga, along with a civilian in a dark suit, walked
up to the coffin and stood looking at it for a few moments.
The colonel had his hands folded on his stomach, his under
lip covered his upper lip, and his eyes were half-closed: it
was the expression he saved for very important occasions.
The lieutenant and the civilian stood on either side of him.
The civilian had a white handkerchief in his hand. The
colonel turned toward Pitaluga and whispered something in
his ear. Then both of them turned toward the civilian, who
nodded two or three times, and they all walked back to the

rear of the chapel. The woman began murmuring again, and even after the lieutenant told them to file out into the patio in front of the chapel, where the second section was waiting to replace them, they were still conscious of her voice.

They went out in single file, walking to the door on tiptoe. As they passed the benches they all looked sidewise, in the hope of seeing the cadet's mother, but their view was blocked by a group of men—the colonel, the lieutenant, and three others—standing around her, all of them looking very solemn. Outside the chapel they met the cadets from the second section, who were also wearing their dress uniforms. The first section fell in a few yards behind them. Their brigadier looked down the lines to make sure they were straight, then went off to report. They waited at attention, but they talked under their breath about the mother, the colonel, the funeral. After a while they began asking each other if Pitaluga had forgotten about them. Arróspide walked back and forth in front of them but without saying a word.

When the lieutenant finally came out of the chapel, the brigadier went up to him, saluted, and asked for instructions. Pitaluga told him to march them back to their barracks, but just as Arróspide was turning to give the command, a voice from the rear said, "Someone's missing." The lieutenant, the brigadier, and the cadets looked back and forth, and other voices said, "Yes," "He's right," "Someone's missing." The lieutenant nodded at Arróspide and the brigadier counted the section, using his fingers to make sure his tally was correct. "Yes, Sir," he said when he finished. "We were twenty-nine before, now we're twenty-eight." "It's the Poet," someone shouted. "Cadet Fernández is missing, Sir," Arróspide said. "Did he go into the chapel with the rest?" Pitaluga asked. "Yes, Lieutenant, I saw him." "I hope *he* isn't dead too," Pitaluga muttered, and gestured to the brigadier to follow him.

They were scarcely inside the door when they saw him. He was in the middle of the chapel—his body hid the coffin from them, but not the wreaths—with his rifle tilted to one side and his head bent over. The lieutenant and the brigadier stopped near the door. "What's that fool doing in here?" the lieutenant asked. "Get him out." Arróspide walked forward, and as he passed a small group of people his eyes met those of the colonel. He nodded respectfully, but he could not tell if the colonel returned the nod because he immediately turned his head toward the front. Alberto did not move when Arróspide took his arm. The brigadier forgot his errand for a moment to look at the coffin. Its cover was also of smooth black wood, but there was a small pane of glass set into it, and he could dimly make out a face and a cap. The Slave's face was wrapped in a white bandage, and was swollen and dark red. Arróspide shook Alberto by the arm. "They're all in formation," he said, "and the lieutenant's waiting at the door. Do you want to be confined again?" Alberto did not answer, and followed Arróspide like a sleep-walker. Outside, the lieutenant said to Alberto, "You bastard, you just love to look at corpses, don't you?" Alberto still kept silent: he walked on to the formation and took his place, while the rest of the section stared at him. A few of them asked him what had happened, but he ignored them. And a few minutes later, as they were marching to the barracks, he seemed not to hear when Vallano, who was beside him, said, "Look, the Poet's crying."

3

She's well again now but she's always going to have a lame leg. There must be something wrong inside, a twisted bone or cartilage or muscle, I've tried to straighten her leg but I can't, it's as stiff as an iron hook, no matter how hard I try I can't do anything with it. And Skimpy starts whining and kicking, so now I leave it alone. She's getting used to it now, little by little. She walks kind of funny, she keeps dipping to the right, and she can't run the way she used to, she takes a few leaps and then stops. It's natural she'd get tired so soon, with only three legs to walk on, she's a real cripple. Besides, it's a front leg, worse luck, so her head weighs the other one down, she'll never be the same again. They've changed her name in the section, they call her Gimpy now, I don't but the others do. I think it must've been the Negro Vallano that started it, he's always making up nicknames. And everything else is different here, just like Skimpy, in all the time I've been here there hasn't been so much happening in such a few days. First they got the peasant Cava for stealing the chemistry exam, they tried him and kicked him out. He must be back in the mountains by now, with the Indians and the guanacos, poor guy. It was the first time they ever kicked anybody out of the section, and when you start having bad luck there isn't any end to it. That's what my mother always says and I know what she means, because right after Cava there was the Slave. You can't be unluckier than that, not only a bullet in your head but all those operations, God knows how many. So the guys in the section aren't the same any more, it's easy to see the difference. Maybe they'll change back again, but right now they all act different, they even *look* different. The Poet's a good example, he's like a stranger, nobody bullies him or says anything to him, it's as if it was normal to see him with that blank face. He never talks any more. It's over four days since his buddy's funeral, he could've got over it by now, but he's even worse. I knew he was broken up when he stayed in there next to the coffin. The truth is, he was his pal. I think he's the only pal the Slave had—I should say, Arana—in the whole Academy. But only recently. Before, the Poet used to haze him like all the rest. What happened, why did they suddenly start going everywhere side by side? They got kidded a lot, Curly told the Slave, "You've found yourself a husband." And that's how it looked. He stuck to the Poet all the time, he followed him up and down and around, looking at him, talking to him in a low voice so nobody could overhear. Or they'd go out to the field so they could talk in peace. And the Poet started defending the Slave when they gave him a bad time. Not straight out, though, because he's very tricky. If somebody started hazing the Slave, a little later the Poet was cracking jokes about the other guy, and he almost always got the best of it, the Poet's real fierce when he makes wisecracks, at least he used to be. Now he just stays by himself, he doesn't crack jokes, it's as if he's walking in his sleep. You can really see the change, he used to razz somebody every chance he got. It was fun to hear his comebacks when somebody razzed him. "Poet, make up a poem about this," Vallano said, grabbing himself in the crotch. "All right," the Poet said, "but give me a minute or two, I've got to get inspired." And a little later he recited it to us:

> What's Vallano holding in his hand?
> If you think it's a peanut, you're wrong.
> It isn't a peanut, it isn't a pea,
> It's just his cute little dong.

He was a card, he could make everybody laugh, he razzed me a lot and sometimes I wanted to murder him. He made up some good poems about Skimpy, I've still got one of them copied in my literature notebook:

> Skimpy, you prick-licking bitch,
> I've never seen a dog so thin.
> How come you don't curl up and die
> When the Boa rams it in?

I almost killed him the night he woke up the whole section and went into the latrine shouting, "Look what the Boa does with Skimpy when he's on guard duty!" He was a card, all right. But he couldn't fight very well, the time he had that fight with Gallo he got flattened. He's somewhat creole, the way the coast people ought to be, and he's so thin I feel sorry for him. There aren't many whiteys in the Academy, the Poet's one of the most passable. They've got the others scared, "Yah, yah, you're a whitey shit, watch out for the half-breeds or you're going to get hit." There's only two of them in our section and Arróspide isn't a bad guy either, but he's a terrible ass-kisser, three years in a row as brigadier. One time I saw Arróspide in town, he was in a big red car and he was wearing a fancy yellow shirt, my jaw dropped a whole foot when I saw how he was dressed, Jesus, I thought, he's a whitey with lots of cash, he must live in Miraflores. It's funny that the two whiteys in the section don't even talk to each other, Arróspide and the Poet never got to be pals, they've always kept apart, I wonder why. If I had money and a big red car like that, I wouldn't've entered the Academy, not even at gun point. What's the good of having money if you're in here getting screwed like just anybody? I remember when Curly asked the Poet, "What are you doing here? You ought to be in a seminary." Curly's always talking about the Poet, maybe he's envious of him, maybe he'd like to be a poet too. He asked me today, "Have you noticed how the Poet's almost like an idiot now?" And it's the plain truth. Not that he does anything idiotic, he just doesn't do anything at all. He stays in his bunk all during free time, sleeping or pretending to sleep. Curly went over and asked him to write him a story, and the Poet said, "I don't write stories any more, leave me alone." I don't know if he writes letters either, before all this he used to hunt for clients like mad, perhaps he's got more than enough money right now. When we get up in the morning, the Poet's already outside. Tuesday, Wednesday, Thursday, and now today, he's been the first one in the patio in the morning, standing there with that long face of his and looking at God knows what, as if he's dreaming with his eyes open. And the guys at his table tell me he doesn't eat. "The Poet's all broken up," Vallano said to Mendoza, "he leaves half his food and doesn't even sell it, he doesn't give a damn when the others grab for it, and he never says a word during the whole meal." He's broken up for sure by his buddy's death. That's how the whiteys are, they've got men's faces and women's hearts. The Poet's sick all right, he's the one that's been hit hardest by the death of the—I mean Arana.

Would he come this Saturday? The Military Academy was grand, and so were the uniforms, but how awful not to know when you could get out. Teresa was walking through the arcades at the San Martín Plaza. The bars and cafés were full of customers; the air was dense with greetings, laughter, and the smell of beer; there were little clouds of smoke over the tables. He told me he isn't going to be a soldier, Teresa thought. But what if he changes his mind and goes to the military school in Chorrillos? What's the use of getting married to an army man, they spend their whole lives on the post, and if there's a war they're the first ones to get killed. Besides, they keep getting transferred, how awful to be living in a city and suddenly get shifted to the jungle, with all those mosquitoes and savages. As she passed the Zela Bar she heard some compliments that alarmed her: a group of older men raised their drinks to her, a young man said hello, and she had to dodge a drunkard who tried to stop her. But no, Teresa thought, he's not going to be a soldier. He's going to be an engineer. But I'll still have to wait five years. That's a long time. And then if he doesn't want to marry me, I'll be too old, nobody falls in love with an old woman. On other days, the arcades were almost deserted. When she passed the empty tables and the news-stands in the middle of the day, she saw only the shoeshine boys on the corners and a paperboy running by. She hurried to catch the streetcar so that she could eat her lunch, quickly, and get back to the office on time. On Saturday, however, she walked through the crowded, noisy arcades at a slower pace, always looking straight ahead, enjoying herself without showing it. The compliments the men gave her were flattering, and it was pleasant not to have to go back to work in the afternoon. But years before, Saturday had been a horrible day. Her mother swore and complained even more than on other days, because her father came home very late. And he arrived like a hurricane, full of rage and alcohol. His eyes burned, his voice thundered, his huge fists were clenched, and he paced back and forth like a wild beast in a cage, staggering, cursing his poverty, tipping the furniture over and pounding on the doors, until finally he collapsed on the floor, his anger exhausted. Then she and her mother undressed him and covered him with a blanket; he was so heavy they could not lift him into bed. Sometimes he brought someone home with him. Her mother dashed at the intruder like a fury, her thin hands trying to scratch her face. Her father set Teresa on his knees and told her with savage glee, "Watch them, this is better than a wrestling match." That was until the day a woman split her mother's forehead open with a bottle and they had to take her to the Public Aid. After that, her mother became resigned and docile. When he came home with another woman, she shrugged her shoulders, took Teresa by the hand, and left the house. They went to stay with the aunt in Bellavista, not returning until Monday. They found their house a stinking graveyard of empty bottles, with her father asleep, his legs spread out, in a great puddle of vomit, muttering in his dreams about the filthy rich and the injustices of life. He was a good man, Teresa thought. He worked like a horse all week. He drank to forget how poor he was. He loved me, he wouldn't have abandoned me. The Lima-Chorrillos streetcar passed the reddish front of the penitentiary, the huge white mass of the Hall of Justice, and suddenly emerged into an open area where there were tall trees with swaying branches, and pools of still water, and winding paths bordered with flowers, and, in the midst of a vast, circular lawn, that enchanted palace with its gleaming white walls, its bas-reliefs, its latticed windows, its many doors with knockers in the shape of human faces: the Garifos Park. But my mother wasn't a bad person either, Teresa thought. It's just that she'd suffered a lot. When her father died in a charity hospital after a long illness, her mother took her one night to the door of her aunt's house, gave her a hug, and said, "Don't knock till I'm gone. I'm fed up with this dog's life. I'm going to live for myself from now on, and may God forgive me. Your aunt will take care of you." The streetcar brought her nearer her house than the express. But to get home from the streetcar stop she had to pass a series of open yards full of ragged, wild-looking men who said insolent things to her and sometimes tried to grab her. This time, no one molested her. She could only see two women and a dog, all of them busily digging in some heaps of rubbish, surrounded by swarms of flies. Otherwise the yards were deserted. I'll do all the housecleaning before lunch, she thought. She was walking through Lince now, among small, worn-out houses. Then I'll have the whole afternoon free.

Half a block from her house, she saw the silhouette of a figure in a dark uniform and a white cap, standing beside a small valise. He was so motionless that she thought at once of the sentries who guarded the high, barred gates of the Government Palace. But the sentries always looked very gallant, they puffed out their chests and stretched their necks, proud of their tall boots and plumed helmets; while Alberto's shoulders drooped, his head was bent, his whole body sagged. Teresa waved to him but he did not see her. The uniform looks good on him, Teresa thought. And how the buttons shine. He looks like a cadet from the Naval Academy. Alberto raised his head when she was a few yards away. Teresa smiled and he lifted his hand. What's happened to him? she wondered. Alberto seemed to have aged, he was almost unrecognizable. There was a deep furrow between his eyebrows, his eyes had dark shadows under them, and his cheekbones seemed about to rip through his pallid skin. His glance wandered and his lips were nearly bloodless.

"Did you just get out?" Teresa asked, scrutinizing his face. "I didn't think you'd come till later."

There was no reply. He looked at her with vacant, defeated eyes.

"You look fine in your uniform," Teresa said softly, after a brief pause.

"I don't like the uniform," Alberto said with a furtive smile. "I take it off as soon as I get home. But I haven't been to Miraflores today." He spoke without moving his lips, and his voice was faint and hollow.

"What's happened?" Teresa asked. "Why are you like this? Are you sick? Tell me, Alberto."

"No," he said, looking away. "I'm not sick. But I don't want to go home right now. I want to see you." He ran his hand across his brow; the furrow vanished, but only for an instant. "I've got a problem."

Teresa waited, leaning toward him slightly, and she looked at him tenderly to encourage him to go on speaking, but Alberto had closed his lips and was slowly rubbing his hands together. What should she say, what should she do to give him confidence in her, how could she cheer him up, what would he think of her afterward? Her heart had begun to beat very rapidly. She still hesitated for a moment. Then, on an impulse, she took a step toward Alberto and grasped his hand.

"Come in the house," she said. "Stay and have lunch with us."

"Lunch?" Alberto said, bewildered. He ran his hand across his brow again. "No, don't bother your aunt. I'll eat something nearby here and come back for you later."

"Come on in," she insisted, picking up his bag. "Don't be so silly. My aunt won't be bothered at all. Come on."

Alberto followed her. At the door, Teresa let go of his

hand. She bit her lip, then said in a whisper, "I don't like to see you unhappy." His eyes seemed to come back to life, and he was smiling at her gratefully. He lowered his face to hers and they kissed each other's lips, very quickly. Teresa knocked on the door. Her aunt thought Alberto was a stranger at first: her little eyes peered at him suspiciously, took in the details of his uniform, and lighted up when she recognized his features. A smile spread across her fat face. She wiped her hand on her skirt and held it out, meanwhile babbling a stream of greetings.

"How are you, how are you, Señor Alberto? What a pleasure, come in, come in! I didn't recognize you in that beautiful uniform you're wearing. I asked myself, Who is he, who is he? and I couldn't tell. I swear I'm going blind, from the smoke in the kitchen, you know, and besides that, I'm getting old. Come in, Señor Alberto, what a pleasure to see you."

They had scarcely entered when Teresa said to her aunt, "Alberto's going to stay and have lunch with us."

"What?" the aunt said, as if thunderstruck. "What's that you said?"

"He's going to stay and have lunch with us," Teresa repeated.

Her eyes begged the woman not to look so shocked, and to make some gesture of assent. But her aunt's expression did not change: her eyes were wide open, her lower lip hung down, her forehead was covered with deep wrinkles, she seemed to be in a trance. Finally she came to, made a bitter face at Teresa, and told her, "Come with me." Then she turned and went to the kitchen, rocking her body as she walked like a ponderous camel. Teresa followed her, closed the curtain, and immediately put her finger to her mouth. But her aunt did not speak, she merely looked at her furiously and made as if to scratch her eyes out.

Teresa whispered in her ear, "The grocer can trust you till Tuesday. Don't say anything now, he'll hear you, I'll explain later. He's got to stay. Please don't be angry, Aunt. Go ahead, I'm sure he'll trust you."

"You idiot!" her aunt bellowed, but in the midst of doing so she lowered her voice and put her finger to her lips. "You idiot," she murmured. "Have you gone crazy, do you want me to die of rage? It's been years since the grocer gave me credit. We owe him money and I can't even stick my head in there. Idiot."

"Beg him," Teresa said. "Do anything you can."

"Idiot," her aunt exclaimed, then spoke in a low voice again. "There's only two soles. What're you going to give him? Soup? There isn't even any bread."

"Go ahead, Aunt," Teresa insisted. "Get whatever you like."

And without waiting for a reply she went back to the living room. Alberto was sitting down. He had put his bag on the floor, with his cap on top of it. Teresa sat down next to him. She saw that his hair was tangled and dirty. The curtain opened again and her aunt came out. Her face was still red with anger, but it was wearing a fixed smile.

"Here I am, Señor Alberto. I'll be right back. I have to go out for a moment or two, just a little errand." She glared at Teresa and said, "Take care of things in the kitchen." She slammed the door as she left.

"What happened to you last Saturday?" Teresa asked. "Why didn't you get out?"

"Arana's dead," Alberto said. "They buried him on Tuesday."

"Who?" she asked. "Arana, the boy on the corner? He's dead? But that's impossible. Do you mean Ricardo Arana?"

"The wake was at the Academy," Alberto said. There was no emotion in his voice, only a certain weariness; his eyes looked vacant again. "They didn't bring him home. It happened last Saturday. In the field exercises. We were having rifle practice. A bullet hit him in the head."

"But. . ." Teresa said when he stopped speaking. She

appeared confused. "I knew him very slightly. But I'm awfully sorry. It's horrible!" She put a hand on his shoulder. "He was in the same section with you, wasn't he? Is that why you're so sad?"

"Yes, partly," he said. "He was my friend. And besides that. . ."

"Yes, yes," Teresa said. "But why are you so different? What else has happened?" She leaned over and kissed his cheek. Alberto did not move and she straightened up, flushing.

"It doesn't seem like much to you?" Alberto asked. "It doesn't seem like much for him to die that way? And I couldn't even talk with him. He thought I was his friend and I. . . It doesn't seem like much to you?"

"Why are you speaking to me in that tone of voice?" Teresa asked. "Tell me the truth, Alberto. Why are you angry at me? Have they been telling you things about me?"

"It doesn't matter to you if Arana's dead? Can't you see I'm talking about the Slave? Why do you change the subject? You only think of yourself and. . ." He stopped shouting because he could see that Teresa's eyes were full of tears, her lips trembling. "I'm sorry," Alberto said. "I'm talking like an imbecile. I didn't mean to shout at you. It's just that so many things have happened, I'm all nerves. Please don't cry, Teresa."

He drew her toward him, she rested her head on his shoulder, and they remained like that for a moment. Then Alberto kissed her cheeks, her eyes, and then, for a long while, her lips.

"Of course I'm sorry about it," Teresa said. "The poor boy. But you looked so different, I was frightened, I thought you were angry at me about something. And when you shouted at me it was terrible, I'd never seen you in a rage before. How your eyes flashed!"

"Teresa," he said, "I want to tell you something."

"Good," she said. Her cheeks were burning red and she

was smiling happily. "Tell me, I want to know all about you."

He closed his mouth abruptly, and his anxious expression dissolved into a timid smile.

"What is it?" she asked. "Tell me, Alberto."

"I love you very much," he said.

When the door opened, they separated so hurriedly that the valise tipped over and his cap fell on the floor. Alberto bent over to pick it up. The aunt smiled at him benevolently. She was carrying a bundle in her hands. Teresa helped to prepare the meal, blowing kisses to Alberto whenever her aunt's back was turned. Then they all talked about the weather, the summer vacation, the latest movies. It was not until they were halfway through lunch that Teresa told her aunt about the death of Arana. The woman bewailed the tragedy in a loud voice, pitying the boy's parents, above all his poor mother, and asserting that God sends the worst misfortunes to the best families, nobody knows why. It seemed as if she was also going to weep, but she limited herself to rubbing her dry eyes and sneezing. When lunch was finished, Alberto said he had to leave.

At the front door, Teresa asked him again, "You really aren't angry at me?"

"No, I swear I'm not. Why should I be angry at you? But perhaps I won't be able to see you for a while. Write to me at the Academy every week. I'll explain everything later."

Teresa watched him until he disappeared from sight. She was puzzled by his last remarks. Why had he left in that manner? Then she had a revelation: He's fallen in love with another girl and he didn't dare tell me because I invited him to lunch.

The first time, we went to La Perla. Skinny Higueras asked me if I'd mind walking instead of taking a bus. We walked down Progreso Avenue, talking about everything except what we were going to do. Skinny didn't seem nervous, he even seemed calmer than usual, and I figured he wanted to give me courage, because I was scared sick. After a while, Skinny took off his jacket, he said it was hot, but I was freezing to death, I kept on shivering and I had to stop three times to take a leak. When we got to the Carrión Hospital, a man came out from among the trees. I jumped back and shouted, "Skinny! The cops!" But it was one of the characters that were with Skinny the night before in that dive on Sáenz Peña. He didn't behave like Skinny, he was very serious, he even looked nervous. They talked in an underworld slang I could hardly understand. We kept on walking, and after a while Skinny said, "This is where we cut across." We left the street and crossed a field. It was dark, and I was almost stumbling along. Before we got to Palmeras Avenue, Skinny said, "We'd better sit down and talk it over so we'll know just what we're doing." We sat down and Skinny told me what I had to do. He said the house was empty and they'd help me get up on the roof. I'd have to climb down into the garden and get inside through a small window that didn't have any glass in it. Then I had to open one of the windows on the street and come back to where we were. They'd meet me there. Skinny repeated what I had to do a number of times and told me exactly where to find the window. He seemed to know the house inside out, he told me where every room was. I didn't ask him anything about the instructions, only about what could happen to me. "Are you sure there isn't anybody in there? And what if there's a dog? What'll I do if I get caught?" Skinny calmed me down, he was very patient with me. A little later he turned to his friend and said, "Go ahead, Jitters." Jitters walked on toward Palmeras Avenue and in a few minutes we lost sight of him. Skinny asked me, "Are you scared?" "Yes," I said, "a little." "So am I," he said, "so don't worry, you're like the rest of us." A moment later we heard a whistle. Skinny got up and said, "Let's go. That whistle means the coast is clear." I started to shake and I told him, "Look, Skinny, I'd better go back to Bellavista."

"Don't be stupid," he said, "we can do it in half an hour."
We walked over to the avenue and Jitters met us again. "It's
just like a graveyard," he said. "Not even a cat." The house
was as big as a castle, and completely dark. We cased the
walls all around, and when we got out back Skinny and
Jitters boosted me up so I could get onto the roof. Once
I was up there I stopped being afraid. I wanted to do everything very quickly. I crossed the roof and I saw that the
tree in the garden was very close to the wall of the house,
the way Skinny said. I got down without making any noise
and without scraping myself. The window was very small
and I was scared again when I saw it was covered with a
wire screen. He double-crossed me, I thought. But the wire
was rusty, I gave it a little push and it fell apart. I had a
hard time getting in, I scratched my shoulders and my legs
and for a few moments I thought I was stuck. I couldn't see
anything when I got inside the house. I bumped into the
furniture and the walls. Every time I went into another room
I thought I was going to see the windows that looked out on
the street, but everything was pitch black. I was so nervous
I made a lot of noise, and I couldn't figure out where I was.
The minutes kept passing and I couldn't find those windows.
I bumped against a table and knocked a vase or something
to the floor, and it broke with a loud crash. I almost bawled
when I saw some narrow streaks of light in one corner. I
hadn't seen the windows because they were covered by
heavy drapes. I peeked out, and there was Palmeras Avenue,
but I couldn't see either Skinny or Jitters and it gave me a
terrible scare. I thought, A cop came along and they left me
here alone. I kept watching for a while, to see if they'd show
up. I began to feel as if I'd been taken in, and I thought,
So what, I'm a minor after all, the worst they can do is send
me to reform school. I opened the window and jumped out
onto the sidewalk. I'd hardly landed when I heard footsteps
and then Skinny's voice. "Good work. Go back to the field
and stay still." I ran across the street and flopped onto the

grass. I started thinking what I'd do if the cops came around. Now and then I forgot where I was and it seemed as if it was all a dream and I was home in bed, I could picture Teresa's face and I wanted to visit her and talk with her. I was so busy thinking about her I didn't notice when Skinny and Jitters came back. We returned to Bellavista through the fields without going on Progreso Avenue. Skinny'd taken a lot of things out of that house. We stopped under the trees in front of the Carrión Hospital, and Skinny and Jitters made up several packages. They said good-by to each other before we got into the city, and Jitters told me, "You passed the acid test, kid." Skinny gave me some packages and I hid them in my clothes. We brushed our trousers and cleaned the dirt off our shoes. Then we went on toward the plaza, walking calmly. Skinny told me some jokes and I laughed like a madman. He walked me to the door of my house, and told me, "You did your part like a real buddy. We'll see each other tomorrow and I'll give you your share." I told him I needed money right away, even if it was just a little. He gave me a ten-sol bill. "That's only part of it," he said. "I'll give you some more tomorrow if I can sell the stuff tonight." I'd never had so much money at one time in all my life. I thought about all the things I could do with ten soles, lots of things occurred to me but I couldn't decide on any of them, I was only sure I'd spend a little for the fare to go into Lima. I thought, I'll bring her a present. I spent hours trying to figure out what she'd like best. I thought of all sorts of things, from notebooks or chalk to caramels or a canary. The next morning when I got out of school I still hadn't made up my mind. Suddenly I remembered the time she borrowed a magazine from the baker to read some stories. I went to a newsstand and bought three magazines, two of them with adventure stories, the other with love stories. I felt very happy in the streetcar and my head was full of ideas. I waited for her again in the store on Alfonso Ugarte and when she got out of school I hurried over to her. We shook hands and began talking about her classes. I had the magazines under my arm. She'd been glancing at them out of the corner of her eye for several minutes, and when we were crossing the Bolognesi Plaza she said, "Have you got some magazines? How nice. Will you lend them to me when you've read them?" I said, "I bought them for you as a present." "Honestly?" she asked. "Of course," I said. "Here, take them." "Thank you," she said, and began to glance through them as we walked along. I noticed she opened the love stories first and spent more time on them. I thought, I should've bought nothing but love stories, she won't be interested in the adventures. As we reached Arica Avenue she said, "I'll lend them to you when I'm finished." I told her that would be fine. We didn't say anything for a few moments. Suddenly she told me, "You're very good." I just laughed and said, "Don't you believe it."

I should've told her and perhaps she'd've given me some advice, do you think what I'm going to do'll make it worse, will they make me the goat? Am I sure, who can be sure? You can't fool me, you son of a bitch, I can see it in your face, I can promise you're going to pay for it. But should I? Alberto looked around and was surprised to see the wide, grassy esplanade where the cadets of the Leoncio Prado assembled on the 28th of July for the grand parade. How had he got there? The empty field, the slight chill in the air, the dusk falling on the city like a dark rain, made him think of the Academy. He looked at his watch: he had wandered aimlessly for three hours. I'll go home, go to bed, call the doctor, take a pill, sleep for a month, forget everything, my name, Teresa, the Academy, be an invalid all my life so as not to remember. He turned and walked back in the direction he had come. He stopped in front of the monument to Jorge Chávez: in the darkness, the compact triangle and its flying figures seemed to be made of tar. A stream of cars filled the avenue, and he waited on the corner with a group of other people. But when the stream halted and the people around him crossed the avenue in front of a wall of bumpers, he stayed where he was, gazing blankly at the red light. If I could start over again and do things differently, that night, for example, I'd ask him where the Jaguar was, he'd say he didn't know, I'd say okay, so long, and that'd be that, and so what if they stole his jacket, everyone has to take care of himself the best he can, that's all there is to it, and I wouldn't be so worried, no problems, just listening to my mother, Albertito, your father's still the same, running around with those women day and night, those prostitutes, he's still the same. Then he was at the express stop on 28th of July Avenue and had left the bar behind him. He had only taken a quick look at it as he went by, but he could recall the noise, the glaring lights, the smoke that drifted out into the street. The express arrived, the people who had been waiting got on, and the conductor asked him, "How about you?" And since Alberto stared at him dully, without moving, he shrugged his shoulders and closed the door. Alberto turned and walked along the same stretch of the avenue for the third time. He reached the door of the bar, and this time he entered it. The noise battered him from every direction, and the glare hurt his eyes and made him blink. He managed to get to the bar, squeezing through men who reeked of tobacco and alcohol. He asked for a telephone book. They're eating him now, little by little. If they started with his eyes, the softest part, they must be down to his neck by now, they've already eaten his nose, his ears, they've got in under his fingernails like chiggers and they're devouring the flesh, what a banquet they must be having. I should've telephoned before they started eating him, before he was buried, before he died, before. The noise upset him, it kept him from concentrating on the name he was looking for. At last he found it. He picked up the receiver quickly, but when he reached out to dial the number, his finger stopped a fraction of an inch away. There was a harsh buzz in his ear. He glanced toward the bar and saw a white jacket with wrinkled lapels. He dialed the number and listened to it ring: silence, a ring, silence, a ring. He looked around him. Someone at a corner table was making a toast, roaring out a woman's name. The others held up their glasses and repeated it. The telephone went on ringing. Then a voice said, "Hello." He was speechless for a moment, he felt as if there were a lump of ice in his throat. The white shadow in front of him moved, came toward him. "I'd like to speak with Lt. Gamboa, please," Alberto said. "American whisky is shit," the white jacket said, "English whisky is good whisky." "Just a moment," the voice said, "I'll call him." The man who had made the toast was now making a speech. "Her name's Leticia and I'm not ashamed to tell you I'm in love with her. Marriage is a serious business, but I love her and I'm going to marry my half-breed." "Whisky," the shadow said. "Scotch. Good whisky. Scotch, English, doesn't matter. Not American. Scotch or English." "Hello," he heard another voice say. He felt himself shivering, and took the receiver a few inches away from his ear. "Hello," Lt. Gamboa said, "who's calling?" "I'm off the booze for good. I've got to behave myself from now on. Got to earn lots of money to keep my half-breed happy." "Lt. Gamboa?" Alberto asked. "Montesierpe pisco," the shadow said, "that's bad pisco. Motocachi pisco, that's good pisco." "Yes, speaking. Who is it?" "So here's to my half-breed and here's to my friends." "A cadet," Alberto said, "a cadet from the Fifth Year." "In my personal opinion," the shadow said, "it's the best pisco in the world," but then he qualified his statement: "Or one of the best, gentlemen, one of the best. Motocachi." "Your name," Gamboa said. "We'll have ten kids, all of them boys, and I'll name every one of them after my friends. Not one of them after myself, just after my friends." "They killed Arana," Alberto said. "I know who it was. Can I come to your house?" "Your name," Gamboa said. "Do you want something really special? Give him Motocachi." "Cadet Alberto

Fernández, Sir, first section. Can I come over?" "Yes, right away. 327 Bolognesi Street, Barranco." Alberto hung up.

Everybody's different now. Maybe I am too, only I don't notice it. The Jaguar's changed so much it's enough to scare you. He's always angry, you can't talk to him, if anybody just goes up and asks him a question or asks him for a cigarette, he acts as if it was an insult and starts saying the worst things he can think of. He hasn't got any patience at all, he gets sore at anything, and then, bang, he laughs the way he does when he fights and you've got to calm him down. Jaguar, what's the matter, I didn't do anything, don't get sore, there isn't any reason to get sore. But no matter how you beg his pardon, he's apt to start swinging, he's beaten up several cadets these last few days. And he isn't like that with just the others in the section, he's like that with me and Curly, it's hard to believe he'd be like that with us, we're in the Circle. But the Jaguar's changed on account of what happened to the peasant, I can tell it for sure. I don't care how much he laughed and made believe he didn't care a damn, it changed him when the peasant Cava was expelled. I've never seen him get so mad before, his whole body trembles, and what things he says, I'll burn everything, I'll kill everybody, I'll burn down the administration building, I want to cut the colonel's belly open and wear his guts for a necktie. It seems like years since the three of us left in the Circle got together, ever since they locked up the peasant and we tried to find the squealer. It isn't fair what's happened, the peasant up there with the alpacas, his whole life screwed up, and the guy that squealed on him scratching his stomach and laughing up his sleeve, I think it's going to be tough to find out who it was. The Jaguar said, "We'll know who it is in two hours, no, in one, just keep sniffing around, you can smell a squealer right away." But that's crap, you only find out a peasant with your nose or your eyes, the other sons of bitches know how to put on an act. That must be what's got him down. But at least he should get together with us two, we've been his pals from the start. I don't know why he stays alone. All you've got to do is go near him and he gives you a dirty look, it's as if he's ready to jump on you and bite you. They gave him a good nickname, it fits him exactly right. I don't think I'll go near him any more, he'll think I'm ass-kissing, but I only tried to speak to him like a friend. It's a miracle we didn't have a big fight yesterday, I don't know why I held back, I should've put him in his place, I'm not afraid of him. When the captain took us to the assembly hall and started talking about the Slave, that you have to pay dearly for your mistakes in the army, get it into your skulls that you're in the armed forces and not a menagerie if you don't want the same thing to happen to you, if we'd been at war that cadet would have been a traitor to the fatherland because he was irresponsible, what horseshit, it made my blood boil to hear him blabbing about a dead guy, Piranha you filthy bastard, you ought to get a bullet in the brain yourself. But I wasn't the only one that got furious, everybody did, you just had to look at their faces. So I said to him, "Jaguar, he shouldn't be talking like that about a dead guy, why don't we start a chant and drown him out?" He said, "Shut up, you're an animal, you always say stupid things. Don't speak to me unless I speak to you first." He must be sick, that isn't the way a sane person behaves, mentally sick, completely out of his mind. Don't think I need to hang around you, Jaguar, I used to follow you because it was a way of passing the time, but I can get along without you, we'll be out of this dump pretty soon and I'll never see you again. When I leave the Academy I'm not going to see anybody here again. Except for Skimpy. Maybe I'll steal her and keep her for my own.

Alberto walked along the quiet streets of Barranco, among big, discolored houses in the style of the beginning of the century; they were separated from the street by deep gardens. The leaves of the tall trees cast spidery shadows on the pavement. Now and then a crowded streetcar went by, its passengers looking out of the windows with a bored air. I should've told her everything, just listen to what's happened, he was in love with you, my father's out with the prostitutes, my mother's telling her beads and holding up her crucifix and confessing to the Jesuit, Pluto and Babe are talking in somebody's house, listening to records in somebody's living room, your aunt's nibbling at her hair in the kitchen, and all the time the worms are eating him because he wanted to see you and his father wouldn't let him out, just think about that, it doesn't seem like much to you? He had got off the streetcar at La Laguna. There were couples or whole families enjoying the evening coolness on the grass under the trees, and the mosquitoes whined at the edge of the pool near the motionless boats. Alberto crossed the park and the playground. The light from the avenue showed him the swings and seesaws; the parallel bars, trapezes, and other games were hidden by shadows. He walked as far as the lighted plaza, but avoided it. He turned toward the Malecón, which he knew was not far off, beyond a mansion with cream-colored walls; it was taller than the others, and bathed in the slanting light of the street light. At the Malécon, he went to the parapet and looked over. The sea at Barranco was not the same as it was at La Perla. There, it always showed signs of life, and murmured angrily at night, but here at Barranco it was silent, waveless, a lake. You're to blame too and when I told you he was dead you didn't cry, it didn't upset you at all. You're to blame too and if I'd told you the Jaguar killed him you'd say, "The poor thing, do you mean a real jaguar?" But you wouldn't cry about that either, and he was absolutely crazy about you. You're to blame too and the only thing that's upsetting you is the serious look on my face. Golden Toes is just a cheap whore but she's got a bigger heart than you have.

It was an old, two-story house, with balconies over a

flowerless garden. A narrow walk led from the rusting gate to the front door; it was an ancient door, carved with dim designs that looked like hieroglyphics. Alberto rapped with his knuckles. He waited a few seconds, noticed the doorbell, pressed his finger on the button and quickly released it. He heard footsteps, and came to attention.

"Come in," Gamboa said, stepping aside.

Alberto entered, and heard the door close behind him. The lieutenant passed him and walked down a long, dark hallway. Alberto followed him on tiptoe. His face was almost touching Gamboa's shoulders, and if the lieutenant had stopped suddenly, he would have bumped into him. But the lieutenant did not stop until he reached the end of the hall-way and opened a door. Alberto waited on the threshold until Gamboa turned on the lights. It was a living room with green walls, and there were pictures in gilt frames. A man gazed fixedly at Alberto from a table top: it was an old, yellowed photograph, and the man sported sidewhiskers, a patriarchal beard, and a pointed mustache.

"Sit down," Gamboa said, nodding toward an armchair.

Alberto sat down, and he felt himself sink into it as into a dream. Then he remembered he was still wearing his cap. He snatched it off, excusing himself in a low voice. But the lieutenant was closing the door and did not hear him. He turned, sat down in front of Alberto on a chair with ornate legs, and said, "Alberto Fernández. From the first section?"

"Yes, Sir." He leaned forward a little and the springs in the armchair creaked.

"All right," Gamboa said, "what's it all about?"

Alberto looked at the floor. The carpet had a blue and cream-colored design, one square within another within another. He counted the bands: twelve, with a gray square in the center. He raised his eyes. There was a cabinet against the wall behind the lieutenant. It had a marble top and the drawer pulls were metal.

"I'm waiting, Cadet," Gamboa said.

Alberto looked at the carpet again. "The death of Cadet

Arana wasn't an accident," he said. "They killed him. It was revenge, Lieutenant."

He raised his eyes. Gamboa had not moved; his face was impassive, there was no sign of surprise or even curiosity. His hands were resting on his knees, his legs were spread. Alberto noticed that the chair in which the lieutenant was sitting had squat, animal feet with cruel talons.

"They murdered him," he said. "It was the Circle. They hated him, the whole section hated him. They didn't have any reason to, he never made trouble for anybody, but they hated him because he didn't like wisecracks and fighting. They drove him crazy, they bullied him all the time, and now they've murdered him!"

"Calm down," Gamboa said. "Tell it in some kind of order. You can speak freely."

"Yes, Sir," Alberto said. "The officers don't know anything about what goes on in the barracks. Everybody was against Arana the whole time, they made him get confined, they didn't leave him alone for a single minute. Now they're happy. It was the Circle, Lieutenant."

"One moment," Gamboa said, and Alberto looked at him. The lieutenant was sitting on the edge of his chair now, with his chin on the palm of his hand. "Are you trying to say that a cadet in your section deliberately fired at Cadet Arana? Is that it?"

"Yes, Sir."

"Before you tell me the name of that person," Gamboa said, "I've got to warn you of something. You're making a very, very serious accusation. I hope you realize all the consequences this affair could have. And I hope you don't have the slightest doubt about what you're going to tell me. An accusation like this isn't any joke. Do you understand?"

"Yes, Lieutenant. I've thought it all over. I didn't speak to you before because I was afraid. Now I'm not." He opened his mouth to continue, then closed it again. He was watching Gamboa's face without lowering his eyes: it had clean-cut features and a look of self-assurance. A few seconds later those strong outlines seemed to dissolve, that dark skin seemed to grow pallid. Alberto closed his eyes and saw the pale, yellowish face of the Slave, his wavering gaze, his weak lips. He opened his eyes again, and when he became conscious of Lt. Gamboa, he remembered the open field, the vicuña, the chapel, the empty bunk in the barracks.

"Yes, Sir," he said. "I'll take the responsibility. The Jaguar killed him to get revenge for Cava."

"What?" Gamboa asked. He had dropped his hand and his eyes now looked interested.

"It was all on account of the confinement, Sir. On account of that pane of glass. It was terrible for him, worse than for anybody else, he hadn't had a pass for two weeks. First they stole his pajamas, and the next week you confined him for trying to help me in the chemistry exam. He was desperate, he *had* to get a pass. Don't you understand, Sir?"

"No," Gamboa said. "Not a single word."

"What I mean is, he was in love, Sir. He kept thinking about this girl. The Slave didn't have any friends, you've got to keep that in mind, he didn't pal around with anybody. He spent almost three years in the Academy all alone, without talking with anybody. They all bullied him. And he wanted to get a pass so he could see that girl. You can't imagine the way they treated him, all the time, they stole his things, they took his cigarettes away, they. . ."

"His cigarettes?" Gamboa asked.

"Everybody in the Academy smokes," Alberto said aggressively. "A pack each a day. Or more. The officers don't know a thing about what goes on. Everybody bullied the Slave. I did too. But finally we got to be friends, I was the only one he ever had. He used to tell me all his troubles. They kept making it hell for him just because he was afraid of fighting. And it wasn't just practical jokes, Lieutenant. They pissed on him while he was sleeping, they cut holes in his uniform so he'd be confined, they spit in his food, they made him get back with the last ones to fall in even though he was the first one there."

"Who did all this?" Gamboa asked.

"Everybody, Sir."

"Calm down a little, Cadet. Explain it in order."

"He wasn't a bad guy," Alberto said, interrupting him. "The only thing he hated was the confinement. When he couldn't get a pass he almost went wild. He didn't get a pass for a whole month. And the girl didn't write to him even once. I treated him like dirt myself, Lieutenant. I admit it."

"Speak slower," the lieutenant said. "Try to get a grip on yourself, Cadet."

"Yes, Sir. Do you remember when you confined him for giving me the answers in the exam? He had a date to take the girl to the movies. He asked me to go to her house and explain. I double-crossed him. She's my girl friend now."

"Ah," Gamboa said. "I'm beginning to understand."

"He didn't know anything about it," Alberto said. "He went crazy when he couldn't get out to see her. He wanted to find out why she didn't write to him. The confinement could've lasted for months, I mean about the windowpane. They'd never find out it was Cava, the officers never find out about anything if we don't want them to, Lieutenant. And he wasn't like the rest of us, he never dared to jump over the wall."

"What did you say?"

"Everybody jumps over the wall. Even the Dogs. There isn't a night that somebody doesn't do it. But not the Slave, Lieutenant, he never did it even once. So that's why he went to Huarina, I mean Lt. Huarina, and told him about Cava. Not because he was a squealer. Just because he had to get a pass. And the Circle found out about it, I'm positive they knew who it was."

"What's this about the Circle?" Gamboa asked.

"They're four cadets in the section, Sir. I mean three, Cava's gone now. They steal exams and uniforms and then sell them. They've also got a steady business going, and they sell everything, cigarettes, liquor, at double the price."

"Are you out of your mind?"

"Pisco and beer, Lieutenant. Didn't I tell you the officers don't know what's going on? The cadets drink more in the Academy than they do when they're on pass. At night, and sometimes even during recess. When the Circle heard that Cava got caught, they were furious. But Arana wasn't a squealer, we've never had squealers in the barracks. That's why they killed him, for revenge."

"Who killed him?"

"The Jaguar, Sir, the leader. The other two, Curly and the Boa, they're a couple of animals all right, but they wouldn't've killed him. I know it was the Jaguar."

"Who is the Jaguar?" Gamboa asked. "I don't know the nicknames of the cadets. Tell me their right names."

Alberto told him, and then went on explaining, with occasional interruptions by Gamboa, who wanted details, names, dates. Much later, Alberto fell silent and hung his head. The lieutenant showed him where the bathroom was. He went in, and came back with his face and hair dripping wet. Gamboa was still sitting in the chair with animal feet, thinking, brooding. Alberto stood in front of him.

"Go home now," Gamboa said. "I'll be at the guardhouse tomorrow morning. Don't go to your barracks, come directly to see me. And give me your word you won't say anything to anybody else. Not even your parents."

"Yes, Lieutenant," Alberto said. "I give you my word."

4

He said he was going to come but he didn't, and I felt like killing him. After I left the mess hall I went up into the summerhouse the way we agreed and I got tired waiting for him. I don't know how long I was there, smoking and thinking. Every now and then I got up to look out but the patio was always empty. Also, Skimpy wasn't with me, she follows me everywhere but she wasn't with me just when I needed her, I wanted to have her beside me there in the summerhouse so I wouldn't feel scared: bark, Skimpy, bark, drive off the evil spirits. Then I got to thinking: Curly's double-crossed me. But it wasn't that, I found out later. It was getting dark and I was still there in a corner of the summerhouse, so I left it and went toward the barracks, almost on the run. I got to the patio just as they blew the whistle, if I'd waited for him any longer they'd've given me six points and he didn't even think of that, I sure wanted to beat him up. I saw he was in the first rank and he turned his head so as not to look at me. His mouth was open, he looked like one of those idiots that wander through the streets talking to the flies. That's when I knew why Curly didn't go to the summerhouse: he was too scared. This time we're screwed for sure, I thought, I'd better start packing my bag, I'll go out and earn my living somehow, I'll jump over the wall before they rip off my insignias, and I'll take Skimpy with me, nobody'll notice she's gone. The brigadier was calling the roll and everybody was saying here. Then he called the Jaguar's name, I can still feel the chill that ran down my spine, my knees are still shaking, I looked at Curly and he looked at me with wide-open eyes and everybody turned to look and I don't know how I had the strength to stand it. The brigadier coughed and went on calling the roll. Afterward the big fuss began, we hardly got into the barracks when the whole section ran up to me and Curly, shouting, "What's happened? Spill it, spill it!" They wouldn't believe us when we told them we didn't know anything and Curly starting pouting, he said, "We don't know any more than you do, stop asking so many questions, damnit." Come here, Skimpy, don't go running off, don't be so grouchy. Look how sad I am, I need your company, come here. Later, when the others went to bed, I went over to Curly and said to him, "You double-crosser, why didn't you go to the summerhouse?

I waited for hours." He was even more scared than before, it made me feel sorry for him, and the worst part was, it was the kind of fear that's catching. Don't let them see us together, Boa, wait till they're all asleep, Boa, I'll wake you up in an hour and tell you everything, Boa, go back to your bunk, get away from me, Boa. I insulted him and I told him, "If you're double-crossing me again, I'll murder you." But I went and lay down and a little later they put out the lights and I saw the Negro Vallano get out of his bunk and come over to mine. He was all sweet-talk, the wise guy, very lovey-dovey, I'm a friend of yours, Boa, tell me what's happened, very buddy-buddy and showing those rat's teeth of his. Even though I was feeling so sad, it made me laugh to see how quick he went away when I just shook my fist at him and made a face. Come here, Skimpy, be good to me, I'm having a bad time, don't go away. I said to myself, I'll go and crack his skull if he doesn't come. But he finally came, when the others were all snoring. He walked up to me very slowly and said, "Let's go in the latrine, we can talk better there." The dog followed me, lapping my feet, her tongue's always hot. Curly was pissing and it seemed as if he'd never finish, I decided he was just stalling so I grabbed him by the neck and shook him, I said, "Okay, now tell me what's happened." And I'm not surprised at all about the Jaguar, I've known all along he doesn't have any feelings, who'd be surprised that he wants to get the rest of us in the soup. Curly says he said, if I get screwed, everybody gets screwed, I'm not surprised at all. Curly doesn't know all about it, stop moving, Skimpy, you're clawing my stomach, but I hoped he'd tell me lots of things and he sure did. He said they were using a Dog's cap as a target to throw stones at, the Jaguar hit it every time from twenty yards away, the Dog said, "You're ruining my cap, Cadets." I remember I saw them in the field but I thought they'd gone out there to have a smoke or I'd've gone out and joined them, I like that kind of target practice and I've got a better aim than Curly and the Jaguar.

And he said the Dog objected too much and the Jaguar told him, "If you keep on talking I'm going to aim at your balls, you'd better shut up." Then he turned to Curly and said, "I've just figured out why the Poet hasn't come back to the Academy: he's dead. This is the year for dying, we'll have some other deaths in the section before it's through." Curly says it made him nervous to hear the Jaguar talking like that, he crossed himself and just then he saw Gamboa. It didn't occur to him that he'd come for the Jaguar, I wouldn't've thought of it either, nobody would've. Curly opened his eyes wide again and said, "I didn't even think he'd come over to us, Boa, I was only thinking about what the Jaguar said about the Poet and more deaths in the section, then I saw he was coming straight at us, Boa, he was looking straight at us." Skimpy, why's your tongue always so hot? It reminds me of the cupping glass my mother used to use to draw out the poisons when I was sick. He said that when Gamboa was about ten yards away the Dog stood up, so did the Jaguar, and the Jaguar came to attention. "I knew something was wrong, Boa, it wasn't just that the Dog didn't have his cap on, anybody'd notice that, but Gamboa only looked at me and the Jaguar, he didn't take his eyes off us, Boa." And he says that Gamboa said, "Hello, Cadets," but not looking at Curly any more, just at the Jaguar, and the Jaguar dropped the stone he had in his hand. "Go to the guard-house," he said, "and report to the Officer of the Day. Take your pajamas, your toothbrush, a towel and a bar of soap." Curly turned pale, but he says the Jaguar was as calm as anything, even insolent, he said, "Me, Lieutenant? Why, Lieutenant?" and the Dog laughed, I hope we find out who he was. Gamboa didn't answer, he only said, "Get going." It's too bad Curly doesn't remember what that Dog looks like, the lieutenant was there so the Dog grabbed his cap and ran away. I'm not surprised by what the Jaguar said to Curly, "If this is about the exam, a lot of people are going to wish they'd never been born," that sounds exactly like him. Then

Curly said he asked him, "Do you think I'm a squealer? Do you think the Boa's a squealer?" And the Jaguar said, "I hope not, for your own good. Remember, you're in this as deep as I am. Tell the Boa the same thing. Tell all the ones that bought exams. Tell everybody." I know the rest of it because I saw him leaving the barracks, he was dragging his pajamas along on the ground, with his toothbrush stuck in his mouth like a pipe. I was surprised because I thought he was going to take a shower and the Jaguar isn't like Vallano, who takes a shower every week, when we were in the Third they called him the frogman. You've got a hot tongue, Skimpy, your tongue's long and burning.

When my mother told me, "School's over for you, let's go see your godfather, he'll get you a job," I said, "I know how to get money without leaving school, don't worry about it." "What do you mean?" she asked me. I got tongue-tied and just stood there with my mouth open. Then I asked her if she knew Skinny Higueras. She gave me a queer look and asked me, "How do you know him?" "We're friends," I told her, "and sometimes I do little jobs for him." She shrugged her shoulders. "You're grown up now," she said, "so do what you like. I don't want to know anything about it. But if you don't bring home any money you'll have to go to work." I could tell that my mother knew what my brother and Skinny Higueras used to do. I'd already gone with Skinny to other houses, we always went at night and each time I earned about twenty soles. Skinny told me, "You just stick by me and I'll make you rich." I had all the money hidden in my notebooks and I asked my mother, "Do you need any money right now?" "I always need money," she said, "give me what you've got." I gave her all of it except two soles. The only things I spent money on were the fares to go wait for Tere every day when she got out of school and my packs of cigarettes, that's when I began buying my own. A pack of Incas would last me three or four days. One time I lit a cigarette in the Bellavista Plaza and Tere saw me from the doorway of her house. She came over and we sat down on a bench to talk. She said, "Teach me how to smoke." I lit another cigarette and she took a few puffs, but she couldn't inhale and right away she started choking. She told me the next day that she'd been sick all night and wasn't going to try smoking any more. I remember those days very clearly, they were the best days in the year. We were almost at the end of the term, exams were beginning, and we studied even more than before. We were practically inseparable. When her aunt was out or was sleeping, we cracked jokes and rumpled each other's hair, and I felt very nervous every time she touched me. I saw her twice a day and I was very happy. I had money, too, so I always brought her a surprise. At night I went to the Bellavista Plaza to meet Skinny, and he'd tell me to be ready on such and such a night. "We've got something real good lined up," he'd tell me.

At first the three of us went out, Skinny and me and the peasant Jitters. One time when we pulled off a job in Orrantia, in a rich man's house, a couple of new guys went with us. But mostly it was just Skinny and me. "The fewer, the better," he said. "That way there's a bigger split. But sometimes we have to take others, if it's a big haul we can't do it by ourselves." Usually we broke into vacant houses. Skinny knew all about them, I don't know how, and he'd explain to me how to get in, by the roof or the chimney or a window. At first I was scared, but later on I could work very calmly. I remember the time we got into a house in Chorrillos. I went in through a garage window after Skinny cut a hole in it with a glass cutter. I passed through the house to open the front door, then I walked down to the corner to wait. A few minutes later I saw the lights go on upstairs and Skinny came shooting out the front door. He grabbed my hand as he went by and said, "Hurry up or we're cooked." We ran for about three blocks, I don't know if they were chasing us but I was plenty scared, and when Skinny told me, "Run down that way, then turn the corner and start walking like nothing happened," I thought I was done for. But I did what he told me and it all worked out all right. I had to walk the whole way home. I was half frozen by the time I got there, and dead tired, and I was afraid Skinny'd got caught. But he was waiting for me in the plaza the next day, and he almost died laughing about it. "What a flop!" he said. "I was opening a dresser drawer when all the lights came on. They damn near blinded me. It's a good thing we've got God on our side."

"Then what?" Alberto asked.

"That's all," the corporal said. "It's just that he started to bleed, and I told him, 'Stop your bellyaching.' So the idiot said, 'I'm not, Corporal, but I'm hurt.' And since all the privates are buddies, they started saying, 'He's hurt, he's hurt.' I didn't believe it, but maybe it was true. Do you know why, Cadet? Because his hair was getting red. I told him to go wash it off so he wouldn't dirty the floor in the barracks. But he was a stubborn bastard, he wouldn't do it. If you want to know the truth, he's a fairy. He just sat there on his bunk, and I gave him a shove so he'd get up. That's the only reason I shoved him, Cadet, but the others started yelling, 'Leave him alone, Corporal, can't you see he's hurt.' "

"And after that?" Alberto asked.

"That's all, Cadet, that's all. The sergeant came in and asked what was the matter with him. 'He fell down, Sergeant,' I said. 'Isn't that right, you fell down?' But the fairy said, 'No, you hit me on the head, Corporal,' and the other bastards started shouting, 'That's right, that's right, the corporal hit him.' What goddamned fairies! So the sergeant sent that idiot to the infirmary and brought me here to the guardhouse. I've been here four days, on bread and water. You can't guess how hungry I am, Cadet."

"Why did you hit him on the head?" Alberto asked.

"Bah," the corporal said with a scornful gesture. "I just

wanted him to clear out the rubbish faster. Want me to tell you something? There isn't any justice. If the lieutenant finds any rubbish in the barracks he restricts me to the grounds for three days or he kicks my ass. But if I give a soldier a bat on the head they put me in the guardhouse. Want to know the truth, Cadet? The officers walk all over the privates, but they're all buddies and they help each other. We noncoms, though, we get it from both sides. The officers treat us like dirt and the privates hate us, they do everything they can to make it tough for us. I was better off when I was a private, Cadet."

The two cells were in back of the guardhouse. They were high and dark, with a grating between them through which Alberto and the corporal could chat comfortably. In each cell there was a small window near the ceiling that let in a few rays of light; there was also a rickety field cot, a straw mattress and a khaki blanket.

"How long're you going to be here, Cadet?" the corporal asked.

"I don't know," Alberto said. Gamboa had not given him any explanation the night before, he had merely said curtly, "And sleep there, I don't want you to go to the barracks." It was scarcely ten o'clock, Costanera Avenue and the patios were deserted, with a silent wind sweeping through them; the cadets who had been confined were in their barracks and the cadets who had gone out on pass would not return until eleven. The privates were sitting together on a bench at the rear of the guardhouse, talking in low voices. They had not even glanced at Alberto when he entered the cell. For a few moments he could not see anything in the darkness, then he made out the shadow of the field cot in one corner. He put his bag on the floor, took off his jacket, shoes and cap, and covered himself with the blanket. He could hear someone snoring, it sounded like an animal growling, but he fell asleep almost at once. He woke up several times during the night, and that snoring still continued, unchanged, powerful. At daybreak he discovered the corporal in the next cell: a tall man with a face as sharp as a knife, sleeping with his cap and leggings on. A little later a soldier brought him a cup of hot coffee. The corporal woke up and gave him a friendly wave from his bunk. That was when they started chatting together, and they were still at it when reveille sounded.

Alberto left the grating and went over to the cell door, which looked out into the main room of the guardhouse. Lt. Gamboa was leaning toward Lt. Ferrero, saying something almost in a whisper. The soldiers rubbed their eyes, stretched, picked up their rifles and went out of the guard-house on the double. When they opened the door, Alberto could see the patio out front and the border of white stones around the monument to the hero. The privates who were going on duty with Ferrero would be waiting out there to come in. Gamboa left the guardhouse without looking toward the cells. Alberto heard a whistle blowing, then another and another, and he knew that the cadets of the different Years were forming ranks in their patios. The cor-poral was still on his cot. He had closed his eyes again, but he was not snoring. When he heard the sound of the bat-talions marching to the mess hall, he whistled in time with their steps. Alberto looked at his watch. He must be in with the Piranha now, Teresita, or else he's already talked with him, they've talked with the major and the commandant, they're going to see the colonel, Teresita, the five of them are talking about me, they'll call the newspapers and I'll be photographed and the first day I get a pass I'll be lynched and my mother'll go crazy, and I won't be able to go to Miraflores any more because they'll all point their fingers at me, I'll have to go away and change my name, Teresita. A few minutes later, they heard the whistles again. The cadets left the mess hall and crossed the field to take their places on the parade ground; in the guardhouse the sound of their footsteps was like a distant murmur. But when they marched to the classrooms the sound was a heavy, martial beat that slowly diminished and finally died away. They know about it now, Teresita, they're saying the Poet didn't come back, Arróspide's put me down as absent, they'll draw lots to see who'll beat me up, it'll all come out and my father'll say, you've dragged my name in the mud, in the police reports in the newspapers, your grandfather and your great-grandfather would've died of shock, we've always been the best in every way and you're a disgrace, we'll run away, Teresita, we'll go to New York and never come back to Peru, they're in the classrooms now and they're looking at my empty place. Alberto stepped back when Lt. Ferrero came to the cell. The metal door opened silently.

"Cadet Fernández?" He was a very young lieutenant, in charge of a company in the Third.

"Yes, Sir."

"Go to the office of your Year and report to Captain Garrido."

Alberto put on his jacket and cap. The morning was clear, with a smell of salt and fish in the wind. He had not heard any rain during the night, but the patio in front of the guard-house was full of puddles and the statue of the hero looked like a sad, wet plant. There was no one on the parade ground, no one in the patio outside his barracks. The office door was open. He pulled his jacket down and rubbed his hand over his eyes. Gamboa was standing, Capt. Garrido was sitting on a corner of the desk; when they saw him, the captain nodded him in. Alberto went in and came to attention. The captain looked him up and down very slowly. For once, his jaw muscles were not working, but they bulged out like abscesses under his ears. His mouth was closed but his bright white teeth stuck out through his lips, that was why they called him the Piranha. The captain nodded again.

"All right," he said, "let's get to the facts. What's it all about, Cadet?"

Alberto opened his mouth, but it was as if he had let in

some poisonous air that destroyed his vitals. What was he going to say? The captain seemed both angry and nervous, he kept fiddling with the papers on his desk. Gamboa was off to one side and he could not see his face. His cheeks burned, he knew-that he must be blushing.

"What are you waiting for?" the captain said. "Haven't you got a tongue?"

Alberto lowered his head. He felt immensely tired and suddenly unsure of himself: the words that rose seemed fragile and deceptive, they retreated or they died on his lips.

Gamboa interrupted his stammering. "Come on, Cadet," he said. "Calm down, get hold of yourself. The captain's waiting. Just repeat what you told me on Saturday. Don't be afraid to speak out."

"Yes, Sir," Alberto said. He took a deep breath. "They killed Cadet Arana because he told on the Circle."

"Did you see it with your own eyes?" the captain asked him crossly. Alberto looked up: the captain's jaws were working now, the muscles moving in rhythm under his greenish skin.

"No, Sir," he said, "but. . ."

"But what?" the captain roared. "How can you dare make an accusation like that without concrete evidence? Do you know what it means to accuse someone of murder? Why have you made up this idiotic story?"

Capt. Garrido's brow was damp and there was a little yellow fire in both of his eyes. His hands gripped the top of the desk, his temples were pulsing. All at once, Alberto recovered himself. He returned the captain's look without blinking, and after a few seconds he could see the officer shift his eyes.

"I haven't made up a thing, Sir," he said, and his voice sounded convincing to his own ears. "Not a thing, Sir. The cadets in the Circle were looking for whoever made Cava get expelled. The Jaguar wanted revenge no matter what happened, he hates squealers worse than anything. And everybody hated Cadet Arana, they treated him like a slave. I'm sure the Jaguar killed him, Sir. If I wasn't sure I wouldn't've said anything."

"One moment, Fernández," Gamboa said. "Explain things in order. Come up closer. Sit down if you want to."

"No," the captain said in a harsh voice, and Gamboa turned to look at him. But Capt. Garrido had his eyes fixed on Alberto. "Stay where you are. And keep talking."

Alberto coughed and wiped his brow with his handkerchief. He began to speak in a faint, unsteady voice, but as he described what the Circle did, and told the story of the Slave, and went on to the liquor and cigarettes, the stealing and selling of exams, the affairs at Paulino's, the jumping over the wall, the poker games in the latrine, the contests, the vengeances, the bets, it was as if the secret life of the section took on the reality of a nightmare, and his voice grew stronger, steadier, even aggressive at times.

The captain turned paler at every revelation, and only interrupted him once: "But what's *that* got to do with it?"

"I'm telling you so you'll believe me, Sir," Alberto said. "The officers don't have any way of knowing what goes on in the barracks. I'm telling you so you'll believe me about the Slave."

Later, when Alberto had finished speaking, Capt. Garrido was silent for a few moments, glaring at all the objects on his desk. His hands twitched at the buttons on his jacket. "All right," he said abruptly. "You mean we should expel the whole section. They're all thieves or drunkards or gamblers. They're all guilty of something. That's just fine. But what about you?"

"We're all guilty, Sir," Alberto said. "Of everything. The only one who wasn't was the Slave. That's why he never had any friends." His voice broke. "You've got to believe me, Sir. The Circle was out to get him. They wanted to get whoever told on Cava. It was revenge, Sir."

"Stop right there!" the captain said. He seemed even more

nervous than before. "That's right where your story falls apart! What nonsense are you trying to hand me? Nobody accused Cadet Cava of anything!"

"It isn't nonsense, Sir," Alberto said. "Ask Lieutenant Huarina if it wasn't the Slave who told on Cava. He was the only one who saw Cava when he left the barracks to steal the exam. He was on guard duty that night. Ask Lieutenant Huarina."

"You haven't got a leg to stand on," the captain said. But Alberto could tell that he was still less sure of himself: one hand was dangling futilely in the air, and his teeth looked even bigger. "It's nonsense, nonsense, Cadet."

"But it was as if they'd told on the Jaguar himself, Sir," Alberto said. "He was raving mad because they expelled Cava, and the Circle met every night. It was revenge. I know the Jaguar and he's capable of. . ."

"That's enough," the captain said. "What you're telling me is absolutely childish. You're accusing a fellow cadet of murder, but without any proof. I wouldn't be surprised if you yourself aren't the one who wants revenge. You can't play that kind of game in the army, Cadet. It could cost you dearly."

"Captain," Alberto said, "the Jaguar was behind the Slave when we attacked the hill."

But then he stopped talking. He had said it without thinking and now he was not sure. He tried feverishly to visualize the scene at La Perla, the hill with the plowed fields around it, the morning light, the formations.

"Are you sure?" Gamboa asked.

"Yes, Sir. He was behind Arana. I'm sure."

Capt. Garrido looked at them: his eyes jumped from one to the other, suspicious, angry. His hands were together now, one of them clenched, the other one covering it. "And what does that mean? Nothing!" he said. "Absolutely nothing!"

The three of them were silent for a few moments. Suddenly the captain straightened up and began pacing back and forth, his arms crossed, his hands on his shoulders.

Gamboa sat where the captain had been sitting and stared at the wall.

"Cadet Fernández," the captain said. He had stopped in the middle of the room and his voice was gentler now. "I'm going to talk to you man to man. You're young and impulsive. That's not a fault, it can even be a virtue. A mere tenth of what you've told me would be more than enough to expel you from the Academy. And that would be a terrible blow for your parents. Am I right?"

"Yes, Sir," Alberto said. Lt. Gamboa was dangling one foot in the air and looking at the floor.

"The death of that cadet has affected you," the captain went on. "I can understand, he was your friend. But even if some parts of what you've said are true, you could never *prove* it. Never. Because it's all based on a sheer hypothesis. The most we can do is investigate the violations you mentioned. . .and if they exist, you'll be the first one we'll expel, of course. However, I'm willing to forget the whole affair if you'll promise me you'll never say another word about it." He gestured as if to clap his brow, but then dropped his hand. "Yes, that's the best thing. We'll forget all these fantasies."

Lt. Gamboa still had his eyes lowered and was still swinging his foot, but now the tip of his shoe was grazing the floor.

"Do you understand?" the captain said, trying to smile.

"No, Sir," Alberto said.

"You don't understand me, Cadet?"

"I can't make that promise," Alberto said. "They killed Arana."

"In that case," the captain said, "I *order* you to keep your mouth shut and stop talking nonsense. And if you don't obey me, you'll soon find out who you're dealing with."

"Excuse me, Sir," Gamboa said.

"I'm speaking, Gamboa, don't interrupt me."

"I'm sorry, Sir," Gamboa said, standing up. He was taller

than the captain and Garrido had to raise his eyes. "Cadet Fernández has the right to make this accusation, Sir. I'm not saying it's true, but he has the right to demand an investigation. That's perfectly clear in the regulations."

"Are you going to teach me the regulations, Gamboa?"

"No, Sir, of course not. But if you aren't going to take any action, I'll hand my report to the major. This is a serious thing and I believe it ought to be investigated."

A little after the last exam, I saw Teresa with two other girls on Sáenz Peña Avenue. They were carrying towels and I called to her and asked her where she was going. "To the beach," she told me. I was in a bad mood that day, and when my mother asked me for money I answered with a coarse remark. She got out the belt she kept under her bed. She hadn't hit me for a long time and I threatened her: "If you touch me, I'll never give you another centavo." It was only a bluff and I never dreamed it'd have any effect. I was stunned when I saw her lower the belt, which was already in mid-air, and throw it on the floor. She muttered a remark as coarse as mine and went into the kitchen without another word. Teresa and the other two girls went to the beach the next day and the days that followed. One morning I decided to spy on them. They went to Chucuito. They had their bathing suits on under their clothes and they undressed on the beach. Three or four boys were waiting for them there. I only looked at the one that talked with Teresa. I watched them all morning from behind the railing. Finally the girls put on their clothes again and went back to Bellavista. I waited for the boys. Two of them left in a short while, but the boy that talked with Teresa stayed there with another one till almost three. Then they headed toward La Punta, walking in the middle of the street, swinging their towels. When they got to an empty block I began throwing stones at them. I aimed at both of them and I hit Teresa's friend square in the face. He said, "Ow!" and bent over, and another stone hit him in the back. They both stared at me and I ran toward them before they had time to think what to do. The other one shouted, "He's a lunatic!" and ran away, but Teresa's friend just stood there and I piled into him. I'd had fights at school and knew what to do, also my brother taught me to use my feet and head while I was still little. "If you lose hold of yourself and just start throwing punches," he told me, "you're done for. It's all right to fight that way if you're a lot stronger than the other guy, you can get him into a corner and break through his guard. But if you aren't, it's bad. You wear yourself out swinging at the air, and you start getting bored, and pretty soon you don't feel like fighting any more. And if the other guy knows what's up, that's when he takes advantage of it and gives you a real beating." My brother taught me how to handle a guy that just swings wildly, how to tire him out, how to keep him away with your feet. Then when he gets careless you grab his shirt and bang him with your head. He taught me how to do it the Callao way, not with your forehead or the top of your head, you hit him with the bone that's right at your hairline, it's harder than the rest, and you drop your hands so he won't bring his knee up and get you in the stomach. "There's nothing like a bang with the head," my brother told me, "one good one can stun the other guy and then you're all set." This time I forgot everything he taught me but I beat them anyway. The one who'd been with Teresa didn't defend himself, he just fell down and started crying. His friend was watching about ten yards away and he shouted, "Don't hit him, you fairy, don't hit him," but I kept on hitting him while he was down. Then I went after the other one, he started running but I caught up with him and hit him and he fell down. He didn't want to fight: the minute I let him loose he got up and ran. I went back to the other one, who was wiping his face. I meant to talk with him but as soon as I saw his face I got furious again and gave him a punch. He began screeching like a parrot. I grabbed him by his shirt and said, "If you go near Teresa again, I'll hit you twice as hard." I insulted his mother and gave him a kick, I might've gone on with it but just then I got grabbed by the ear. It was a woman, she started hitting me on the head and shouting, "You savage, you animal!" and the other one took the chance to run away. She finally let go of me and I went home to Bellavista. It was like before the fight, I didn't feel as if I'd got revenge. I'd never felt that way before. The other times I didn't see Teresa I just felt unhappy or I wanted to be alone, but this time I felt angry and unhappy all at once. I knew that when Teresa heard what I did, she'd hate me. I went to the Bellavista Plaza but I didn't go in my house. I walked on to the bar on Sáenz Peña, and Skinny Higueras was there, talking to the bartender. "What's the matter?" he asked me. I'd never told him anything about Tere, but now I had to spill it out to somebody I could trust. I told Skinny everything, from the time she came to live next door to us four years earlier. Skinny listened to me very seriously, he didn't laugh even once. All he said was, "Really, man?" and "Christ!" and "So then what?" All at the right places. When I was through, he said, "You're head over heels in love. I was about your age the first time I fell in love, but I didn't take it so hard. Love's the worst thing there is. You start acting like an idiot, you don't look out for yourself. Everything seems different and you do the craziest things just on the spur of the moment. I mean that men do. Women, they're different, they're smarter, they only fall in love when it suits them. If they figure their man isn't right for them, they fall out again and look for another one. And it doesn't bother them at all. But don't worry. I swear to God I can cure you right now, today, I know just the medicine you need." He had me drinking pisco and cerveza till it got dark, then he made me throw up, squeezing my stomach to help me. After that he took me to a tavern in Callao, he made me take a shower in the patio and I had to eat things with lots of chili in them, the dining room was full

of people. We got into a taxi and he gave the driver an
address. "Ever been to a whorehouse?" he asked me. I
shook my head. "It's the sure cure," he said. "You wait and
see. But maybe they won't let you in." And that's what
almost happened: the woman that opened the door knew
Skinny all right, but she got mad when she saw me. "You're
crazy if you think you can bring this kid in," she said, "there's
a stool pigeon here every five minutes cadging a beer." They
argued for a while but she let me in with Skinny. "All right,"
she said, "but go straight to the room and don't come out of
it till morning." Skinny rushed me through the downstairs
room, I didn't even have time to look at the people that were
there. We went up the stairs and the woman opened a door,
and before Skinny could turn on the light she said, "I'm
going to send you a dozen beers. I'll put up with the kid
here but you've got to spend some money. The girls'll be up
right away. You know Sandra, she likes these snot-nosed
babies." The room was large and dirty. There was a bed in
the middle of it, with a red mattress, and a chamber pot,
and two mirrors. One of them was on the ceiling over the
bed, the other one was on the wall next to it. The rest of the
walls were covered with drawings of naked men and women,
some of them in pencil or ink, some of them scratched with
a knife. Then two women came in with a lot of bottles of
beer. They were friends of Skinny's and they both kissed
him, they pinched him and sat on his lap and used words like
ass and whore and prick. One of them was thin, she was part
Negro and she had a gold tooth, the other one was plump,
with light-colored skin. They made fun of me and told
Skinny he was corrupting a minor. They started drinking
beer and a little later they opened the door part way so they
could hear the music from downstairs, then they danced. At
first I didn't say a word to anybody but after I'd had some
beer I felt happier. I danced with the light-skinned one and
she pushed my head against her tits, they were outside her
dress. Skinny got drunk and told the other one to put on a

show for us. She danced a mambo in just her panties and suddenly Skinny went up to her and dumped her onto the bed. The light-skinned one grabbed my hand and took me to another room. "Is this the first time?" she asked me. I told her no but she could tell I was lying. She looked happy about that and she came over to me naked and said, "I hope you bring me good luck."

Lt. Gamboa left his room and walked quickly across the parade ground. He reached the classroom building at the moment that Pitaluga, the Officer of the Day, was blowing his whistle: the first class of the morning had just ended. The cadets were in the classrooms, and a steady roar emerged from the gray walls of the building: it was like a vast, round monster hovering over the patio. Gamboa paused a moment on the stairs, then went on to the office. Pezoa, the noncom on duty, was there, leafing through his notebook.

"Come on, Pezoa."

The noncom followed him, stroking his thin mustache with one finger. He walked with his legs apart, as if he were in the cavalry. Gamboa respected him because he was alert and efficient, especially during the field exercises.

"When they get out of classes, tell the first section to fall in. With their rifles. March them out to the stadium."

"An arms inspection, Sir?"

"No. I want them to form up in combat groups. Look, Pezoa, they didn't get out of position during the exercises, did they? I mean, they advanced in the proper order, the first group first, then the second, then the third."

"No, Sir," Pezoa said. "The captain told us to put the shortest ones in the front line."

"Yes." Gamboa thought for a moment. "Yes, you're right. Anyway, I'll be waiting for you in the stadium."

The noncom saluted and left. Gamboa returned to his quarters. The morning light was clearer, with almost no fog, and the sea wind barely stirred the grass on the open field where the vicuña was wandering in circles. It was almost summer, the Academy would be empty, life would be easier, softer: he would have fewer hours on duty, fewer things to worry about, he could go to the beach at least three times a week. And his wife would be all right again, they could take the baby out for a ride. And he could also study harder for the exams, he had had only eight months to get ready, that was too little: twenty candidates would be promoted to captain, but a hundred lieutenants had applied.

A few moments later, he went to the captain's office. Garrido was sitting at his desk, reading reports, and did not look up when he entered. At last he said, "Lieutenant?"

"Yes, Sir?"

"What's it all about?" Capt. Garrido was scowling at him. Gamboa hesitated before answering.

"I'm not sure, Sir," he said. "It's hard to say what really happened. I've started investigating. Perhaps I can find out."

"I'm not thinking about that," the captain said. "I'm thinking about the consequences. Aren't you?"

"Yes," Gamboa said. "It could be serious."

"Serious?" The captain smiled. "I'm sure you haven't forgotten I'm in charge of the battalion. And I'm sure you haven't forgotten you're in charge of the company. Whatever happens, we'll take the rap, the two of us."

"I've thought about that, Sir," Gamboa said. "You're right, of course. And believe me, I don't like it."

"When do you expect a promotion?"

"Next year."

"So do I," the captain said. "The exams are going to be tough, there's less and less room at the top. Let's face the facts, Gamboa. We've both got excellent records. There isn't a single black mark against us. But they'll hold us responsible for this. The cadet seems to believe you're backing him up. Talk with him. Convince him we're right. The only thing to do is to forget the whole affair."

Gamboa looked the captain in the eyes. "May I speak to you frankly, Sir?"

"That's exactly what I've been doing, Gamboa. I'm treating you as a friend, not a subordinate."

"I'm as interested in a promotion as you are, Sir. I'll do all I can to get it. I don't want to be stuck here at the Academy any more than you do. I can't feel I'm in the army when I'm bossing these kids around. But if I didn't learn anything else at the Military School, I learned the importance of discipline. Without that, everything breaks down, everything falls to pieces. Why is our country the way it is? Lack of discipline. Lack of order. The only part of it that stays strong and healthy is the army, because of its structure, its organization. If it's true they killed that boy, if it's true about the liquor and the sale of exams and the rest, I feel I've got a duty, Captain. I feel it's my duty to find out if there's any truth in that story."

"You're exaggerating, Gamboa," the captain said. He began to pace back and forth as he had done during his interview with Alberto. "I don't say we should cover up everything. We'll have to punish them for the liquor and the exams. But remember, the first thing you learn in the army is to be a man. And what do men do? They smoke, they drink, they gamble, they fuck. The cadets all know they get expelled if they're discovered. *If*, Gamboa. We've already expelled quite a few. But the smart ones don't get caught. If they're going to be men, they have to take chances, they have to use their wits. That's the way the army is, Gamboa. Discipline isn't enough. You've got to have guts, and you've also got to have brains." He paused for a moment. "But we can discuss all that some other time. What's worrying me right now is the main accusation. It's asinine, of course, but it could still do us a lot of harm if it gets to the colonel."

"Excuse me, Captain," Gamboa said, "but. . .well, I agree with you that the cadets in my company can do what they want as long as I don't know about it. But now I *do* know about it, and I'd be neglecting my duty if I tried to pretend I didn't. I'm positive there's something very wrong. Cadet Fernández showed me that the whole company has been laughing in my face all along. They've made a fool of me."

"But that's because they're men now, Gamboa," the captain said. "When we first get them, they're sniveling little brats. And look at them!"

"Then I'm going to make better men of them," Gamboa said. "By the time I get through investigating I'll have the whole company court-martialed if I have to."

The captain stopped pacing. "You talk like a religious fanatic," he said, raising his voice. "Do you want to wreck your career?"

"A soldier can't wreck his career by doing his duty, Sir."

"Very well," the captain said, beginning to pace again. "I can't stop you. But surely you realize you'll end up holding the bag. You aren't stupid, in one way, Gamboa: you know I won't back you up, you know you're doing this on your own."

"Of course, Sir. Excuse me."

Gamboa saluted and left the office. In his room there was a photograph of a woman on the nightstand. It had been taken before they were married. He had met her at a party, while he was still at the Military School. The picture had been taken in the countryside, but Gamboa did not know where. She was slimmer then, and wore her hair loose. She was standing under a tree, smiling, and there was a river in the background. Gamboa studied it for a few moments, then re-examined the reports and the punishment orders. A little before noon he went back to the patio. Two soldiers were sweeping out the barracks of the first section. When they saw him approaching they came to attention.

"At ease," Gamboa said. "Do you sweep out this barracks every day?"

"Yes, Sir, I do," one of the soldiers said. He pointed to the other and added, "He sweeps out the second."

"Come with me."

Out in the patio, the lieutenant stared at him for a moment and then said, "You've screwed yourself, you idiot."

The soldier automatically came to attention, and opened his eyes wider. His face was coarse and beardless. He seemed to accept it as a fact that he had done something wrong.

"Why haven't you turned in a report?" Gamboa asked.

"But I have, Sir. Thirty-two beds. Thirty-two lockers. But I turned it in to the sergeant."

"I'm not talking about that. And don't pretend you don't know. Why didn't you report the bottles of liquor, the cigarettes, the dice, the cards?"

The soldier opened his eyes even wider, but without replying.

"Which lockers?" Gamboa asked.

"I don't understand, Lieutenant."

"Which lockers had cards and liquor in them?"

"I wouldn't know, Sir. It must've been in another section."

"If you lie to me, you'll be confined to the grounds for two weeks," Gamboa said. "Which lockers had cigarettes in them?"

"I'm not sure, Sir." But then he lowered his eyes and said, "All of them, I think."

"And liquor?"

"Just in a few, I think."

"And dice?"

"Just in a few, I think."

"And why haven't you reported it?"

"I haven't seen a thing, Sir. I can't open the lockers. They're all locked, and the cadets've got the keys. I only think those things are there. I haven't seen them."

"All right," Gamboa said. "This afternoon I take over as Officer of the Day. I want you and the other privates on the clean-up detail to report to me at the guardhouse at three o'clock."

"Yes, Sir," the soldier said.

5

You could tell that nobody'd escape, the whole thing was like witchcraft. They had us standing in formation, then they took us into the barracks, and I said to myself, some stool pigeon's been singing, I don't like to believe it but it's as clear as day, the Jaguar's told on us. They told us to open our lockers, my heart sank like a stone, "Keep hold of yourself," Vallano said, "this is the end of the world," and he was right. "Clothing inspection?" Arróspide asked, the poor guy looked like a corpse. "Don't try to be a Pelopidas," Pezoa said, "keep quiet, just stick your tongue up your ass, please." I was so nervous I had cramps, and the guys were all like sleepwalkers. Everything was like a bad dream, with Gamboa standing on one locker, the Rat on another, and the lieutenant shouted, "All right, open your lockers, but that's all, no one's to stick his hand in." And who would've dared, they had us screwed, at least it was good to know the Jaguar got screwed first. Who else could've told them about the bottles and the cards? But it's very confusing, I still don't understand all that about the stadium and the rifles. Was Gamboa in a bad mood, did he want to take it out on us? And some of them even laughed, it's a shame there's guys like that, they don't know what the word disgrace means. Though the truth is, it was funny enough, the Rat began diving into the lockers, he got right inside them, and since he's practically a dwarf the clothes hid him from sight. He got down on all fours, the ass-kissing bastard, so Gamboa'd know he was making a thorough search, he fished in every pocket, opened everything, smelled every bottle, he was having a wonderful time. "Here's a pack of Incas, and Jesus, this one's high society, he smokes Chesterfields, and here's another bottle, were they going to throw a party?" We were all scared, but at least they found something or other in every one of the lockers, that made it a little better. Of course the guys that had bottles'll get screwed the worst, mine was almost empty and I told him to notice that and the bastard said, "Shut up, stupid." All through it, Gamboa was happy as a pig, you could tell from the way he'd ask, "How many did you say?" "Two packs of Incas, two boxes of matches, Lieutenant." And Gamboa'd write it down in his notebook, slowly, slowly, to make the pleasure last longer. "A half full bottle of what?" "Of pisco, Sir. Sol de Ica brand." Every time Curly looked at me he swallowed hard, that's right, buddy, we're screwed for sure. It was pitiful to see the look on the faces of the other guys. Where the Christ did they get the idea of inspecting the lockers? After Gamboa and the Rat went away, Curly said, "It's got to be the Jaguar. He said himself, 'If I get screwed, everybody gets screwed.' He's a fairy and a squealer." He shouldn't've said it like that, not without proof, even though it's got to be true.

The one thing I can't figure out is why they took us to the stadium, I suppose the Jaguar's to blame for that too, he must've told them what we did with the chickens sometimes, I bet the lieutenant said he'd take care of those wise guys, the Rat came into the classroom and said, "Fall in on the double, I've got a surprise for you." We all shouted, "Rat! Rat!" He said, "It's an order from the lieutenant. Fall in and quick-march to the barracks. Or do you want me to call him?" We fell in and he marched us to the barracks, and when we got to the door he said, "Get your rifles, I'll give you one minute to fall in again. Brigadier, write down the names of the last three out." We said everything we could think of about his mother and none of us knew what the story was. Out in the patio the cadets from the other sections made fun of us. Who ever saw a section with rifles going out for field exercises in the stadium in the middle of the day? Maybe Gamboa's lost some of his marbles. He was waiting for us on the soccer field, he looked sort of eager like. "Halt!" the Rat said. "Take your field positions." We all

objected, it was like a nightmare to have to do field exercises
in your regular uniform, and on an empty stomach besides,
go tell your mother to flop around on the wet grass after
three straight hours of classes. Gamboa broke in with that
big voice of his, he said, "Form three lines, group three in
front, group one at the rear." And that ass-kissing Rat said,
"Come on, you fuck-ups, get moving." Then Gamboa said,
"Attack formation. Each man ten yards apart." Maybe there's
going to be a war, maybe the Minister told them to speed
up our training. We'd all go, even if they just made us noncoms, but we'd probably be officers, I'd love to march into
Arica all blood and thunder and put up the Peruvian flag all
over the place, on the rooftops, in the windows, in the streets,
they say Chilean women are the most beautiful in the world,
I wonder if that's true. But I don't think there's going to be
a war, or they'd be drilling the others too, not just the first
section. "What's the matter?" Gamboa bellowed. "You in
groups one and two, are you deaf or just plain stupid? I
said ten yards, not twenty. You Negro there, what's your
name?" "Vallano, Sir," and I could've died laughing to see
Vallano's face when Gamboa called him a Negro. "All right,"
the lieutenant said, "why're you twenty yards away when
I told you ten?" "There's a cadet missing, Sir," Pezoa said.
"Oh?" Gamboa said. "Then give him six points." "That's
impossible, Sir. The missing cadet is deceased. Cadet Arana,
Lieutenant." What a stupid bastard the Rat is. And everything kept going wrong, Gamboa was furious. "Very well,"
he said, "I want the cadet in the second line to move up." A
few moments later he shouted, "Why don't you little shits
obey my orders?" We all looked at each other and Arróspide
came to attention and said, "That cadet's missing too. The
Jaguar." "Take his place," Gamboa said. "And don't bitch
about it. Orders should be carried out without questions or
complaints." That last was for all of us. Then he made us
advance from one end of the field to the other, jump up
when you hear the whistle, charge forward, flop on your

belly again, you lose track of time, you even forget your own body in exercises like that, and when we started getting winded Gamboa marched us back to the barracks. The lieutenant got up on one locker and the Rat on another, Pezoa's so small he sweat blood to get up there, and they told us, "Stand at attention in your regular places," and right then I said to myself, the Jaguar's sold us out to save his own skin, there aren't any decent people in this world, who'd've thought he'd do a thing like that. "Open your lockers and then take one step forward. Anybody who puts his hand inside is done for," as if we were magicians to hide a bottle right under the lieutenant's nose. Then they got a big bag and went away with everything they found, we were all silent and I went and lay down on my bunk. Skimpy wasn't around, it was chow-time and she must've gone to the kitchen to look for scraps. Too bad she wasn't with me so I could scratch her head, that's restful, it calms me down, I think of her as a girl. It must be something like that when you're married. Say I come home tired out, and my woman sits down beside me, very quiet and comfortable, and I don't say anything at first, I fondle her, I scratch her, I tickle her and she laughs, I pinch her and she squeals, I tease her, I play with her lips, I make curls in her hair with my fingers, I hold her nose and let go when she's gasping, I rub my hands on her neck, her tits, her shoulders, her back, her ass, her legs, her belly, then I kiss her and tell her she's my little half-breed, my little whore. Suddenly somebody yelled, "You guys are to blame!" I yelled back, "What do you mean by you guys?" "The Jaguar and you others," Arróspide said. I jumped up and headed for him but they stopped me before I got there. "I said you guys, you guys." He was shouting as if he'd gone crazy, the spit ran down his chin and he didn't even notice. "Let go of me," I told them, "I'm not afraid of him, I'll beat the shit out of him once and for all." But they kept holding me back so I'd calm down, "It's better not to fight right now," Vallano said, "not with things like they are, we've got to stick together, it's going to be bad for all of us." "Arróspide," I said, "you're the worst fairy I've ever seen, the minute things get rough you start in blaming your own buddies." "You're a liar," Arróspide said, "I'm with all of you against the officers, if I can help anybody I'll do it. But the Jaguar and you and Curly are to blame for what's happened, because you played dirty. There's something we don't know about yet. It's quite a coincidence, they hardly got the Jaguar in the guardhouse when Gamboa knew what was in our lockers." I didn't know what to say, and Curly sided with the rest. They all said, "That's right, the Jaguar's the squealer," and, "We'll get revenge," things like that. Then the whistle blew for going to the mess hall, and I think it was the first time in the Academy I could hardly eat anything, because the food stuck in my throat.

When the soldier saw Gamboa approaching, he stood up and fished out the key to open the cell door. But the lieutenant took the key out of his hand and said, "Go away, leave me alone with the cadet." He waited while the soldier walked out onto the soccer field in the direction of the classroom building. Then he opened the door. The cell was in almost total darkness: night was falling and the only window seemed a mere slit. At first he could not see anyone, and had the sudden idea that the cadet had escaped. Then he discovered him stretched out on the cot. He walked over to him, and saw that his eyes were closed, that he was asleep. The lieutenant studied his motionless features, trying to remember him, but it was useless: he confused his face with others, although it was vaguely familiar, not because of any particular feature but because it looked prematurely adult, with clenched jaws, a solemn frown, a cleft chin. When the soldiers and cadets were in the presence of a superior they put on a stern expression, but this cadet did not know he was there. Also, his face was different. Most of the cadets had dark skin and angular features, but what Gamboa saw was a white face and almost blond hair and lashes. He reached out a hand and grasped the Jaguar's shoulder. He was surprised at himself, because the gesture had lacked energy, he had touched him gently as if waking up a comrade. He felt the Jaguar's body contract under his hand, and his arm was pushed away by the violence with which the Jaguar sat up. But then he heard the click of heels: he had been recognized, and all was normal again.

"Sit down," Gamboa said. "We've got lots to talk about."

The Jaguar sat down. The lieutenant could see his eyes now in the darkness: they were not large, but they were brilliant and penetrating. The cadet did not move or speak, but there was something in his rigidity and silence that annoyed Gamboa.

"Why did you enroll in the Military Academy?"

There was no reply. The Jaguar's hands were gripped on the edge of the cot. His expression did not change: it was still calm and serious.

"They sent you here against your will, right?"

"Why, Lieutenant?"

His voice was exactly like his eyes. The words were not disrespectful, and he pronounced them slowly, almost with a touch of sensuality, but the tone of his voice suggested a hidden arrogance.

"Because I want to know," Gamboa said. "Why did you enroll in the Academy?"

"I wanted to be an army officer."

"'Wanted'?" Gamboa asked. "Have you changed your mind?"

Gamboa was uncertain. He knew that when an officer asked a cadet what his plans were, he always said that he wanted to be an officer in the army. But he also knew that only a handful ever appeared for the entrance exams at the Military School in Chorrillos.

"I'm still not sure, Sir," the Jaguar said. "Perhaps I'll try to get into the Air Force School."

There was a brief pause, during which they looked each other in the eyes, as if waiting for the other to say something.

Then Gamboa asked him harshly, "You know why you're in prison, don't you?"

"No, Sir."

"Really? You don't know the reasons?"

"I haven't done a thing," the Jaguar said.

"Your locker was enough," Gamboa said. "Cigarettes. Two bottles of pisco. A set of skeleton keys. Isn't that enough?"

The lieutenant watched him closely, but it was no use: the Jaguar remained motionless and silent. He seemed neither surprised nor frightened.

"We'll skip the cigarettes," Gamboa added. "They'd only make you lose one pass. But the liquor's something else. The cadets can get drunk outside, in the bars, in their own homes. But they're not permitted to drink a single drop of alcohol inside the Academy." He paused. "And the dice? The first section is a gambling den. And the skeleton keys? Do you know what they mean? They mean stealing. How many lockers have you opened? When was the last time you stole from your comrades?"

"Me?" Gamboa was disconcerted for a moment, and the Jaguar gave him an ironic look. Then, without lowering his eyes, he repeated: "Me?"

"Yes," Gamboa said. He felt as if he could not control his anger. "Who the shit else?"

"Everybody," the Jaguar said. "The whole Academy."

"That's a lie," Gamboa said. "You're a coward."

"I'm not a coward," the Jaguar said. "You're mistaken, Lieutenant."

"And a crook," Gamboa added. "And a drunkard. And a gambler. But above all, a coward. Do you know what I'd like to do if we were civilians?"

"Would you like to hit me?" the Jaguar asked.

"No," Gamboa said. "I'd grab you by the ear and take you to the reformatory. That's where your parents should've sent you. You've screwed yourself now. Do you remember three years ago? I ordered the Circle to break up, to stop playing bandits. Do you remember what I told you that night?"

"No," the Jaguar said. "I don't remember."

"Yes you do," Gamboa said. "But it doesn't matter. You think you're pretty wise, don't you? Well, in the army the wise guys get what's coming to them sooner or later. You've got away with all this for three years. But now your time's up."

"Why? I haven't done a thing," the Jaguar said.

"The Circle," Gamboa said. "Thefts of exams. Thefts of clothing. Disrespect for your superiors. Bullying the cadets in the Third. Do you know what you are? You're a juvenile delinquent."

"That's not true," the Jaguar said. "I haven't done a thing. I've just done what the others do."

"All right, who?" Gamboa asked. "Who else has stolen exams?"

"Everybody," the Jaguar said. "Some guys didn't have to steal them, because they had enough money to buy them. But everybody was mixed up in it."

"Names," Gamboa said. "Give me some names. Which cadets in the first section?"

"Are they going to expel me?"

"Yes. And it might be even worse than expulsion."

"I see," the Jaguar said, with no change in his voice. "Everybody in the first section has bought exams."

"Oh?" Gamboa said. "Including Cadet Arana?"

"What, Sir?"

"I said Arana. Cadet Ricardo Arana."

"No," the Jaguar said. "I don't think he ever bought any. He was a teacher's pet. But all the others did."

"Why did you kill Arana?" Gamboa asked. "Answer me. Everybody knows you did it. Why?"

"What's the matter with you?" the Jaguar asked. He had only blinked once.

"Answer my question."

"Are you a real man?" the Jaguar asked. He had stood up, and his voice shook. "If you are, take off your insignias. I'm not afraid of you."

Gamboa reached out, as quick as lightning, and grasped the collar of his shirt, and in the same movement he pushed him up against the wall with his other hand. Before the Jaguar began choking, Gamboa felt a blow on his shoulder: the Jaguar, trying to hit him in the face, had grazed his elbow and the punch had gone astray.

The lieutenant released him and took a step backward. "I could kill you," he said. "I'd be within my rights. I'm your superior and you tried to hit me. But the court-martial's going to take care of you."

"Take off your insignias," the Jaguar said. "Maybe you're stronger than I am, but I'm not afraid of you."

"Why did you kill Arana?" Gamboa repeated. "Stop acting crazy and answer me."

"I haven't killed anybody. Why do you say that? Do you think I'm a murderer? Why would I want to kill the Slave?"

"Somebody's accused you," Gamboa said. "You're done for."

"Who?" The Jaguar's eyes were glowing like lamps.

"Don't you see?" Gamboa asked. "You're admitting it."

"Who said that?" the Jaguar demanded. "He's the one I *am* going to kill."

"From behind," Gamboa said. "Arana was ahead of you, twenty yards away. You shot him like a coward. Do you know the punishment for that?"

"I haven't killed anybody. I swear I haven't, Lieutenant."

"We'll see," Gamboa said. "It'd be better for you to confess the whole thing."

"I haven't got anything to confess!" the Jaguar shouted. "It's true about the exams and the stealing. But I'm not the only one. Everybody did it. Except for the assholes that paid others to steal for them. But I haven't killed anybody."

"You'll find out," Gamboa said. "He'll say it to your face."

The next day, I got home at nine in the morning. My mother was sitting in the doorway. She didn't move when she saw me coming. I told her, "I stayed with my friend in Chucuito." She didn't say anything. She just gave me a strange look, with a little bit of fear in it, as if she thought I was going to do something to her. Her eyes wandered up and down my body and I felt very uncomfortable. I had a headache and my throat was dry, but I didn't dare go to sleep in front of my mother. I didn't know what to do, I glanced through my notebooks and textbooks, that wasn't any good, then I started rummaging through a chest, and she was standing behind me all the time, watching me. I turned around and said, "What's the matter, why do you keep looking at me?" She said, "You're hopeless. I wish you were dead." And she went out the front door. She sat for a long time on the steps, her elbows on her knees, her face in her hands. I could see her from the window of my room, I could see the rips and mends in her blouse, the wrinkles on her neck, her tangled hair. I went out to her, very slowly, and said, "If you're angry about something, I hope you'll forgive me." She looked at me again. Her face was wrinkled too, and there were white hairs sticking out of her nostrils. "You'd do better to ask God to forgive you," she said. "But it wouldn't be worth the trouble. You're damned to Hell already." "Do you want me to promise you something?" I asked her. She said, "Why? You're damned, I told you. I can see it in your face. The best thing you could do is go in and sleep off your drunk."

I didn't lie down, I wasn't sleepy any more. After a while I left the house and went to the beach at Chucuito. When I got to the wall I could see two of the boys who'd been there the day before. They were stretched out on the rocks, smoking cigarettes, with their heads on their bundled clothes. There were lots of kids on the beach. Some of them were at the edge of the water, throwing flat stones so they'd skip across the surface. A little later, Teresa and her friends arrived. They went over to the boys and shook hands with them. They got undressed and sat in a circle, and that same boy was next to Teresa the whole while, as if I hadn't done a thing to him. Finally they went into the water. Teresa shrieked, "It's cold! I'm freezing to death!" and the boy scooped up water with his hands and started wetting her. She screeched even louder but she didn't get mad. Then they went further out. Teresa swam better than he did, as smooth and easy as a fish, he did a lot of splashing but he kept going under. In a little while they came out again and sat down on the rocks. Teresa stretched out and the boy made a pillow for her out of his clothes, he sat beside her, turned half way around so he could see her whole body. All I could see was Tere's arms raised up to the sun, but I could see his skinny back, and the way his ribs stuck out, and his crooked legs. They went back into the water at about noon. He made believe he was a fairy and when she splashed him he screamed. Then they swam some more, and Teresa pretended she was drowning. He dove under and she began waving her arms and shouting, "Help, help!" but you could tell it was only in fun. Suddenly he bobbed up like a cork, with his hair plastered down on his face, and let out a Tarzan yell. I could hear them laughing, they laughed so loud. When they came out of the water again, I was waiting for them next to their piles of clothing. I don't know where Teresa's friends and the other boy were, I didn't pay any attention to them. It was as if everybody'd disappeared. They came near, and Teresa saw me first. The boy was behind her, acting crazy. Her expression didn't change, she didn't look any happier or sadder than she was before. And she didn't offer to shake hands, she just said, "Hello. Were you on the beach too?" When she said that, the boy suddenly noticed me and recognized me. He stopped dead, backed up, picked up a stone and aimed at me. "Do you know him?" Teresa asked the boy, laughing, and she said, "He's my neighbor." "He thinks he's quite a killer," the boy said, "but I'm going to smash his face in so he won't play that game any more." I judged the distance wrong, or rather I forgot I was up on the rocks. I jumped, my feet sank into the sand, and I didn't get half way, I fell down about a yard from him, and then the boy came up and threw the stone square in my face. It was as if the sun broke into my head, everything was white and I seemed to be floating. I don't think it lasted very long. When I opened my eyes, Teresa was looking terrified and the boy was standing there with his mouth open. He was stupid, if he'd used his advantage he could've trampled on me all he wanted, but my face was bleeding and he just stood still, trying to see how bad I was hurt, and I lunged at him, jumping over Teresa. He wasn't any good in a real fight, I could tell it the minute I got him down, he was weak as a rag and didn't try to hit me. We didn't roll over even once, I stayed on top of him and kept punching him in the face and he just covered his face with his hands. I picked up a handful of pebbles and started scrubbing his head and forehead with them, and when he lifted his hands I got them into his eyes and mouth. They didn't separate us until the cop came. He grabbed me by the shirt and yanked, and I could feel something rip. He gave me a slap in the face and that's when I hit him in the chest with a stone. "You son of a bitch, I'll murder you," he said. He lifted me up like a feather and gave me half a dozen good whacks. Then he said, "Look what you've done, you bully." The boy was still lying on the sand, whining. Some women and some other people were trying to comfort him. The women were all furious at me, they said to the cop, "He's wrecked the boy's face, he's a savage, take him to the reformatory." I didn't care a thing about what the women said, but just then I saw Teresa. Her face was flushed and she was looking at me with sheer hatred in her eyes. "You're wicked," she said, "you're brutal." And I told her, "It's your fault, for being such a whore." The cop banged me in the mouth and shouted, "Don't insult this girl, you little thug!" She looked at me very astonished and I turned around and the cop said, "Stop, where do you think you're going?" I began to kick him and punch him until he dragged me off the beach. At the police station, the lieutenant told the cop, "Give him a good whipping and let him go. We'll have him back pretty soon for something big. He's headed for the pen, you can tell it from his face." The cop took me into a patio, took off his leather belt, and started to whip me with it. I ran away from him and the other cops almost died laughing when they saw how he lumbered around and couldn't catch me. Then he dropped the belt and trapped me in a corner. The other cops came over and said, "Let him go. You can't punch a little kid." I left the station and didn't go back home. I went to live with Skinny Higueras.

"I don't understand a word of it," the major said. "Not a word."

He was fat and red-faced, with a little mustache that did not reach the ends of his lips. He had read the report carefully, from beginning to end, blinking the whole time. Before looking up at Capt. Garrido, who was standing in front of the desk with his back to the window, to the dark fields and gray sea of La Perla, he reread a few paragraphs in the ten typewritten pages.

"I don't understand," he repeated. "Explain it to me, Captain. Somebody's gone crazy, and I don't think it's me. What's happened to Lieutenant Gamboa?"

"I don't know, Sir. I'm as surprised as you are. I've talked with him several times about this affair. I've tried to show him that a report like this is ridiculous."

"Ridiculous?" the major said. "You shouldn't have let him put those boys in the guardhouse, and you shouldn't have let him make out a report like this. We've got to put an end to the matter right away. There isn't a minute to lose."

"Nobody knows about it, Sir. The cadets are incommunicado."

"Call Gamboa in," the major said. "Tell him to get here on the double."

The captain hurried out. The major picked up the report again. As he reread it, he tried to bite the reddish hairs of his mustache, but he had very small teeth and he only succeeded in scratching and irritating his lip. One of his feet was tapping nervously. A few minutes later the captain returned, followed by the lieutenant.

"Good morning," the major said, in a voice that rose and fell because of his annoyance. "I'm very surprised, Gamboa. You're an outstanding officer, your superiors think a great deal of you. What ever led you to hand in this report? You've lost your mind, man. This is a bomb. A real bomb."

"What it says is true, Sir." The captain glared at him, his jaws working furiously. "But some things still aren't clear. I've found out everything I can. The court-martial will have to. . ."

"What?" the major said, interrupting him. "Do you think there'll be a court-martial? Don't talk nonsense, man. The Leoncio Prado is an Academy, we're not going to have any scandals. I really think there's something wrong with your head, Gamboa. Do you actually believe I'd let this report get to the Ministry?"

"That's what I've told the lieutenant, Sir," the captain said. "But he insists."

"We'll see," the major said. "We've got to keep hold of ourselves, we've got to act calmly. We'll see. Who's the boy that made the accusation?"

"Fernández, Sir. A cadet in the first section."

"Why did you put the other one in the guardhouse without waiting for orders?"

"I had to begin the investigation, Sir. It was important not to question him until I had separated him from the rest of the cadets. Otherwise the whole Year would have heard about it. I've also been careful to keep the two of them apart."

"The accusation is idiotic, preposterous," the major said. "And you shouldn't have given it the slightest importance. This is kid stuff, nothing else. How could you put any trust in such a fantastic story? I never thought you'd be so credulous, Gamboa."

"Possibly you're right, Sir. But let me make one comment. I was like you, I didn't believe they stole exams, formed gangs of thieves, brought cards and liquor into the Academy. But I've proved these things personally, Sir."

"That's something else," the major said. "Obviously the Fifth Year doesn't have any respect for discipline. No doubt about it. But in this instance, you're the ones responsible. Captain Garrido, you and Lieutenant Gamboa are in plenty of trouble. The boys have made fools of you. Just picture the colonel's face when he hears what goes on in the barracks. There's nothing I can do, I'll have to hand on the report and straighten things out as best as possible." He tried to bite his mustache again. "But the other matter is out. It's completely absurd. The boy shot himself by accident. The incident is closed."

"Excuse me, Sir," Gamboa said, "but it hasn't been proved that the boy shot himself."

"No?" the major said, his eyes flaming. "Would you like me to show you the official report on the accident?"

"The colonel explained the reason for that report, Sir. It was to avoid complications."

"Ah!" the major said with a triumphant gesture. "Exactly. And did you submit this horror story to avoid complications?"

"It's different now, Sir," Gamboa said calmly. "Everything's changed. Before, the accident theory was the likeliest one, or rather, the only one. The doctors said the bullet hit him from behind, but I and the other officers thought it must have been a stray shot, an accident. If that was the case, it was all right to blame the mistake on the victim himself, so as not to damage the Academy's reputation. In fact, Sir, I even thought Cadet Arana *was* to blame, at least partly, for having been out of position, or for being too slow. But everything's changed now that someone tells us a crime was committed. The accusation isn't really ridiculous, Sir. The cadets' positions. . ."

"Nonsense," the major said angrily. "You must like to read novels, Gamboa. We're going to clear up this mess right now and stop wasting time. Go to the guardhouse and send the two cadets back to their barracks. Tell them that if they say a word about all this, they'll be expelled without any academic credits. And write a new report, omitting what you said about Cadet Arana's death."

"I can't do that, Sir," Gamboa said. "Cadet Fernández won't withdraw his accusations. As far as I've been able to discover, he's telling the truth. The cadet he accuses was directly behind Arana in the exercises. I'm not saying there's proof of murder, Sir, but technically the accusation is admissible. The only way to decide is to hold a court-martial."

"I'm not interested in your opinions," the major said contemptuously. "I'm giving you an order. Keep these fantasies to yourself and do what you're told. Or do *you* want a court-martial too? Orders are orders, Lieutenant."

"Court-martial me if you want, Sir," Gamboa said in a quiet voice. "But I'm not going to change my report. And please remember your obligation to hand it on to the commandant."

The major stood up. He had turned pale with anger, and he tried desperately to reach his mustache with his teeth, making astonishing faces.

"All right!" he said, his eyes glittering. "You don't know me, Gamboa. I'm easygoing when I'm treated right. But I'm a dangerous enemy, as you'll soon find out. You're going to pay dearly for all this. Right now, don't leave the Academy until everything's cleared up. I'll hand on your report, but

I'll also report the way you behave toward your superiors. Now get out."

"Yes, Sir," Gamboa said and walked out of the office.

"He's crazy," the major said. "He's gone mad. But I'll cure him, just wait."

"Are you going to submit his report, Sir?" the captain asked.

The major stared at him, as if surprised to find him there. "I can't do anything else," he said. "And you'll get screwed too, Garrido. It won't look good on your service record."

"But Major," the captain stammered, "it isn't my fault. It's all happened in the first company, and that's Gamboa's. The others behave perfectly, as if they were running on rails, Sir. I've always followed the book to the very letter."

"Lieutenant Gamboa is your subordinate," the major said. His tone was curt. "If it takes a cadet to tell you what goes on in your battalion, where have you been all the time? What kind of officers are you? You can't even discipline a bunch of schoolboys. Take my advice and try to straighten out the Fifth. All right, that's all."

The captain turned away, and it was not until he reached the door that he remembered he had not saluted. He whirled about and clicked his heels, but the major was rereading the report again, moving his lips and scowling. Garrido walked quickly, almost trotted, toward the office of the Fifth Year. When he reached the patio he blew his whistle as hard as he could. A few moments later the non-com Morte ran in through the office door.

"Tell the officers and noncoms of the Fifth to get here," the captain said. He rubbed his hand over the violent twitching of his jaws. "You're all to blame, nobody else, and by God you'll get what's coming to you. Why are you standing there with your mouth open? Go do what I told you."

6

Gamboa hesitated, unable to decide whether to open the door. He was upset. Was it because of these troubles, he asked himself, or because of the letter? He had received it a few hours earlier. "I miss you terribly. I shouldn't have made this trip. Didn't I tell you it would be better for me to stay in Lima? I couldn't keep from vomiting in the plane and everybody looked at me and I felt even worse. Cristina and her husband were waiting for me at the airport. I've already told you how nice he is. They took me straight to their house and called a doctor. He said the trip wasn't good for me but everything would be all right. But my headache didn't go away and I still felt sick, so they called him again and he said I'd be better off in the hospital. They've got me under observation. They've given me lots of injections and I have to stay in bed without any pillow, that bothers me a lot, you know how I like to sleep almost sitting up. Mamma and Cristina are with me all day and my brother-in-law comes to see me as soon as he gets off his job. They've all been very good to me but I wish you were here, that's the only way I could really feel right in my mind. I'm a little better now but I'm awfully afraid of losing the baby. The doctor says the first time is complicated but everything will go all right. But I'm very nervous and I think about you all the time. Please take care of yourself. You miss me, don't you? Not as much as I miss you." As he read it, he began to feel his confidence draining away. And as he was rereading it, the captain came to his room with a peevish look on his face. "The colonel knows the whole story," he told him. "He isn't happy about what you've done. The commandant wants you to get Fernández out of the guardhouse and take him to the colonel's office." Gamboa was not alarmed, but he felt a complete lack of spirit, as if the affair were suddenly none of his concern. It was not often that he allowed himself to be overcome by apathy and disgust. He folded the letter, put it in his wallet, and opened the door. No doubt Alberto had seen him coming, for he was waiting at attention. The cell received more light than the one the Jaguar was in, and Gamboa could see that Alberto's khaki pants were ridiculously short. They clung to his legs like a ballet dancer's tights, and only half the buttons on his fly were buttoned. His shirt, on the other hand, was far too big for him: the shoulders drooped, and it bulged out behind as if he were humpbacked.

"Where did you change from your dress uniform?" Gamboa asked him.

"Right here, Sir. I had my regular uniform in my bag. I take it home on Saturday to have it washed."

Gamboa could see his white cap and the shiny buttons of his jacket lying on the cot.

"Don't you know the regulation?" he asked brusquely. "Your regular uniform gets washed at the Academy, you can't take it outside. And what's the matter with that uniform you're wearing? You look like a clown."

Alberto became nervous. With one hand he tried to button the top buttons on his pants, sucking in his stomach as far as possible, but he could not do it.

"The pants shrank and the shirt stretched," Gamboa said in a flat voice. "Which one did you steal?"

"Both of them, Sir."

Gamboa was somewhat startled: the captain was right, this cadet considered him an ally. "Shit," he said, as if speaking to himself. "Don't you realize you're in for it? Even Jesus couldn't save you. You're worse off than anybody else. I'm going to tell you something. You did me a bad turn by coming and telling me your problems. Why didn't you go to Huarina or Pitaluga?"

"I don't know, Sir," Alberto said. Then he quickly added, "You're the only one I trust."

"I'm not your friend," Gamboa said, "or your accomplice, or your protector. I've simply done my duty. Now it's in the hands of the colonel and the court-martial. Come with me, the colonel wants to see you."

Alberto turned pale, and his eyes widened.

"Are you afraid?" Gamboa asked.

Alberto did not answer. He was standing rigid, blinking.

"Come on," Gamboa said.

They walked to the administration building, and Alberto was surprised to see that Gamboa did not return the salutes of the soldiers on guard. It was the first time he had ever been inside the building. It resembled the other Academy buildings on the outside—tall, gray, moldy walls—but everything within was different. There was a thick carpet in the vestibule that silenced their footsteps, and the artificial light was so strong that Alberto closed his eyes several times, half blinded. There were pictures on the walls; as he went by, he thought he recognized some of the persons whose pictures were in his history book. They were acting out their supreme moments: Bolognesi firing the last shot, San Martín raising a flag, Alfonso Ugarte leaping into the abyss, the President of the Republic receiving a medal. Beyond the vestibule there was a large, empty, brightly lighted room, with diplomas and sports trophies on the walls. Gamboa led him to a corner and they entered the elevator. The lieutenant pushed the button for the fifth floor, which was probably the top one. Alberto thought how ridiculous it was that in almost three years he had never noticed how many floors there were to this building. It was off limits to the cadets, a grayish monster that was somewhat satanic because it was where the confinement lists were made out and where the Academy authorities had their dens. In the minds of the cadets it seemed as distant from the barracks as the archbishop's palace or the beach at Ancón.

"Step out," Gamboa said.

They were in a narrow corridor with gleaming walls. Gamboa opened a door. Alberto saw a desk, and behind it, next to a portrait of the colonel, a man in civilian clothes.

"The colonel is expecting you," the man told Gamboa. "You can go right in, Lieutenant."

"Wait here," Gamboa told Alberto. "They'll call for you."

Alberto sat down in front of the civilian, who was studying some papers. The pencil in his hand moved back and forth in the air, as if it were following the rhythm of a secret melody. He was a short man, well dressed, with an anonymous face. His collar seemed to bother him: he kept jerking his head, and his Adam's apple leaped up and down like an excited animal. Alberto tried to make out what was being said in the next room, but he could not hear a word. Therefore he started to daydream: Teresa was smiling at him from the Raimondi stop. Her image had haunted him ever since they had removed the corporal from the cell next to his. He could only picture the girl's face, suspended against the pale walls of the Italian school at the edge of Arequipa Avenue; he could not see her body. He had spent hours and hours trying to remember her body. He thought up elegant dresses for her, and jewelry, and exotic coiffures. Then he blushed, telling himself he was playing at dressing a doll, like a little girl. He searched for a sheet of paper in his pockets and his bag, but it was no use, and he could not write her a note. Instead, he composed imaginary letters, full of grandiloquent phrases, in which he spoke of the Military Academy, love, the death of the Slave, his guilt feelings, the future. Suddenly he heard a bell. The civilian answered the phone, nodding his head as if the person on the other end of the line could see him. He hung up with a delicate gesture and turned to Alberto.

"Are you Cadet Fernández? Go into the colonel's office, please."

He went to the door and rapped three times with his knuckles. There was no response. He pushed the door open, and saw a huge room with fluorescent lighting; it was so brilliant that it hurt his eyes. Ten yards away, there were three officers seated in leather armchairs. He glanced around, and noted a large desk, a floor lamp, diplomas, banners, pictures. There was no rug on the floor, and it was so highly polished that his boots slid as if he were walking on ice. He approached the officers slowly, afraid of slipping and falling down. He kept his eyes on the floor, and only looked up when he saw a khaki-clad leg and the leather-covered arm of a chair. Then he came to attention.

"Fernández?" It was the same voice that jangled in the gray air when the cadets drilled in the stadium, the high-pitched voice that kept them on and on in the assembly hall, lecturing them about patriotism and the spirit of sacrifice. "Fernández who?"

"Fernández Temple, Sir. Cadet Alberto Fernández Temple."

The colonel studied him. He was a plump little man, impeccably uniformed, with his gray hair neatly combed out and plastered to his skull.

"Are you related to General Temple?" he asked. Alberto tried to guess the colonel's mood from the tone of his voice. It was cold, but not threatening.

"No, Sir. I think General Temple is from Piura. My mother was born in Moquegua."

"Yes," the colonel said. "He's from the country." He turned his head, and Alberto, following his eyes, saw that the commandant, Altuna, was sitting in one of the armchairs. "So am I. So are most of the officers in the army. It's a known fact that the best officers come from the villages. By the way, Altuna, where do *you* come from?"

"I was born in Lima, Sir. But I don't think of myself as a Limeño. My family comes from Ancash."

Alberto tried to see Gamboa's face, but the lieutenant was sitting with his back to him, and all he could make out were his arm and his gently tapping foot.

"All right, Cadet Fernández," the colonel said. His voice had become solemn. "Now we're going to talk about more important things, more serious things." Earlier, the colonel had been leaning back in his armchair; now he perched on its edge, with his stomach bulging. "Are you a real cadet, a sensible, intelligent, educated person? We'll assume that you are. Therefore, you wouldn't bother all the officers in the Academy with something trivial. And, in fact, the report Lieutenant Gamboa has submitted is not a matter for the officers to handle alone. I'll have to send it on to the Ministry of War. And they'll have to take it up with the Ministry of Justice. If I'm not mistaken, you accuse one of your comrades of murder."

He coughed briefly, with a certain elegance, and was silent for a moment.

"It occurs to me," he said, "that a cadet in the Fifth Year isn't a child any more. After three years in the Military Academy he's had more than enough time to become a man. And if a man, a rational human being, wants to accuse someone of murder, he'll naturally have absolute, irrefutable proof. That is, unless he's out of his mind. Or unless he's ignorant of judicial matters and doesn't know what false testimony is, doesn't know that slander is clearly defined by law and severely punished. I've studied this report with the closest attention. And unfortunately, Cadet, there's not a shred of evidence anywhere. That caused me to say to myself, this cadet is prudent, cautious, he doesn't want to disclose his evidence until the last moment, that is, to me in person, so I can present it to the court-martial. Very well, Cadet, that's why I've summoned you. Tell me your evidence."

Alberto stared for a moment at the colonel's tapping foot. It moved up and down, up and down, up and down.

"Sir," he said, "I only. . ."

"Yes, yes," the colonel said. "You're a man now. You're a cadet from the Fifth Year at the Leoncio Prado Military Academy. You know what you're doing. So let me hear your evidence."

"I've told everything I know, Sir. The Jaguar wanted to get revenge on Arana for having accused. . ."

"We'll talk about that later," the colonel broke in. "Your

anecdotes are very interesting, and your theories show you have a creative spirit, a captivating imagination." He paused, and repeated with relish, "captivating. But right now we're going to review the documentation. Give me all the necessary juridical material."

"I don't have any evidence, Sir," Alberto admitted. His voice was weak and unsteady. He bit his lip and then said, "I only told what I knew. But I'm sure. . ."

"What?" the colonel said with a gesture of surprise. "Are you trying to make me believe that you don't have concrete and authentic evidence? Be a little more serious, Cadet. This is no moment for joking. Do you really mean that you don't have even a single valid document? Come, speak up."

"Sir, I thought it was my duty to. . ."

"Ah!" the colonel said. "So it *is* a joke. I don't disapprove. You have a right to a little diversion, and besides that, a show of high spirits in the young is a healthy thing. But there are limits to everything. You're in the army, Cadet. You can't make fun of the armed forces. And it isn't only a military matter. In civilian life, too, you have to pay dearly for jokes like this. If you want to accuse someone of murder, you have to base your charge on something—how shall I say it?—sufficient. That is, on sufficient evidence. And you haven't got any evidence at all, sufficient or otherwise, yet you come here to make this gratuitous, this fantastic accusation, one that slings mud at one of your own comrades, not to mention the Academy. Don't make us think you're a dunce, Cadet. And what do you think *we* are, eh? Imbeciles, or lunatics, or what? Don't you know that four doctors and a group of ballistics experts all agree that the bullet that killed the poor cadet was fired from his own rifle? Don't you realize that your superiors, who have more experience and more responsibility than you do, made a thorough investigation of the cadet's death? Stop, don't speak, let me finish. Do you imagine we'd sit still after that accident and wouldn't investigate, make inquiries, try to find out what errors and failures were the cause of it? Do you think we earn our ranks as officers by sitting around wishing for them? Do you think the lieutenants, the captains, the major, the commandant, I myself, are such a pack of idiots that we'd simply fold our arms when a cadet died under those circumstances? This is really disgraceful, Cadet Fernández. I say 'disgraceful' to avoid using a stronger word. Think for a moment and then tell me if it isn't disgraceful."

"Yes, Sir," Alberto said, and immediately he felt relieved.

"Too bad you didn't realize it earlier," the colonel said. "Too bad it required my personal attention to make you see the consequences of your adolescent prank. Now we're going to talk about something else, Cadet. Because without knowing it, you've started an avalanche. And its first victim will be you yourself. You have a lively imagination, right? You've just finished giving us a convincing demonstration of that. Unfortunately, your murder story isn't the only proof. I have other evidence of your fantasies, your inspirations. Will you please bring us those papers, Commandant?"

Alberto saw Commandant Altuna get to his feet. He was a tall, fleshy man, very different from the colonel. The cadets called them Fat and Skinny. Altuna was a reserved and silent person who rarely entered the barracks or the classrooms. He went to the desk and came back with a handful of papers. His shoes creaked like the boots of the cadets. The colonel took the papers and held them up in front of Alberto's eyes.

"Do you know what these are, Cadet?"

"No, Sir."

"Of course you do. Take a look at them."

Alberto read a few lines, and only then understood what they were.

"Now do you recognize them, Cadet?"

Alberto saw a head appear over the back of a chair: Lt. Gamboa was looking at him. He blushed violently.

"Obviously you recognize them," the colonel said, almost

with a laugh. "They're documents, they're concrete evidence. Now, then, read us a little of what they say."

Alberto suddenly thought of the initiation of the Dogs. For the first time in almost three years he had that deep feeling of impotence and humiliation that he had experienced when he entered the Academy. But this was even worse, because he was suffering it alone.

"I told you to read something to us," the colonel said.

Alberto forced himself to start reading. His voice was weak and at moments it broke. "She had big, hairy legs, and her ass was so enormous that she looked more like an animal than a woman, but she was the most popular whore in the fourth block because all the worst characters wanted her." He stopped and waited tensely, expecting to hear the colonel's voice ordering him to continue. But the colonel remained silent. Alberto felt profoundly tired. This, he thought, was like the contests in Paulino's cave: it was so humiliating that it exhausted him, weakened every muscle, clouded his brain.

"Return those papers to me," the colonel said. Alberto handed them to him. The colonel leafed through them slowly. His lips moved and he murmured some of the words and phrases. Alberto could see portions of titles he hardly remembered, some of them written the year before: "Lulu, the Incorrigible Flirt," "The Mad Woman and the Burro," "The Whore and the Whoremaster."

"Do you know what I should do regarding these papers?" the colonel asked. His eyes were half closed and he seemed crushed by some painful but inescapable obligation. His voice sounded weary and rather bitter. "I shouldn't even order a court-martial, Cadet. I should expel you this very minute, for being a degenerate. And I should talk with your father so that he could take you to a clinic. Perhaps the psychiatrists—do you understand what I'm saying, Cadet? —could cure you. This is a scandalous affair, scandalous. Only a twisted mind, a diseased mind, could write this sort of filth. These papers are a disgrace to the Academy, a disgrace to all of us. Have you anything to say, Cadet? Speak up, speak up."

"No, Sir."

"Of course not," the colonel said. "How could you defend such disgusting documents. You couldn't. Now answer me frankly, man to man. Don't you deserve to be expelled? And shouldn't we inform your parents that you're a degenerate who also corrupts others? Yes or no?"

"Yes, Sir."

"These papers have ruined you, Cadet. Do you think any school is going to admit you after you've been expelled from here as a delinquent with a perverted mind. You've ruined your career. Yes or no?"

"Yes, Sir."

"What would you do if you were in my place, Cadet?"

"I don't know, Sir."

"But I know what I *should* do, Cadet. I have a duty to perform." He paused. His expression became less belligerent, became almost kind. He settled back into the armchair again, and his stomach contracted and seemed more normal. He scratched his chin as he glanced about the room; it was as if he were debating a number of conflicting ideas. The commandant and the lieutenant were silent and motionless. Alberto waited for the decision, concentrating his attention on the colonel's foot: the heel of his shoe rested on the polished floor, but the toe was raised. He was afraid that at any moment the colonel would start tapping his foot once more.

"Cadet Fernández Temple," the colonel said in a solemn voice. Alberto raised his eyes. "Are you sorry about what you've done?"

"Yes, Sir," Alberto said without hesitating.

"I'm a sensitive man," the colonel said. "And I find these documents extremely painful. They're a blatant insult to the Academy. Look me in the eye, Cadet. You have the appearance of a real soldier. You're not like the riffraff we usually get. So I want you to behave like a man. Do you understand me?"

"Yes, Sir."

"And will you turn over a new leaf? Will you try to be a model cadet?"

"Yes, Sir."

"Good. But seeing is believing," the colonel said. He paused again. "I've decided to forget my duty. Just for this once. My duty is to expel you right now. But I'm not thinking about you, I'm thinking about the Academy. To me, the Academy is sacred. I like to think of the Leoncio Prado as one big family. Therefore, I'm going to give you a last chance. I'll keep these papers, these incriminating documents, and I'll also keep a sharp eye on you. If your superiors tell me at the end of the year that you've earned the trust I'm giving you now, that your record is completely clear, I'll burn these papers and forget the whole sordid story. But, Cadet, if you commit a single misdemeanor—and one will be more than enough—you'll be expelled in disgrace. Do you understand?"

"Yes, Sir." Alberto lowered his eyes and added, "Thank you, Colonel."

"So you realize what I'm doing for you?"

"Yes, Sir."

"That's all, then. Go back to your section and behave yourself as you should. Be a true Leoncio Prado cadet. Respect your superiors and yourself. Dismissed."

Alberto saluted and started to walk toward the door, but he had only taken three steps when the colonel's voice halted him.

"One moment, Cadet. Naturally you'll keep absolutely quiet about what we've been saying. I mean, about these papers, and the imaginary murder, and everything. And from now on, keep your fantasies under control. The next time you feel like playing detective, remember that you're in the army, that your superiors make sure that everything is carefully investigated and carefully judged. That's all."

Alberto saluted again and left the room. The civilian did not even look up as he went by. Instead of taking the elevator, he walked down, thinking. The stairs glittered like all the rest of the building.

It was not until he was outside, in front of the statue of the hero, that he remembered his bag. It was still in the guardhouse, along with his dress uniform. He walked slowly over to the guardhouse. The lieutenant on duty nodded to him.

"I've come to get my things, Sir," Alberto said.

"What?" the lieutenant asked. "You're still a prisoner. Gamboa's orders."

"But they told me to go back to my barracks."

"No, Cadet," the lieutenant said. "Not a chance. Don't you know the regulations? I can't let you go without written authorization from Gamboa. So you go back in."

"Yes, Sir."

"Put him in the cell with that other cadet," the officer told the sergeant. "I've got to make room for the soldiers Capt. Bezada wants to punish for whatever it was they did." He scratched his head. "This place isn't an Academy, it's a prison."

The sergeant was a solidly-built man with Oriental features. He opened the cell door, kicking it back with his foot. "All right, get in, Cadet." And he added in a low voice, "Don't worry, I'll bring you something to smoke when they change the guard."

Alberto entered. The Jaguar was sitting on the cot, looking at him.

Then there was the time Skinny Higueras hung back, he didn't want to go with us, it was as if he suspected that something was sure to go wrong. A few months before, the Bull sent him a message saying, "Either you work with me or you stay out of Callao if you don't want to get your face pushed in," and Skinny said to me, "He's back, I knew this'd happen." He'd worked with the Bull when he was a kid, in fact it was the Bull who taught Skinny and my brother how to be crooks. Then the Bull got caught and the two of them went on by themselves. Five years later the Bull got out of jail and formed another gang. Skinny kept ducking him but one day two toughs from the gang ran across him in a bar and made him go with them to see the Bull. Skinny told me they didn't do anything to him, the Bull put his arm around his shoulder and said, "I love you like a son." Later they got drunk together and said good-by like old friends. In about a week, though, he got that message. Skinny didn't want to operate in a gang, he said it was bad business, but he also didn't want to have the Bull for an enemy. So he told me, "I'm going to join up. After all, the Bull doesn't cheat. But you don't have to go with me. If you want my advice, go back home with your mother and study to be a doctor. You must've saved plenty of money by now." I didn't have a single centavo and I said so. "Do you know what you are?" he said. "You're a whoremaster, that's what you are. Did you spend all your money in the brothels?" I told him yes. He said, "You've still got a lot to learn. It isn't worth it to spend all you've got on the whores. You should've saved at least something. Well, what do you want to do?" I told him I'd stay with him. That same night we went to see the Bull. He was in a real dump of a bar, and the waitress only had one eye. The Bull was an old man, a half-breed, and he hardly knew what he was saying because he kept calling for another shot of pisco. The others, five or six of them, half-breeds and Chinks and peasants, kept giving Skinny dirty looks, but the Bull always listened to him when he talked, and laughed at all his jokes. He hardly even looked at me. We started working and at first everything went all right. We cleaned out houses in Magdalena and La Punta, San Isidro and Orrantia, Salaverry and Barranco, but not in Callao. They used me as a lookout and never sent me inside to open the door. When they divvied up, the Bull gave me the measliest share he could, but afterward Skinny gave me part of what he got. We formed a pair and the rest of the characters in the gang didn't trust us. One time we were all in a whorehouse and Skinny and the half-breed Pancracio started fighting over one of the whores, and Pancracio took out a knife and slashed my friend on the arm. That made me sore and I went at him. Another half-breed jumped in and said he'd take me on. The Bull told everybody to stand back and give us room, and the whores all screamed. At first the half-breed insulted me, that was while we were sizing each other up, he laughed and said, "You're the mouse and I'm the cat," but I gave him a couple of good butts with my head and then we had a real fight. The Bull bought me a drink and said, "My hat's off to you. Who taught you how to fight like that?"

After that, I fought with the half-breeds and Chinks and peasants in the gang for any reason at all. Sometimes I took a beating, but sometimes I held my own and even got the best of it. Every time we got drunk we ended up fighting. And we fought so much we finally got to be friends. They invited me to drink with them, they took me with them to the whorehouse or the movies. I remember we went to the movies the night before it happened. The Bull was waiting for us outside, and he was more excited than I'd ever seen him. We went to a bar and when we got there he said, "This is it, this is the best deal yet." But then when he said that the Priest had looked him up and suggested a job, Skinny interrupted him. "Not with those guys, Bull. They'd screw us for sure. They're big-time operators." The Bull didn't pay any attention to him, he went on explaining the setup. He was very proud that the Priest wanted him, because he had a large gang and everybody was jealous of them. They lived like respectable people, they had good houses and they all owned cars. Skinny wanted to argue about it some more but the others made him shut up. It was set for the next night, and it sounded easy. We met at the Quebrada de Armendáriz at ten o'clock at night, the way the Bull told us to, and a couple of the Priest's men were there waiting for us. They both had mustaches and were very well dressed, they smoked imported cigarettes, it looked as if they were going to a party. We waited there till midnight and then went to the streetcar line, walking in pairs. Another guy from the Priest's gang was waiting. "It's all set," he told us. "The house is empty. They left just now. We can start right away." The Bull showed me where to be a lookout, off at one side of the house behind a wall. I asked Skinny, "Who goes in?" He said, "Me, the Bull and the Priest's men. The rest of you are lookouts. That's the way they work. This is what you call a sure thing." I couldn't see anybody from where I was, not even any lights in the houses, but before we got there, Skinny stopped talking and looked pretty worried about what was coming. Pancracio showed me the house as we went by. It was enormous, and the Bull said, "There should be enough money in there to make a whole army rich." Quite a while later I heard the whistle blasts, the shots and the yells, and I started running in that direction, but then I saw the three patrolmen on the corner. I turned around and escaped. I got on a streetcar at the Marsano Plaza and in Lima I took a taxi. When I got to the bar I only found Pancracio. "It was a trap," he said. "The Priest tipped off the cops. I think they caught everybody. I saw them beating up the Bull and Skinny on the ground. The four guys from the Priest's gang were laughing, some day they'll get what's coming to them. Right now we'd better clear out." I told him I was flat broke. He gave me five soles and told me, "Go and live in a different neighborhood and don't come back here. I'm going to get out of Lima for a while."

That night I went to the fields at Bellavista and slept in a ditch. Or rather, I lay on my back, staring into the darkness, freezing to death. As soon as it was daylight I went to the Bellavista Plaza. I hadn't been there for two years. Everything looked the same, except the door of my house had a new coat of paint. I knocked, but nobody answered. I knocked harder, and somebody inside shouted, "Wait a minute, damn it!" A man came to the door and I asked for Señora Domitila. "I don't know who she is," he said. "Pedro Caifás lives here, and that's me." Then a woman came up beside him and said, "Señora Domitila? An old lady that lived here all alone?" "Yes," I said; "I think so." "She's dead," the woman told me. "She lived here before we came, but that was quite a while ago." I thanked them and went and sat down in the plaza. I spent the whole morning watching the door of Teresa's house to see if she'd come out. About noon, a boy came out. I went over and asked him, "Do you know the address of the woman and girl that used to live in your house?" "I don't know a thing," he said. I went back to my old house and knocked again. The woman came to the door. I asked her, "Do you know where Señora Domitila is buried?" "No," she said. "I never even met her. Was she related to you?" I was going to tell her she was my mother, but then I remembered the cops were looking for me and I said, "No, I just wanted to find out."

"Hello," the Jaguar said.

Apparently he was not surprised to see him there. The sergeant closed the door and the cell was dark.

"Hello," Alberto said.

"Have you got any cigarettes?" the Jaguar asked. He was seated on the cot with his shoulders resting against the wall. Alberto could see one half of his face clearly, because it was in the small shaft of light that entered through the window; the other half was a dark blur.

"No," Alberto said. "But the sergeant's going to bring me some a little later."

"Why'd they put you in here?" the Jaguar asked.

"I don't know. And you?"

"Some son of a bitch went and squealed to Gamboa."

"Who was it? What did he say?"

"Listen," the Jaguar said, lowering his voice. "You're sure to get out of here quicker than me. Do me one favor. But come up close, I don't want them to hear me."

Alberto went over to him and stood a few inches away, so close that their knees touched.

"Tell Curly and the Boa there's a squealer in the section. I want them to find out who it is. Do you know what he told Gamboa?"

"No."

"The guys in the section, what do they think I'm in here for?"

"On account of the stolen exams."

"Yes," the Jaguar said. "That's part of it. He told Gamboa about the exams, the Circle, the stolen clothing, the gambling, the liquor. Everything. We've got to find out who it was. Tell them that they're screwed too if they don't find out. And so are you, and the whole barracks. It's somebody in the section, nobody else would've known."

"They're going to expel you," Alberto said. "Maybe they'll even send you to jail."

"That's what Gamboa told me. And I'm sure they're going to screw Curly and the Boa too, on account of the Circle. Tell them to find out who it was and then toss a piece of paper through the window here with the squealer's name on it. If I'm expelled, I won't have a chance to see them."

"What can you gain by that?"

"Nothing," the Jaguar said. "I'm already fucked. But I have to get revenge."

"You're a shit, Jaguar," Alberto said. "I'd like to see them send you to prison."

The Jaguar made a slight movement: he was still sitting on the cot, but straight up now, without leaning against the wall, and he turned his head a few inches to look straight at Alberto. His whole face became visible.

"Did you hear what I said?"

"Don't shout," the Jaguar said. "Do you want the lieuten-ant to come? What's the matter with you?"

"A shit," Alberto whispered. "A murderer. You killed the Slave."

Alberto had taken a step backward and was standing in a crouch, but the Jaguar did not attack him, did not even move. Alberto could see his blue eyes shining in the dark-ness.

"That's a lie," the Jaguar said, also in a very low voice. "A slander. They said that to Gamboa just to screw me. Whoever squealed is someone who wants to ruin me, some coward, some fairy. Can't you see it? Tell me something: does everybody in the barracks think I killed Arana?"

Alberto did not reply.

"They couldn't," the Jaguar said. "Nobody'd believe it. Arana was just a poor devil, anybody could push him around. Why would I want to kill him?"

"He was a lot better than you," Alberto said. The two were speaking secretively, and the effort they made to keep their voices down caused their words to sound forced and theat-rical. "You're a murderer, you're the one who's a poor devil. The Slave was a good guy, you wouldn't know what that means. He was decent, he never bothered anybody. You screwed him all the time, day and night. He was normal enough when he got here to the Academy, but you and the others gave him such a hard time you made an idiot out of him. And just because he didn't know how to fight. Well, your luck's run out, Jaguar. They're going to expel you. Do you know what your life's going to be like? You'll just be a cheap crook, and sooner or later you'll land in prison."

"That's what my mother told me." Alberto was surprised, he had not expected a confidence. But he understood that the Jaguar was talking to himself: his voice was a dull mut-ter. "So did Gamboa. My life is my own business. But I wasn't the only one that screwed the Slave. Everybody bullied him, you too, Poet. Everybody screws everybody in the Academy if you let them get away with it. It isn't my fault. The reason they couldn't fuck me was, I'm more of a man. It isn't my fault."

"No, Jaguar," Alberto said, "you're not more of a man. You're a murderer, but I'm not afraid of you. You'll see when we get out of here."

"Do you want to fight with me?" the Jaguar asked.

"Yes."

"You don't know how," the Jaguar said. "Tell me, are they all mad at me in the barracks?"

"No," Alberto said. "I'm the only one. And I'm not afraid of you, I told you."

"Shhh, don't shout. If you want, we'll fight outside the Academy. But I'm warning you, you can't handle me. You're just excited. I didn't do anything to the Slave. I only hazed him like everybody else. I didn't have any grudge against him, I was only having fun."

"What difference does that make? You bullied him and the rest of them imitated you. You made his life sheer hell. And then you killed him."

"Don't shout, you idiot, they'll hear you. I didn't kill him. When I get out of here, I'll find the squealer and make him confess in front of everybody that that's a lie. You wait and see."

"It isn't a lie," Alberto said. "I know for sure."

"Don't shout, goddamn it."

"You're a murderer."

"Shhh."

"I'm the one that squealed on you, Jaguar. I know you killed him."

This time, Alberto did not move, although the Jaguar had crouched as if to spring from the cot.

"You told that to Gamboa?" the Jaguar asked very slowly.

"Yes. I told him everything you've done, everything that goes on in the barracks."

"Why did you do it?"

"Because I felt like it."

"Let's see if you're the man you think you are," the Jaguar said, and stood up.

7

Lt. Gamboa left the colonel's office, nodded to the civilian, and waited a few moments for the elevator. When it failed to arrive, he walked down the stairs, taking them two at a time. In the patio he discovered that the morning had grown clear under a shining sky. There were many white clouds on the horizon, standing motionless above the glitter of the sea. He walked quickly to the barracks of the Fifth Year and opened the office door. Capt. Garrido was at his desk, hunched over like a porcupine. Gamboa saluted him from the doorway.

"Yes?" the captain asked, leaping up.

"The colonel told me to tell you not to register the report I submitted, Sir."

The captain's face relaxed, and his eyes, which had been hard, smiled with relief. "Of course," he said, thumping the desk. "I haven't even bothered to register it. I knew what the decision would be. What happened, Gamboa?"

"The cadet withdrew his accusation, Sir. The colonel tore up the report. We're to forget about the whole thing, that is, about the supposed murder, Sir. As for the rest, we're to maintain stricter discipline."

"Stricter?" The captain laughed loudly. "Come here, Gamboa. Look." He held up a sheaf of papers. "See this? More paperwork in three days than during all last month. Sixty cadets confined, that's almost a third of the Year. The colonel doesn't have to worry. We'll get them back in line, and we'll see that they stay there. As for the exams, I'm going to take special precautions. I'll keep them in my own room until the moment they're needed in the classrooms. Let the cadets come looking for them if they dare. I've doubled the cadet sentries and the patrols by the soldiers. The noncoms will ask for reports every hour. We'll hold a clothing inspection twice a week, and the same goes for their rifles. Do you think they'll keep on cutting up?"

"I hope not, Sir."

"And who was right?" the captain asked him, leaning forward with a triumphant smile. "You or me?"

"It was my duty," Gamboa said.

"You're too fussy about the regulations," the captain said. "I'm not criticizing you, Gamboa, but sometimes it's better to be practical. That is, sometimes it's better to forget the regulations and use your common sense."

"I believe in the regulations," Gamboa said. "I'm going to confess something to you: I can recite them from memory. And I want you to know I don't regret anything I've done."

"Cigarette?" the captain asked. Gamboa accepted one. The captain smoked imported cigarettes; they were made from black tobacco that gave off a dense, fetid cloud. The lieutenant fondled the oval cigarette for a few moments before putting it to his mouth.

"We all believe in the regulations," the captain said. "But you have to know how to interpret them. Above all, we soldiers have to be realists, we have to act according to the situation at hand. You can't make facts fit the rules, Gamboa. It's the other way around. The rules have to be adapted to fit the facts." The captain's hand made circles in the air; he clearly felt inspired. "Otherwise, life would be impossible. Stubbornness does more harm than it does good. What are you going to gain from having stood up for that cadet? Nothing, absolutely nothing. You simply got yourself in trouble. If you'd only listened to me, the results would be the same and we'd have avoided a lot of problems. Don't think for a minute that I'm glad about what's happened to you. You know how much I respect you. But the major's furious and he'll try to make trouble for you. The colonel must be thoroughly disgusted also."

"Bah," Gamboa said scornfully. "What can they do to me? Besides, I don't care what they do. My conscience is clean."

"A clean conscience might help you get into heaven," the captain said in an amiable voice, "but it won't help your career. In any case, I'll do what I can to prevent all this from causing you harm. Now, then, what did they decide about the two cadets?"

"The colonel said they were to return to their barracks."

"Go and see them. Give them a little advice. Tell them to keep their mouths shut if they don't want a lot more trouble. They're the ones who'll gain the most by forgetting the whole affair. But watch out for the one you've been protecting. He's plain insolent."

"Protecting?" Gamboa said. "A week ago I didn't even know he existed."

The lieutenant walked out without asking the captain's permission. The barracks patio was empty, but it was almost noon and the cadets would come back from the classrooms like a swelling, roaring, overflowing river, and then the patio would be all noise and turmoil. Gamboa took the letter out of his wallet, held it in his hand for a moment, and replaced it without opening it. If it's a boy, he thought, he won't be a soldier.

At the guardhouse, the lieutenant on duty was reading a magazine, and the soldiers sitting on the bench were looking at each other with vacant eyes. When Gamboa entered, they stood up like automatons.

"Good morning."

"Good morning, Sir."

Gamboa's manner toward him was easy and friendly, but the young lieutenant had served under him and still treated him with a certain respect.

"I've come for the two cadets from the Fifth."

"Yes," the lieutenant said. "One of them wanted to leave, but he didn't have a written order. Shall I bring them out? They're in the right-hand cell."

"Together?" Gamboa asked.

"Yes. I needed the other one. There's some soldiers being punished. Should I have kept them apart?"

"Give me the key. I'm going to talk with them."

Gamboa opened the door of the cell slowly, but entered with a bound, like a lion tamer. He saw two pairs of legs dangling in the shaft of light that came in through the window, and heard the heavy breathing of the cadets, but his eyes were not accustomed to the darkness and he could barely make out their silhouettes and the shape of their faces. He took a step toward them and shouted, "Attention!"

They stood up, but without any haste.

"When a superior enters," Gamboa said, "his inferiors come to attention. Have you forgotten? Six points for each one. Take your hand away from your face and come to attention, Cadet!"

"He can't, Sir," the Jaguar said.

Alberto removed his hand, but immediately put it over his eye again. Gamboa pushed him gently toward the light. He could see the swelling over the cadet's cheekbone and the drying blood on his nose and mouth.

"Take your hand away," Gamboa said. "Let me see it."

Alberto lowered his hand, and winced with pain. His eye had been forced shut by a huge violet-colored bruise, and his swollen eyelid looked as if it had been scorched. Gamboa also saw the splotches of blood on his shirt. Alberto's hair was matted with sweat and dust.

"Come here."

The Jaguar obeyed. The fight had not left many marks on his face, but the wings of his nostrils were trembling and there was a crust of dried saliva around his lips.

"Go to the infirmary, both of you," Gamboa said. "After they take care of you, go to my room. I'll be waiting for you. I've got some things to tell you."

Alberto and the Jaguar left the cell. The lieutenant on duty turned toward them when he heard their footsteps. His vague smile abruptly became an expression of astonishment, of shock.

"Halt!" he bellowed. "What's going on? Don't make a move!"

The soldiers had run forward toward the cadets and were staring at them.

"It's all right," Gamboa said. Then he told the cadets, "Get going."

Alberto and the Jaguar left the guardhouse. The lieutenants and the soldiers watched them walk away through the clear noonday light. They walked shoulder to shoulder but without turning their heads, not speaking, not looking at each other.

"He wrecked that kid's face," the young lieutenant said. "I don't understand it."

"You didn't know what was going on?" Gamboa asked.

"No." The lieutenant seemed completely confused. "And I was right here the whole time." He looked at the soldiers. "What about you? Did you hear anything?"

The four soldiers shook their heads.

"They fought without letting out a grunt," the lieutenant said. He had recovered from his surprise and confusion, and even sounded a little like a sports fan. "I'd've broken it up if I'd heard them, but I didn't. What a pair of gamecocks! It's going to be a long while before that kid's face looks all right. What were they fighting about?"

"Nothing," Gamboa said. "Nothing serious."

"But how did he take such a beating without making a sound? His face is a real mess. We'll have to put the whitey on the Academy boxing team. Or is he on it already?"

"No," Gamboa said. "I don't think so. But you're right, we'll have to put him somewhere."

The rest of that day I just wandered around, and a woman gave me some bread and a little milk. When it got dark I slept in a ditch again, near Progreso Avenue. This time I really got some sleep, and didn't wake up until the sun was high. There wasn't anybody around, but I could hear the cars going by on the avenue. I was starving, I had a headache, and I kept shivering the way you do when you're coming down with the grippe. I walked into Lima and got to Alfonso Ugarte about noon. I waited for Teresa to come out of school with the other girls, but she didn't appear. I walked around in the center of town, in places where there were lots of people, the San Martín Plaza, Unión Street, Grau Avenue. Later I went to the Reserva Park, dead tired. I drank some water from a faucet in the park, but it made me vomit. I lay down on the grass, and in a little while I saw a cop coming toward me, making signals from a distance. I got up and ran as fast as I could, and he didn't chase me. It was already dark by the time I got to my godfather's house on Francisco Pizarro Avenue. I thought my head was going to split and I was shaking all over. It wasn't wintertime and I thought, I must be sick. Before knocking, I thought, His wife's going to answer the door and turn me away. If she does, I'll go to the police station. At least they'll give me something to eat. But it was my godfather that came to the door. He stood there looking at me, not recognizing who I was, though it was only two years that he hadn't seen me. I told him my name. He was blocking the doorway with his body. There were lights inside and I could see his round, bald head. "You?" he said. "I can't believe it, godson. I thought you were dead too." He told me to come in, and inside he asked me, "What's wrong, godson, what's the trouble?" I said, "Excuse me, godfather, but I haven't had anything to eat for two days." He grasped my arm and called his wife. They gave me a bowl of soup, a steak with beans, dessert. Afterward they both asked me lots of questions. I made up a story for them: "I ran away from home to work in the jungle with this guy and I was there two years, it was a coffee plantation, then they fired me and I got back to Lima without a centavo in my pocket." Later I asked them about my mother and my godfather told me she'd died six months ago, from a heart attack. "I paid all the funeral expenses," he said. "Don't worry about that. It was a very good funeral." And he added, "Tonight you can sleep in the back patio, and tomorrow we'll see what we can do with you." His wife gave me a blanket and a mat. Next day, my godfather took me to his store and put me to work behind the counter. We were the only two that worked there. He didn't pay me anything, but at least I had food and shelter, and they treated me well, even though I had to work hard all day. I got up before six, made breakfast, and took it to their bedroom. Then I went to the market with a shopping list she made out for me. After that, I went to the store and waited on customers all day. At first, my godfather stayed with me all the time, but later on he left me in charge and didn't come in, and at night I'd have to show him my accounts. When I got back to the house I fixed supper—his wife taught me to cook—and then I went to bed. I didn't think about leaving, even though I was fed up with not having any money. I had to cheat the customers the best I could, overcharging them or shortchanging them, that was the only way I could buy a pack of Nacional, and I had to smoke on the sly. The reason I didn't leave was that I was still afraid of the police. After a while, things got a lot better. My godfather had to go up into the mountains on business, and he took his daughter with him. I was scared when I heard he was taking a trip, because I remembered his wife didn't like me. Still, she hadn't made any trouble for me during all the time I'd been living with them, she just told me to do this, do that. And on the very day my godfather left, she changed. She was friendly with me, told me stories, laughed all the time. And when she went to the store at night and I started to show her my accounts, she said, "Never mind, I know you're not a thief." One night she showed up at the store before it was nine o'clock. She seemed very nervous. I could tell right away what she was up to. She was using all the gestures and looks and giggles of the whores in the Callao whorehouses when they're drunk and on the make. I felt good, because I remembered how many times she'd turned me away when I was looking for my godfather, and I thought, Now I can get revenge. She was fat and ugly, and she was taller than me besides. She said, "Look, close the store and let's go to the movies. I'm inviting you." We went to a movie house in the center of town. She said it was showing a wonderful picture, but I could tell she didn't want them to see us together in the neighborhood, because everybody knew how jealous my godfather was. It was one of those horror films, so she acted scared, grabbed my hands, nudged me with her knee. Or she put her hand on my thigh, pretending it was an accident, and left it there for a while. I wanted to laugh out loud. But I just played stupid and didn't respond to her advances. She must've been furious. When the movie let out we walked back to the house and she began to talk to me about women, she told me filthy stories though without using any bad words, then she asked me if I'd ever had any love affairs. I said no and she said, "Liar! You men are all alike." She made sure I understood she was treating me as a man. I wanted to tell her, You look just like one of the whores at "Happy Land," the one they call Emma. When we got to the house I asked her if she wanted me to fix supper, but she said, "No. Let's have some fun. There's never any fun in this house. Open a bottle of beer." Then she started telling me how bad my godfather was. She hated him: he was a miser, an old imbecile, I forget what else. She made me drink by myself. She wanted to get me drunk to see if I'd pay more attention to her. A while later she turned the radio on and said, "I'm going to teach you to dance." She grabbed me in a bear-hug and I let her drag me around, but I kept on playing stupid. Finally she asked me, "Haven't you ever been kissed by a woman?" She didn't have a speck of shame, she rammed her stinking tongue down to my tonsils and pinched me all over. Then she hauled me into her room and got undressed. She didn't look so ugly when she was naked, she still had a good firm body. She was embarrassed because I was looking at her without coming near her, so she turned out the light. She made me sleep with her the whole time my godfather was away. "I love you," she said, "you make me very happy." She never stopped talking about how she hated her husband. She gave me money, and bought me clothes, and after he came back she made him take me along with them every week when they went to the movies. She'd hold my hand in the darkness when my godfather couldn't see what she was doing. One day I told her I wanted to enter the Leoncio Prado Military Academy and I asked her to persuade her husband to pay the tuition and the other expenses. She almost went crazy, she tore her hair and called me selfish, ungrateful, cruel. I told her I'd clear out if she didn't do it and finally she agreed. One morning a few days later my godfather said to me, "Do you know what, my boy? We've decided to make a real man out of you. I'm going to enroll you in the Military Academy."

"Don't move, even if it burns," the attendant said. "If it gets in your eye you'll be seeing fireworks."

Alberto saw the iodine-soaked wad of gauze approaching his face, and he gritted his teeth. A fierce pain ran through his whole body like a shudder; he opened his mouth and shrieked. Then the pain restricted itself to his face. With his good eye he could see the Jaguar over the attendant's shoulder. The Jaguar looked back at him, indifferently, from a chair at the far side of the room. Alberto felt dizzy from the smell of iodine and alcohol. It almost made him vomit. The infirmary was white, and the tile floor reflected the blue-white glare of the fluorescent lights. The attendant had thrown away the piece of gauze and was soaking another one, meanwhile whistling between his teeth. Would it hurt as much this time? When he was being punched by the Jaguar on the floor of the cell, struggling in silence, he had not felt any pain, only humiliation. Because almost as soon as they began fighting, he knew he would lose: his fists and boots hardly touched the Jaguar, he grappled with him and knew almost at once that he should release that hard and amazingly elusive body which advanced and retreated, always present, always evading his blows. The worst part was the butting: Alberto raised his elbows, tried to jab with his knees, went into a crouch, and it was all useless, the Jaguar's head rammed against his arms, separated them, and found its way to his face. He thought confusedly of a hammer pounding an anvil. Then he let himself drop to the floor, in order to catch his breath. But the Jaguar would not wait until he got up, would not stop proving he had won. He leaped on top of him and continued to beat him with those tireless fists until Alberto managed to stand up and run to the far corner of the cell. Seconds later he was down on the floor again. The Jaguar straddled him and went on punching him until he lost consciousness. When Alberto opened his eyes he was sitting on the cot beside the Jaguar, hearing him gasp for breath. He had scarcely had time to gather his wits when Gamboa's voice boomed in the cell.

"There you go," the attendant said. "Now we'll have to wait till it dries. Then I'll bandage it. Don't move around, and don't touch it with your dirty fingers."

The attendant left the room, still whistling between his teeth. Alberto and the Jaguar looked at each other. Alberto felt curiously calm: his anger had vanished. Even so, he tried to speak in an insulting tone.

"Why are you looking at me?"

"You're a squealer," the Jaguar said. His pale eyes regarded Alberto coldly. "That's the rottenest thing a man can be. There's nothing worse, nothing filthier. A squealer! You make me puke."

"Some day I'll get even," Alberto said. "You think you're real tough, right? I promise you, some day you'll be kneeling at my feet. Do you know what you are? You're a criminal. You ought to be in prison."

"Squealers like you," the Jaguar said, without paying any attention to what Alberto was saying, "should never've been born. Maybe they'll screw me on account of what you told them. But I'm going to tell the whole section, the whole Academy, that you're a squealer. You ought to be dying of shame for what you've done."

"I'm not ashamed," Alberto said. "And as soon as I can get out of the Academy, I'm going to tell the police you're a murderer."

"You're crazy," the Jaguar said in a flat voice. "You know I haven't killed anybody. Everybody knows the Slave shot himself accidentally. You know it too, you squealer."

"You're not worried at all, are you? Because the colonel, the captain, everybody here, they're all like you, they're your accomplices, they're just a gang of bastards. They don't want anybody to talk about what happened. But I'm going to tell the whole world that you killed the Slave."

The door opened. The attendant was carrying a bandage and a roll of adhesive tape. He bandaged Alberto's whole face, only leaving open his good eye and his nose and mouth. The Jaguar laughed.

"What's the matter?" the attendant asked him. "What're you laughing at?"

"Nothing," the Jaguar said.

"Nothing? Don't you know that only lunatics laugh at nothing?"

"Really?" the Jaguar said. "I didn't know that."

"There," the attendant said to Alberto. "Okay, you're next."

The Jaguar sat down in the chair where Alberto had been. The attendant, whistling even more enthusiastically, dipped a cotton swab in the iodine. The Jaguar only had a few scratches on his face and a small bruise on his neck. The attendant began swabbing his face with elaborate care. He was whistling furiously now.

"You shit!" the Jaguar yelled, pushing the attendant away with both hands. "You stupid Indian! You peasant!"

Alberto and the attendant laughed.

"You did it on purpose," the Jaguar said, covering his eye with his hand. "Damn fairy."

"Why did you move your head?" the attendant asked. "I told you if it got in your eye it'd burn like hell." He made him raise his face. "Take your hand away. Let some air get at it, that'll stop the burning."

The Jaguar removed his hand. His eye was red and full of tears. The attendant treated it. He had stopped whistling, but his tongue, just the tip of it, protruded from between his lips like a small, pink snake. After using a swab of iodine, he put on some small bandages. Then he washed his hands and said, "That's it. Now sign right here."

Alberto and the Jaguar signed the report book and left the infirmary. The day was even clearer now, and except for the wind that swept across the field, it was as if summer had finally, definitely arrived. The cloudless sky seemed infinitely deep. They walked across the parade ground. No one was in sight, but when they passed the mess hall they could hear the voices of the cadets and the rhythms of a creole waltz. As they walked by the officers' quarters they met Lt. Huarina.

"Halt," he told them. "What's all this?"

"We fell down, Sir," Alberto said.

"You won't get passes for a month, not looking like that."

They went on toward the barracks, in silence. The door of Gamboa's room was open, but they hesitated to enter, standing outside and looking at each other.

"Well, what're you waiting for?" the Jaguar asked. "He's your bosom buddy."

Alberto knocked once.

"Come in," Gamboa said.

The lieutenant was sitting down, holding a letter. He put it away quickly as soon as they entered, then stood up, walked over to the door, and closed it. He motioned toward the bed with a brusque gesture. "Sit there."

Alberto and the Jaguar sat down on the edge of it. Gamboa picked up a chair and set it in front of them; it was turned around, and when he sat facing them he rested his arms on its back. His face looked damp, as if he had just finished washing it. His eyes were tired, his shoes were dirty, and his shirt was partly unbuttoned. He rested his cheek on one hand, while the other drummed on his knee. He looked at the two cadets intently.

"All right," he said after a moment, with a gesture of impatience. "Now you know what it's all about. I suppose I don't need to tell you what you've got to do."

"I don't know anything, Sir," the Jaguar said. "I only know what you told me yesterday."

The lieutenant questioned Alberto with his eyes.

"I haven't told him a thing, Sir."

Gamboa stood up. It was obvious that he felt uncomfortable, that he disliked the interview.

"Cadet Fernández presented an accusation against you. You know what it was. The authorities have decided that it lacks a foundation." He spoke slowly, seeking impersonal words and phrases; now and then there was a small, stiff smile on his lips. "This affair isn't to be discussed any further, not even here and now. It's something that both harms and offends the Academy. Since the matter is closed, you're to go back to your section and behave with the most absolute discretion. The smallest infraction you commit will be severely punished. The colonel in person ordered me to tell you that if there's any indiscretion, you'll both suffer the consequences."

The Jaguar had listened to Gamboa with his head bowed. But when the officer finished, he raised his eyes to his.

"Now do you see, Sir? I told you it was just a slander this dirty squealer made up." He nodded contemptuously toward Alberto.

"It wasn't a slander," Alberto said. "You're a murderer."

"Shut up!" Gamboa roared. "Shut up, you little farts!"

Automatically, Alberto and the Jaguar came to attention.

"Cadet Fernández," Gamboa said, "two hours ago—in my presence—you withdrew your accusation against your comrade. You can't bring up this affair again without suffering a very harsh punishment. And I'll see to that punishment myself. I think I've made the situation perfectly clear."

"But Lieutenant," Alberto stammered, "when I was in front of the colonel I didn't know what to do, that is, I couldn't do anything else. He didn't give me a chance to do anything. Besides. . ."

"Besides," Gamboa said, interrupting him, "you're in no position to accuse anybody, to judge anybody. If I were running this Academy, you'd be out in the street. I hope that from now on you'll stop selling your pornography, unless you don't want to graduate."

"Yes, Sir. But that's something else. I. . ."

"You told the colonel you withdraw the accusation. So shut your mouth and keep it shut." Gamboa turned to the Jaguar. "As for you, I guess it's possible you didn't have anything to do with the death of Cadet Arana. But you're still in plenty of trouble. I can tell you right now, don't laugh at the officers any more. I'll be watching you, believe me. Now get out, both of you, and don't forget what I've told you."

Alberto and the Jaguar departed, and Gamboa closed the door behind them. Outside, they could hear the far-off confusion of voices and music. The waltz had given way to a *marinera*. They crossed the parade ground. The wind had died, and as they walked across the field each blade of grass was erect and motionless.

"The officers are shits," Alberto said without looking at

the Jaguar. "All of them. Even Gamboa. I thought he was different."

"Did they find out about the stories?" the Jaguar asked.

"Yes."

"You've screwed yourself."

"No," Alberto said. "They blackmailed me. I agreed to withdraw the accusation, they agreed to forget about the stories I used to sell. The colonel didn't put it like that, but that's what he meant, all right. It's hard to believe they could be such sons of bitches."

"Are you crazy?" the Jaguar asked. "Since when have the officers protected me?"

"Not you. They're protecting themselves. They don't want any trouble. They're a bunch of shits. They don't give a damn about what happened to the Slave."

"You're right," the Jaguar said, nodding. "I heard they wouldn't even let his parents see him when he was in the infirmary. Just think what it must be like to be dying and only see lieutenants and doctors. They stink, all of them."

"You didn't care if he died either," Alberto said. "You just wanted to get revenge because he told on Cava."

"What?" the Jaguar said, stopping dead and looking at Alberto. "What's that?"

"What's what?"

"The Slave accused the peasant?" His eyes were glowing.

"Don't be a shit," Alberto said. "Don't be a phoney."

"I'm not a phoney," the Jaguar said. "I didn't know he squealed on Cava. It's a good thing he's dead. All the squealers ought to be dead."

Alberto could not see well with one eye bandaged, and could not judge the distance. He reached out to grab him by the front of his shirt, but his hand closed on empty air.

"Swear to me you didn't know the Slave accused Cava. Swear it in the name of your mother. Tell me she can drop dead if you did know. Swear it."

"My mother's dead already," the Jaguar said. "But I didn't know."

"Swear it, if you're a man."

"I swear I didn't know."

"I thought you knew," Alberto said. "I thought you killed the Slave on account of it. If you really didn't know I was wrong. Excuse me, Jaguar."

"It's kind of late to be sorry," the Jaguar said. "But from now on, don't squeal on anybody. There's nothing worse than a squealer."

8

After lunch, the cadets returned to the barracks like a river in flood. Alberto could hear them coming: they crossed the empty field with a rustle of trodden grass, then clattered across the parade ground, and suddenly the patio was a wild torrent of sound, from the hundreds of boots that hammered on the pavement. The noise became more and more frenetic until the double door swung wide open and familiar figures surged into the barracks. As they entered, Alberto heard them pronouncing his own name and the Jaguar's. The tide of cadets divided into two currents, one of them racing toward his bunk, the other toward the far end where the Jaguar was. Vallano was at the head of the group that came over to him; they were all gesturing and their eyes were bright with curiosity. He felt dazed by so many stares and such a babble of questions. For a moment he had the impression they were going to lynch him. He tried to smile, but it was pointless: they could not see it as the bandages almost covered his face. They called him Dracula, the Monster, Frankenstein, Rita Hayworth. Then there were more questions. He decided to talk in a hoarse, weak voice, as if the bandages were suffocating him. "I had an accident," he murmured. "I just got out of the hospital this morning." "It looks to me as if you're going to be uglier than ever," Vallano said in a friendly voice, and another predicted, "You're going to lose an eye, and then we won't call you the Poet, we'll call you One-Eye." They stopped asking him questions, no one wanted the details of the accident, they engaged in a tacit contest to invent ridiculous and brutal nicknames for him. "I got hit by a car," Alberto said. "It knocked me down on 2nd of May Avenue." But now the group around him was growing restless; some of them went to their bunks, others came up closer and laughed at his bandages. Suddenly someone shouted, "I bet it's all a lie. The Jaguar and the Poet had a fight." A roar of laughter shook the barracks. Alberto felt grateful to the attendant at the infirmary: the bandage covering his face was a perfect mask, no one could read the truth from his features. He was sitting on his bunk watching Vallano, who was in front of him, and Arróspide and Montes. He could only see them rather cloudily, and had to guess what the rest of them were doing; but he heard them making wisecracks about the Jaguar and himself. "What've you done to the Poet, Jaguar?" one of them asked. "Poet," another asked, "do you fight with your fingernails like a woman?" Alberto tried to make out the Jaguar's voice in the hubbub, but he could not hear him. He could not see him either, because the bunks, the lockers and the bodies of his comrades were in the way. The jokes continued, with Vallano's voice standing out, a venomous, treacherous hiss. The Negro was inspired, and shot off burst after burst of sarcasm and humor.

Suddenly the Jaguar's voice dominated the barracks. "That's enough! Leave him alone!" The loud talk died down at once, and there were only a few mocking snickers, furtive, timid. With his one free eye, which dizzily opened and closed, Alberto watched the cadet who moved near Vallano's bunk, who leaned his arms on the upper bunk and pulled himself up and then climbed onto a locker. After that, Alberto could only see his long legs, with blue socks falling down over chocolate-colored boots. The other cadets had not noticed anything yet; the hidden snickers continued. When he heard Arróspide's thundering words, Alberto did not think that anything unusual was happening, but his body understood better: it grew tense, and his shoulder pressed so hard against the wall that it ached. Arróspide repeated his bellow: "Stop, Jaguar! Don't shout, Jaguar. One moment." There was complete silence now, the whole section had turned to look at the brigadier, but Alberto could not see his face: the bandages made it hard to raise his head, and his blinking cyclops eye saw only that motionless pair of boots, then the darkness behind its lid, then the boots again. Arróspide went on saying angrily, "Stop there, Jaguar! One moment, Jaguar." Alberto heard a rustle of bodies as the cadets who were lying on their bunks sat up and craned their necks toward Vallano's locker.

"What's the matter?" the Jaguar asked at last. "What's up, Arróspide. What's on your mind?"

Alberto, without moving, watched the cadets nearest to him. Their eyes were like pendulums, swinging back and forth from one end of the barracks to the other, from Arróspide to the Jaguar.

"We're going to talk," Arróspide yelled. "We've got lots to say to you. In the first place, don't shout. Do you understand, Jaguar? Lots of things have happened in the barracks since Gamboa sent you to the guardhouse."

"I don't like to have people speak to me in that tone," the Jaguar said, calmly but in a low voice. If the other cadets had not remained silent, his words could scarcely have been heard. "If you want to talk to me, get down off that locker and come here. Like a gentleman."

"I'm not a gentleman," Arróspide screamed.

He's furious, Alberto thought. He's dying of rage. He doesn't want to fight with the Jaguar, what he wants is to shame him in front of everybody.

"Yes, you're a gentleman," the Jaguar said. "Of course you are. Everybody from Miraflores is a gentleman."

"Right now I'm talking to you as a brigadier, Jaguar. Don't try to start a fight, don't be a coward, Jaguar. Afterward, anything you want. But right now we're going to talk. Strange things have been happening, do you hear me? They'd hardly put you in the guardhouse and do you know what happened? The lieutenants and noncoms suddenly went wild. They came to the barracks, opened all the lockers, took out the cards, the bottles, the dice. Then a steady stream of orders and confinements. Almost the whole section is going to have to wait a long time to get passes, Jaguar."

"So?" the Jaguar said. "What's that got to do with me?"

"You're still asking?"

"Yes," the Jaguar said quietly. "I'm still asking."

"You told Curly and the Boa that if you got screwed, you'd fuck the whole section. And that's what you've done, Jaguar. Do you know what you are? You're a squealer. You've screwed all of us. You're a traitor, a coward. I'm speaking for the rest when I tell you you don't even deserve to have us beat you up. You're a shit, Jaguar. Don't think anybody's afraid of you. Did you hear me?"

Alberto hitched over a little on his bunk and then leaned his head back. In that way he could see him: Arróspide, up there on the locker, looked taller than ever; his hair was disheveled, and his long arms and legs accentuated his thinness. He was standing with his feet apart, his eyes wide open and hysterical, his fists clenched. What was the Jaguar waiting for? Once again, Alberto could only see things through a sort of mist, because his eyelid twitched without stopping.

"You're trying to say I'm a squealer?" the Jaguar asked. "Is that it? Go ahead, Arróspide. Is that what you're trying to say, that I'm a squealer?"

"I've already said it," Arróspide shouted. "And I'm not

the only one. Everybody says so, the whole barracks, Jaguar. You're a squealer."

Suddenly Alberto heard a rapid pounding of boots: someone was running through the middle of the barracks, among the lockers and the motionless cadets. The figure stopped within his range of vision. It was the Boa.

"Get down, you fairy," the Boa shouted. "Get down, get down."

He was standing in front of the locker, and his head with its shock of hair was swaying like a tuft of plumes a few inches from Arróspide's boots. I know what's going to happen, Alberto thought. He's going to grab his feet and dump him on the floor. But the Boa did not raise his hands, he merely challenged him: "Get down, get down."

"Go away, Boa," Arróspide said without looking at him. "I'm not talking to you. Go away. Don't forget that you suspected the Jaguar too."

"Jaguar," the Boa said, glaring at Arróspide out of his inflamed little eyes, "don't believe what he says. I doubted you for a moment but not any more. Tell him it's all a lie and you're going to kill him. Get down from there, Arróspide, if you're a man."

He's his friend, Alberto thought. I never dared to stand up for the Slave like that.

"You're a squealer, Jaguar," Arróspide repeated. "And I'll say it again. You're a dirty squealer."

"He's just making it up, Jaguar," the Boa said. "Don't believe him. Nobody thinks you're a squealer. Nobody'd dare. Tell him it's a lie and break his jaw."

"Cut it out, Boa," the Jaguar said. His voice remained calm and measured. "I don't need anybody to defend me."

"Cadets," Arróspide shouted, pointing at the Jaguar, "there's the one that squealed. Look at him. He doesn't even dare deny it. He's a squealer and a coward. Did you hear me, Jaguar? I said you're a squealer and a coward."

What's he waiting for? Alberto wondered. A few moments

before, his whole face had begun to throb with pain under
the bandages, but he scarcely noticed it. He was resigned
to what he was sure would happen, and waited impatiently
for the Jaguar to toss his name out into the barracks the
way you toss a scrap of meat to the dogs. Then everyone
would turn to him, surprised and infuriated.

But the Jaguar said, in an ironic voice, "Who goes along
with that Miraflores gentleman? Don't be cowards, damn it,
I want to know who else is against me."

"Nobody, Jaguar," the Boa shouted. "Don't pay any attention to him. Can't you see he's a damned queer?"

"Everybody," Arróspide said. "Look at their faces and
you can tell it, Jaguar. Everybody hates you."

"All I can see is a bunch of cowards," the Jaguar said.
"That's all. Just cowards and fairies."

He doesn't dare, Alberto thought. He's afraid to accuse
me.

"Squealer!" Arróspide shouted. "Squealer! Squealer!"

"We'll see," the Jaguar said. "I'm tired of all these cowards.
Why doesn't anybody else start shouting? Don't be scared."

"Start shouting," Arróspide said. "Tell him what he is to
his face. Tell him."

They won't, Alberto thought. They wouldn't dare.
Arróspide chanted, "Squealer! Squealer!" frenetically, and
from various parts of the barracks, anonymous allies joined
him, repeating the word in low voices and almost without
opening their mouths. The chant spread as it did in their
French classes, and Alberto began to distinguish some of
the voices that stood out in the chorus: Vallano's thin
piping, the songlike voice of Quiñones, others. The chant
was loud and general now. He sat up and looked around
him. Their mouths were opening and closing in unison. He
was fascinated by the spectacle, and suddenly he was no
longer afraid that his name would explode in the barracks,
that the hatred which the cadets were directing at the
Jaguar would be turned toward him. His own mouth, from

the mask of the bandages, started whispering, "Squealer, squealer." He closed his eye, because it was now like a burning abscess, and did not see what happened until the brawl was almost at its height. The pushing, the shoving, the collisions. The lockers rattled, the bunks creaked, the curses broke up the rhythm of the chant. And yet it had not been the Jaguar who started it. He learned afterward that it was the Boa: he had seized Arróspide by the ankles and tumbled him to the floor. It was only then that the Jaguar had acted, running up from the far end of the barracks. No one tried to stop him, but they all kept up the chant, shouting it even louder as he ran past them. They let him reach the Boa and Arróspide, who were struggling on the floor halfway under Montes' bunk; they even stayed still when the Jaguar, without leaning over, began to kick the brigadier, savagely, as if he were no more than a bag of sand. Then Alberto was aware of confused shouting, a sudden charge: the cadets ran from all sides to the center of the barracks. He had dropped back on his bunk, to keep from being hit, with his arms over his face as a shield. By peering between his arms with his free eye, he could see the cadets surround the Jaguar, drag him away from Arróspide and the Boa, then crash him to the floor in the middle of the aisle. The noise and commotion grew wilder, but Alberto made out the faces of Vallano and Mesa, Valdivia and Romero, and heard them egging each other on: "Hit him hard!" "Dirty squealer!" "Beat the shit out of him!" "He thinks he's tough, the bastard!" They're going to kill him, he thought. And the Boa too. But a moment later it was all over. There was the blast of a whistle, the noncom in the patio roared that the last three out in each section would be written down, and the tumult stopped as if by magic. Alberto ran out of the barracks and was one of the first to get into the formation. He turned around and tried to locate Arróspide, the Jaguar and the Boa, but they were not there. Someone said, "They've gone to the latrine. It's better they don't come out here till they've washed their faces. And the hell with any more fighting."

Lt. Gamboa left his room, and paused for a moment in the hallway to wipe his forehead with his handkerchief. He had just finished writing a letter to his wife, and now he was going to the guardhouse to give it to the Officer of the Day so that it would be sent out with the rest of the mail. When he reached the parade ground, he turned, almost without thinking, toward "La Perlita." As he crossed the open field he could see Paulino opening rolls with his dirty fingers: he would put sausage meat in them and sell them during recess. Gamboa wondered why he had not taken any measures against Paulino, despite the fact that his report had mentioned the half-breed's illegal sale of liquor and cigarettes. Was Paulino the real owner of "La Perlita," or merely a front? But he was bored by these thoughts. He looked at his watch: in two hours he would be off duty and would have twenty-four hours of freedom. Where should he go? He was not interested in the idea of shutting himself up in his solitary house in Barranco; he would be worried and restless. He could visit some of his relatives, they were always happy to see him and scolded him for not coming more often. At night, perhaps he would go to the movies: there was always a war or gangster picture in the movie houses in Barranco. When he was a cadet, he and Rosa went to the movies every Sunday afternoon and evening, and sometimes they sat through the picture twice. He used to make fun of her because the Mexican melodramas frightened her and she grasped his hand in the darkness, as if seeking protection; but actually that sudden contact thrilled him. It was hard to believe that eight years had gone by since then. Until a few weeks ago, he had never remembered the past, spending his off hours in making plans for the future. Thus far he had realized his objectives, and no one had taken away the post he obtained when he graduated from the Military School. Why was it, he wondered, that ever since these recent problems arose, he thought constantly, and with a certain bitterness, of his youth?

"What'll you have, Lieutenant?" Paulino asked with a respectful nod.

"A cola."

The warm sweet drink almost made him gag. Had it been worth the while to spend so many hours learning those dust-dry pages by heart? To give the same importance to his study of the rules and regulations as he gave to strategy, logistics and military geography? Justice is constituted of order and discipline, he recited to himself with a wry smile, and these are the indispensable instruments of a rational collective life. Order and discipline are obtained by accommodating the facts to the laws. Capt. Montero had made them memorize the regulations, even the introductions. They used to call him the Lawyer because he was forever citing them. A good teacher, Gamboa thought. And a fine officer. Is he still rotting away in that garrison at Borja? When he left the Military School at Chorrillos, Gamboa imitated Capt. Montero in everything. His first assignment was at Ayacucho, and almost at once he had a reputation for keeping strictly to the book. The officers nicknamed him the Judge, the troops nicknamed him the Whip. They all made jokes about his strictness, but he knew that at heart they respected and even admired him. His company was the best trained, the best disciplined. It was not even necessary to punish the soldiers under his command: after telling them exactly what he expected of them, and reminding them of it from time to time, he never had any trouble. It was as easy to impose discipline on others as it was to impose it on himself. And he thought it would be the same in the Military Academy. Now he was full of doubts. How could he maintain his blind faith in authority after what had happened? Perhaps it would be more sensible to go along with the rest. Capt. Garrido was surely right when he said that the regulations had to be interpreted according to the situation at hand, and that above all you had to keep an eye on your own security, your career. He remembered that incident with the corporal, shortly after he came to the Leoncio Prado. The corporal was an insolent peasant who laughed in his face while he bawled him out. Gamboa slapped him hard, and the corporal said, "If I were a cadet, you wouldn't have hit me, Sir." He wasn't so stupid after all, Gamboa thought.

He paid for his cola and went back to the parade ground. Earlier that morning he had presented four reports: the stealing of exams, the bottles of liquor, the gambling in the barracks, the jumping over the wall. Theoretically, more than half of the cadets in the First should be court-martialed. They should be severely punished, and some of them should be expelled. And his reports only referred to the first section. There was no point in inspecting the others, because the cadets had had plenty of time to get rid of their cards and bottles. Gamboa had not even mentioned the other companies: after all, they had their own officers.

Capt. Garrido read the reports in his presence, looking more and more disturbed and hostile.

"What's the meaning of all these reports, Gamboa?"

"I don't understand your question, Sir."

"The case is closed. And we've taken every precaution to keep it closed."

"The case of Cadet Fernández is closed, Sir. But not the rest."

The captain waved his hand in disgust. He picked up the reports again and leafed through them, his jaw muscles working tirelessly and spectacularly.

"I asked you, Gamboa, why all these reports? You've already given me an oral report. Why write it all out? We've already confined almost the whole first section. What more do you want?"

"If there's a court-martial, Sir, they'll demand written reports."

"Ah!" the captain said. "You can't get the idea of a court-martial out of your head, I see. Do you want us to punish the whole Year?"

"I've only reported on my own company, Sir. The others don't concern me."

"All right," the captain said. "You've given me your reports. Now forget the whole matter and leave it in my hands. I'll take care of everything."

Gamboa left. From that moment, the discouragement he had been feeling grew worse. This time, he was resolved not to concern himself with the matter any longer, not to take the initiative again. The best thing I could do tonight, he thought, is get good and drunk. He went to the guardhouse and handed the letter to the officer on duty, asking him to send it by registered mail. As he left the guardhouse, he saw the commandant, Altuna, standing in the doorway of the administration building. Altuna signaled to him to come over.

"Hello, Gamboa," he said. "Come on, I'll go with you."

The commandant had always been very cordial with Gamboa, although their relations were strictly professional. They walked toward the officers' mess.

"I've got to give you some bad news, Gamboa." The commandant walked with his hands behind his back. "This is private information, between friends. You know what I mean by that, don't you?"

"Yes, Sir."

"The major is very angry with you, Gamboa. So is the colonel. I advise you to get to the Ministry as fast as you can. They've requested your immediate transfer. I'm afraid the thing's pretty far along, so you haven't got much time. Your fine service record protects you, but you know yourself that influence is always useful in cases like this."

She won't be happy about leaving Lima, not now, Gamboa thought. I'll have to leave her here for a while, with her family. Until I find a house and a servant.

"I'm very grateful to you, Sir," he said. "Can you tell me where they might send me?"

"I wouldn't be surprised if it was a jungle garrison. Or way up in the mountains. They don't change personnel at this time of year except when there are posts to fill in the more difficult garrisons. So don't lose any time. Perhaps you can get yourself assigned to one of the larger cities— Arequipa, say, or Trujillo. Oh, and don't forget that what I'm telling you is confidential, friend to friend. I don't want to get into hot water."

"Don't worry, Sir," Gamboa interrupted. "And thanks again."

Alberto watched him leave the barracks: the Jaguar came down the aisle without paying any attention to the hateful or mocking looks of the other cadets, who were stretched out on their bunks smoking cigarettes and flicking the ashes into scraps of paper or empty matchboxes. He walked slowly, without looking at anyone but without lowering his eyes. When he reached the door he pushed it open with one hand and then slammed the door behind him. Alberto asked himself again how it was possible that the Jaguar's face remained unmarked after what they did to him. However, he still walked with a slight limp. On the day of the brawl, Urioste claimed in the mess hall, "I'm the one that gave him that limp." But on the following day, Vallano asserted that he was the one who had done it, and so did Núñez, Revilla, and even the weakling, García. They argued the question at the top of their voices in the Jaguar's presence, as if they were talking about someone who was not there. The Boa, on the other hand, had a swollen mouth and a deep, bloody scratch on his neck. Alberto searched for him with his eyes: he was lying on his bunk, with Skimpy stretched out on top of him, licking the scratch with her long pink tongue.

The strange thing is, Alberto thought, he doesn't talk

with the Boa either. I can understand why he doesn't have anything to do with Curly, because Curly ran away, but the Boa defended him and took an awful beating. He doesn't know what gratitude means. Also, the section appeared to have forgotten the Boa's part in the affair. They talked with him, swapped wisecracks with him, just as before, and handed him their cigarettes when they were smoking in a group. The strange thing is, Alberto thought, they didn't get together and agree to give him the cold shoulder. And it's better they didn't. That day, during recess, Alberto had watched him from a distance. The Jaguar left the patio of the classroom building and strolled around in the field, kicking pebbles, with his hands thrust in his pockets. The Boa went over to him and started walking at his side. No doubt they had an argument, because the Boa shook his head and waved his fists. Then he left him. During the second recess, the Jaguar did the same thing. This time it was Curly who went over to him, but the Jaguar gave him a shove and Curly returned to the patio with a red face. In class, the cadets talked, insulted each other, bombarded each other with spitballs, interrupted the teachers by neighing, snorting, grunting, miaowing, barking: life was normal again. But they all knew there was an exile among them. His arms crossed on the desk, his blue eyes fixed on the blackboard, the Jaguar spent the hours in the classroom without opening his mouth, without taking any notes, without turning his head to look at the other cadets. It's as if he was giving us the cold shoulder, Alberto thought, not the other way around. It's as if he was punishing us. Alberto had been waiting for the Jaguar to ask him for explanations, to force him to tell the others what really happened. But the Jaguar ignored him, just as he did everyone else. Therefore Alberto supposed that the Jaguar was preparing a terrible vengeance.

He got up and left the barracks. The patio was full of cadets. It was that ambiguous, indecisive hour when the

THE TIME OF THE HERO 377

afternoon and the night are in balance and seem to neutral-
ize each other. The shadows confused the perspectives of
the barracks, and although the outlines of the cadets in
their heavy jackets were still clear, their faces were dark
blurs. The patio, the walls, the parade ground, the empty
fields were all the same, ashen gray. The deceptive light
also falsified motions and noises: everyone seemed to walk
more swiftly or more slowly in that dying glow, and to
speak between clenched teeth, or murmur, or shriek; and
when two bodies came close together, they appeared to be
caressing or fighting each other. Alberto walked toward
the field, turning up the collar of his jacket. He knew the
ocean must have grown calm, because he could not hear
any trace of surf. When he came across a body sprawled
on the grass, he asked, "Jaguar?" Either there was no answer
or they insulted him: "I'm not the Jaguar, but if you're looking for a nice long dick, I've got one right here. Come on."
He went to the latrine in the classroom building. It was in
darkness, and all he could see were the little red dots that
hovered over some of the toilets. "Jaguar!" he called from
the doorway. No one answered, but he knew they were all
looking at him: the red dots of their cigarettes had become
motionless. He returned to the field and went to the latrine
near "La Perlita." No one used it at night because it
swarmed with rats. From the doorway he could see a glowing dot and a silhouette.

"Jaguar?"

"What?"

Alberto walked in and lit a match. The Jaguar was standing up, fastening his belt. There was no one else. He
dropped the burnt match.

"I want to talk with you."

"We haven't got anything to talk about," the Jaguar said.
"Go away."

"Why haven't you told them I'm the one that reported
them to Gamboa?"

The Jaguar laughed that ironic, mirthless laugh which Alberto had not heard since before the Slave was wounded. There was a frantic scurrying of small feet in the darkness. His laugh even frightens the rats, Alberto thought.

"Do you think everybody's like you?" the Jaguar asked. "You're wrong. I'm not a squealer and I don't talk with squealers. Get out of here."

"Are you going to let them go on thinking it was you?" Alberto found himself speaking respectfully, almost cordially.

"I taught all of them how to be men," the Jaguar said. "Do you think I care about them? They can go fuck themselves for all I care. I'm not interested in what they're thinking. Or you either. Go away."

"Jaguar," Alberto said, "I've been looking for you because I want to tell you I'm sorry about what's happened. Honest, I'm very sorry."

"Are you going to start crying?" the Jaguar said. "Don't speak to me again. Not a word. I've already told you I don't want to have anything to do with you."

"Don't act like that," Alberto said. "I want to be your friend. And I'll tell them you didn't do it, I did. Let's be friends."

"I don't want to be your friend," the Jaguar said. "You're a rotten squealer and you make me vomit. Get out."

This time, Alberto obeyed him. He did not return to the barracks. He lay down in the field until the whistle blew for chow.

EPILOGUE

. . . in each lineage/deterioration exercises its dominion.

—CARLOS GERMÁN BELLI

When Lt. Gamboa reached the door of the office of the Fifth Year, Capt. Garrido was putting a notebook into a cabinet. He had his back to him, and Gamboa noticed that his tie was so tight it wrinkled his collar. He said, "Good morning, Sir," and Garrido turned around.

"Hello, Gamboa," he said, smiling. "Ready to leave?"

"Yes, Sir." The lieutenant entered the room. He was wearing his dress uniform, and when he took off his cap there was a thin furrow running across his brow and his temples. "I've just said good-bye to the colonel, the commandant, and the major. You're the only one missing."

"When's the trip?"

"Early tomorrow morning. But I've still got a lot of things to do."

"It's getting hot already," the captain said. "We're going to have a wicked summer this year. But what do you care about that? Up in the mountains, summer and winter are the same."

"If you don't like the heat," Gamboa joked, "we could swap places. I'll stay here in your job and you go to Juliaca."

"Not for all the money in the world," the captain said, taking him by the arm. "Come on, I'm standing you to a drink."

They left the office. In the doorway of one of the barracks, a cadet with the purple badge of a sentry was counting a stack of clothes.

"Why isn't that cadet in class?" Gamboa asked.

"You'll never change," the captain said with a chuckle. "What do you care what the cadets do now?"

"You're right. It's practically a vice."

They went into the officers' club and the captain ordered a bottle of beer. He filled the two glasses himself, and they clinked them together before drinking.

"I've never been in Puno," the captain said, "but I hear it isn't a bad city. You can get there from Juliaca by train or car. And now and then you could spend a leave in Arequipa."

"Yes," Gamboa said. "I'll get used to it."

"I'm really very sorry for you," the captain said. "You don't believe it, but I regard you very highly. Remember the advice I gave you. And from now on, remember that in the army you teach lessons to your subordinates, not your superiors."

"I don't like you to be sorry for me, Sir. I didn't become a soldier to lead an easy life. The garrison at Juliaca or the Military Academy, it's all the same to me."

"So much the better. All right, we won't argue. Bottoms up."

They drank what was left of the beer in their glasses and the captain refilled them. They could see the open field from the window. The grass seemed taller and brighter. The vicuña ran past the window several times; it seemed irritable, and kept looking from side to side with its intelligent eyes.

"It's the heat," the captain said, pointing at the vicuña with his finger. "She can't get used to it. Last summer she acted half crazy."

"I'll be seeing lots of vicuñas in Juliaca," Gamboa said. "And maybe I'll learn to speak Quechua."

"Do you know anybody up there?"

"Muñoz. He's the only one."

"That burro Muñoz? He's a good guy. What a drunk!"

"I'd like to ask you a favor, Sir."

"Why, of course, man. Just tell me."

"It's about one of the cadets. I have to talk with him in private, outside the Academy. Could you give him permission?"

"For how long?"

"Half an hour at the most."

"Aha!" the captain said with a malicious grin.

"It's a personal matter."

"I can see that. Are you going to hit him?"

"I don't know," Gamboa said, smiling. "Probably."

"Is it Fernández?" the captain asked in a low voice. "If so, it's a waste of time. There's a better way of taking care of him. Just leave it to me."

"Not him," Gamboa said. "The other one. And anyway, you can't do anything to him now."

"Why not?" the captain asked in a serious voice. "What if he has to repeat the year? Isn't that something?"

"It's too late," Gamboa said. "The exams ended yesterday."

"Bah," the captain said, "that's nothing. They still haven't made out the report cards."

"Do you really mean that?"

The captain quickly recovered his good humor. "I'm joking, Gamboa," he said with a laugh. "Don't worry, I won't do anything unjust. Take that cadet outside and do what you want with him. But look, don't hit him in the face. I don't want any more trouble."

"Thank you, Sir." Gamboa put on his cap. "I've got to leave now. I hope we'll meet again soon."

They shook hands. Gamboa went to the classroom building, spoke to one of the noncoms, and then returned to the guardhouse, where he had left his suitcase. The lieutenant on duty came out to meet him.

"Here's a telegram for you, Gamboa."

He opened it and read it hurriedly. Then he put it in his pocket. He sat down on the bench—the soldiers got up and moved away—and remained motionless, a far-off look in his eyes.

"Bad news?" the officer on duty asked him.

"No, no," Gamboa said. "Family matters."

One of the soldiers was making coffee, and the lieutenant asked Gamboa if he would like a cup; he nodded. A moment later, the Jaguar appeared in the guardhouse doorway. Gamboa gulped his coffee and stood up.

"The cadet is going outside with me for a minute," he said. "He has the captain's permission."

He picked up his suitcase and went out onto Costanera Avenue. He walked along the level ground at the edge of the cliff, with the Jaguar following him a few steps back. They reached Palmeras Avenue. When the Academy was out of sight, Gamboa put down his suitcase and took a piece of paper out of his pocket.

"What's the meaning of this note?" he asked.

"It's clear enough, Sir," the Jaguar said. "I don't have anything else to say."

"I'm not an Academy officer any more," Gamboa said. "Why did you address it to me? Why not to the captain of your Year?"

"I don't want anything to do with the captain," the Jaguar said. He was rather pale, and his eyes avoided Gamboa's look. There was no one near them. The roar of the surf sounded very close. Gamboa pushed his cap back and wiped his brow.

"Why did you write this?" he asked.

"That doesn't concern you," the Jaguar said in a soft, docile voice. "The only thing you have to do is take me to the colonel. Nothing else."

"Do you think things are going to get settled as easily as the first time?" Gamboa asked him. "Is that what you think? Or are you just having some fun at my expense?"

"I'm not like that," the Jaguar said with a scornful gesture. "But I'm not afraid of anybody, Sir, the colonel or anybody else. When we entered the Academy, I defended them from the cadets of the Fourth. They were scared to death of the initiations, they trembled like women, and I taught them how to be men. And now they've turned against me. Do you know what they are? They're a pack of traitors, that's what they are. All of them. I'm fed up with the Academy, Sir."

"Never mind your stories," Gamboa said. "Tell me the truth. Why did you write this note?"

"They think I'm a squealer," the Jaguar said. "Do you understand what I'm saying? They didn't even try to find out the truth. The minute the lockers were inspected, they turned their backs on me. Have you seen the walls in the latrines? 'Jaguar the Squealer,' 'Jaguar the Coward,' everywhere. What could I gain? Let's see if you can tell me, Sir. Nothing, isn't that right? Everything I did was for the section. I don't want to be with them for another moment. They were like a family to me, that's why they make me even sicker."

"That isn't true," Gamboa said. "You're lying. If their opinion means so much to you, would you rather have them know you're a murderer?"

"I don't care about their opinion," the Jaguar said quietly. "It's their ingratitude that bothers me, that's all."

"All?" Gamboa asked with a mocking smile. "For the last time, I'm asking you for the truth. Be frank. Why didn't you tell them it was Cadet Fernández who made the accusation?"

The Jaguar's whole body seemed to fold up, as if surprised by a sudden stab of pain.

"But his case is different," he said hoarsely, forcing out the words. "It isn't the same at all, Sir. The others betrayed me out of plain cowardice. He wanted revenge for the Slave. He's a squealer and that's the worst thing you can be, but he did it to get revenge for a friend. Don't you see the difference, Sir?"

"Get out of here," Gamboa said. "I don't feel like wasting any more time with you. I'm not interested in your ideas about loyalty and revenge."

"I can't sleep," the Jaguar stammered. "That's the truth, Sir, I swear to God it is. I didn't know what it was like to have everybody against you. Don't get angry, try to understand me, I'm not asking a big favor. They all say, 'Gamboa's the strictest of the officers, but he's the only one that's just.' Why won't you listen to what I'm saying?"

"All right," Gamboa said. "I'm listening. Why did you kill that cadet? Why have you written me this note?"

"I was wrong about the others, Sir. I wanted to rid them of a character like that. Think about what happened and you'll see how anybody could be wrong. He had Cava expelled just so he could get outside. He didn't care if he ruined a buddy's career as long as he got a pass. That'd make anybody sick."

"And why have you changed your mind?" Gamboa asked. "Why didn't you tell me the truth when I questioned you in the guardhouse?"

"I haven't changed my mind," the Jaguar said. "It's just that I. . ." He hesitated for a moment, then nodded as if to himself. "It's just that I understand the Slave better now. To him, we weren't his friends, we were his enemies. Haven't I told you I didn't know what it was like to have everybody against you? We all bullied him, so much we sometimes got tired of it—and I was the worst of all. I can't forget his face, Sir. I swear to you, I don't know in my heart how I came to do it. I'd been thinking of beating him up, of giving him a scare. But that morning I saw him right in front of me, with his head up, so I aimed and fired. I wanted to get revenge for the section, Sir. How could I know the rest were worse than he was? I think the best thing is to put me in prison. Everybody said that's where I'd end up, my mother, you too. You can be happy now, Sir."

"I can't remember him," Gamboa said, and the Jaguar

stared at him in amazement. "I mean, his life as a cadet. I know all the others, I remember how they performed during the field exercises, how they wore their uniforms. But not Arana. And he was in my company for three years."

"Don't give me any advice," the Jaguar said, confused. "Don't tell me anything, please. I don't like. . ."

"I wasn't talking to you," Gamboa said. "Don't worry, I'm not thinking of giving you any advice. Go on, now. Go back to the Academy. Your pass is only good for half an hour."

"Sir," the Jaguar said. He stood with his mouth open for a moment, then repeated, "Sir."

"The Arana case is closed," Gamboa said. "The army doesn't want to hear another word about it. It would be easier to bring Arana back to life than to convince the army it's made an error."

"You aren't going to take me to the colonel?" the Jaguar asked. "Then they wouldn't send you to Juliaca, Sir. Don't look so surprised. Do you think I don't know they've screwed you on account of this business? Take me to the colonel."

"Don't you know what useless objectives are?"

"What did you say?" the Jaguar murmured.

"Look, when an enemy lays down his arms and surrenders, a responsible soldier doesn't fire at him. Not only for moral reasons, for military reasons too: for economy. Even in war there shouldn't be any useless deaths. You understand what I mean. Go back to the Academy, and from now on try to see to it that the death of Cadet Arana serves some use."

He tore the piece of paper he had in his hand and dropped it on the ground.

"Go on," he added. "It's almost time for lunch."

"You aren't coming back, Sir?"

"No," Gamboa said. "Maybe we'll see each other some day. Good-by."

He picked up his suitcase and walked down Palmeras Avenue in the direction of Bellavista. The Jaguar stood watching him for a moment. Then he picked up the pieces of paper at his feet. Gamboa had torn the note in half, but he was surprised to find there were two other pieces besides those of the leaf from his notebook on which he had written: "Lieutenant Gamboa: I killed the Slave. You can make out a report and take me to the colonel." The other two halves were a telegram: DAUGHTER BORN TWO HOURS AGO STOP ROSA AND BABY DOING FINE STOP CONGRATULATIONS STOP LETTER FOLLOWS. ANDRES. He tore the four scraps into little bits, and strewed them along the ground as he walked toward the wall that ran along the cliffs. As he passed one of the houses, he stopped for a minute: it was a large house, with a wide garden in front, the house where he had committed his first robbery. He walked on until he reached Costanera Avenue. He looked at the sea far below: it was less gray than usual, and the waves broke on the shore and died almost instantaneously.

There was a penetrating white light that seemed to burst from the roofs of the houses and ascend straight up into the cloudless sky. Alberto had the feeling that his eyes would explode from the reflections if he stared hard at those wide windows that caught and shot back the sun. His body was sweating under his light silk shirt, and every few minutes he had to mop his face with his towel. The avenue was strangely deserted: usually, at that hour, there was already a stream of cars heading toward the beaches. He looked at his watch, but neglected to notice the time: his eyes were too fascinated by the glitter of the hands, the dials, the case, the goldplated band. It was a beautiful watch, with a solid gold case. The night before, in Salazar Park, Pluto had said, "It looks just like a chronometer." "It *is* a chronometer," he told him. "And besides that, it's waterproof and shockproof." They pretended not to believe him, so he took the watch off and handed it to Marcela: "Drop it on the pavement and you'll see." She was afraid to, and kept letting out little squeals. Pluto, Helena, Emilio, the Babe and Paco all egged her on. "Do you really and truly want me to?" "Yes," Alberto told her, "go ahead and drop it." When she let it fall, the others were all silent, waiting for it to shatter in a thousand pieces. But it just gave a little bounce, and when Alberto picked it up it was intact, without a scratch on it and still running. Then Alberto himself submerged it in the park fountain, to show them it was waterproof. Alberto smiled as he remembered the incident, thinking: I'll wear it in swimming today at Herradura. His father had given it to him for Christmas. "For your good marks in the exams," his father told him. You're finally beginning to live up to the family name. I doubt if any of your friends has a watch like this. You can put on airs." And he was right: the night before, in the park, the watch had been the main topic of conversation. My father knows what life's all about, Alberto thought.

He turned down Primavera Avenue. He felt lively and contented as he walked between that double row of mansions, each with its broad, carefully-tended garden, and he enjoyed seeing the tangles of light and shadow that ran up and down the trunks of the trees or quivered in the boughs. How wonderful summer is, he thought. Tomorrow's Monday, but for me it'll be just like today. I'll get up at nine and meet Marcela and we'll go to the beach. In the afternoon, the movies, and at night, the park. And the same on Tuesday, Wednesday, Thursday, every day till the end of summer. And after that I won't have to return to the Academy, just pack my bags. I'm sure I'm going to like the United States a lot. He glanced at his watch again: nine-thirty. If the sun was already so bright, what would it be like at noon? A perfect day for the beach, he thought. He was carrying his bathing trunks in his right hand, rolled up in a white-bordered green towel. Pluto would be meeting him at ten o'clock: he was early. Before he entered the Academy, he always arrived late at the neighborhood get-togethers. Now it was the opposite, as if he wanted to make up the lost hours. And to think he had spent two summers shut up in his house, without seeing anybody! Yet the neighborhood was so close that he could have left the house any morning, gone to the corner of Colón and Diego Ferré, and re-established his friendships with a few words of explanation. "Hello. I haven't been around this year on account of the Academy. But now I've got a three-month vacation and I want to spend it with you people and not think about the confinements, the officers, the barracks." But what did the past matter now? The morning stretched out before him as a luminous, protective reality. His unhappy memories were like snow: the golden heat would melt them away.

But the thought of the Academy still awoke that inevitable feeling of revulsion and gloom which made his heart contract like the mimosa. Now, however, those states of utter misery were much more ephemeral, like a speck of dust in his eye: a few minutes later he was feeling fine again. Two months earlier, if he remembered the Leoncio Prado he felt nothing but disgust, confusion, and despondency for the rest of the day. Now he could remember many of the events as if they had been episodes in a motion picture, and for days at a time he could avoid thinking of the Slave.

He crossed Petit Thouars Avenue, stopped in front of the second house, and whistled. The front garden overflowed with blossoms and the damp lawn shone in the sunlight. A girl's voice said, "I'll be right down!" He could not see anyone: Marcela must have called from the stairs. Would she ask him in? Alberto intended to suggest that they take a stroll until it was ten o'clock. They would walk toward the streetcar tracks, under the trees that lined the avenue. Perhaps he would be able to kiss her. Then Marcela appeared at the far side of the garden; she was dressed in slacks and a loose blouse with garnet and black stripes. She came toward him with a smile, and he thought, How lovely she is. Her dark eyes and hair contrasted with her white, white skin.

"Hello," Marcela said. "You're early."

"If you want, I'll go away," he said. He felt very much in command of himself. At the beginning, especially in the days after the party at which he had asked Marcela to be his girl friend, he felt somewhat timid in that world of his boyhood, after the three-year parenthesis in which he had been separated from everything that was pleasant and good. He always felt sure of himself now: he could keep up a steady stream of jokes, and consider himself an equal among equals, or even, at times, a bit superior.

"Stupid," she said.

"Do you want to take a walk? Pluto isn't coming till ten."

"Yes, let's," Marcela said. She raised a finger to her temple. What was the meaning of that gesture? "My folks are still asleep. They went to a party last night, in Ancón. It was awfully late when they got home. And I came back from the park before nine o'clock."

When they were a few yards away from the house, Alberto clasped her hand. "Have you noticed the sun?" he asked her. "It's perfect for the beach."

"I've got to tell you something," Marcela said. Alberto looked at her: she was smiling at him, impertinently, maliciously, charmingly. He thought, She's absolutely lovely.

"What is it?"

"I saw your sweetheart last night."

Was this a joke of some sort? He had still not adjusted completely to the group: sometimes there was an allusion which everyone from the neighborhood caught but which left him ignorant, blind, lost. And how could he retaliate? Not with the kind of jokes they had cracked in the barracks, certainly. In his mind's eye he saw the Jaguar and the Boa spitting on the Slave while he was asleep.

"Who?" he asked in a cautious voice.

"Teresa," Marcela said. "The girl that lives in Lince."

He had forgotten about the heat, but suddenly he was aware of its aggressive, powerful, crushing strength. He felt that it was suffocating him.

"Teresa, you said?"

Marcela laughed. "Why do you think I asked you where she lives?" There was a note of triumph in her voice: she was proud of her accomplishment. "Pluto took me there in his car, after we left the park."

"To her house?" Alberto stammered.

"Yes," Marcela said. Her dark eyes were flashing. "Do you know what I did? I knocked on the door and she answered it herself. I asked her if this was where Señora Grellot lived. Do you know who the señora is? My next-door neighbor!" She paused for a moment. "So I got a good look at Teresa."

He smiled as best he could, and murmured, "You're crazy." But once again he felt uneasy and even humiliated.

"Tell me the truth," Marcela said. Her voice was still sweet, but still mischievous. "Were you really in love with that girl?"

"No," Alberto said. "Of course not. It was just that I was in the Academy."

"She's ugly!" Marcela said. "She's an ugly little nobody!"

Alberto still felt confused, but he was also gratified. Marcela's crazy about me, he thought. She's as jealous as anything.

"You know I only love you," he said. "I've never loved anybody else the way I love you."

Marcela squeezed his hand. He stopped, reached out his arm, and pulled her toward him; but she resisted, turning her head from side to side to make sure no one was watching. There was no one in sight. Alberto merely brushed her lips with his. They went on walking.

"What did she tell you?" Alberto asked.

"Her?" Marcela laughed an elegant little laugh. "Nothing. She told me Señora Somebody-or-Other lived there. It was a peculiar name, I can't remember it. Pluto almost died laughing. He began to make remarks from the car and she shut the door. That's all. You haven't gone back to see her?"

"No," Alberto said. "Of course not."

"Tell me, did you take her to the Salazar Park?"

"I didn't even have time. I only saw her a few weekends, at her house or in Lima. I never took her to Miraflores."

"And why did you break up with her?"

It was unexpected. Alberto opened his mouth but no words came out. How could he explain to Marcela what he could not wholly explain to himself? Teresa was a part of those three years at the Military Academy, one of those corpses it was best not to revive.

"Bah," he said. "When I got out of the Academy I realized I didn't care for her. I didn't go back to see her."

They had reached the streetcar line. They walked down Reducto Avenue. He put his arm around her shoulder, and under his hand he could feel her warm, smooth skin, which he touched only lightly and carefully, as if it were fragile. Why had he told Marcela about Teresa? Everybody in the neighborhood talked about their girl friends and boy friends, and Marcela herself used to date a boy from San Isidro; therefore he had not wanted them to think he was a beginner. The fact that he had graduated from the Leoncio Prado Academy gave him a certain prestige in the neighborhood: they regarded him as a prodigal son, a person who returned to his home after living through grand adventures. What would have happened if he had not run across the neighborhood boys and girls that afternoon, there on the corner of Diego Ferré?

"A ghost!" Pluto said. "Yes, sir, a ghost!"

Babe embraced him, Helena smiled at him, Tico introduced him to the ones he had never met, Molly said, "We haven't seen him for three years, he forgot all about us," and Emilio called him a snob and patted him on the shoulder affectionately.

"A ghost," Pluto repeated. "Aren't you afraid of him?"

Alberto was wearing civilian clothes. His uniform was on a chair in his room, although his cap had fallen on the floor.

His mother was out, the empty house bored him, he wanted to smoke, he had only been free for two hours and he was disconcerted by the infinite possibilities for spending his time that had opened up in front of him. I'll buy some cigarettes, he thought, and then I'll go see Teresa. But after he had gone out and bought cigarettes, he did not get on the express; instead, he wandered for a long while through the streets of Miraflores like a tourist or a tramp. Larco Avenue, the Malecones, the Diagonal, the Salazar Park, and suddenly he came across Babe, Pluto, Helena, a great ring of smiling faces that welcomed him back.

"You returned just in time," Molly said. "We need another man, we're going to Chosica in a few days. Now we're all set, eight couples."

They stayed there talking until nightfall, and arranged to go to the beach in a group on the following day. After he said good-by to them, Alberto went home, walking slowly, absorbed with new concerns. Marcela—Marcela who? he had never seen her before, she lived on Primavera Avenue, she was new in Miraflores—had asked him, "But you'll be sure to come, won't you?" His bathing trunks were old and faded, he would have to persuade his mother to buy him a new pair the first thing in the morning, so he could wear them on the Herradura beach.

"Isn't that something?" Pluto said. "A flesh-and-blood ghost!"

("That's right," Lt. Huarina said. "But go and see the captain, on the double."

They can't do anything to me now, Alberto thought. They've already given us our grades. I'll tell him what he is to his face. But instead of doing so, he came to attention and saluted respectfully. The captain smiled at him, examining his dress uniform. It's the last time I'll put it on, Alberto thought. But he was not completely overjoyed by the thought of leaving the Academy forever.

"That's fine," the captain said. "Just wipe the dust off your shoes, then go to the colonel's office right away."

He climbed the stairs with a foreboding of disaster. The civilian asked him his name, then hastened to open the door for him. The colonel was sitting at his desk. Once again, Alberto was impressed by the glossiness of the floor, the walls, the furniture. Even the colonel's skin and hair seemed to have been waxed.

"Come in, come in, Cadet," the colonel said.

Alberto was still uneasy. What was hidden behind that benevolent tone, that friendly look? The colonel congratulated him on his grades. "You see?" he told him. "A little extra effort pays big dividends. Your academic record is very good." Alberto listened to these praises in a motionless silence: he was waiting. "In the army," the colonel said, "justice always triumphs sooner or later. It's something inherent in the military system, as you've had opportunity to observe for yourself. Just consider, Cadet Fernández: you were on the verge of ruining your life, of soiling an honorable name, an illustrious family tradition. But the army gave you a last opportunity to mend your ways. I don't regret having placed so much confidence in you. Let me shake your hand, Cadet," The colonel's hand was as soft and flabby as a sponge. "You've turned over a new leaf," the colonel went on. "A new leaf. That's why I sent for you. Tell me, what are your plans for the future?" Alberto told him he was going to become an engineer. "Good," the colonel said. "That's very good. Our country has a great need for technicians. You're taking the right path, it's a most useful profession. I wish you the best of luck." Alberto smiled timidly and said, "I don't know how to thank you, Sir. I'm very grateful to you." "You can leave now," the colonel said. "Ah, but don't forget to join the Alumni Association. It's important for the cadets to maintain their ties with the Academy. We're all one great big family." The colonel stood up and accompanied him to the door, but then he remembered something else. "I forgot," he said, waving his hand in the air. "There's one more small detail." Alberto stiffened to attention.

"Do you recall certain pages you wrote? You know what I'm referring to. A very unpleasant business."

Alberto lowered his eyes and mumbled, "Yes, Sir."

"I've kept my word," the colonel said. "I always keep my word. There isn't a single blot on your record. I destroyed those documents."

Alberto thanked him effusively, saluted again, and left, while the colonel smiled at him from the doorway of his office.)

"A ghost," Pluto kept saying. "Alive and kicking."

"That's enough," Babe said. "We're all glad that Alberto's here. But give us a chance to talk."

"Yes," Molly said. "We've got to make plans for the outing."

"Correct," Emilio said. "Right now."

"An outing with a ghost," Pluto said. "That's really something!"

Alberto walked home, absorbed, perturbed. The dying winter was saying farewell to Miraflores with a sudden fog that reached the tops of the trees along Larco Avenue, weakening the glow of the street lights. It spread everywhere, enfolding and dissolving objects, persons, memories: the faces of Arana and the Jaguar, the barracks, the confinements, all lost actuality, and instead a forgotten group of boys and girls returned in his memory, he talked with those dream images on the little square of grass at the corner of Diego Ferré, and nothing seemed to have changed, their words and gestures were familiar, life seemed pleasant and harmonious, time passed smoothly and evenly, and was as sweet and exciting as the dark eyes of that unknown girl who joked with him so cordially, a small, gentle girl with black hair and a soft voice. No one was surprised to see him there again, a grown-up now. They were all grown-ups now, living in a larger world, but the atmosphere had not changed and Alberto recognized the topics and concerns of those earlier days: sports, parties, the movies, the beaches, love affairs, well-bred humor, refined malice. His room was in darkness, and as he lay on the bed, he dreamed with his eyes open. It had only taken a few seconds for the world he had abandoned to open its doors and receive him again without question, as if the place he once occupied among them had been jealously guarded for him during those three years. He had regained his future.

"And you didn't feel ashamed?" Marcela asked.

"Of what?"

"Of being seen with her in public?"

He could feel the blood rushing to his face. How could he explain that he had never felt ashamed, that on the contrary he had felt proud to be seen with Teresa? How could he explain that actually the one thing he felt ashamed of during that period was not to be from Lince like Teresa, that at the Leoncio Prado it was a humiliating disadvantage to be from Miraflores?

"No," he said, "I didn't feel ashamed."

"Then you must have been in love with her," Marcela said. "I hate you."

He squeezed her with his hand; the girl's hip touched his, and at that brief contact Alberto felt a sudden rush of desire. He stopped walking.

"No," she said. "Not here, Alberto."

But she yielded to him and he was able to give her a long kiss on the mouth. When they parted, Marcela's face was rapturous and her eyes were shining.

"What about your parents?" she asked.

"My parents?"

"What did they think of her?"

"They didn't know about her."

They were in the Ricardo Palma Park. They walked

through the middle of it, in the mottled shadows that the tall trees cast on the walks. There were a few other people strolling in the park, and a flower seller under an awning. Alberto took his arm from Marcela's shoulder and clasped her hand. In the distance, a long line of cars was entering Larco Avenue. They're going to the beach, Alberto thought.

"Do they know about me?" Marcela asked.

"Yes," he said. "And they're very happy about it. My father says you're beautiful."

"And your mother?"

"The same."

"Really?"

"Of course. Do you know what my father told me the other day? He told me that before I leave I should invite you to spend a Sunday with us at one of the good beaches in the south. Just my parents and you and me."

"There you go," she said. "Talking about it again."

"Yes, but I'll be back for vacations. Three whole months every year. And besides, it's not going to take very long. It isn't like here in the United States. Everything's quicker there, more efficient, more businesslike."

"You promised not to talk about it, Alberto," she protested. "I hate you."

"I'm sorry," he said. "I wasn't thinking. Did you know my parents are getting along very well these days?"

"Yes, you told me. And does your father stay home now? He's to blame for everything. I don't know how your mother puts up with it."

"She's a lot calmer now," Alberto said. "They're looking for another house, a more comfortable one. But sometimes my father goes out and doesn't come back till the next day. He's incurable."

"You aren't like him, right?"

"No," Alberto said. "I'm very serious."

She looked at him tenderly. Alberto thought, I'll study hard and be a good engineer. When I come back, I'll work with my father, and I'll have a convertible and a big house with a swimming pool. I'll marry Marcela and be a Don Juan. I'll go to the Grill Bolívar every Saturday for the dancing, and I'll do a lot of traveling. After a few years I won't even remember I was in the Leoncio Prado.

"What's the matter?" Marcela asked. "What are you thinking about?"

They were at the corner of Larco Avenue. There were people around them: the women were wearing bright-colored skirts and blouses, white shoes, straw hats, sunglasses. In the passing convertibles they could see men and women in bathing suits, talking and laughing.

"Nothing," Alberto said. "I don't like to remember the Military Academy."

"Why not?"

"I was always getting punished. It wasn't exactly good fun."

"The other day," she said, "my father asked me why they sent you to that Academy."

"To make me behave," Alberto said. "My father told me I could cut up with the priests but not with the military."

"Your father must be a heretic."

They went up Arequipa Avenue. As they got to 2nd of May, someone shouted to them from a flashy red car: "Hi, there, Alberto, Marcela!" They could see a young man waving his hand to them, and they waved back.

"Did you hear the news?" Marcela said. "He's broken off with Ursula."

"Oh? I didn't know about it."

Marcela told him the details. He only half listened, because he had begun to think, against his will, about Lt. Gamboa. He'll have to stay up there in the mountains. He treated me fair and square and that's why they sent him away from Lima. All because I didn't have enough guts. Maybe he'll lose his chance at promotion and stay a lieutenant for years. Just for having believed in me.

"Are you listening to me or not?" Marcela asked.

"Of course," Alberto said. "Then what?"

"He called her on the telephone dozens of times, but the moment she recognized his voice she hung up. She did right, don't you think?"

"Yes," he said. "Exactly right."

"Would you treat me the way he treated Ursula?"

"No," Alberto said. "Never."

"I don't believe you," Marcela said. "You men are all bandits."

They were back on Primavera Avenue. In the distance they could see Pluto's car. Pluto was standing near it, shaking his fist at them. He was wearing a bright blue shirt, khaki trousers rolled up above his ankles, moccasins and cream-colored socks.

"You're a pair of stinkers!" he shouted. "Stinkers!"

"Isn't he gorgeous?" Marcela said. "I adore him."

She ran up to him and Pluto pretended theatrically to behead her. Marcela laughed, and her laugh seemed like a fountain cooling the hot morning. Alberto smiled at Pluto, who punched him affectionately on the shoulder.

"I thought you'd run off with her, man," Pluto said.

"Wait just a second," Marcela said. "I've got to go in and get my bathing suit."

"Hurry up or we'll leave you behind," Pluto said.

"That's right," Alberto said. "Hurry up or we'll leave you behind."

"And what did she say to you?" Skinny Higueras asked.

She was motionless, stunned. He forgot his agitation for a moment, thinking: She still remembers. In the gray light that drifted down like a thin, gentle rain on that street in Lince, everything seemed made of ashes: the afternoon, the old houses, the pedestrians who slowly came and went, the identical lampposts, the uneven sidewalks, the dust hanging in the air.

"Nothing. She just stood looking at me with wide-open eyes, as if she was afraid of me."

"I don't believe it," Skinny Higueras said. "That I don't believe. She had to say something to you. Hello, at least, or how've you been, or how are you. Anyway, something."

But no, she had not said anything until he spoke to her again. His first words when he came across her were sudden and imperious: "Hello, Teresa. Do you remember me? How are you?" The Jaguar smiled, to show her that there was nothing unusual about this meeting, that it was a flat and banal episode with no mystery about it. But that smile cost him a tremendous effort, and he was aware of a sick feeling that had suddenly grown in his stomach like those white mushrooms with yellow caps that spring up on damp wood. Then the sickness attacked his legs: they wanted to take a step backward, forward, to one side or the other. And his hands wanted to plunge into his pockets or touch his face. Also, strangely, his heart was filled with a brute terror, as if any one of those impulses, if carried out, would unleash a catastrophe.

"What did you do?" Skinny Higueras asked.

"I repeated, 'Hello, Teresa. Don't you remember me?'"

And then she said, "Of course. I didn't recognize you at first."

He breathed a sigh of relief. Teresa smiled and reached out to shake his hand. The contact was very short, his fingers scarcely grazed hers, but his whole body grew calm, the fear and sickness and nervousness all vanished at once.

"What suspense!" Skinny Higueras said.

He was standing on a corner, looking distractedly about him while the ice-cream vendor served him a double cone of chocolate and vanilla. A few steps away, the Lima-Chorrillos streetcar stopped with a brief squeal next to the wooden shelter, and the people waiting on the cement platform surged forward and blocked the door, so that the passengers getting out had to push their way through them.

Teresa appeared on the top step of the streetcar, behind two women loaded down with bundles. In the midst of that jostling crowd she looked as if she were in danger. The vendor held out the cone, and as he took it, one of the scoops of ice cream fell off and landed on his shoe. "Damn!" the vendor said. "But it's your own fault. I'm not going to give you another one." He gave a kick and the scoop of ice cream sailed a few yards through the air. He turned and entered a side street, but seconds later he stopped and looked back. The streetcar was disappearing around the corner. He ran back and saw Teresa in the distance, walking alone. He followed her, hiding behind the pedestrians, thinking: Now she'll go in one of the houses and I'll never see her again. He made a decision: I'll take a turn around the block, and if I see her when I get to the corner, I'll go up to her. He started running, slowly at first, then like a madman. As he turned a corner he knocked down a pedestrian, who cursed his mother from the sidewalk. When he stopped, he was gasping and sweating. He wiped his brow with his hand, and between his fingers he could see Teresa coming toward him.

"What next?" Skinny Higueras asked.

"We talked," the Jaguar said. "We had a talk."

"A long one?" Skinny Higueras asked. "How long?"

"I don't know," the Jaguar said. "Just a short while, I guess. I walked her home."

She walked on the inner side of the sidewalk, he on the outer. Teresa walked slowly, sometimes turning to look at him, and he discovered that her eyes were steadier and surer than before, sometimes even bold, and that her glance was more sparkling.

"It's been five years, hasn't it?" Teresa said. "Or maybe more."

"Six," the Jaguar said. He lowered his voice a little. "And three months."

"How the time flies!" Teresa said. "Pretty soon we'll be old."

She laughed, and the Jaguar thought, She's a woman now.

"And your mother?" she asked.

"Didn't you know? She died."

"That was a good chance," Skinny Higueras said. "What did she do?"

"She stopped," the Jaguar said. He was smoking a cigarette, and he watched the dense cone of smoke that emerged from his mouth; one of his hands was drumming on the grimy table. "She said, 'I'm very sorry. The poor thing.'"

"You should've kissed her right then, and told her something," Skinny Higueras said. "It was the right moment."

"Yes," the Jaguar said. "The poor thing."

They walked for a little while in silence. He had his hands in his pockets and was glancing at her furtively. Suddenly he said, "I wanted to talk to you. I mean, a long time ago. But I didn't know where you were."

"Ah!" Skinny Higueras said. "You finally got up the courage!"

"Yes," the Jaguar said, staring at the smoke ferociously. "Yes."

"Yes," Teresa said. "I haven't gone back to Bellavista since we moved. I don't know how long it's been."

"I wanted to beg your pardon," the Jaguar said. "I mean for what happened on the beach that time."

She remained silent, but gave him an astonished look. He avoided her eyes and mumbled, "That is, to pardon me for insulting you."

"I'd already forgotten about it long ago," Teresa said. "It was just kid stuff. Better not to remember it. Besides, I felt awful after the cop took you away. Yes, honestly I did." Her eyes met his, but the Jaguar could tell that she was actually looking at the past, that it was opening out in her memory like a fan. "I went to your house that afternoon and told your mother everything that happened. She went to the police station to look for you and they told her they let you go. She was at my house all night, crying and crying. What happened? Why didn't you come back?"

"That was a good moment too," Skinny Higueras said. He had just finished drinking a shot of pisco, and still had the shotglass near his lips, holding it with two fingers. "A real sentimental moment, I'd think."

"I told her everything," the Jaguar said.

"What's everything?" Skinny Higueras asked. "That you came looking for me with a face like a whipped dog? That you turned into a thief and a whoremonger?"

"Yes," the Jaguar said. "I told her about all the robberies, at least the ones I remembered. I told her about everything except the presents, but she guessed right off."

"It was you," Teresa said. "All those packages. You sent them to me."

"Ah!" Skinny Higueras said. "You spent half your earnings in the whorehouse and the other half sending her presents. What a character!"

"No," the Jaguar said. "I didn't spend hardly anything in the whorehouse. The women didn't charge me."

"Why did you do that?" Teresa asked.

The Jaguar did not answer. He took his hands out of his pockets and began twiddling his fingers.

"Were you in love with me?" she asked. He looked at her. She was not blushing, her expression was tranquil and gently questioning.

"Yes," the Jaguar said. "That's why I fought with that guy on the beach."

"Were you jealous?" Teresa asked. There was something in her voice that disconcerted him: an indefinable presence, an unexpected force, both gentle and proud.

"Yes," the Jaguar said. "That's why I insulted you. Have you forgiven me?"

"Yes," Teresa said. "But you should've come back. Why didn't you look me up?"

"I was ashamed," the Jaguar said. "But I did come back once, after Skinny got caught."

"You told her about me too!" Skinny Higueras said happily. "Then you really did tell her everything."

"But you'd moved," the Jaguar said. "There were other people living in your house. In mine too."

"I never stopped thinking about you," Teresa said. And she added, in a knowing voice, "Remember that boy? The one that hit you when we were at the beach? I didn't see him again."

"Not ever?" the Jaguar asked.

"No," Teresa said. "He never came back to the beach." She laughed, and apparently she had forgotten all about the robberies and the brothels: her eyes were smiling, unworried and contented. "You scared him away. He must've thought you'd hit him again."

"I hated him," the Jaguar said.

"Remember how you used to wait for me outside my school?" Teresa asked.

The Jaguar nodded. He was walking very close to her, and at times his arm touched hers.

"The girls all thought you were my sweetheart," Teresa said. "They called you the Old Man. Because you were always so serious."

"What was she doing all that time after the fight?" Skinny Higueras asked.

"She didn't finish school," the Jaguar said. "She got a job as secretary in an office. She still works there."

"What else?" Skinny Higueras asked. "How many boy friends did she have?"

"I had a boy friend," Teresa said. "You'll probably go and beat him up too."

They both laughed. They had walked around the block several times. They stopped at the corner, and then, without either of them suggesting it, they began another turn.

"Good!" Skinny Higueras said. "That was good going. Did she tell you anything else?"

"Her boy friend stood her up," the Jaguar said. "He broke a date and never came back. A while later she saw him walking hand in hand with a real fancy girl, you know what I mean, real upperclass. He was wearing his dress uniform, he was a cadet from the Leoncio Prado. She says she didn't sleep a wink that night. She even decided to be a nun."

Skinny Higueras howled with laughter. He had finished another shot of pisco, and he motioned to the waiter to bring him a refill. "She was in love with you, that's for sure," he said. "Otherwise she wouldn't've told you. You know how proud women are. And then what?"

"I'm glad he stood you up," the Jaguar said. "Now you know how I felt when I saw you on the beach with that guy."

"What did she say?" Skinny asked.

"All you think about is revenge," Teresa said.

She pretended she was going to hit him, but her raised fist hung in the air and her eyes were shining and challenging. The Jaguar grasped her fist. Teresa let him pull her toward him, and leaned her head against his chest, hugging him with her free hand.

"It was the first time I'd kissed her," the Jaguar said. "I mean on her lips. And she kissed me back."

"Of course," Skinny said. "Naturally. When did you get married?"

"A little later," the Jaguar said. "About two weeks later."

"What a rush!" Skinny said. He had another shot of pisco in his hand, tilting it back and forth with the casual ease of an expert. The liquor kept mounting to the brim and sinking back.

"The next day, she waited for me outside the bank. We took a walk, then we went to the movies. And she told me that night that she'd told her aunt everything. Her aunt was furious and didn't want her to see me again."

"She's a good girl," Skinny Higueras said. He had been sucking a half of a lime, and now he raised the shot of pisco again. His eyes were bright and greedy. "What did you do?"

"I asked the bank for some salary in advance. The boss is really okay. He gave me a week off. 'I love to see people stick their heads in a noose,' he told me. 'Go ahead and get married if you want, but I'll expect you to show up on Monday morning at eight o'clock sharp.' "

"Tell me about that sainted aunt of hers," Skinny Higueras said. "Did you go and see her?"

"Afterward," the Jaguar said. "That same night, after the movies, I asked Teresa if she wanted to marry me."

"Yes," Teresa said. "Yes, I do. But what about my aunt?"

"She can go fuck herself," the Jaguar said.

"Is that what you really said?" Skinny Higueras asked.

"Yes," the Jaguar said.

"Don't talk like that in front of me," Teresa said.

"She's a good girl, all right," Skinny Higueras said. "I can tell. You shouldn't've said what you did about her aunt."

"I get along fine with her now," the Jaguar said. "But when we went to see her after we got married, she slapped my face."

"She must be something special," Skinny Higueras said. "Where did you get married?"

"In Huacho. The priest didn't want to marry us. He kept talking about banns and God knows what else. He gave me a bad time."

"I'll bet he did," Skinny Higueras said.

"Can't you see we've run away?" the Jaguar asked. "Can't you see we haven't got much money? How do you think we can wait for eight whole days?"

The door of the sacristy was open, and beyond the priest's bald head the Jaguar could see a portion of the side wall of the church. It was covered with ex votos, small scraps of painted tin half hidden by grime and dust. The priest had folded his arms on his breast, with his hands snuggling together under his chin. Teresa pressed against the Jaguar, a look of terror in her eyes. Then she began sobbing.

"I got mad when I saw her crying," the Jaguar said. "So I grabbed the priest by the neck."

"No!" Skinny said. "By the neck?"

"Yes," the Jaguar said. "You should've seen how his eyes popped out."

"Do you know what it costs?" the priest said, rubbing his throat.

"Thank you, Father," Teresa said. "Thank you very much."

"What's your price?" the Jaguar asked.

"How much money have you got?" the priest asked.

"Three hundred soles," the Jaguar said.

"Give me half," the priest said. "Not for myself. For the poor."

"And he married us," the Jaguar said. "He even sent out for a bottle of wine, and we drank it in the sacristy. Teresa got a little drunk."

"But what about her aunt?" Skinny asked. "Come on, tell me what you did."

"We came back to Lima the next day and we went to see her. I told her we'd got married and I showed her the certificate the priest gave me. That's when she slapped me. Teresa got mad, she told her she was selfish, stupid, I forget what else. They ended up crying, because her aunt said we were leaving her to die like a dog. I promised her she could live with us, and that calmed her down. She even went out and invited the neighbors to a party. She isn't as bad as you'd think. We get along fine now."

"Maybe," Skinny Higueras said. "I couldn't stand living in the same house with an old woman." He had suddenly lost all interest in the Jaguar's story. "When I was a kid I lived with my grandmother, and she was as crazy as they come. She spent the whole day talking to herself and trying to catch her chickens. Trouble was, she didn't *have* any chickens. Every time I see an old woman I think of my grandmother. I couldn't live in the same house with one of them, they're all a little crazy."

"What're you going to do now?" the Jaguar asked.

"Me?" Skinny Higueras said, surprised. "I don't know. Right now I'm going to get drunk. I'll decide later. I want to have some fun. It's been a long time since I got around anywhere."

"If you want, you can stay at my house," the Jaguar said. "Until you find something."

"Thanks," Skinny Higueras said with a laugh. "But I just told you I can't stand having an old woman around. Besides, your wife must hate me. The best thing is not even let her know I got out. Some day I'll pick you up at your job and we'll go have a drink. You know how I like to talk with my friends. But we can't get together very often. You've turned decent all of a sudden, and I don't try to mix with decent people."

"Are you going back to the same thing?" the Jaguar asked.

"Stealing, you mean?" Skinny Higueras shrugged his shoulders. "I suppose so. What else can I do? But I'll have to stay out of Lima for a while."

"I'm your friend," the Jaguar said. "Let me know if there's anything I can do for you."

"Yes, there is," Skinny said. "You can pay for my drinks. I'm flat broke."